The Magic Wheel

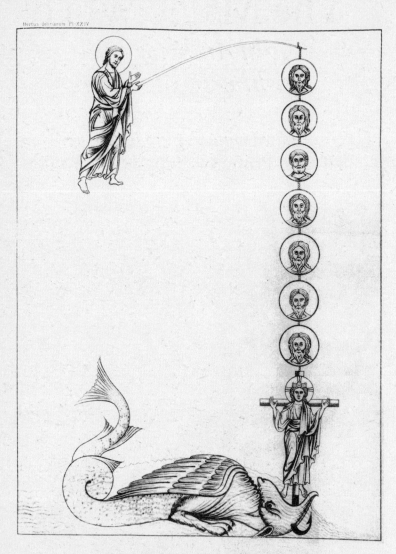

GOD ANGLING FOR LEVIATHAN.
From *Hortulus Deliciarum* (1901 edition).

The Magic Wheel

An Anthology of Fishing in Literature

Edited with an Introduction by
David Profumo and Graham Swift

HEINEMANN : LONDON

William Heinemann Ltd
10 Upper Grosvenor Street, London W1X 9PA
LONDON MELBOURNE TORONTO
JOHANNESBURG AUCKLAND

First published by William Heinemann Ltd 1986
in association with Pan Books Ltd

SBN 434 75331 9

Photoset by Parker Typesetting Service, Leicester
Printed and bound in Great Britain by
Richard Clay (The Chaucer Press) Ltd, Bungay, Suffolk

For Candice and Helen

Acknowledgements

Every effort has been made to contact copyright holders; in the event of an inadvertent omission or error, the editorial department should be notified at William Heinemann Ltd, 10 Upper Grosvenor Street, London W1X 9PA.

The editors wish to thank the following writers, publishers and literary representatives for their permission to use copyright material:

Extract from *The Poems of Leonidas of Tarentum*, translated by Edwyn Bevan (1931), reprinted by permission of Oxford University Press.

Extracts from Aelian, *De Natura Animalium*, translated by A. E. Schofield, published by The Loeb Classical Library (Harvard University Press: William Heinemann Ltd).

Extracts from Ausonius, *Mosella*, translated by E. H. Blakeney, reprinted by permission of Eyre & Spottiswoode Ltd.

'The Green Stream' and 'Taking the Cool of the Evening' are reprinted by permission of Penguin Books Ltd from Wang Wei, *Poems*, translated by G. W. Robinson (Penguin Classics, 1973), pp. 49, 129. © G. W. Robinson, 1973.

'Fishing in the Wei River' by Po Chui-I is reprinted from *Chinese Poems* by A. Waley, published by George Allen & Unwin.

'Fisherman's Song' by Li Yu (translated by Hsiung Ting) is reprinted from *The White Pony: An Anthology of Chinese Poetry* (ed. Robert Payne), published by Mentor Books (The New American Library of World Literature) by arrangement with The John Day Company.

The sixteenth-century spell (anon.) is from Sloane MS 3846, f. 54, British Museum. It is in the public domain, but is reprinted here by permission of the British Library Board.

Extract from Jacopo Sannazaro, *Piscatorial Eclogues*, translated by Ralph Nash, 1966, published by Wayne State University Press.

Extract from *The Arte of Angling* (anon.), ed. Gerald E. Bentley, © 1956 by Princeton University Library.

Extract from *The Fables of La Fontaine*, translated by Edward Marsh, published by William Heinemann Ltd.

Extract from Christopher Smart, *Jubilate Agno* (ed. William Force Stead) published by Jonathan Cape Ltd, by permission of the Executors of the William Force Stead Estate.

Extract from Gerard Manley Hopkins, *Journals* (ed. H. House) published by Oxford University Press, 1959.

Extracts from Arthur Ransome, *Rod and Line* (including 'The Fisherman Growing Old' by Sergei Aksakov) reprinted by permission of the Arthur Ransome Estate, Sergei Aksakov, and Jonathan Cape Ltd.

'Two Friends': © 1922 and renewed 1950 by Alfred A. Knopf Inc. Reprinted from *The Collected Novels and Stories of Guy de Maupassant*, translated by Ernest Boyd and others, by permission of the publishers.

'The Little Fishes' from *Sugar for the Horse* by H. E. Bates, published by Michael Joseph Ltd, reprinted by permission of Lawrence Pollinger Ltd and the Estate of H. E. Bates.

Extract from Alan Sillitoe, *Saturday Night and Sunday Morning* by permission of W. H. Allen & Co PLC © Alan Sillitoe 1958.

Extract from *Shark Attack* by Victor Coppleson, reproduced with the permission of Angus & Robertson (UK) Ltd.

Extract from A. A. Luce, *Fishing and Thinking*, reprinted by permission of Hodder and Stoughton Ltd.

'Pike' and the extract from *Poetry in the Making* are reprinted by permission of Faber and Faber Ltd from *Lupercal* and *Poetry in the Making* by Ted Hughes © Ted Hughes 1960, 1967.

The extract from *Jonah's Dream, a Meditation on Fishing*, published by J. M. Dent, is reprinted by permission of Sven Berlin.

Extract from Hugh Falkus, *The Stolen Years* (1965, revised edn. 1979, H. F. & G. Witherby Ltd).

'Trout' and 'Bait' are reprinted by permission of Faber and Faber Ltd from *Death of a Naturalist* and *Door into the Dark* © Seamus Heaney 1966, 1969.

'The Hunchback Trout' is reprinted from *Trout Fishing in America* by Richard Brautigan by permission of Jonathan Cape Ltd.

Extract from Howard Marshall, *Reflections on a River* by permission of H. F. & G. Witherby Ltd © Howard Marshall, 1967.

'The Ballad of the Long-Legged Bait' is reprinted from *Collected Poems* by Dylan Thomas, published by J. M. Dent.

Charles Ritz extract reprinted by permission of The Bodley Head from *A Flyfisher's Life*.

Extract from Hunter S. Thompson, *The Great Shark Hunt* published by Pan Books. For Canada: © 1974 by Hunter S. Thompson. First published by *Playboy* magazine. Reprinted by permission of ICM.

Extract from Frank Tuohy, *Live Bait and Other Stories* published by Macmillan & Co Ltd. Reprinted by permission of A. D. Peters & Co. Ltd.

'The Birderman' from *Waving at Trains* by Roger McGough, published by Jonathan Cape Ltd.

'The Fish are Retrograde' from *King Horn* by Michael Baldwin (Routledge & Kegan Paul, 1983).

Extract from *The River Why* © 1983 by David James Duncan. Reprinted by permission of Sierra Club Books.

Additional Acknowledgements

Many people have offered advice and encouragement during the making of this book, and the editors would particularly like to thank the following for their help: Professor John Brewer, the late Jack Chance, Julian Evans, Alasdair Fraser, Helen Fraser, Tim Gates, Hugh Haughton, Christopher Hawtree, Alan Hollinghurst, Alan Jenkins, Caradoc King, Peter Lapsley, Hermione Lee, Maggie Noach, Dr David Nokes, Dieter Pevsner, Christopher Priest, Jo Rippier, Dr Gareth Roberts, Candice Rodd, Catherine Sharrock, Sue Stannard, Lisa Tuttle, Merlin Unwin, Professor Brian Vickers, Charles Walker and Dermot Wilson; *Books and Bookmen*, *The Literary Review* and *Punch*; the staff of the British Library, including the Manuscript Department; the Librarian of the Flyfishers' Club, and the National Book League.

Finally, a word of thanks to Tim Binding, David Godwin and Adam Lively for their editorial guidance.

D. J. P.
G. S.

(1985)

List of Illustrations

God Angling for Leviathan. From *Hortulus Deliciarum* (1901 edition).
ii

'The Happy Fisherman.' Attributed to the artist Chachrylion. From *Die Griechischen Meisterschalen* by P. Hartwig (1893).
22

Frontispiece to *A Treatyse of Fysshing with an Angle.* From *The Boke of St Albans*, attributed to Dame Juliana Berners (1496).
46

Frontispiece to *The Experienc'd Angler* by Robert Venables (1662).
72

Frontispiece by William Hogarth to *Dr Brook Taylor's Method of Perspective Made Easy* (1754).
128

'Beginning Early' by Sir Francis Chantrey. Frontispiece to *Maxims and Hints for an Angler and Miseries of Fishing* by Richard Penn (1839 edition).
166

'Black Bass Fishing in the Adirondacks, State of New York.' From a woodcut after R. F. Zogbaum (1884). From *Angling in British Art* by Walter Shaw Sparrow (1923).
234

'Fisches Nachtgesang' (Fish's Nightsong). From *Galgenlieder* (*Gallows Songs*) by Christian Morgenstern (1905).
328

'Three Worlds' by M. C. Escher (1955).
390

The woodcuts which appear at the head of each section are from Thomas Bewick's *History of British Birds* (1797–1821).

Contents

A birr! a whirr! the salmon's off!—
  No, no, we still have got him;
The wily fish is sullen grown,
And, like a bright imbedded stone,
  Lies gleaming at the bottom.
  Hark to the music of the reel!
    'Tis hush'd, it hath forsaken;
  With care we'll guard the magic wheel,
    Until its notes rewaken.

      from *The Taking of the Salmon* by
      Thomas Todd Stoddart (1835).

Introduction

'I felt receptive to every sight, every colour and every sound, as though I had walked through a world from which a veil had been withdrawn.' So wrote the fishing writer J. W. Hills about the pursuit which was his lifetime's passion; and in her little-known, posthumously published essay *Fishing*, Virginia Woolf (scarcely a writer, despite her watery death, whom one associates with rods and lines) quoted the same words as a prelude to a remarkably ambitious claim for the connections between angling and writing:

> Is it possible that to remove veils from trees it is necessary to fish? – our conscious mind must be all body, and then the unconscious mind leaps to the top and strips off veils? It is possible that, if to bare reality is to be a great poet, we have, as Mr Yeats said the other day, no great poet because since the war farmers preserve or net their waters, and vermin get up? Has the deplorable habit of clubs to fetter anglers with ridiculous restrictions, to pamper them with insidious luxuries, somehow cramped our poets' style?

The very health of literature itself, it seems, is dependent on good fishing. And this is not such a tongue-in-cheek conceit as might appear. The whole essay – prompted by a reading of Hills – is written in a marvelling, breathless tone which precludes sarcasm and, indeed, is proof of the very point it strives to make: fishing, quite simply, *inspires*.

This anthology, it is hoped, will bear out Virginia Woolf's enthralled reflections. It is not just that there happens to have been some fine writing about fishing, or that some fine writers, from Ovid to Orwell, happen to have loved fishing. It is rather that the habits and attitudes which make literature, echo to an extraordinary degree, as they do with few other specific pastimes, the habits and attitudes of fishing. Literature in general has a fondness for the piscatorial, while fishing has developed its own extensive sub-literature.

The sub-literature is not, of course, uniformly good, and there has been much to debar from this selection. Many experts in the field have glided into print on the subject, unable to write for toffee; inferior piscatorial literature, feverish with enthusiasm or entangled in its own jargon is dully predictable stuff, bristling with clichés, folksiness and bucolic warblings. This is, perhaps, most common in the verse, of which there has been a great deal. Thomas Westwood, compiler of the monumental *Bibliotheca Piscatoria* (1883), remarked of these angling poets:

> To some three or four of them may be assigned a place – shall we say midway, by courtesy? – on the ledges of Parnassus; the rest are innocent of all altitudes whatsoever, except those of Grub Street garrets, or the stilts of an absurd vanity.

Not confined to works exclusively on fishing itself, this collection also includes passages from poems, letters, tracts and prose fiction primarily devoted to other subjects. Writing about fishing is not confined to any one genre, although there does exist at least one form that is uniquely its own – the 'piscatory eclogue', in which the stock features of the more familiar Pastoral – (swains and nymphs, the blend of eroticism and unworldliness) – are replaced with fishers and aquatic trappings. Its most influential exponent was, perhaps, the Italian Jacopo Sannazaro, writing in the early sixteenth century; though Dr Johnson, over two hundred years later, in an essay in *The Rambler* in 1750, still takes it seriously enough to discuss its demerits as against the true Pastoral. There have even been instances of the piscatory drama, though nothing of much independent literary interest. Ben Jonson had in mind an intriguing project, as recorded in his conversations with William Drummond: 'he heth intention to writt a fisher or Pastorall play and sett the stage of it in the Lowmond Lake', a spectacle that was, alas, never realized.

Why then this singular affinity between the angler's and the writer's art? The answer lies partly in the nature of the craft itself, and partly in the image of the fisherman as it has evolved through the centuries. In his foreword to Walter Shaw Sparrow's stylish *Angling in British Art* (1923), H. T. Sheringham referred to angling as a 'branch of human activity with its roots in culture as well as hunger'. Men have fished for as long as they have hunted; indeed, as Robert Burton observed, 'Fishing is a kind of hunting by water'. And while the modern sport has become highly specialized and the image of the fisherman subsumed by civilized concerns, fishing literature remains a blend of sophistication and tenacious primitivism. The primitive element is most epically alive in Melville's *Moby Dick*, not a book, it is true, strictly about fishing, but surely an apotheosis of the 'hunt by water'. And, repeatedly, the best fishing writers evoke that naked sense of awe, that strange emotional fusion in which the fearsome and the desirable, the hunter and the hunted combine, which seems at the heart of all great fishing experience. William Scrope hooks a *'monstrum horrendum ingens of a fish'*, while T. H. White once played a salmon described as 'lovely and terrible, like a shark'; Gilfrid Hartley's fish was 'a fearful sight to behold', and Ted Hughes's pike-angler 'cast and fished/With the hair frozen on my head/For what might move, for what eye might move . . .' Fishing is not a game.

Almost as ancient as this fascination with fish is the fascination with techniques of catching them. Angling with a rod appears to have been invented by about 2,000 BC. It was certainly known to Homer and the Old Testament prophets. In the field of technical innovation, the Orient has often been in advance of the Occident, with the Chinese developing the fishing-reel, for example, by the end of the thirteenth century (probably as a result of their textile industry) whereas it was not until the seventeenth century that British anglers had the use of a running line – the method for playing a fish before then was to heave the wooden rod into the water and let the fish tow it around until exhausted. While the disciples of Walton were doing this, the feudal Japanese had already refined the practice of angling into a pastime of aristocratic delicacy, where their nobles, ensconced in special temples, fished with a line made of a single human hair.

In practice, the actual mechanics of fishing comprise a relatively minor part of the whole business, and what makes fishing books interesting to the non-fisher is that they are seldom just about fishing. *Piscator non solum piscatur* runs the motto of the Flyfishers' Club – there is more to fishing than catching fish; a dictum which is sometimes interpreted as a mere safety-valve to excuse the unsuccessful angler any embarrassment. The American Ed Zern, one of the funniest of all writers on the subject, summarizes such an interchange nicely:

> You say well, where are the fish, ha, ha, they say look, bub, can't you get it through your thick skull there is more to fishing than catching fish.

The philosopher J. W. Dunne observed that fishing is unlike any other sport, since, in effect, the opponent is 'Nature, wayward, cheating, laughing, alluring, infinitely diversified, entrancingly mutable'; and from its origins, from Aristotle and Pliny onwards, the literature of fish and fishing (halieutic writing) has been indivisible from Natural History at large, concerned with pisciculture, hydrography, the weather, entomology and psychology. Renaissance writers such as Mascall and Taverner presented it in the context of husbandry and nutrition, while

Du Bartas and Montaigne delved through the wonders of the subsurface world as part of their enquiries into natural philosophy. Today, much of this writing is of additional interest for its scientific credulity. The freshwater pike, in particular, seemed to seize upon the popular imagination: in one seventeenth-century tract there is reference made to 'a Pike that when taken was found to have an infant child in its stomach'. Piscatory writing of the pre-specialist age was 'par excellence' the literature of a fanciful curiosity. We find fish copulating with goats, swallowing books, turning inside out and going to church. People continue to be unempirical: when asked why he never drank water, W. C. Fields remarked, 'Fish fuck in it'. Which they don't. Quite.

The fisherman as a distinct literary type emerges in classical times. In contrast to the fishy wonders he may haul up, he is a lowly, simple, grimly patient figure; and this image of a schizoid experience, of the angler as a drab, mundane, if stubborn soul, hopefully or pathetically attempting to engage the marvels beneath the surface, seems to have stuck. The classical fisherman is frequently destitute, old and worn out, and peculiarly prone to the extremities of chance. Another notion which appears perennially to dog the fisherman, is that of his 'luck'. The fickleness of the waters brings at times great bounty, at others it works his destruction. In Herodotus's tale of Polycrates, the fish and the ring, as in similar tales in the Arabian Nights and other folklore, the fisherman is the recipient of, or agent for, omens and sudden changes of fortune – a tradition plainly echoed in the miraculous aspects of fishing in the Bible.

The Biblical and Christian influences are of fundamental importance. If shepherds were the first to be told of the birth of Christ, fishermen were the first disciples. Thereafter, both trades became sacrosanct. Time and again, from Walton onwards, writers wishing to commend or defend angling adduce the fact that Christ chose fishermen for his followers – Gervase Markham gushingly described fishing as 'the Sport and Recreation of God's Saints'. These zealots forget, perhaps, that Peter and Andrew fished for their living, not their pleasure, yet the image of the 'fishers of men', drawn from Matthew's Gospel, only gives authority to the growing contention, in Renaissance times, that fishing has, anyway, its spiritual aspect, instilling virtue and peace, if not actual holiness.

This undoubtedly reaches its peak in the fraught religiosity of the seventeenth century, and is itself a somewhat vexed matter. The angler, it is argued, is drawn to the love of God through the contemplation, in the scenes of his pastime, of God's creation; while the simplicity, quiet and patience of his craft, mirror the ways of the hermit. On a secular level, Charles Cotton's song, 'Farewell, thou busy world' (from Book 2 of the 1676 version of *The Compleat Angler*) epitomizes this view of the fisherman as innocent recluse; while the retirement theme is common, too, in the 'country house' sub-genre of the seventeenth century – Jonson's 'To Penshurst' and Marvell's 'Upon Appleton House', both celebrated topographical poems, frame the angler in an idyllic setting of rural England. But the notion of the angler as a blessed being is curiously confused by certain contrary and inescapable aspects of fishing. The mechanics of angling, after all, suggest not virtue but treachery. Conrad Heresbach wrote, succinctly enough, in 1631, that angling is 'the art of deceiving fish'; and the hook and line are stock-in-trade emblems of cunning and fraud.

The seventeenth-century writers show considerable ingenuity in attempting to circumvent this problem. Thus, we are told, the angler is privileged to behold, in the deception of the fish, an image of the deception of man by the false lures of this world. If this seems to put angling in an essentially devilish light, we are reminded that God too 'angles' for the souls of men – the point, indeed, of the 'fishers of men' image. The seventeenth century is, in fact, the great age of angling allegorized, of angling as (sometimes rather tortured) metaphor. God and the Devil fish. Bunyan employs the image of the fisherman in his Apology to *The Pilgrim's Progress*. An anonymous poem begins 'Death is a fisherman' and goes on to elaborate the image of the world as his fish-pond. The acme of this sort of writing is perhaps to be found in the grandiloquent convolutions of Donne's sermon on Matthew 4, 18–20, preached in 1619 and revised in 1630, which elaborates the Biblical imagery of fishing to an almost dizzying extent.

Yet the presiding genius of the seventeenth century, and the figure to whom we owe our lasting impression, wrapped in visions of meadows and milkmaids, of that century as the golden age of angling, is of course Isaak Walton. The history of his *Compleat Angler* is a classic example of small beginnings taking on a near-mythical status. When it first appeared in 1653 the *Angler* was nothing more than a slender handbook, small enough to slip into a pocket for bankside consultation. The action beginning, as it does, on May Day, this most innocuous of books must have seemed positively subversive to the repressive Puritan regime of the Interregnum, with its total ban on festivities. By 1676,

Walton had so augmented and repointed the original, that, with the assistance of his talented young protégé Charles Cotton, who fashioned the second part, it had become the opinionated anthology-cum-manual that is so widely known even today. Like most fishing books, it is quirky, brimful with oddities, and digressive. To be sure, many readers find it a tiresome, fussy book, but it is an historically unique mishmash of received lore, 'new' scientific knowledge, and robustly Royalist sentiments, a period piece of apparently timeless appeal, and infused with that gentle capacity for wonder that the author's personality lent it. Walton's 'Piscator', quite unwittingly, has become the stereotype of the fisherman in print: garrulous, inquisitive, courteous, eclectic, humorous, a shade childlike, sybaritic, a touch Polonian, and terribly English. Whatever its precise chemistry, the book became such a cult that it overshadowed everything else, although, without denying its charm, it is in fact not so exceptional as it appears.

And it would be a mistake, though he is popularly seen as such, to regard Walton as the founding father of English angling literature. It is in fact a moot scholarly point how much Walton cribbed from others. Shameless plagiarizing, it should be said, is a marked feature of angling writing, and if some extracts in the earlier sections of this anthology echo each other, the trend will be illustrated. *The Compleat Angler* is certainly, in part, an amalgam, if a happy one, of earlier writers, such as John Dennys, Thomas Barker, Gervase Markham (also a literary stealer of some scope) and Janus Dubravius. For the real *fons et origo* we should perhaps turn to the late fifteenth-century *Boke of St Albans* 'Enprynted at Westmestre by Wynkyn the Worde the yere of thyncarnacon of our Lorde MCCCCLVI' which includes the *Treatyse of Fysshynge wyth an Angle*, attributed, quite spuriously, to an aristocratic nun, Dame Juliana Berners. Even here, the author refers to earlier advice 'founde wryten in bokes of credence', but the authority and influence of the *Treatyse* are undeniable. It is not only one of the first printed works to give extensive instruction in how to fish, but it is the first to inculcate, in prose still lucidly persuasive, the 'spirit' of angling. Its seminal status is borne out by the fact that, even in the late eighteenth century, writers such as Charles Bowlker and Thomas Best are still, whether they know it or not, drawing upon it.

The eighteenth century, late or early, cannot be called distinguished for its contribution to piscatorial literature. Technical manuals proliferate, many of them clumsy revampings of Walton, but prose of intrinsic literary merit is scarce. More interesting is the verse, such as that of Gay in *Rural Sports* or Thomson in *The Seasons*, and a certain fascination with angling in the visual arts, in the work of such painters as Zoffany and Morland. The English gentleman who likes to be immortalized in oils before the appurtenances of his estate – his horses, dogs and landscaped parkland – clearly includes angling rods and spilling creels of fish amongst the necessary props; and this is only a sign of the times. In that century, angling emerges as a genuine recreation or sport, as opposed to a possibly pleasurable way of getting one's supper; and as early as 1724, James Saunders in *The Compleat Fisherman* is keen to emphasize not only that angling is 'Sport', rather than 'Work', but is 'Sport' fit for a 'Gentleman'. Such a rigid distinction between the inferior Fisherman of Trade and the superior Angler of Leisure, Walton, with his constant sense of the humility of the craft, would scarcely have entertained. But Saunders goes further still, for he argues that the man of 'Business' who neglects his employment to go fishing, is positively stooping to vice.

Thus, in typically English fashion, a potentially democratic pastime is hedged round with moral reservation and social stigma. Saunders, at least, though he distinguishes those who should or should not angle, does not introduce a ranking system amongst anglers themselves. The most pronounced and snobbish notions of piscatorial hierarchy belong to the century which follows his. The dominant feature, indeed, of nineteenth-century angling, and perhaps the most significant theoretical innovation since Walton's time, is the emphatic division of fresh-water fishing into game (salmon and trout) and coarse (other fish) categories, with an implied equivalent social distinction between the practitioners of each kind. Barker or Walton would have as soon fished for a carp as a trout, and, wise in the ways of fish-cooking, as soon ate one too. Purist fly-fishermen from Victorian times onwards, one feels, would have found both catching and eating a carp equally tasteless.

The causes of this state of affairs are complex and not merely the product of blind prejudice. Dietary changes have much to do with it – it should be remembered that salmon, like oysters, were once a cheap and plentiful food, not a prized delicacy – and these in turn were the product of involved causes: the ownership and restriction of fishing rights; the urbanization of society; the pollution caused by industrial expansion. The coming of gaslight to London in the 1820s produced an effluent that annihilated the once legendary Thames salmon (only now are they returning). And to compare Sir Humphry Davy's idyllic treatment in *Salmonia* (1828) of the Wandle – once famed Surrey trout stream, where Nelson fished (with one arm) and even the poet Donne may have cast a line – with Ruskin's lament in *The Crown of Wild Olive* (1866) for the virtual death of a river, is to observe the grim rapidity of ecological change.

The Industrial Revolution, of course, even for anglers, brought its benefits. As in so many fields, not least the reading of books, technology produced a healthy popularization. It was only with improved methods of transport that fishing really began to enjoy the mass following that has been the case ever since. In the new conurbations of the Midlands (a whole style of fishing belongs to Nottingham and the Trent) and in the metropolis, associations and working-men's clubs were widely organized, and regular competitions and matches arranged, on a surprisingly large scale, on the canals and other waters now within reach. At the same time – around the 1830s – the idea of sea-angling began to become popular, and another new branch of the sport started to take shape.

Yet as this general following gathered momentum, the division between game-fishing – patrician and accessible only to the privileged – and coarse-fishing – open to the 'hoi polloi' – became correspondingly more entrenched. Operating as part cause and part symptom of this was the development, to a highly sophisticated level, of fly-fishing, particularly dry fly-fishing, with the consequent wrapping around it of an aristocratic mystique. This mystique is unjustified. Fly-fishing has been practised at least since the time when Aelian, around the turn of the second century AD, first made written reference to it, without elitist claims being made. And while it is an undoubted art, the near-fetishism and exclusiveness of late Victorian and Edwardian days have no valid foundation.

This said, the fishing writing of the nineteenth century is rich and varied, refreshingly so after the dearth of the eighteenth century. Old forms and conventions still persist. The Waltonian ethos is re-evoked in the bucolic effusions of the Newcastle Fishers' Garlands, or in the by now quaint dialogue form adopted by several writers, such as Davy, in homage to the *Angler*.

Yet if angling literature of this period has one pervasive characteristic, this might be called its 'adventurousness'. A strenuous, restless, even downright athletic quality emerges which is not to be found in the peaceable Walton or the cheerful buoyancy of Gay. Writers thrust at us their knowledge, their delight in tales of physical prowess; they seem at all times anxious to prove their heartiness and indefatigability. It is possible to see, in this dominant tone, the same assertive spirit that moves through much Victorian moralizing, as it moves through Victorian commerce and Victorian imperialism: the insatiable need for monumental achievement, the compulsion to prove tirelessly, the desire to do, find and make Work, even out of Pleasure. It is no accident that one of the great angling writers of the age was Charles Kingsley, muscular Christian to beat them all. Nor is it an accident that this is the age in which, helped by the vogues of tweed cloth and whiskey, Scottish angling, with all its implications of ruggedness of scenery and attitude, comes into its own, notably in the works of William Scrope, Thomas Tod Stoddart and Professor John Wilson (alias Christopher North). To dip at random into any of these writers is to encounter a very different angling ambience from that of the seventeenth century. Yet the achievement of these authors is solid and original. Scrope's *Days and Nights of Salmon-fishing in the Tweed*, in particular, is a sustained blend of vigorous scene-painting, chafing humour, gusty anecdotalism and arrogantly imparted knowledge: one begins by being intimidated and ends galvanized. If any book can stand as the active, extrovert counterpart to *The Compleat Angler*'s essentially contemplative, quiescent spirit, this is surely it.

Out of the Romantic appeal of the North and the mountain regions there arose the phenomenon of the angling or full-scale sporting tour, of which those two trigger-happy colonels, Thornton and Hawker, were exemplars. Different in temperament, they both epitomize a certain nineteenth-century masculine ethos, a ceaseless desire to track down wildlife to the ends of the earth. Hawker, who, when not shooting stag-beetles or feeding his dying child with port, found time to compile one of the most lively diaries ever written, made the obligatory excursion to the Lakes despite the fact that, living in Hampshire, he had some of the best fishing in the world on his doorstep. Kingsley, too, seems to 'discover' the now ultra-exclusive south country waters only, as it were, by way of a journey from the north.

Simple ease of accessibility, replacing the formidable logistics of the grand tour, has much to do with this strangely circuitous geographical drift. Kingsley alludes to the boon of the railways (though opting himself for the 'cosy four-wheel'); and the historian Froude, writing in 1879 about the Buckinghamshire Ches, makes the same point that there is good fishing only a short distance from London. We have moved by now into a modern world of mobility, town–country schizophrenia, and rapid shuttling between the domains of business and pleasure – typified, in angling terms, by the City gent who can leave his office on a summer evening and, by way of Waterloo, be in Hampshire in time for the evening rise.

Nowadays those Hampshire vales, of the Test and the Itchen, constitute an angling Nirvana which most anglers can only dream – or read – about, and only the very wealthy actually enjoy. They also evoke a soft, green landscape which is quintessentially English. In 1820, the American, Washington Irving (by his own admission a would-be, bungling fisherman), wrote that angling was 'an amusement peculiarly adapted to the mild and cultivated scenery of England'. But, by the latter half of the century, it would be a mistake to regard this comment too narrowly, as it would be to suppose that in the haven of the chalk streams the questing, outgoing qualities of contemporary angling writing were finally brought to rest. Even when describing those tranquil waters, Kingsley still writes a prose of torrential energy. Moreover, as he trots in his four-wheel into the bosom of England, his intrepid compatriots in the corners of Empire are pursuing the mahseer or the Nile perch; while the compatriots of Washington Irving are encountering a genuine, adventure-full wilderness. By the mid-nineteenth century the American literature of angling is already well established, though it is as much a literature of exploration – of trackless forests and uncharted, canoe-pierced waters – as a literature of actual fishing. Domestication and 'tourism', it is true, followed swiftly in the path of pioneering. Charles Hallock describes how the prime fishing region of the Maine Lakes was rapidly exploited as holiday territory, complete with fishing lodges, tackle traders and guides ready to fleece the city excursionists. And it is interesting to note that the fishing societies or 'companies', such as that on the Schuilkill mentioned as early as 1798 by Andrew Burnaby, were not merely incidental institutions catering for a specialist interest, but often a significant socializing influence on the early river-dependent communities.

Nonetheless, the vast extent of the American and Canadian territories ensured that there would be no shortage of 'wildness'. The American angler remains something of a backwoodsman, and American angling literature draws frequently on the spirit of Fennimore Cooper. And while the forests and mountains beckoned, the sea provided a further challenge. In Britain, sea fishing remains overshadowed by the freshwater tradition, in America the wonderful opportunities of the Gulf and the Pacific establish a major vogue. By the turn of the century, anglers – among them the redoubtable Charles Frederick Holder – are to be found in plenty on the quays of Florida and California, preparing to combat the tarpon, the tuna, the sword fish and the giant sea bass, and to tackle sharks along the way. These powerful adversaries offer undeniable adventure, no small amount of danger, and genuine aquatic battle: angling finds its equivalent of the safari.

If one feature of nineteenth-century angling literature was a certain bravado, another, not unrelated feature was its increasing 'numeracy'. Accounts of fishing are peppered with figures, measurements, avoir-dupois. The record books are out. Walton may have appreciated a good-sized fish, but he seems not to have produced the scales at every opportunity. The statistical obsession is a modern obsession – the final extract in this anthology, from David James Duncan's recent *The River Why*, pays ironical tribute to it – yet it is rooted in the nineteenth century. So too is that other phenomenon of which statistics are only a symptom. If the seventeenth century transformed fishing from a trade into a pastime, and the eighteenth century transformed it into sport or recreation, the nineteenth century and our own have transformed it, to its own cost many anglers would argue, into competition. Competition, that is, not between angler and fish but between angler and angler.

The days of Saunders' Gentlemen of Leisure are indeed numbered. The angler, impelled as he may be by a competitive obsession which owes more to 'Trade' than 'Leisure', is hemmed in, in any case, by the rapacious pace of modern life. He gets his fishing when he can and regards it as a respite. Small wonder that the late nineteenth century sees some writers, such as Herbert Spencer, valuing angling less for its excitements and more as a precious 'sedative'. Yet out of this pressurized existence, in the very final year of the century, is born what to many minds is *the* great modern fishing classic. Lord Grey's aristocratic pedigree would doubtless have more than satisfied Saunders, but, as Foreign Secretary, Grey was an intensely busy man, with onerous duties. His *Fly Fishing*, however, is like a gentle, irresistible rebuff to the fervour of so much fishing writing before him. It breathes that rare thing, peace of spirit; yet a peace of spirit simultaneously, and movingly, aware of the fragility of a pastime before those very forces of the world for which it is, potentially, a sovereign antidote. It is tempting to say that *Fly Fishing* is imbued with a consciousness of a much wider vulnerability; for it was Grey who, fifteen years after the first publication of *Fly Fishing*, declared, 'the lamps are going out all over Europe'.

If the Great War extinguished so many things, it would be wrong to see it as casting an eternal shroud over angling's silver age. The twenties and thirties were another hey-day for angling literature, the years 1920 to 1925 alone producing Skues's *The Way of a Trout with a Fly*, *A Summer on the Test* by J. W. Hills – who so fascinated Virginia Woolf – and Harry Plunket-Greene's *Where the Bright Waters Meet:* all classics of fishing writing. And if these books have a certain Edwardian tone, a nostalgic tendency, as in so much else produced in the twenties, to sustain vicariously an era and a mood that has effectively vanished, they are far from being enervated or secondhand.

George Orwell, writing under the shadow of the Second World War in *Coming Up For Air*, is much more overtly, even angrily repining. His narrator's memories of fishing as a boy are symbolic of a civilization 'just about at its last kick':

> As soon as you think of fishing you think of things that don't belong to the modern world. The very idea of sitting all day under a willow tree beside a quiet pool – and being able to find a quiet pool to sit beside – belongs to the time before the war, before the radio, before aeroplanes, before Hitler. There's a kind of peacefulness even in the names of English coarse fish . . . They're solid kind of names. The people who made them up hadn't heard of machine guns, they didn't live in terror of the sack or spend their time eating aspirins, going to the pictures, and wondering how to keep out of the concentration camp.

This is a strong and seemingly despairing indictment. If it does not confirm that the age of fishing is over, it indirectly lays fishing open to the charge, in future, of being a kind of wilful burying of one's head in the sand – or water. Yet the claim that any private, peace-bringing recreation must be invalidated by the violent and woeful nature of the times is questionable. During Walton's life there were political upheavals and civil war in England, raging religious intolerance and persecution throughout Europe and a great plague which killed in thousands. Orwell's gloom can no more be taken as final than Virginia Woolf's implicit assertion that the age of great writing has passed because the fishing is no longer what it was. The fishing, in fact, still flourishes, in the era of aspirins and machine guns, beating even the watching of football as Britain's most popular pastime. And it still brings peace to many, in contrast to football's occasional contributions to contemporary violence.

This brief historical survey of angling's place in culture still leaves unexplained the central mystery with which we began and which so exercised Virginia Woolf: angling's inherent affinity for literature. Some reasons are perhaps fairly self-evident. That angling induces a thoughtfulness which may have a creative aspect follows from the solitary nature of the pastime and the fact that it involves long periods of waiting, of apparent inactivity. As Sillitoe's Arthur Seaton says in *Saturday Night and Sunday Morning*, 'it was marvellous the things that came to you in the tranquillity of fishing'. Ted Hughes in *Poetry in the Making* (1967) dismisses the popular notion that this 'thoughtfulness' is really only an idle stupor; indeed, he makes a quite direct link between the fisherman's mood of concentration and aroused imagination and the condition – a simultaneous settling and excitement of the mind – in which poetry is written.

Following from this state of heightened attention, it need scarcely be emphasized that angling brings one remarkably close to nature and can make one peculiarly sensitive to it. For hours at a stretch one may be focussing on a tiny, specific portion of it, and, almost involuntarily, one sees and absorbs more like this than does the deliberately investigative observer. It should be no surprise that angling has produced a wealth of very fine nature writing – writing seldom sentimental or cloying, but invariably marked by a marvellous concreteness and clarity of observation.

There are other reasons. Once divested of its technical details, there is, in angling, much with which everyone can identify. It is in essence a mythopoeic activity, the shapes of its experience being representative of experience elsewhere. As a paradigm of the individual struggle, it often mounts to heroic proportions, particularly in the duel between huge sea-fish and lone angler, the description of such maritime sagas (at the hands of, say, Hemingway) deriving power from the vast hostility of the surroundings being as old as written literature itself. There are only three fish in fresh water formidable enough to give rise to a proper gladiatorial contest – the pike, the sturgeon and the salmon. Ted Hughes in *Pike*, Longfellow in Hiawatha's surreal onslaught on the sturgeon, and Bishop Browne's lost giant are all exceptional examples of this mode, and the latter, with its understated passion, perhaps best illustrates how naturally the business of catching a fish lends itself to story-telling – the inherent narrative shape, the commingling of action and reflection, silence and speech, and, above all, the real suspense at the outcome. That instant of deep despair experienced by even the hardiest of anglers when a fish he has set his heart on gets away is a recognizable emblem of disillusionment at large. Jonathan Swift certainly thought so, still recalling in his sixties a fish he lost as a child: 'the disappointment vexeth me to this very day, and I think it was the type of all my future disappointments'. The one that gets away is an archetype of failure and loss.

On the other hand, an early triumph over a fish seems to lodge in the memory of many writers as an unforgettably formative experience: Andrew Lang and F. M. Halford are just two who recreate this childhood elation, where the atavistic thrills of the hunt and of victory are so strong. There is something peculiarly satisfying (especially in view of his later calling) about the earliest entry in the Diary of Rev. Smythe, when he was only twelve: 'Coming back from church, caught a minnow with my hands. I ate minnow'. Few sentences in the *Bibliotheca Piscatoria* have distilled the spirit of the sport – or of childhood – so neatly.

There remains, however, perhaps one abiding and underlying reason for angling's literary dimension, which may be put in this way: the writer repeatedly attempts to transform the world, to see the world anew, to approach it, indeed, as if it were *another* world; the repeated experience of the angler is precisely of a confrontation with another world, or, of what may stand for it, another element. Water, in short, is all. More than anything, it is that glinting, tantalizing horizontal veil, the surface of water, dividing so absolutely one realm from another, which gives angling its mystery, its magic, its endless speculation. 'Water and meditation', wrote Melville in a splendidly hydrolatrous chapter in *Moby Dick*, 'are wedded for ever', and even the most casual lingerer on bridge or jetty will testify to this truth. The angler becomes curiously affected by and attuned to his watery surroundings; he seems to acquire, as Hills observed, a new perception, to slip beneath the mental surface. It is this sense of blending into the natural ambience and rhythm of his environment which is the subject of *The Fisherman* by W. B. Yeats, himself a keen angler:

> A man who does not exist,
> A man who is but a dream . . .

and it is perfectly evoked by another fishing poet, Ted Hughes, when he describes float fishing:

> You are aware, in a horizonless and slightly mesmerized way, like listening to the double-bass in orchestral music, of the fish below there in the dark.

The encounter with water, furthermore, is dual in nature. If fishing is a meeting with, a peering into another universe, there goes with it a Narcissus-like in-peering, inescapably yearning, entranced, nostalgic. Time and again the strain of paradise lost (sometimes to be regained) finds expression in the literature of angling, frequently focused in the writer's love for a particular hallowed water – Lang's Tweed, Plunket-Greene's Bourne, Patrick Chalmers' summer-drowned Thames. Yet whatever the specific occasion, the general fact remains true: in water we see the dream, the mystery of ourselves.

And we also see fish. It is little wonder that these creatures so often embody, as in Kingsley's *Water Babies*, our fantasies of passing into another world; that the literature of fishing is characterized, as Virginia Woolf noted, by a 'confusion between fish and men'; or that Sven Berlin should, in his *Jonah's Dream*, see the Jonah legend as the archetypal myth of the angler. At the very heart of the sport lies a curious imaginative circuitry between fisherman and fish, for the former has to try to think like the latter, the angler has to *be* part fish.

At a more immediate level, it is not surprising that fish, for the most part (except to fishermen) invisible beings known only from their dead forms on fishmongers' slabs or from their notional forms in books, should embody our ideas of the mysterious and the magical, of regions not wholly within our power or ken. St Anthony, in his famous sermon, praised the fishes for having been selected by God for a miraculous destiny; and, both within and without the Christian tradition, fish legends and fish magic abound. The identification, for example, of fish with fertility and procreation is a very ancient one, common to many cultures, where a complicated aura of connotations surrounds the fish in astrology, heraldry, magic and ichthyolatry. Revered for their aphrodisiac and fecundative powers, fish were traditionally eaten on Venus' Day (Dies Veneris), a practice admirably perpetuated by the Roman Catholic Church. Phallic symbols apart, sexual matters seem always to have had a fishy aspect. In the old German folk tale of the Fisherman and the Flounder, it is the fish that gives the low-down on the relations of the sexes. Some of Shakespeare's most inventive bawdy is piscine ('groping for trout in a peculiar river'); and it is Shakespeare who enshrines the piscatorial trick played by Cleopatra on Antony, first recorded in Plutarch, and repeated by Nell Gwynne on that enthusiastic angler and lover, Charles II. John Gay's delightful verses *To a Young Lady with a Dish of Lampreys* only endorse an ancient fish-superstition curiously at odds with the notion of fish as the Lenten fare of self-denial.

The science of ichthyology, as we have seen, emerged but tardily from the mists of legend, and the great Renaissance zoologists extracted only a little of the hocus-pocus. As late as 1862 David Cairncross, a crank of some commitment, could devote most of his life to the confident claim that the common eel issues from a beetle. And the more sober nineteenth-century natural historians, such as Couch and Yarrell, seem unable to resist mentioning those classic fish legends which have at least half a footing in truth.

In addition to such natural, or unnatural marvels, fishing literature inevitably abounds in exotic recipes. The formulae for compounding special baits are quite as bizarre as those for dressing the catch for the table, and some of the ingredients (especially those advocated by James Chetham, who seems to have frequented graveyards) offer outlandish evidence of the human being at his most inventive. Fish-epicurism (or 'opsophagy') is an elaborate ritual in itself – the Ancient Romans were extremely partial to such feasts, and liked to see the fish dying and changing colour before being prepared – but even the instructions for cooking the most ordinary of fish often make lively reading on their own. Walton offered a succulent recipe for his favourite 'minnow tansy', while for the author of *Barker's Delight*, himself a cook, this final stage of the piscatorial cycle was virtually the 'raison d'être' of the matter. 'Sometimes', he grumbled, 'I see slovenly scullions abuse good fish most grossly.' The art of cooking is but one of several others that is embraced by the art of angling.

The history of the elaborate strategies and methods designed to catch fish is one index of human ingenuity through the ages, and this constant sense of busy cogitation mixed with hope, runs like a vibrant current through the literature. Glow-worms, candlesticks, mummy, spades, dogs, horses, cobwebs, kites, birds and innumerable potions have all been pressed into service by fishermen along with the more usual weaponry of nets, lines and hooks. And yet despite so many centuries of scientific 'progress', little of the mystery and none of the fascination has gone out of the subject.

Anglers, of course, have a vested interest in preserving the magical and arcane nature of their craft. Actual fisherman's spells exist in plenty, and the whole notion of fishing as a species of subtle sorcery permeates the writing. The conceit is seen in the timorous figure in Gay's witty *Rural Sports*, who unexpectedly hooks a prodigious salmon; a hydromancer, deploying his wooden wand and his magic hair (in those days the material for lines) to charm fish from the safety of their element, he has now conjured a power greater than he had bargained for: 'Now he turns pale and fears his dubious art'. Similarly, in Stoddart's rousing poem *The Taking of the Salmon*, the tackle is likened to mystical apparatus:

> With care we'll guard the magic wheel
> Until its notes rewaken.

Yet, setting aside all other wizardry, it would be strange indeed if the following pages did not reveal the simple fact that anglers are in love with fish, these denizens of another, perpetually strange world, and that if no other magic is to be found, it should yet exist in the verbal magic with which angling writers describe fish. No angler or ex-angler can read T. H. White's evocations of trout fishing in *England Have My Bones* without feeling, too, that those trout are in his 'nose and ear and spine'. But anglers and non-anglers alike will surely appreciate Walton's exquisite portrait of the bleak: 'a Fish that is ever in motion, and therefore called by some the *River Swallow* . . . his back is of a pleasant sad or Sea-water green, his belly white and shining as the Mountain snow'.

Two last points need to be made. Though a selection from classical works and a sprinkling of foreign authors have been included, this is essentially an anthology of English, or at least Anglo-Saxon writing, a fact which largely justifies itself. John Buchan noted in his *Musa Piscatrix* (1896) that 'the celebration of angling by the poets is a very English characteristic'; and if other nations have their practising devotees, the literary tradition is unique to our language. *The Compleat Angler* is one of those rare books   like perhaps *The Pilgrim's Progress* or *Robinson Crusoe* – which finds a special place in the English consciousness, even for those who have never read it. Yet while it has run through numerous editions, it is seldom translated.

The reasons for this Anglo-Saxon bias are many, but it is difficult not to invoke the basic factors of national topography and temperament. Goldsmith in his *History of the Earth and Animated Nature* anticipated Washington Irving when he wrote: 'Happy England! Where the sea furnishes an abundant and luxurious repast, and the fresh waters an innocent and harmless pastime; where the angler, in cheerful solitude, strolls by the edge of the stream, and fears neither the coiled snake nor the lurking crocodile'. Such an observation, it is true, could be as readily made about, say, France; but with temperament we are on more special ground. Walton's 'Study to be Quiet' has a deep appeal to a people noted for their reticence and reserve, and the quality inseparably linked with silence in angling – solitude – strikes an equally rich chord with a nation that has enshrined the cult of solitude in its Romantic, Wordsworthian traditions and has never been famed for demonstrative sociability. In any case, taciturnity and an often lonesome tenacity are distinct features of both the English and Scottish characters, and they are qualities which angling both requires and instils. Perhaps the very reserve and caution of the pursuit demands, in compensation, the companionability and loquacity of, at least, the written word. And this, possibly, is how much English literature has been written: it is the silent vociferation of a naturally quiet people.

Finally, since this is an anthology for general readers, not just for anglers, we have included several examples of anti-angling writing, of which there is a not insignificant amount, with some illustrious proponents. The main arguments blame angling for its cruelty, its mendacity, or its sheer folly. Of these, the first must be taken seriously, though not all the attacks bear close scrutiny. Byron's famous jibe in *Don Juan* – 'No angler can be a good man' – acquires a new perspective when set against his letter of 7 September 1814: 'I have caught a great many perch and some carp . . .' The counter-argument by the practitioners, that the angler has often a much greater respect for fish, rivers and nature than the anti-angler and is more concerned for the preservation of all three, is usually laughed at by the opponents. At any rate, the defences countering the cruelty charge can be at least as persuasive and often more intelligent than the attacks.

That all anglers are congenital liars, and that, uniquely in the animal kingdom, the fish enjoys a pronounced degree of posthumous growth, are commonplace themes of a more light-hearted aspect of angling satire, and ones which on the whole the angler–writer responds to spiritedly. Hyperbole and a certain allowable amplification of detail are indelible characteristics of most piscatorial writing, and there has been no attempt to launder such fictions from this collection. The uncharitable cynic may prefer to greet the more extravagant accounts in the manner of Defoe, who once concluded, 'All this story I see so little ground to give the least credit to, that I look upon it, and't shall please you, to be no better than a FIB'.

As to the indictment of folly, this seems unlikely ever to be wholly rebutted. The collective unconscious harbours a composite stereotype of the angler as a sedentary simpleton, a deranged yokel, hypnotized by the tiny tip of his float, hunched Rodin-still on the bank of a river, probably in the rain, possibly inebriated, and invariably fishless. Some renowned lovers of angling, such as the painter Turner, with his convertible fishing-rod-cum-umbrella, seem positively to encourage this image; and when asked by a childhood friend who had later become a successful businessman, what he was now doing in life, Thomas Tod Stoddart replied, 'Doing? *Doing?* Mon . . . I'm an angler'. R. L. Stevenson wrote of an immobile rank of bankside anglers: 'You might have trepanned every one of their innocent heads and found no more than so much coiled fishing line below their skulls'. And the French classify deeply eccentric people as 'capable de pêcher à lá ligne'. Whatever the justice of such observations, they testify to the inherent comic potential of the sport, which its literature has readily utilized. The unsuccessful and frustrated angler, the fisherman incommensurately proud of his diminutive catch, the drenched, defeated and demented angler are stock figures in the cast of caricatures.

The most famous of all remarks on angling-folly, that of Dr Johnson about the worm and the fool, is, at least, apocryphal, properly belonging to Martial Guyet, who lived a century before Johnson. Johnson, in fact, could quote Walton by heart, and, through his encouragement of Moses Browne as editor, we owe to him the first eighteenth-century reprint of the *Angler*. In any case, to judge from many examples in this book, anglers have a fine enough sense of self-irony to immunize themselves safely against the slander of lunacy, which really only exists for those who voice it, for the lunatic, if such he is, hardly minds being accused of lunacy. Perhaps – to pay one final tribute to the muse of angling – what the Greeks believed of poetry is also true of fishing: anything which brings us such great pleasure must contain a touch of madness.

'Leviathan with an hook?'

The Ancient Tradition

'THE HAPPY FISHERMAN.' Attributed to the artist Chachrylion.
From *Die Griechischen Meisterschalen* by P. Hartwig (1893).

HOMER: from *The Iliad, Book XXIV* (? 8th century BC).
Translated from the Greek by Alexander Pope, 1715–20.

           And *Iris* from the Skies
Swift as a Whirlwind, on the Message flies,
Meteorous the Face of Ocean sweeps,
Refulgent gliding o'er the sable Deeps.
Between where *Samos* wide his Forests spreads,
And rocky *Imbrus* lifts its pointed Heads,
Down plung'd the Maid; (the parted Waves resound)
She plung'd, and instant shot the dark Profound.
As bearing Death in the fallacious Bait
From the bent Angle sinks the loaden Weight;
So past the Goddess thro' the closing Wave,
Where *Thetis* sorrow'd in her secret Cave:
There plac'd amidst her melancholy Train
(The blue-hair'd Sisters of the sacred Main)
Pensive she sate, revolving Fates to come,
And wept her god-like Sons's approaching Doom.

HOMER: from *The Odyssey, Book XII* (? 8th century BC).
Translated from the Greek by Alexander Pope, 1725–6.

Struck with despair, with trembling hearts we view'd
The yawning dungeon, and the tumbling flood:
When lo! fierce *Scylla* stoop'd to seize her prey,
Stretch'd her dire jaws and swept six men away;
Chiefs of renown! loud echoing shrieks arise;
I turn, and view them quivering in the skies;
They call, and aid with out-stretch'd arms implore:
In vain they call! those arms are stretch'd no more.
As from some rock that overhangs the flood,
The silent fisher casts th' insidious food.
With fraudful care he waits the finny prize,
And sudden lifts it quivering to the skies:
So the foul monster lifts her prey on high,
So pant the wretches, struggling in the sky,
In the wide dungeon she devours her food,
And the flesh trembles while she churns the blood.
Worn as I am with griefs, with care decay'd;
Never, I never, scene so dire survey'd!
My shiv'ring blood congeal'd forgot to flow,
Aghast I stood, a monument of woe!

THE HOLY BIBLE: from *Habakkuk* (c. 625–585 BC).

13 *Thou art* of purer eyes than to behold evil, and canst not look on iniquity: wherefore lookest thou upon them that deal treacherously, and holdest thy tongue when the wicked devoureth *the man that is* more righteous than he?

14 And makest men as the fishes of the sea, as the creeping things, *that have* no ruler over them?

15 They take up all of them with the angle, they catch them in their net, and gather them in their drag: therefore they rejoice and are glad.

16 Therefore, they sacrifice unto their net, and burn incense unto their drag; because by them their portion *is* fat, and their meat plenteous.

17 Shall they therefore empty their net, and not spare continually to slay the nations?

THE HOLY BIBLE: from *Job* (6th or 5th century BC).

Canst thou draw out leviathan with an hook? or his tongue with a cord *which* thou lettest down?

 2 Canst thou put an hook into his nose? or bore his jaw through with a thorn?

 3 Will he make many supplications unto thee? will he speak soft *words* unto thee?

 4 Will he make a covenant with thee? wilt thou take him for a servant for ever?

HERODOTUS (? born 484 BC): from *The Histories*.
Translated from the Greek by George Rawlinson, 1858.

Book II, Chapter 70

The modes of catching the crocodile are many and various. I shall only describe the one which seems to me most worthy of mention. They bait a hook with a chine of pork and let the meat be carried out into the middle of the stream, while the hunter upon the bank holds a living pig, which he belabours. The crocodile hears its cries, and, making for the sound, encounters the pork, which he instantly swallows down. The men on the shore haul, and when they have got him to land, the first thing the hunter does is to plaster his eyes with mud. This once accomplished, the animal is despatched with ease, otherwise he gives great trouble.

Book II, Chapter 93

Gregarious fish are not found in any numbers in the rivers; they frequent the lagunes, whence, at the season of breeding, they proceed in shoals towards the sea. The males lead the way, and drop their milt as they go, while the females, following close behind, eagerly swallow it down. From this they conceive, and when, after passing some time in the sea, they begin to be in spawn, the whole shoal sets off on its return to its ancient haunts. Now, however, it is no longer the males, but the females, who take the lead: they swim in front in a body, and do exactly as the males did before, dropping, little by little, their grains of spawn as they go, while the males in the rear devour the grains, each one of which is a fish. A portion of the spawn escapes and is not swallowed by the males, and hence come the fishes which grow afterwards to maturity. When any of this sort of fish are taken on their passage to the sea, they are found to have the left side of the head scarred and bruised: while if taken on their return, the marks appear on the right. the reason is, that as they swim down the Nile seaward, they keep close to the bank of the river upon their left, and returning again up stream they still cling to the same side, hugging it and brushing against it constantly, to be sure that they miss not their road through the great force of the current. When the Nile begins to rise, the hollows in the land and the marshy spots near the river are flooded before any other places by the percolation of the water through the river banks; and these, almost as soon as they become pools, are found to be full of numbers of little fishes. I think that I understand how it is this comes to pass. On the subsidence of the Nile the year before, though the fish retired with the retreating waters, they had first deposited their spawn in the mud upon the banks; and so, when at the usual season the water returns, small fry are rapidly engendered out of the spawn of the preceding year. So much concerning the fish.

Book III, Chapters 40–3

The exceeding good fortune of Polycrates did not escape the notice of Amasis, who was much disturbed thereat. When therefore his successes continued increasing, Amasis wrote him the following letter, and sent it to Samos. 'Amasis to Polycrates thus sayeth: It is a pleasure to hear of a friend and ally prospering, but thy exceeding prosperity does not cause me joy, forasmuch as I know that the gods are envious. My wish for myself, and for those whom I love, is, to be now successful, and now to meet with a check; thus passing through life amid alternate good and ill, rather than with perpetual good fortune. For never yet did I hear tell of any one succeeding in all his undertakings, who did not meet with calamity at last, and come to utter ruin. Now, therefore, give ear to my words, and meet thy good luck in this way: bethink thee which of all thy treasures thou valuest most and canst least bear to part with; take it, whatsoever it be, and throw it away, so that it may be sure never to come any more into the sight of man. Then, if thy good fortune be not thenceforth chequered with ill, save thyself from harm by again doing as I have counselled.'

41 When Polycrates read this letter, and perceived that the advice of Amasis was good, he considered carefully with himself which of the treasures that he had in store it would grieve him most to lose. After much thought he made up his mind that it was a signet-ring which he was wont to wear, an emerald set in gold, the workmanship of Theodore, son of Têlecles, a Samian. So he determined to throw this away; and, manning a penteconter, he went on board, and bade the sailors put out into the open sea. When he was now a long way from the island, he took the ring from his finger, and, in the sight of all those who were on board, flung it into the deep. This done, he returned home, and gave vent to his sorrow.

42 Now it happened five or six days afterwards that a fisherman caught a fish so large and beautiful that he thought it well deserved to be made a present of to the king. So he took it with him to the gate of the palace, and said that he wanted to see Polycrates. Then Polycrates allowed him to come in, and the fisherman gave him the fish with these words following – 'Sir king, when I took this prize, I thought I would not carry it to market, though I am a poor man who live by my trade. I said to myself, it is worthy of Polycrates and his greatness: and so I brought it here to give it to you.' The speech pleased the king, who thus spoke in reply – 'Thou didst right well, friend, and I am doubly indebted, both for the gift, and for the speech. Come now, and sup with me.' So the fisherman went home, esteeming it a high honour that he had been asked to sup with the king. Meanwhile the servants, on cutting open the fish, found the signet of their master in its belly. No sooner did they see it than they seized upon it, and hastening to Polycrates with great joy, restored it to him, and told him in what way it had been found. The king, who saw something providential in the matter, forthwith wrote a letter to Amasis, telling him all that had happened, what he had himself done, and what had been the upshot – and despatched the letter to Egypt.

43 When Amasis had read the letter of Polycrates, he perceived that it does not belong to man to save his fellow-man from the fate which is in store for him: likewise he felt certain that Polycrates would end ill, as he prospered in everything, even finding what he had thrown away. So he sent a herald to Samos, and dissolved the contract of friendship. This he did, that when the great and heavy misfortune came, he might escape the grief which he would have felt if the sufferer had been his bond-friend.

ARISTOTLE (384–21 BC): from *Historia Animalium, Book VI, Chapter XV*.
Translated from the Greek by Richard Cresswell, 1862.

Eels are not produced from sexual intercourse, nor are they oviparous, nor have they ever been detected with semen or ova, nor when dissected do they appear to possess either seminal or uterine viscera; and this is the only kind of sanguineous animal which does not originate either in sexual intercourse or in ova. It is, however, manifest that this is the case, for, after rain, they have been reproduced in some marshy ponds, from which all the water was drawn and the mud cleaned out; but they are never produced in dry places nor in ponds that are always full, for they live upon and are nourished by rain water. It is plain, therefore, that they are not produced either from sexual intercourse or from ova. Some persons have thought that they were productive, because some eeels have parasitical worms, and they thought that these became eels.

This however, is not the case, but they originate in what are called the entrails of the earth, which are found spontaneously in mud and moist earth. They have been observed making their escape from them, and others have been found in them when cut up and dissected. These originate both in the sea and in rivers wherein putrid matter is abundant: in those places in the sea which are full of fuci*, and near the banks of rivers and ponds, for in these places the heat causes much putridity. This is the mode of generation in eels.

*Seaweeds.

THEOCRITUS (310–250 BC): from *Idyll XXI*.
Translated from the Greek by Francis Fawkes, 1767.

Asphalion

Last evening, weary with the toils of day,
Lull'd in the lap of rest secure I lay;
Full late we supp'd, and sparingly we eat;
No danger of a surfeit from our meat.
Methought I sat upon a shelfy steep,
And watch'd the fish that gambol'd in the deep:
Suspended by my rod, I gently shook

The bait fallacious, which a huge one took;
(Sleeping we image what awake we wish;
Dogs dream of bones, and fishermen of fish)
Bent was my rod, and from his gills the blood,
With crimson stream, distain'd the silver flood.
I stretch'd my arm out, lest the line should break;
The fish so vigorous, and my hook so weak!
Anxious I gaz'd, he struggled to be gone;
'You're wounded – I'll be with you friend,
      anon—
Still do you teise me?' for he plagu'd me sore;
At last, quite spent, I drew him safe on shore,
Then graspt him with my hand, for surer hold,
A noble prize, a fish of solid gold!
But fears suspicious in my bosom throng'd,
Lest to the god of ocean he belong'd;
Or, haply wandering in the azure main,
Some favourite fish of Amphitrite's train.
My prize I loos'd, and strictest caution took,
For fear some gold might stick about the hook;
Then safe secur'd him, and devoutly swore,
Never to venture on the ocean more;
But live on land, as happy as a king:
At this I wak'd: what think you of the thing!
Speak free, for know, I am extremely loth,
And greatly fear, to violate my oath.

Friend

Fear not, old friend; you took no oath, for why;
You took no fish – your vision's all a lye.
Go search the shoals, not sleeping, but awake,
Hunger will soon discover your mistake;
Catch real fish; you need not, sure, be told,
Those fools must starve who only dream of gold.

LEONIDAS OF TARENTUM: *Poem LVIII* (early 3rd century BC).
Translated from the Greek by Edwyn Bevan, 1931.

Parmis son of Calligrotus, on sea-shore, by river-sides
   Ever angling wrasse and scar-fish – master hand in strike and
      throw –
Greedy perch that gulp the bait down, everything that lurks and glides
   In sea-cave or weedy hollow or the deeper rocks below,

On a day for first catch landed, little evil prickly thing,
   An iulis, which he lifted to his teeth, to hold for bait:
That destroy'd him: from his fingers, ere he knew it, slithering,
   With one wriggle down his gullet it was gone as sure as fate.

There by rod and hooks and tackle how he flung himself about,
   Choking, groaning, writhing, rolling! All in vain– the destined
      thread
Of his life was spun and ended: all in vain: his breath gave out;
   And this mound a fellow-fisher raised above the fisher dead.

THE HOLY BIBLE: *The Apocrypha to the Old Testament: Book of Tobit,
Chapter VI* (c.200–100 BC).

6 Now as they proceeded on their way they came at evening to the
Tigris river and camped there.

Then the young man went down to wash himself. A fish leaped up
from the river and would have swallowed the young man; and the angel
said to him, 'Catch the fish'. So the young man seized the fish and threw
it up on the land. Then the angel said to him 'Cut open the fish and take
the heart and liver and gall and put them away safely'. So the young man
did as the angel told him; and they roasted and ate the fish.

And they both continued on their way until they came near to
Ecbatana. Then the young man said to the angel, 'Brother Azarias, of
what use is the liver and heart and gall of the fish?' He replied, 'As for the
heart and the liver, if a demon or evil spirit gives trouble to any one, you
make a smoke from these before the man or woman, and that person will
never be troubled again. And as for the gall, anoint with it a man who has
white films in his eyes, and he will be cured'.

OVID: from *Metamorphoses* (1–8 AD), *Book III*.
Translated from the Latin by Joseph Addison, 1717.

From high Meonia's rocky shores I came,
Of poor descent, Acœtes is my name;
My sire was meanly born; no oxen plough'd
His fruitful fields, nor in his pastures low'd.
His whole estate within the waters lay,
With lines and hooks he caught the finny prey;
His art was all his livelihood, which he
Thus with his dying lips bequeath'd to me:
'In streams, my boy, and rivers take thy chance;
There swims,' said he, 'thy whole inheritance'.

MARTIAL (38–41 – c. 103 AD): *Ad Piscatorem*. From *Epigrams, Book
IV, 30*.
Translated from the Latin by Robert Louis Stevenson, c. 1883–4.

For these are sacred fishes all
Who know that lord who is lord of all;
Come to the brim and nose the friendly hand
That sways and can beshadow all the land.
Nor only so, but have their names, and come
When they are summoned by the Lord of Rome.
Here once his line an impious Libyan threw;
And as with tremulous reed his prey he drew,
Straight, the light failed him.
He groped, nor found the prey that he had ta'en.
Now as a warning to the fisher clan
Beside the lake he sits, a beggarman.
Thou, then, while still thine innocence is pure,
Flee swiftly, nor presume to set thy lure;
Respect these fishes, for their friends are great
And in the waters empty all thy bait.

PLINY THE ELDER: from *Natural History* (77 AD).
Translated from the Latin by Philemon Holland as *The History of the*
World: commonly called the Natural History of C. Plinius Secundus (1601).
From *Book IX: Of Fishes and Creatures of the Water: Of the Fish Anthias,*
and How He is Taken.

I think it not meet to conceale that, which I perceive many do beleieve
and hold, as touching the fish Anthias*. We have in our Cosmographie
made mention of the Isles Cheldoniae in Asia, situate in a sea full of
rocks under the promontory of Taurus; among which are found great
store of these fishes: and much fishing there is for them, but they are
suddenly taken, and ever after one sort.

For when the time serveth, there goeth forth a fisher in a small boat
or barge for certain daies together, a pretty way into the sea, clad
alwaies in apparel of one and the same colour, at one houre, and to the
same place stil, where he casteth forth a bait for the fish: but the fish
Anthias is so craftie and warie, that whatsoever is thrown forth, he
suspecteth it evermore, that it is a means to surprise him. He feareth
therefore and distrusteth: and as he feareth, so is he as warie: untill at
length, after much practise and often using this devise of flinging meat
into one place, one above the rest groweth so hardy and bold, as to bite
at it, for now by this time he is grown acquainted with the maner
thereof and secure. The fisher takes good mark of this one fish,
making sure reckoning that he wil bring more thither, and be the
means that he shall speed his hand in the end. And that is no hard
matter for him to do, because for certain daies together, that fish, and
none but he, dare adventure to come alone unto the bait. At length this
hardy captaine meets with some other companions, and by little and
little he cometh every day better accompanied than other, until in the
end he brings with him infinite troups and squadrons together, so as
now the eldest of them all (as crafty as they be) be so well used to know
the fisher, that they will snatch meat out of his hands.

Then hee espying his time, putteth forth an hook with the bait,
somwhat beyond his fingers ends, flieth and siezeth upon them more
truly; then catcheth them, and speedily with a quick and nimble hand
whippes them out of the water within the shadow of the ship, for feare
the rest should perceive, and giveth them one after another to his
companion within, who, ever as they be snatcht up, latcheth them in a

*Probably the wrasse.

course twillie or covering, and keeps them sure enough from strugling or squeaking, that they should not drive the rest away. The speciall thing that helpeth this game and pretty sport, is to know the captain from the rest, who brought his fellows to this feast, and to take heed in any hand that he be not twitcht up and caught. And therefore the fisher spareth him, that he may flie and goe to some other flock for to train them to the like banket. Thus you see the maner of fishing for these Anthae.

Now it is reported moreover, that one fisher upon a time of spightfull minde to do his fellow a shrewd turn laid wait for the said captain fish, the leader of the rest for he was very wel known from all others and so caught him: but when the foresaid fisher espied him in the market to be sold, and knew it was he: taking himself misused and wronged, brought his action of the case against the other, and sued him for the dammage, and in the end condemned him.

PLUTARCH (c. 50–100 AD):
from *The Life of Antonius*. From *The Lives of The Noble Greeks and Romans*. Translated from the French of Jacques Amyot by Thomas North, 1579.

But now again to Cleopatra, Plato writeth that there are four kinds of flattery: but Cleopatra divided it into many kinds. For she, were it in sport, or in matters of earnest, still devised sundry new delights to have Antonius at commandment, never leaving him night nor day, nor once letting him go out of her sight. For she would play at dice with him, drink with him, and hunt commonly with him, and also be with him when he went to any exercise or activity of body. And sometimes also, when he would go up and down the city disguised like a slave in the night, and would peer into poor men's windows and their shops, and scold and brawl with them within the house: Cleopatra would be also in a chambermaid's array, and amble up and down the streets with him, so that oftentimes Antonius bare away both mocks and blows. Now, though most men misliked this manner, yet the Alexandrians were commonly glad of this jollity, and liked it well, saying very gallantly, and wisely: That Antonius shewed them a comical face, to wit, a merry countenance: and the Romans a tragical face, to say, a grim look. But to reckon up all the foolish sports they made, revelling in this sort, it were too fond a part of me, and therefore I will tell you one among the rest. On a time he went to angle for fish, and when he could take none, he was as angry as could be, because Cleopatra stood by. Wherefore he secretly commanded the fishermen, that when he cast in his line, they should straight dive under the water, and put a fish on his hook which they had taken before: and so snatched up his angling rod, and brought up fish twice or thrice. Cleopatra found it straight, yet she seemed not to see it, but wondered at his excellent fishing: but when she was alone by her self among her own people, she told them how it was, and bade them the next morning to be on the water to see the fishing. A number of people came to the haven, and got into the fisher-boats to see this fishing. Antonius then threw in his line and Cleopatra straight commanded one of her men to dive under water before Antonius' men, and to put some old salt-fish upon his bait, like unto those that are brought out of the country of Pont. When he had hung the fish on his hook, Antonius thinking he had taken a fish indeed, snatched up his line presently. Then they all fell a-laughing. Cleopatra laughing also, said unto him: Leave us (my Lord) Egyptians (which dwell in the country of Pharus and Canobus) your angling rod: this is not thy profession: thou must hunt after conquering of realms and countries.

THE HOLY BIBLE: Matthew (100–10 AD).

4, 18–22

18 And Jesus, walking by the sea of Galilee, saw two brethren, Simon called Peter and Andrew his brother, casting a net into the sea: for they were fishers.

19 And he saith unto them: Follow me, and I will make you fishers of men.

20 And they straightway left *their* nets, and followed him.

21 And going on from thence he saw other two brethren James *the son* of Zebedee, and John his brother, in a ship with Zebedee their father, mending their nets; and he called them.

22 And they immediately left the ship and their father, and followed him.

17, 24–7

24 And when they were come to Capernaum, they that received tribute *money* came to Peter, and said, Doth not your master pay tribute?

25 He saith, Yes. And when he was come into the house, Jesus prevented him, saying. What thinkest thou, Simon? of whom do the kings of the earth take custom or tribute? of their own children, or of strangers?

26 Peter saith unto him, Of strangers. Jesus saith unto him, Then are the children free.

27 Notwithstanding, lest we should offend them, go thou to the sea, and cast an hook, and take up the fish that first cometh up; and when thou hast opened his mouth, thou shalt find a piece of money: that take, and give unto them for me and thee.

OPPIAN (? latter half of 2nd century AD): from *Halieuticks of the Nature of Fishes and Fishing of the Ancients, Book III*.
Translated from the Greek by John Jones, 1722.

The scenting *Mullet* creeps with slow Advance,
And views the Bait with coy retorted Glance
Irresolute; as when some Traveller meets
The branching Angle of diverging Streets,
Anxious he stands, but sends his Eyes around,
And oft reviews the puzzling Tract of Ground;
Perplexing Thoughts distract his wav'ring Mind,
Each Path's prefer'd, and each as soon declin'd.
At length where partial Fancy points the Way,
His Will determines, and his Feet obey.
Such Doubts the *Mullet's* thinking Part divide;
Alternate Fears and Appetite preside.
    As when some little lisping Miss alone,
When kind Occasion prompts, and Mother's gone,
Attempts the Shelf where hoarded Sweetmeats lie,
But fears the Rod that nods tremendous by;
Each infant Passion struggles in her Soul,
Now Resolution fires, now Fears controll;
Fixt on the Door she keeps her constant Eyes,

And dreads in ev'ry Sound the dire Surprize.
Thrice to the Prize her silent Pace aspires,
Thrice sinks her Courage and her Foot retires.
Thus fluctuates the Fish, till urgent Sense
Sways all his Mind, and draws Discretion thence.
First with his Tail he feels the Bait, and tries
If vital Warmth the beating Pulse supplies,
(For *Mullets* always spare the living Prize.)
Then slightly nibbles, but perceives too late
The doubted Fraud, and feels the pungent Fate.
As when the fi'ry Steed with wild Disdain
Asserts his Freedom, and disputes the Rein;
Thus writhes the *Mullet*; but the Fisher's Hand
Extends the panting Captive on the Sand.

AELIAN (c. 170–235 AD): from *De Natura Animalium*.
Translated from the Greek by A. E. Scholfield, 1958–60.

Book XIV, Chapter 1

In the Ionian Sea close to Epidamnus where the Taulantii live, there is
an island and it is called 'Athena's Isle', and fisher folk live there.
There is also a lagoon in the island where shoals of tame Mackerel are
fed. And the fishermen throw in food to them and observe a treaty of
peace with them; so the fish are free and immune from pursuit and
attain to a great age; there are even ancient Mackerel living there. Yet
they do not feed without making any return, nor do they fail in
gratitude for their food, but after they have been fed by the fishermen
in the morning they too of their own accord go to join the pursuit, as
though they were paying for their maintenance. And advancing beyond
the harbour they set out to meet the strange Mackerel. When they have
encountered them as it were in a company or in line of battle, they
swim up to them as being of the same family and the same kind, nor do
the strangers flee from them, nor do the tame fish attempt to divert
them but bear them company. Presently the tame fish surround the
newcomers, and having encircled them, close their ranks and cut off
the fish in their midst, amounting to a great number, and prevent them
from escaping; they wait for their keepers and provide the fishermen

with a feast in return for the satisfaction of their own appetites. For the fishermen arrive, catch the strangers, and perpetrate a massacre. But the tame fish return with all haste to the lagoon, dive into their lairs, and wait for their afternoon meal, which the fishermen bring, if they want allies and loyal friends as fellow-hunters. And this happens every day.

Book XIV, Chapter 8

There is another city not far away which they call Vicetia, and past it there flows a river of the name of Eretaenus: it traverses a considerable area and then falls into the Eridanus, to which it imparts its waters. Now in the Eretaenus there are Eels of very great size and far fatter than those from any other place, and this is how they are caught. The fisherman sits upon a rock jutting out in some bay-like spot on the river where the stream widens out, or else upon a tree which a fierce wind has uprooted and thrown down close to the bank – the tree is beginning to rot and is no use for cutting up and burning. So the eel-fisher seats himself and taking the intestine of a freshly slaughtered lamb which measures some three or four cubits and has been thoroughly fattened, he lowers one end into the water, and keeps it turning in the eddies; the other end he holds in his hands, and a piece of reed, the length of a sword-handle, has been inserted into it. The food does not escape the notice of the Eels, for they delight in this intestine. And the first Eel approaches, stimulated by hunger and with open jaws, and fastening its curved, hook-like teeth, which are hard to disentangle, in the bait, continues to leap up in its efforts to drag it down. But when the fisherman realises from the agitation of the intestine that the Eel is held fast, he puts the reed to which the intestine has been attached to his mouth and blows down it with all his might, inflating the intestine very considerably. And the downflow of breath distends and swells it. And so the air descends into the Eel, fills its head, fills its windpipe, and stops the creature's breathing. And as the Eel can neither breathe nor detach its teeth which are fixed in the intestine, it is suffocated, and is drawn up, a victim of the intestine, the blown air, and thirdly of the reed. Now this is a daily occurrence, and many are the Eeels caught by many a fisherman. This then is what I have to say of the habits peculiar to these fishers.

Book XV, Chapter 1 (The first-known reference to fishing with a fly).

I have heard and can tell of a way of catching fish in Macedonia, and it is this. Between Beroea and Thessalonica there flows a river called the Astraeus. Now there are in it fishes of a speckled hue, but what the natives call them, it is better to enquire of the Macedonians. Now these fish feed upon the flies of the country which flit about the river and which are quite unlike flies elsewhere; they do not look like wasps, nor could one fairly describe this creature as comparable in shape with what are called *Anthedones* (bumble-bees), nor even with actual honey-bees, although they possess a distinctive feature of each of the afore-said insects. Thus, they have the audacity of the fly; you might say they are the size of a bumble-bee, but their colour imitates that of a wasp, and they buzz like a honey-bee. All the natives call them *Hippurus*. These flies settle on the stream and seek the food that they like; they cannot however escape the observation of the fishes that swim below. So when a fish observes a Hippurus on the surface it swims up noiselessly under water for fear of disturbing the surface and to avoid scaring its prey. Then when close at hand in the fly's shadow it opens its jaws and swallows the fly, just as a wolf snatches a sheep from the flock, or as an eagle seizes a goose from the farmyard. Having done this it plunges beneath the ripple. Now although fishermen know of these happenings, they do not in fact make any use of these flies as baits for fish, because if the human hand touches them it destroys the natural bloom; their wings wither and the fish refuse to eat them, and for that reason will not go near them, because by some mysterious instinct they detest flies that have been caught. And so with the skill of anglers the men circumvent the fish by the following artful con-trivance. They wrap the hook in scarlet wool, and to the wool they attach two feathers that grow beneath a cock's wattles and are the colour of wax. The fishing-rod is six feet long, and so is the line. So they let down this lure, and the fish attracted and excited by the colour, comes to meet it, and fancying from the beauty of the sight that he is going to have a wonderful banquet, opens wide his mouth, is entangled with the hook, and gains a bitter feast, for he is caught.

CASSIANUS BASSUS (ed.): from *Geoponika* (? 2nd century AD), *Book XX*.
Translated from the Greek by Rev. T. Owen, 1805.

Recipe XVII: Bait for Sea Mullets

Put the member of a ram into a new pot, and having covered it with another pot, stop it so that it may have no vent, and send it to the glass furnace to be set on from the morning to the evening, and you will find it become quite tender; then use it for bait.

Recipe XVIII: A Convenient Preparation, that the Fish may come to the same Spot

Take three limpets, that are produced on rocks, and having taken out the fish, inscribe on the shell the words which follow, and you will immediately see the fish come to the same place, in a suprising manner. The words are, 'the God of Armies', and the fishermen make use of them.

AUSONIUS: from *Mosella* (c. 370 AD).
Translated from the Latin by E. H. Blakeney, 1933.

O Naiad, dweller by the river's bank,
Declare these scaly tribes; from thy moist bed
Tell now the hosts that haunt this azure stream.
   The scaly Chub gleams amid grass-grown sands,—
Tender of taste, crammed thick with bones, yet fit
To keep for banquets less than six hours' space.
Here dwells the Trout, whose back with scarlet spots
Is starred; the Roach, with no sharp spines to wound;
The Grayling, too, swift-darting out of sight.
And thou, O Barbel, along passage-ways
Of winding Saar much harassed (there six piers
Of massy stone confront the current), when
Its waters sweep thee onward to a stream
Of noble name, art wont to swim more free.
Of thee Time takes no toll; to thee alone
Of all things living falls a lauded age.

Nor would I leave thee unsung, thou rosy red
Salmon, whose broad tail from the middle depth
Ripples the surface, when thy hidden course
Bewrays its motion. Thou, with scaly coat
Of mail, tho' smooth in front, art doomed to grace
Some noble banquet, still untainted kept
Despite of long delay. Upon thy head
How notable the markings, while to the stream
Thy belly swings, swollen with coils of fat!
Thou too, O Burbot, in Illyricum
And Ister's marish caught (an easy prey
Thanks to the foam that marks thy dwelling place)
Art brought to our broad waters, lest Moselle
Defrauded be of fosterling so famed.
What native colours thine! thy shoulders sleek
Gleam with dark spots, circled with orange rings.
Thy back is marked with azure; for one half
Thy length, full-fleshed we find thee, but from thence
To the tail's end the skin grows rough and dry.
  Nor shalt thou go unsung, joy of the board,
O Perch, thou peer of fish that swim the sea,
Sole rival of red mullets; rich in taste,
And in thy firm flesh all the parts cohere
In flakes: the ridge-bones sever each from each.
Here, too, that lover of the marish haunts
Pools dark with sedge and mud, that deadly foe
To croaking frogs – the Pike, in jesting named
Lucius: a title borne by sons of Rome.
Scorned at the banquets of the rich, he's cooked
In taverns smoking with his greasy fume.
  The green Tench, solace of the vulgar, who
Shall know not them, or Bleak, a prey for hooks
Of urchins? or the Shadfish as they hiss
Upon the hearth – a food for common folk?

* * *

Here where the bank an easy access yields
A throng of spoilers through the river-depths
Are busy, probing everywhcrc (poor fish,
Alack, ill guarded by the inmost stream!);
One in mid water, trailing his moist lines

Far from the bank, sweeps off the finny droves
Caught in his knotted seine; another, where
The river floats along in tranquil course,
Spreads wide his drag-net buoyed on floats of cork.
A third, bent o'er the waters slumbering far
Beneath the boulders, dips the arching top
Of his lithe rod, casting upon the stream
Hooks sheathed with deadly baits. The wandering tribes,
Unwary, rush thereon with gaping jaws:
Too late their open mouths feel, deep within,
Stings of the hidden barb; they writhe; down drops
The float; the rod jerks to the quivering twitch
Of vibrant line. Enough! with one sharp stroke
The prey is hooked, and slantwise from the flood
The lad has flicked his prey. A hissing wind
Follows the blow, as when a lash is plied
And a wind whistles through the stricken air.
The dripping victims flounder on the rocks;
In terror of the sunlight's deadly rays
They quake; the fire that moved them while they lived
Down in their native element, expires
Beneath our sky; gasping, they yield up life.

WANG WEI (699–761 AD): Two Poems.
Translated from the Chinese by G. W. Robinson, 1973.

Taking the Cool of the Evening

Thousands of trunks of huge trees
Along the thread of a clear stream
Ahead the great estuary over which
Comes the far wind unobstructed
Rippling water wets white sands
Silver sturgeon swim in transparency
I lie down on a wet rock and let
Waves wash over my slight body
I rinse my mouth and wash my feet
Opposite there's an old man fishing.
How many fish come to the bait–
East of the lotus leaves–useless to think about it.

The Green Stream

To get to the Yellow Flower River
I always follow the green water stream
Among the hills there must be a thousand twists
The distance there cannot be fifty miles
There is the murmur of water among rocks
And the quietness of colours deep in pines
Lightly lightly drifting water-chestnuts
Clearly clearly mirrored reeds and rushes
I have always been a lover of tranquillity
And when I see this clear stream so calm
I want to stay on some great rock
And fish for ever on and on.

PO CHÜ-I: *Fishing in the Wei River* (811 AD).
Translated from the Chinese by A. Waley.

In waters still as a burnished mirror's face,
In the depths of Wei, carp and grayling swim.
Idly I come with my bamboo fishing-rod
And hang my hook by the banks of Wei stream.
A gentle wind blows on my fishing-gear
Softly shaking my ten feet of line.

Though my body sits waiting for fish to come,
My heart has wandered to the Land of Nothingness.
Long ago a white-headed man
Also fished at the same river's side;
A hooker of men, not a hooker of fish,
At seventy years, he caught Wên Wang*.
But *I*, when I come to cast my hook in the stream,
Have no thought either of fish or men.
Lacking the skill to capture either prey,
I can only bask in the autumn water's light.
When I tire of this, my fishing also stops;
I go to my home and drink my cup of wine.

*The Sage T'ai-kung sat till he was seventy, apparently fishing, but really waiting for a prince who would employ him. At last Wên Wang, king of Chou happened to come that way and at once made him his counsellor.

LI YU (936–78 AD): *Fisherman's Song.*
Translated from the Chinese by Hsiung Ting, 1947.

Foam resembling a thousand drifts of snow.
Soundless, the peach and pear trees form their battalions of spring.
With one jug of wine
And a fishing line,
On this earth how many are as happy as I?
I dip the oar – in the spring winds the boat drifts like a leaf.
A delicate hook on the end of a silk tassel,
An island covered with flowers,
A jugful of wine.
Among the ten thousand waves I wander in freedom!

'The dysporte of fysshynge'

The Middle Ages

Frontispiece to *A Treatyse of Fysshynge with an Angle*. From *The Boke of St Albans*, attributed to Dame Juliana Berners (1496).

AELFRIC (d?1020 AD): *Colloquy.*
Translated by Benjamin Thorpe, from *Analecta Anglo-Saxonica*, 1834.

M: What trade are you acquainted with?
P: I am a fisherman.
M: What do you get by your trade?
P: Food, clothes, and money.
M: How do you catch the fish?
P: I go out in my boat, put forth my nets in the river, throw forth the hook and the baskets, and whatever they catch I take.
M: What do you do if the fish happen to be unclean?
P: I throw out the unclean and take the clean ones to eat.
M: Where do you sell your fish?
P: In the city.
M: Who buys them?
P: The citizens: I am unable to catch as many as I can sell.
M: What kind of fish do you catch?
P: Eels, pike, minnows, eel pouts, trout, and lampreys, and as many other kinds as swim in the river.
M: Why don't you fish in the sea?
P: I do sometimes, but not often, because it is a long voyage to the sea.
M: What do you catch in the sea?
P: Herrings, salmon, dolphins, sturgeons, oysters, crabs, mussels, periwinkles, cockles, plaice, soles, lobsters, and many others of a similar kind.

M: Would you like to catch a whale?
P: No, I should not.
M: Why?
P: Because it is dangerous to catch whales. It is safer for me to go to the river with my boat, than go hunting whales with many boats.
M: Why so?
P: Because I prefer to catch a fish, which I am able to kill, rather than one, who is able to sink and kill with one stroke, not only myself, but also my companions.
M: But nevertheless many men catch whales, and so obtain great profit.
P: You speak truly, but I dare not owing to the sluggishness of my spirit.

GIRALDUS CAMBRENSIS: from *Itinerarium Cambriae* (c. 1207?). Translated from the Latin by Sir Richard Colt Hoare and Rev. Thomas Wright, 1863.

On the highest parts of these mountains are two lakes worthy of admiration. The one has a floating island in it, which is often driven from one side to the other by the force of the winds; and the shepherds behold with astonishment their cattle, whilst feeding, carried to the distant parts of the lake. A part of the bank naturally bound together by the roots of willows and other shrubs may have been broken off, and increased by the alluvium of the earth from the shore; and being continually agitated by the winds, which in so elevated a situation blow with great violence, it cannot reunite itself firmly with the banks. The other lake is noted for a wonderful and singular miracle. It contains three sorts of fish – eels, trout and perch, all of which have only one eye, the left being wanting; but if the curious reader should demand of me the explanation of so extraordinary a circumstance, I cannot presume to satisfy him. It is remarkable also, that in two places in Scotland, one near the eastern, the other near the western sea, the fish called mullets possess the same defect, having no left eye.

ST ANTHONY OF PADUA (1195–1231): *St Anthony to the Fishes*.
Translated by Joseph Addison in *Remarks on Several Parts of Italy*, 1705.

When the heretics would not regard his preaching, St Anthony betook himself to the seashore, where the river Marecchia disembogues itself into the Adriatic. He here called the fish together in the name of God, that they might hear his holy word. The fish came swimming towards him in such vast shoals, both from the sea and from the river, that the surface of the water was quite covered with their multitudes. They quickly ranged themselves, according to their several species, into a very beautiful congregation, and, like so many rational creatures, presented themselves before him to hear the word of God. St Anthony was so struck with the miraculous obedience and submission of these poor animals, that he found a secret sweetness distilling upon his soul, and at last addressed himself to them in the following words.

'Although the infinite power and providence of God (my dearly beloved Fish) discovers itself in all the works of his creation, as in the heavens, in the sun, in the moon, and in the stars, in this lower world, in man, and in other perfect creatures; nevertheless the goodness of the Divine Majesty shines out in you more eminently, and appears after a more particular manner, than in any other created beings. For notwithstanding you are comprehended under the name of reptiles, partaking of a middle nature between stones and beasts, and imprisoned in the deep abyss of waters; notwithstanding you are tost among billows, thrown up and down by tempests, deaf to hearing, dumb to speech, and terrible to behold: notwithstanding, I say, these natural disadvantages, the Divine Greatness shows itself in you after a very wonderful manner. In you are seen the mighty mysteries of an infinite goodness. The holy scripture has always made use of you, as the types and shadows of some profound sacrament.

'Do you think that, without a mystery, the first present that God Almighty made to man, was of you, O ye Fishes? Do you think that without a mystery, among all creatures and animals which were appointed for sacrifices, you only were excepted, O ye Fishes? Do you think there was nothing meant by our Saviour Christ, that next to the paschal lamb he took so much pleasure in the food of you, O ye Fishes? Do you think it was by mere chance, that when the Redeemer of the World was to pay a tribute to Caesar, he thought fit to find it in the mouth of a fish? These are all of them so many mysteries and sacraments, that oblige you in a more particular manner to the praises to your Creator.

'It is from God, my beloved Fish, that you have received being, life, motion, and sense. It is he that has given you, in compliance with your natural inclinations, the whole world of waters for your habitation. It is he that has furnished it with lodgings, chambers, caverns, grottoes, and such magnificent retirements as are not to be met with in the seats of kings, or in the palaces of princes. You have the water for your dwelling, a clear transparent element, brighter than crystal; you can see from its deepest bottom everything that passes on its surface; you have the eyes of a lynx, or of an argus; you are guided by a secret and unerring principle, delighting in everything that may be beneficial to you, and avoiding everything that may be hurtful; you are carried on by a hidden instinct to preserve yourselves, and to propagate your species; you obey, in all your actions, works and motions, the dictates and suggestions of nature, without the least repugnancy or contradiction.

'The colds of winter, and the heats of summer, are equally incapable of molesting you. A serene or a clouded sky are indifferent to you. Let the earth abound in fruits, or be cursed with scarcity, it has no influence on your welfare. You live secure in rains and thunders, lightnings and earthquakes; you have no concern in the blossoms of spring, or in the glowings of summer, in the fruits of autumn, or in the frosts of winter. You are not solicitous about hours or days, months or years; the variableness of the weather, or the change of seasons.

'In what dreadful majesty, in what wonderful power, in what amazing providence did God Almighty distinguish you among all the species of creatures that perished in the universal deluge! You only were insensible of the mischief that had laid waste the whole world.

'All this, as I have already told you, ought to inspire you with gratitude and praise towards the Divine Majesty, that has done so great things for you, granted you such particular graces and privileges, and heaped upon you so many distinguishing favours. And since for all this you cannot employ your tongues in the praises of your Benefactor, and are not provided with words to express your gratitude; make at least some sign of reverence; bow yourselves at his name; give some show of gratitude, according to the best of your capacities; express your thanks in the most becoming manner that you are able and be not unmindful of all the benefits he has bestowed upon you.'

He had no sooner done speaking, but behold a miracle! The fish, as though they had been endued with reason, bowed down their heads with all the marks of a profound humility and devotion, moving their bodies up and down with a kind of fondness, as approving what had been spoken by the blessed Father St Anthony.

The legend adds, that after many heretics, who were present at the miracle, had been converted by it, the saint gave his benediction to the fish, and dismissed them.

BARTHOLOMAEUS ANGLICUS: from *De Proprietibus Rerum*
(c. 1250).
Translated from the Latin by John Trevisa, 1397.

Fyshe, hyghte pisces, and hathe that name of Pascendo, fedynge, as Isodore sayth *libro xii. ca. vi.* Fyshe licketh the erthe and watry herbes, and so get they meete and nouryshynge. Also they benne called Reptilia, crepying, bycause in swimmynge they seme as they did crepe: for in swymming they crepe, though they synke downe to the bottom. Wherof speketh Ambrose in Exameron, and saythe, that bitwene fyshe and water is great nighnes of kynred. For withoute water they may not long lyue; and they lyue not longe with onelye brethynge, withoute drawynge of water. And they haue a maner lyknes and kynd of crepyng, for, whyle a fyshe swymmeth, by shrynkyng and drawynge together of his body, he draweth and gathereth hym selfe in to les length, and anone stretcheth hym selfe agayne, and entendeth to passe forth in the water; and by that dyligence he putteth the water backewarde, and passeth itself forwarde. Therfore he vseth finnes in swymmynge, as a foule vseth fethers in fleenge. But all other wyse in swymmynge a fyshe meueth his fynnes fro the hynder parte dounwarde, and as it were with armes, or ores, he clippeth the water, and holdeth it, and stretcheth hym selfe forwarde. But a byrde meueth his fethers vpwarde, and gadereth thayre, and compelleth it to passe out backeward by large stretchynge of wyndes, and so by violente puttynge of ayre backewarde the bodye meuith forwarde.

GEOFFREY CHAUCER: from *The Complainte of Mars*
(14th century).

To what fyn made the God that sit so hye,
Benethen him, love other companye,
And streyneth folk to love, malgre her hed?
And then her joy, for oght I can espye,
Ne lasteth not the twynkelyng of an ye,
And somme han never joy til they be ded.
What meneth this? What is this mystihed?
Wherto constreyneth he his folk so faste
Thing to desyre, but hit shulde laste?

And thogh he made a lover love a thing,
And maketh hit seme stedfast and during,
Yet putteth he in hyt such mysaventure
That reste nys ther non in his yeving.
And that is wonder, that so juste a kyng
Doth such hardnesse to his creature.
Thus, whether love breke or elles dure,
Algates he that hath with love to done
Hath ofter wo then changed ys the mone.

Hit semeth he hath to lovers enmyte,
And lyk a fissher, as men alday may se,
Baiteth hys angle-hok with som plesaunce,
Til many a fissh ys wod til that he be
Sesed therwith; and then at erst hath he
Al his desir, and therwith al myschaunce;
And thogh the lyne breke, he hath penaunce;
For with the hok he wounded is so sore
That he his wages hath for evermore.

ANON: *The Dialoges of Creatures Moralysed: Dialogo XLVIII: Of a
Fissher and a Lytyll Fissh* (1460).

A fissher as he fisshed he cawght a lytell fissh and whan he wolde haue
kylled him he spake and sayde. O gentyll Fissher haue mercye uppon

me, for yf thou kyl me thou shalt haue but lytel auauntage of me. But and if thou wilt suffre me to go fre and delyuer me from this daunger and captiuitye I promise to God and to the, that I shall cawse the to haue greate wynnynge, for I shal retourne unto the daylye withe greate multitude of fisshes and I shall lede them in to thy nettis. To whom the fissher sayd. How shal I mowe knowe the emonge so many fisshes. Then sayd ye fissh. Cut of a lytell of my tayle that thou mayst know me emong al othir. The fissher gaue credence to his woordis and cut of his tayle and let him go. This lytel fissh was euer uncurteys, for contrary to his promyse he lettyd the fissher as oftyn as he shuld fissh, and withdrewe ye fisshes from him and sayd, faders and worshipfull sen-yours be ye ware of that deceyuar for he deceyuyd me, and cut of my tayle, and so shall he serue you if ye be not ware. And, yf ye beleue not me, beleue his workis that apere upon me. And thus saynge the fissh shewyd them his tayle that was cut. Wherfor the fisshes abhorryd ye fyssher and fled from him in al possible haste. The fissher usid no more fysshinge, wherfore he leuyd in great pouerte. Of fortune it happid so that a long while aftir the fissher cawght agayne the same fissh emonge othir. And whan he knew he kylled him cruelly and sayde

He that hath a good turn and is uncurteys agayn
It is veray rightfull that he be therfore slayne.

JOHN LELAND: from *De Rebus Britannicis Collectanea, Volume VI*. Banquet Given in 1466. (1744 edition. Written in late 16th century).

The great feast at the intronization of the reverende father in God George Nevell, Archbishop of York, and Chauncelour of Englande in the sixth yere of the raigne of kyng Edwarde the fourth.

And first the goodly provision madc for the same.
Here foloweth the servyng of fishe in order.

The First Course

First potage, Almonde butter, Red Herrynges, Salt fysch, Luce salt, Ele, Kelyng, Codlyng, and Hadocke boyled, Thirlepoole* rost. Pyke in Rarblet, Eeles baked, Samon chynes broyled, Turbut baked, And Fritters fryed.

*A species of whale.

The Seconde Course

Freshe Samon jowles, salt Sturgion, Whytynges, Pylchers, Eeles, Makerels, Places fryed, Barbelles, Conger rost, Troute, Lamprey rost, Bret†, Turbut, Roches, Samon baked, Lynge in gelly, Breame baked, Tenche in gelly, Crabbes.

The Third Course

Jowles of freshe Sturgion, Great Eels, Broyled Conger, Cheuens**, Breames, Rudes, Lamprones, Small Perches fryed, Smeltes rost, Shrympes, Small Menewes, Thirlepoole baked, and Lopster.

†Brill.   **Chub.

ALFRED DENISON: from *A Literal translation into English of the Earliest Known Book on Fowling and Fishing Written Originally in Flemish and Printed at Antwerp in the Year 1492* (published in 1872).

The xx chapter teaches how to make a bait and shows how men in the water should do to have all the fishes coming to their hands.

Item, take in May of new honey ås much as thou likest, and add to it red snails with their small houses as much as thou thinkest fit for the purpose and put them in a small clean plate, and add to it ammoniac salt or common salt that dissolves the snails, and take then of glow-worms one pound, and thou shalt make with that a paste, then take of the honey twice as much as of the snails, and take a half pound of them and make of it a paste, and mix it well together, and keep the paste in a small box and when thou wilt fish rub thy hands with the paste and thou shalt see wonders.

DAME JULIANA BERNERS (attrib.): from *A Treatyse of Fysshynge with an Angle*. From *The Boke of St Albans* (1496).

Thus me semyth that huntying and hawkynge and also fowlyngc ben so laborous greuous that none of theym maye perfourme nor bi very meane that enduce a man to a mery spyryte: whyche is cause of his longe lyfe acordynge unto ye sayd parable of Salamon: Dowteles thene folowyth it that it must nedes be the dysporte of fysshynge with an angle. For all other manere of fysshyng is also laborous and greuous: often makynge folkes full wete and colde, whyche many tymes hath be seen cause of grete Infirmytees. But the angler maye haue no colde nor no dysease nor angre, but yf he be causer hymself. For he maye not lese at the moost but a lyne or an hoke: of whyche he may haue store plentee of his owne makynge, as this symple treatyse shall teche hym. So thenne his losse is not greuous, and other greyffes may he not haue, sauynge but yf only fisshe breke away after that he is take on the hoke, or elles that he catche nought: whyche ben not greuous. For yf he faylle of one he maye not faylle of a nother, yf he dooth as this treatyse techyth; but yf there be nought in the water. And yet atte the leest he hath his holsom walke and mery at his ease. A swete ayre of the swete sauoure of the meede floures: that makyth hym hungry. He hereth the melodyous armony of fowles. He seeth the yonge swannes: heerons: duckes: cotes and many other foules wyth theyr brodes; whyche me semyth better than alle the noyse of houndys: the blastes of hornys and the scrye of foulis that hunters: fawkeners and foulers can make. And yf the angler take fysshe: surely thenne is there noo man merier than he in his spyryte. Also who soo woll vse the game of anglynge: he must ryse erly, whiche thyng is prouffytable to man in this wyse, That is to wyte: moost to the heele of his soule. For it shall cause hym to be holy. And to the heele of his body, for it shall cause him to be hole. Also to the encrease of his goodys. For it shall make hym ryche. As the olde englysshe prouerbe sayth in this wyse: who soo woll ryse erly shall be holy helthy and zely. Thus have I prouyd in myn entent that the dysporte and game of anglynge is the very meane and cause that enducith a man in to a mery spyryte: Whyche after the sayde parable of Salomon and the sayd doctryne of phisyk makyth a flourynge aege and a longe. And therefore to al you that ben vertuous: gentyll: and free borne I wryte and make this symple treatyse folowynge: by whyche ye may haue the full crafte of anglynge to dysport you at your luste: to the entent that your aege maye the more floure and the more lenger to endure.

* * *

The thyrde good poynt is whan the fysshe bytyth that ye be not to hasty to smyte nor to late, For ye must abide tyll ye suppose that the bayte be ferre in the mouth of the fysshe, and thenne abyde noo longer. And this is for the groude. And for the flote whan ye se it pullyd softly vnder the water: or elles caryed vpon the water softly: thenne smyte. And loke that ye neuer ouersmyte the strengthe of your lyne for brekynge. And yf it fortune you to smyte a grete fysshe with a small harnays, thenne ye must lede hym in the water and labour him there tyll he be drownyd and ouercome. Thenne take hym as well as ye can or maye. And euer be waar that ye holde not ouer the strengthe of your lyne. And as moche as ye may lete hym not come out of your lynes ende streyghte from you: But kepe hym euer vnder the rodde, and euermore holde hym streyghte: soo that your lyne may susteyne and beere his lepys and his plungys wyth the helpe of your cropp: and of your honde.

* * *

Here folowyth the order made to all those whiche shall haue the understondynge of this forsayd treatyse and vse it for theyr pleasures.

Ye that can angle and take fysshe to your pleasures as this forsayd treatyse techyth and shewyth you: I charge and requyre you in the name of alle noble men that ye fysshe not in noo poore mannes seuerall water: as his ponde: slewe: or other necessary thynges to kepe fysshe in wythout his lycence and good wyll. Nor that ye vse not to breke noo mannys gynnys lyenge in theyr weares and in other places due vnto theym. Ne to take the fysshe awaye that is taken in theym. For after a fysshe is taken in a mannys gynne yf the gynne be layed in the comyn waters: or elles in suche waters as he hireth, it is his owne propre goodes. And yf ye take it awaye ye robbe hym: whyche is a ryght shamfull dede to ony noble man to do yt that theuys and brybours done: whyche are punysshed for theyr evyll dedes by the necke and otherwyse whan they maye be aspyed and taken. And also yf ye doo in lyke manere as this treatise shewyth you: ye shall haue no nede to take of other menys: whiles ye shal haue ynough of your owne takying yf ye lyste to labour therefore, whyche shall be to you a very pleasure to se the fayr bryght shynynge scalyd fysshes dysceyved by your crafty meanes and drawne vpon londe. Also that ye breke noo mannys heggys in goynge abowte your dysportes: ne opyn noo mannes gates but that ye shytte theym agayn. Also ye shall not vse this forsayd crafty dysporte for no covetysenes to thencreasynge and sparynge of your money oonly, but pryncypally for your solace and to cause the helthe of your body, and specyally of your soule. For whanne ye purpoos to goo on your disportes in fysshyng ye woll not desyre gretly many persones wyth you, whiche myghte lette you of your game. And thenne ye maye serue God deuowtly in sayenge affectuously youre custumable prayer.

And thus doynge ye shall eschewe and voyde many vices, as ydylnes whyche is pryncypall cause to enduce man to many other vyces, as it is ryght well knowen.

Also ye shall not be to rauenous in takyng of your sayd game as to moche at one tyme: whiche ye maye lyghtly doo yf ye doo in euery poynt as this present treatyse shewyth you in euery poynt: whyche lyghtly be occasyon to dystroye your owne dysportes and other mennys also. As whan ye haue a suffycyent mese ye sholde coveyte nomore as at that tyme. Also ye shall besye yourselfe to nouryssh the game in all that ye maye: and to dystroye all such thynges as ben devourers of it. And all those that done after this rule shall haue the blessynge of god and saynt Petyr, whyche he theym graunte that wyth his precyous blood vs boughte.

ANON: sixteenth-century spell to take fish. From the British Museum
(Sloane ms. 3846, f.54).

If thou wilt take fish in great quantity, when thou beginnest let the moon be Aquarius, Cancer or Pisces and putt one of these sigills* in the nett the first tyme that thou doest fish, saying, I will gather by this same incense a multitude of fish of this water round about that they come unto this nett of taking by the power of the Angell of Luna, hee fore-seeing them to come by his vertue and working, when thou hast done thus thou shalt see a mervaile for within a little space of tyme, there shal come many fishes to the nett that are within the circuite about.

*Occult signs.

JACOPO SANNAZARO: from *Piscatorial Eclogues: Eclogue 5: Herpylis
the Sorceress* (1526).
Translated from the Latin by Ralph Nash, 1966.

Herpylis walked down to the liquid waves of Sebeto, Herpylis not least of the Euboides, whom her father Alcon taught, Alcon known to the Muses and to Phoebus. Also her likeminded sister came to take her part in the joint labour and bore the vessel according to custom. Herpylis with flowing locks and left foot naked murmurs low and long over her potions and thus she speaks:

'Set up the altar and draw living water from the stream, and pluck the hoary wormwood from the neighbouring field. Him, him will I try to inflame with magic spells who left me wretched, robbed of all my heart. Now, now, my thread, revolve the spinning reel.

'Let the brazen reel be summoned to the arts of Haemony, that has the power to make the rain to cease, to drive the clouds from the sky, to draw up fearful fishes from the deep. Revolve, my thread, revolve the spinning reel.

'First this seaweed, spindrift of the swelling sea, is cast about for you, and, being dry, consumed by the swift flames: thus, Maeon, thus for me, may you burn to the marrow. Now, now, my thread, revolve the spinning reel.

'Three times this moss, Clearista, three times burn this crab without a pincer, and say the while "With these I burn the guts of Maeon". Revolve, my thread, revolve the spinning reel.

'Now the sponge is moistened with my tears. Ah good sponge, born in the great sea, drink up my tears with a will, and even as you draw them up thirstily, so draw up all sensation from the breast of Maeon, of ungrateful Maeon. Now, now, my thread, revolve the spinning reel.

'Let him grow fat as the pumice stone is fat, let him rest like a wave of the open sea borne hither and thither, driven and battered by the winds. But why should I, alas, my bosom stricken with grievous sorrow, make imprecation and hurl out my laments to the empty winds? Shall I repay Maeon as many words as Maeon does me injuries? Revolve, my thread, revolve the spinning reel.

'Hither, come hither, fierce stingaree*, who purpose wounds with rigid tail, and you echeneis†, whose nature it is to arrest in their courses the sailing ships; strive thou to hold back the swift feet of Maeon, and thou to transfix his heart. Now, now, my thread, revolve the spinning reel.

'Braise together the liver and spume of the black torpedo**. Tomorrow I shall send this deadly drink to him. May he drink and

*Sting ray.
†Remora, or sucker-fish.
**Cramp fish.

straightway his pallid limbs grow numb. Revolve, my thread, revolve the spinning reel.

'Rip up the sea-hare by hand; the venom of the sea-hare is penetrating. This one was born in the Eastern waves; Aegle brought it, learned Aegle, and bade me touch with it mine enemy's threshold. Run now, touch, smear as you touch; tomorrow that faithless fellow will pay me his penalties, Maeon will groan on his own threshold. Now, now, my thread, make cease the spinning reel.

'Pound to bits the halcyon's nest for me; it is said to disperse the winds and to tame the savage storms of the open sea. Haply this will settle the storms of my heart. Make cease, my thread, make cease the spinning reel.'

GEORGE CLARK: *An act for the preservation of the spawn and fry of fish, 1599.* From *The Game Laws, from King Henry III to the Present Period* (published 1786).

For the preservation hereafter of spawn, fry, and young breed of eels, salmons, pikes, and of all other fish, which heretofore hath been much destroyed in rivers and streams, salt and fresh, within this realm, in so much, that in diuers places, they feed swine and dogs with the fry and spawn of fish, and otherwise (lamentable and horrible to be reported) destroy the same, to the great hinderance and decay of the common wealth; be it therefore enacted, That no person or persons, of what estate, degree, or condition, socver he or they may be, within any manner of net, weel, but, taining, kepper, lime, crele, raw, sagnet, trolnet, trimenet, trimbote, saltbote, weblister, seur, lammet, or with any device or engine made of hair, wool, line or canvas, or shall use any heling-net or trim-boat, or by any other device, engine, cawtel, ways or means whatsoever, heretofore made or devised, hereafter to be made or devised, shall take and kill any young brood, spawn, or fry of eels, salmon, pike or pikerel, or of any other fish, in any floudgate, pipe at the tail of a mill, weare, or in any straites, streams, brooks, rivers, fresh or salt, within this realm of England, Wales, Berwick, or the marches thereof, nor shall, by any of the ways and means aforesaid, or otherwise, in any river or place above specified, take or kill any salmons or trouts, not being in season, being kepper salmons, or kepper trouts, shedder salmons, or shedder trouts.

SIR JOHN MANDEVILLE: from *The Voiage and Trauaile of Syr John Maundeville: Ca. lviii: Of the Kingedome of Talonach, The King Thereof Hath Many Wyves* (1568).

Then is there an other yle that men call Talonach that is a great lande, and plenteous of goods, and fyshes, as you shall hereafter heare.

And the king of the lande hath as many wives as he will, a thousande and mo, and lyeth never by one of them but once, and that lande hath a marvayle that is in no other land, for all maner fyshes of the sea cometh there once a year, one after an other, and lyeth him nere the lande, sometime on the lande, and so lye three days and men of that lande come thither and take of them what he will, and thane go those fyshes awaye and an other sorte commeth, and lyeth also three dayes and men take of them, and thus doe all maner of fyshes tyll all have bene there, and menne have taken what they wyll. And menne wot not the cause why it is so. But they of that countrey saye, that those fyshes come so thyther to do worship to theyr king, for they saye he is the most worthiest king of the worlde for he hath so many wives and geateth so many children of them. And that same kings hath xiiii M. Oly fauntes* or mo, which be all tame, and they bee all fedde of the men of his countrey, for his pleasure bicause that he may have them redy to his hande whan he hath any warre against any kyng or prince, and than he doth put uppon theyr backs castels and men of warre as the use is of the lande, and lykewyse do other kyngs and princes there about.

*Elephants.

ANON (?WILLIAM SAMUEL): from *The Arte of Angling* (1577).

Piscator: In the year of our Lord 1497, a pike was taken in a lake about Haslepurn, the imperial city of Swethland, and a ring of copper found in his gills, under his skin; and a little part thereof seen shining, whose figure and inscription about the compass of it was such in Greek as we here exhibit, which John Dalburg, Bishop of Worms, did expound it thus 'I am the first fish of all, put into this lake by the hands of Frederick the Second, ruler of the world, the fifth day of October, in the year of our Lord 1230'. Thereupon is gathered the sum of 267 years. And, verily, before it was of Frederick the Emperor so marked, a good while it had lived, and, if as yet it had not been taken, it would have lived a longer time.

And now to return to the chevin. When I dwelled in Savoy, the overmost parts of Switzerland, in angling in a part of Losana Lake and the ditch of Geneva, but chiefly in the swift Rodanus, I took sometime the chevin and very fair, the people marveling at my pastime (for that recreation is not there used). They much more marvelled that I or any of my countrymen would eat of them, for they do as much despise them as the Frieser in Friesland doth abhor to eat calves' flesh.

Viator: How kill you the chevin?

Piscator: He will bite very well at a minnow, the great red worm, the white worm in the dead ash, the grasshopper, the young unhaired mouse, the black snail, slit in the back that her grease may hang out, the hornet, the great bear worm in a swift stream or at a mill-tail with heavy gears, the marrow in the ridge-bone of a loin of veal, yea, and rather than fail, at a piece of bacon, I mean the fat.

Viator: I have heard say that he will not stick to bite at a frog.

Piscator: I know not that, but this I tell you, you must stand close, for he hath a quick eye and will fly like an arrow out of a bow to his den or hole, which he is never far from. Your line must be strong and your hook well hardened. Well, now, after grace we will sit by the fire.

GUILLAUME DE SALUSTE DU BARTAS: from *La Semaine* (1578).
Translated from the French by Joshua Sylvester as *Devine Weekes* (1605).

The *Cramp-fish*, knowing that she harboureth
A plague-full humour and fell banefull breath,
A secret *Poppie*, and a sence-lesse Winter,
Benumming all that dare too-neere her venter:
Poures forth her poyson, and her chilling Ice
On the next Fishes, charm'd so in a trice,
That she not onely stayes them in the Deepe,
But stunnes their sence, and lulls them fast a-sleepe,
And then (at fill) she with their flesh is fed,
Whose frozen limbes (still liuing) seeme but dead.
'Tis this *Torpedo*, that when she hath tooke
Into her throat the sharpe deceitfull hooke,
Doth not as other Fish, that wrench and wriggle,
When they be prickt, and plunge, and striue, and struggle,

And by their stirre, thinking to scape the Angle,
Faster and faster on the hooke doo tangle:
But wily, claspping close the Fishing Line,
Sodainly spewes onto the siluer Brine
Her secret-spreading, sodaine-speeding bane
Which vp the Line, and all along the Cane,
Creepes to the hand of th' Angler, who with-all
Benumm'd and sencelesse, sodainly lets fall
His hurtfull pole, and his more hatefull prize:
Becomne like one that as in bed he lies,
Seemes in his sleepe to see some gastly Ghost;
In a cold sweat, shaking, and swelt almost,
He calls his Wife for ayde, his friends, his folkes,
But his stuft stomack his weake clamour choakes:
Then would he strike at that he doth behold,
But sleepe and feare his feeble hands doo hold:
Then would he runne away; but as he striues,
He feels his feete fetter'd with heauie Gyues.

   But if the *Scolopendra* haue suckt in
The sower-sweet morsell with the barbed Pinne,
She hath as rare a trick to ridd her from-it:
For instantly, she all her guts doth vomit,
And hauing clear'd them from the danger, then
She faire and softly sups them in againe,
So that not one of them within her wombe
Changeth his Office or his wonted roome.

   The thriuing *Amia* (neere *Abydus* breeding)
And suttle *Sea-Foxe* (in Seeds-loue exceeding)
Without so vent'ring their deare life and lyning,
Can fro the Worme-claspe compasse their vntwining!
For sucking in, more of the twisted haire,
Aboue the hooke they it in sunder sheare,
So that their foe, who for a Fish did looke,
Lifts up a bare line, rob'd of bait and hooke.

   But timorous *Barbels* will not taste the bit
Till with their tayles they haue vnhooked it,
And all the baytes the Fisher can deuise
Cannot beguile their warie iealousies.

MICHEL DE MONTAIGNE: from *Essais, Second Booke XII: An Apologie to Raymond Sebond* (1580–8).
Translated from the French by John Florio, 1603.

We share the fruits of our prey with our dogges and hawkes, as a meed of their paine and reward of their industry. As about *Amphipolis* in *Thrace*, faulkners, and wilde hawks divide their game equally: And as about the *Maeotide*-fennes, if fishers doe not very honestly leave behind them an even share of their fishings for the Woolves that range about those coasts, they presently run and teare their nets. And, as we have a kinde of fishing, rather managed by sleight, than strength, as that of hooke and line about our Angling-rods, so have beasts amongst themselves. *Aristotle* reporteth, that the Cuttle-Fish, casteth a long gut out of her throat, which like a line she sendeth forth, and at her pleasure pulleth it in againe, according as she perceiveth some little fish come neere her, who being close-hidden in the gravell or stronde, letteth him nible or bite the end of it, and then by little and little drawes it in unto her, untill the Fish be so neere, that with a sodaine leape she may catch it.

* * *

In the manner of the Tunnies life, may be discovered a singular knowledge of the three parts of the Mathematikes. First for Astrologie, it may well be said that man doth learne it of them: For, wheresoever the winter Solstitium doth take them, there do they stay themselves, and never stir till the next Æquinoctium, and that is the reason why *Aristotle* doth so willingly ascribe that art unto them: Then for Geometrie and Arithmetike, they alwaies frame their shole of a Cubike figure, every way square: and so forme a solide, close and wel-ranged battailon, encompassed round about of six equall sides. Thus orderly marshaled, they take their course and swim whither their journey tends, as broad and wide behind as before: So that he that seeth and telleth but one ranke, may easily number all the troope, forsomuch as the number of the depth is equall unto the bredth, and the bredth unto the length.

THOMAS COGHAN: from *The Haven of Health, Chapter 177: The Nature of the Troute* (1584).

The tenth is a Troute, which is so sound in nourishing, that when we would saie in English, that a man is throughly sound, we use to say that he is sound as a Troute. This fish of nature loueth flatterie; for being in the water it will suffer it selfe to be rubbed and clawed, and so to be taken. Whose example I would wish no maydes to folow, lest they repent after clappes.

THOMAS HARIOT: *A Briefe and True Report of the New Found Land of Virginia* (1588).

They have likewise a notable way to catche fishe in their Rivers, for whereas they lacke both yron, and steele, they faste unto their Reedes or longe Rodds, the hollowe tayle of a certain fishe like to a sea crabb in steede of a poynte, wehrwith by nighte or day they stricke fishes, and take them opp into their boates. They also know how to use the prickles, and pricks of other fishes. They also make weares, with settinge opp reedes or twigges in the water, which they soe plant one within another, that they growe still narrower, and narrower, as appeareth by this figure. Ther was never seen amonge us soe cunninge a way to take fish withall, whereof sondrie sortes as they fownde in their Rivers, unlike unto ours, which are also of a verye good taste. Doubtless yt is a pleasant sighte to see the people, somtymes wading and goinge somtymes sailing in those Rivers which are shallowe and not deepe, free from all care of heapinge opp Riches for their posterite, content with their state, and livinge frendlye together of those things which God of his bountye hath given unto them, yet without givinge hym any thanks according to his desarte.

LEONARD MASCALL: from *A Booke of Fishing with Hooke and Line, and all other instruments thereunto belonging* (1590).

The Carpe

The Carpe also is a straunge and daintie fish to take, his baites are not well knowne, for he hath not long beene in this realme. The first bringer of them into England (as I have been credibly informed) was maister Mascoll of Plumsted in Sussex, who also brought first the planting of the Pippin in England: but now many places are replenished with Carpes, both in poundes and rivers, and because not knowing well his cheefe baites ine each moneth, I will write the lesse of him. He is a straunge fish in the water, and very straunge to bite, but at certaine times to wit, at foure a clocke in the morning, and eight at night be his chiefe byting times, and he is so strong enarmed in the mouth, that no weake harness will hold him, and his byting is very tickle: but as touching his baytes, having small knowledge by experience, I am loth to write more then I know and have prooved. But well I wote, the red worme and the Menow bee good baites for him in all times of the yeare, and in June with the cadys or water worme: in July, and in August with the Maggot or gentyll, and with the coale worme, also with paste made with hony and wheate flower, but in Automne, with the redde worme is best, and also the Grashopper with his legs cut off, which he wil take in the morning, or the whites of hard egges steeped in tarte ale, or the white snaile.

To take much fish by a light in the night

Ye shall distill in a lembeck of glasse, a quantitie of glowormes that shineth at night, with a soft fire, and put the distilled water into a thin viall of glasse, and thereunto put foure ounces of quicksilver, that must be purged or past thorough leather, or Kidde skinne. Then stoppe the glasse that no water enter, and tie it in the midst of your bow net for breaking, and so cast it in the water, and the fish will soone come unto the light, and covet to enter into the net, and so ye shall take many. And some doth suppose if ye doe but take a certaine of those glowormes, and put them in a thinne viole or glasse, and then stoppe it close, and tie it in the net, they will shine as well and give as much light. But then I doubt they will not long be alive without meate, except ye put herbes unto them in the day and let them feede, and use them in the night as before. So yee may reserve them for your purpose (I thinke) a long time.

THOMAS BASTARD: from *Chresteleros, Seven Bookes of Epigrames written by T. B.* (1598).

Book IV, Epigram 39: Ad Henricum Wottonem

Wotton, my little Beere dwels on a hill,
Under whose foot the silver Trowt doth swim,
The Trowt silver without and goold within,
Bibbing cleere *Nectar*, which doth aye destill
From *Nulams* lowe head; there the birds are singing,
And there the partiall sunne still gives occasion,
To the sweete dewes eternal generation:
There is greene ioy, and pleasures ever springing.
O iron age of men, O time of rue.
Shame ye not that all things are goold but you?

Book VI, Epigram 14: De Piscatione

Fishing, if I a fisher may protest,
Of pleasures is the sweet'st of sports the best,
Of exercises the most excellent.
Of recreations the most innocent.
But now the sport is marde, and wott ye why?
Fishes decrease, and fishers multiply.

JANUS DUBRAVIUS: from *A New Booke of Husbandry* (1599).

Of Cyprinus, in Englysh a Carpe.

Somewhat I doubted (I confesse) whether I might tearme that fish Cyprinus, which is commonly called Carpo: the occasion of this doubt was, because Plinie would have it a Sea fish. Oppinianus also in his verses wryteth of it as a Sea fish, affirming that he spauneth five times in one yeere: But Plinie sayth six times, when as his opinion is that Carpo casteth spaune but once in a yeere, or twice at the most, and to haunt every Ponde and River. But at the last Aristotles bookes *De Natura Animalium*, resolved me of this doubt, in which Aristotle reckoneth sometymes Cyprinus as well amongst the Sea-fysh, as amongst these that live in Rivers and Ditches, describing him according to the proportion and figure of Carpo, having foure guilles on either side the head, a grosse mouth, a thicke and fast tongue, a belly full of frye about the bignesse of Millet. Also he sheweth, that as the nature of Carpo is, such also is the nature of Cyprinus: for he howseleth him selfe by the bank sides, and when he spawneth, coveteth shallow places, and is blasted at the rysing of the Dogge starre: which all are peculiar and proper to the Carpo: not because these two be onely like one another, but one and the self same with Cyprinus; differing in name and not in nature. And for because this worde Carpo is barberous, I will alto-gether reiect it, and in stead thereof, use this worde Cyprinus: which is indifferently used of the Grecians and Latines. And let no man be troubled in searching the cause why his frye is oftner found in the Sea then in Pondes, for how it hapneth, I will declare in a more apt place. Now it pertayneth more to purpose, diligently to marke the conditions and qualities of Cyprinus, for as much as nature instituted and made him live amongst other fish, without damage doing, and hurting no kinds of thing that lyveth in the water. Besides this he hath no gaping mouth armed with teeth, but close and tender: and as often as he gapeth, his mouth is round, and shyning like a ring. He hath onely two teeth in his mouth, and those very blunt. Blunt also is his back-bone, and soft be his finnes: and a light male covereth all his body, by reason of the continuall coniunction and ioyning together of the scalles. Such a thing also is his forked tayle, with the which he as quickly swimmeth over al the Ponde, as if he were roed in a Boate: and there lyveth of his owne iuice, without any cost to his Maister, bringing this commoditie, that where as he is fatted of his owne, he most delicately feedeth his maister with the pleasant and sweete foods of his body, whether it be rosted, baken, sodden, or salted.

Of the Fish Lucius, in English a Pike

Also the name of the fish Lucius, seemeth in olde time not very famous, for ye shall scarcely repeate an ancienter writer then Aus-onius, that so tearmeth him. And this Ausonius by hap rather ridicu-lously, then by any good ground of reason, mooved with the name of a certaine man called Lucius, in his worke *De Mosella*, writeth thus:

> To crooking Frogges a deadly plague, Lucius by nature is,
>> The secret hooles he sets about, that none his furie misse:
> Yet he him selfe is nothing worth, nor fit for tables use,
>> But sod in smoke with filthy stench, the sence doth foule abuse.

So peradventure it was in times past, but now the fish Lucius is made hot in more lightsome and greater fiers, and a chosen meate for Noble mens tables: not that which feedeth on frogges, or lyes lurking in myrie holes, but that which in pure and cleere Pondes is feede and fatted with the frye of Carpe, and therefore sweete, without all unsaverie tastes, as Martiall sayth:

No Gilt-head sure deserveth price, or yet is worth the dish,
    If that the same devowreth not of Lucryne meere the fysh.

So commendable and delectable a fish is the Pike, to whom in Pondes Carpes frye is foode: and thereof both quickly and tenderly increaseth. And no doubt, if Ausonius has tasted of him thus fed, he would have refrayned from so unmodest a slaunder. In nature and disposition he is lyke unto a Wolfe: for he is like ravening, like greedy and hurtfull, and so eger, that oft times he is cruell to his owne kind, and in extreme hunger feedeth on earth: for this cause, many rather call him Lupus, a Wolfe; then Lucius, a Pike, when as amongst ravening fish there is mo kindes of Wolves than one, as witnesseth Collumella, who councelleth to put into Pondes ravening fish of one disposition, rather then divers of conditions. But some men will heere peradventure aske, Why we put into Pondes the Pike, being a spoyler and an enemie to Carpes frye: Marie to liten and ease the Ponde, unprofitably loden and combred with too much frye, that the Carpes preserved for increase and fatnes, whylest they feede more freely through the smalnes of the number, may sooner to our use waxe great and thicke, and so with the fat and thicke Pikes, may be solde for more money: for if a Pond were free and cleere of the great swarme of young fishes, it should be neither profitable nor needefull, to commit Sheepe (as the proverbe is) unto a Wolfe. I can not choose, but must needes in this place commit to wryting that spectacle which once I saw with mine eyes at the Pondes nigh to the Castle Cremsiris, when as I accompanied Byshop Stanislane Thurzo: There lay lurking in a corner of the Pondes side a frogge at variance with a Pike, and when as by fortune the Pike like unto an idle loyterer, litely with his tayle to and fro, forrowed the toppe of the water, til at the last he came neere unto the place where the frogge lay in wayte: the frogge overslipped not this occasion, but as soone as he saw opportunitie to assault his enemie, with swollen cheekes and angrie eyes, at unawares he lept upon his head, and stretching abrode his feete, imbraced his forehead (marke the wylines of the beast) especially assayled the Pikes eyes, tearing with his teeth his tender partes. The Pike mooved with anguish and paine, sometimes swiftly swam in the water, sturring up the waves; sometimes with whorling turned about, some times rubbed him against the shrubbes and reedes that appeared above the water, trying all these meanes to be delivered from this evill, and to shake from his brow the enemie, being of no force, in comparison to his: But all his labour was in vaine, so violently the frogg bit his brow, and so stoutly tooke revengement on his tormentour and troublour, till such time as strength fayling through much wrestling, the Pike vanquished, shrunke downe, and sunke with the frogge to the bottom. Wee all this while standing in the same place, and looking after the wrestlers that shewed us this pastime, wherein we tooke no small delight, beholde sodaynly the frogge riseth to the toppe, reioycing and crooking like a conquerour, getteth him againe to his cave. The Byshop straight commaunded the fisher-men to be called, if they searching with their nettes, and finding the Pike, might declare what had happened. The Pike is drawen foorth blinde on both eyes, not without our great admiration: but the fisher-men willed us to leave and cease from marveyling, for as much as they have often happened on such frayes, and often have taken Pikes made blinde on both their eyes by frogges, and those to be very leane, because they being deprived of their eyes, could not hunt after their pray, but onely ballasse their bellies with barren and unfruitfull sand.

THOMAS NASHE: from *Lenten Stuffe* (1599).

Be of good cheere, my weary Readers, for I haue espied land, as *Diogenes* said to his weary Schollers when he had read to a waste leafe. Fisher-men, I hope, wil not finde fault with me for fishing before the nette, or making all fish that comes to the net in this history, since, as the Athenians bragged they were the first that inuented wrastling, and one *Ericthonius* amongst them that he was the first that ioyned horses in collar couples for drawing, so I am the first that euer sette quill to paper in prayse of any fish or fisherman.

Not one of the Poets aforetime could giue you or the sea a good word: *Ouid* sayth, *Nimium ne credite ponto* – the sea is a slippery companion, take heed how you trust him: And further, *Periurij poenas repetit ille locus* – it is a place like Hel, good for nothing but to punish periurers; with innumerable inuectiues more against it throughout in euery book.

Plautus in his *Rudens* bringeth in fishermen cowthring and quaking, dung wet after a storme, and complaining their miserable case in this forme, *Captamus cibum e mari; si euentus non venit, neque quicquam captum est piscium, salsi lautique domum redimus clanculum, dormimus incaenati* – All the meate that we eate we catch out of the sea, and if there wee misse, wel washed and salted, wee sneake home to bed supperlesse: and vpon the taile of it hee brings in a parasite that flowteth and bourdeth them thus: *Heus vos familica gens hominum vt viuitis? vt peritis?* hough, you hungerstarued gubbins or offalles of men, how thriue you, howe perish you? and they, cringing in their neckes, like rattes smothered in the holde, poorely replicated, *Viuimus fame, speque, sitique* with hunger, and hope, and thirst wee content our selues. If you would not misconceit that I studiously intended your defamation, you should haue thicke haileshot of these.

Not the lowsie riddle wherewith fishermen constrayned (some say) *Homer*, some say another Philo-sopher, to drowne hymselfe, because he could not expound it, but should be dressed and set before you *supernagulum*, with eight score more galliarde crosse-poynts, and kickshiwinshes of giddy eare-wig brains, were it not I thought you too fretfull and chollericke with feeding altogether on salt meates, to haue the secrets of your trade in publique displayed. Will this appease you, that you are the predecessors of the Apostles, who were poorer Fishermen than you, that for your seeing wonders in the deepe, you may be the sonnes and heires of the Prophet Ionas, that you are all Caualiers and Gentlemen since the king of fishes vouchsafed you for his subiects, that for your selling smoake you may be courtiers, for your keeping of fasting dayes Friar Obseruants, and lastly, that, looke in what Towne there is the signe of the three mariners, the huff-cappest drink in that house you shal be sure of alwayes?

No more can I do for you than I haue done, were you my godchildren euery one: God make you his children and keepe you from the Dunkerks, and then I doubt not but when you are driuen into harbour by foule weather, the kannes shall walke to the health of *Nashes* Lenten-stuffe and the praise of the redde Herring, and euen those that attend vppon the pitch-kettle will bee druncke to my good fortunes and recommendums.

'Study to be quiet'
The Seventeenth Century

Sold by Rich Marriott in St Dunstans Church yard

Vaughan sculp

Frontispiece to *The Experienc'd Angler* by Robert Venables (1662).

LADY MARGARET HOBY: from *The Diary* (Tuesday, 20 May 1600).

After priuat praers I talked with a good christian touchinge sundrie
infirmetes that our humaine nature is subiect vnto: after, I brak my
fast, wrought, hard Mr Rhodes Read, took a lector and, when I had
praied, I went to dinner: after, I wrought a whill and then walked a
fisshinge – after I Came home I went to priuat medetation and praier:
after, to supper: then I walked abroad and then Came to the lecture:
after, I went to priuat praers and so went to bed.

JOHN TAVERNER: from *Certaine Experiments Concerning Fish and
Fruite* (1600).

The causes moving to have a pond lie but one yeare with water and
fish, and the next yeare emptie and drie, do hereafter ensue. First by
that meanes you shall avoid supcrfluous number of frie, which greatly
hinder the growth and goodness of your greater fish. Secondly, by that
meanes you shall so proportion your pond, that it shall never be
overstored. Thirdly, by that meanes your water shall always be excellent sweete, by reason it overfloweth such ground as hath taken the
sunne and ayre all the sommer before: wherein also if cattell do feede,
or especially be fodered and lie, their dung and stale together with the
naturall force of the Sunne at the next Spring overflowing with water,
will breede an innumerable number of flies, and bodes of diverse kinds

and sorts, which in a faire sunshine day in March or Aprill, you shall see in the water as thicke as motes in the Sunne, of which bodes and flies the fish do feed exceedingly. Also great store of seedes, of weedes, and grasse, shedding that sommer that it lieth drie, is a great feede to your fish the next Sommer after, when it is overflowne with water. The sayd bodes do for the most part breede of the blowings and seede of diverse kinds of flies and such like living creatures in the Sommer when your pond lieth drie, in the dung of cattell, and otherwise: and take life and being the next Spring time by the naturall heate of the Sunne, together with the moisture of the fat and pleasant water, as aforesaid: for surely many and sundrie kinds of flies that flie about in the ayre in Sommer time, do take life in the water overflowing such ground where they have bene left by the blowings and seede of other flies. And I have often observed and beheld in a sunshine day, in shallow waters, especially where any dung or fatte earth is therewith mingled: I say, I have seene a young flie swimme in the water too and fro, and in the end come to the upper crust of the water and assay to flie up: howbeit not being perfectly ripe or fledge, have twice or thrice fallen downe againe, into the water: howbeit in the end receiving perfection by the heate of the sunne, and the pleasant fat water, hath in the ende within some halfe houre after taken her flight, and flied quite awaie, into the ayre. And of such young flies before they are able to flie awaie, do fish feede exceedingly. Fourthlie, your fish shall everie yeare have feeding in proportion to their increasing in bignesse: for it standeth with reason, that Carpes or other fish of twelve inches long, will require more feeding than so many of five inches long will do: but chieflie by means aforesayd of sewing everie yeare, you shall have oportunitie to be rid of the great increase of frie, and your greater fish more sweete and fat than any other hath by farre.

Fish will live in a manner in any pond, and without any feeding, or such other industrie as aforesayd: but then they are forced to live uppon the muddie earth and weedes that grow in such ponds, and being so fedde, they will eate and taste accordingly: and there is as great difference in taste between fish that is kept as aforesaid, and other fish that is kept in a standing pond without feeding or other industrie, as is betweene the flesh of a Larke, and the flesh of a Crow or Kite. And I suppose that that is the cause that most men are out of love with all pond fish, because they never tasted of any good or well ordered pond fish.

That Sommer that your pond lieth drie, as aforesaid, if there happen to grow any sower or rancke weedes therein (as many times there will) it is good to cut them up, and being dried with the sunne, to burne them, so shall you have sweete grasse, or young weedes come in their place, that cattell will feede on, and also the heate of the sunne shall much amend your ground. Also trench out the water, that it may lie as drie as may be possible: and if you can plough it, and have Sommer corne therein, as buche or barley that Sommer that it lieth drie, I thinke it very good.

I have heard the common people in the fenne countries affirme, and that very earnestly, that their fishes do feede of ashes, by reason that in a drie Sommer, when much of their fenne grounds lie drie, and are pastured with cattel, then towards the winter time such ranke grasse, sedge, reedes, or weedes, as the cattel do leave uneaten, they will burne them with fire, to the end that the next Sommer such old sedge, reedes, or weedes, may not annoy the coming up of young and better sedge, reedes, or grasse. And the common people find by experience, that after such a drie Sommer, as aforesaid, all the next Winter the water overflowing those grounds, their fish will be exeeding fat and good: and therefore (say they) surely the fish do feede uppon the ashes of the weedes, and suchlike burnt as aforesaid. But the truth is, in such a drie Sommer as aforesaid, the cattell then feeding in such grounds as then lie drie, do bestow therein great quantities of dung and stale, wherein is bred great abundance of such bodes, flies, and wormes, as aforesayd: as also the naturall and livelie heate of the Sunne piercing such grounds, doth make the same pleasant and fat, and to bring forth the next Sommer many herbes and weedes, the seedes of which do yeeld unto fishes verie great foode and nourishment, and not barren drie ashes, as afore is imagined.

FRANCIS THYNNE: *Flatterers*. From *Emblemes and Epigrames*
(1600).

> There is a kinde of men, whome hell hath bredd,
> Deceit hath nourc'd, and doble speech hath fedd;
> naked of vertue, and impudent of face,
> abhord of all, exilde from everie place,
> ffalse flatterers nam'd, themselves which change
> to every fashion though never soe strange.

These doth the fishe *Polipus* represent,
in his conditions *which* be impudent,
Turning his cullor to everie kinde of Hue,
of everie obiect offerd to his viewe,
wherebye he maye, with bayt of cloked change,
deceyve the fishe w*hich* in the deepe do range,
Therbye more lightlie for to winn his praye,
to gorge his gluttenous mawe with foode allwaye.
Soe the false Parisites themselves doe wynde
to divers formes, as tyme and place they fynde,
Changinge themselves to ech mans severall vayne,
foode, wealth, or clothinge, therbye to attayne,
Deceyvinge such as in them put their trust,
paynelesse to serve their Hungrye mawe and lust,
and without labour to releeve their need,
worse then the Crowes on carrion w*hich* doe feed,
for they, dead bodies onlie doe devoure,
when these, the livinge doe consume ech hower.

WILLIAM SHAKESPEARE: from *Antony and Cleopatra, II. v.* (? 1606–7).

Enter Cleopatra, Charmian, Iras, and Alexas.

Cleopatra   Give me some music: music, moody food
Of us that trade in love.

Omnes   The music, ho!

Enter Mardian the Eunuch.

Cleopatra   Let it alone, let's to billiards: come, Charmian.

Charmian   My arm is sore; best play with Mardian.

Cleopatra   As well a woman with an eunuch played
As with a woman. Come, you'll play with me, sir?

Mardian   As well as I can, madam.

Cleopatra	And when good will is showed, though't
	come too short,
	The actor may plead pardon. I'll none now.
	Give me mine angle, we'll to th' river: there,
	My music playing far off, I will betray
	Tawny-finned fishes. My bended hook shall pierce
	Their slimy jaws; and as I draw them up,
	I'll think them every one an Antony,
	And say, 'Ah, ha! y' are caught!'

Charmian   'Twas merry when
You wagered on your angling, when your diver
Did hang a salt fish on his hook, which he
With fervency drew up.

Cleopatra   That time – O times! –
I laughed him out of patience; and that night
I laughed him into patience; and next morn,
Ere the ninth hour, I drunk him to his bed;
Then put my tires and mantles on him, whilst
I wore his sword Philippan.

EDWARD TOPSELL: from *Of the Sea-serpents*. From *The History of Serpents* (first published 1608) from *The History of Four-footed Beasts and the History of Serpents* (1658).

In the *Germane* Ocean there is found a Serpent about the bignesse of a mans leg, which in the tayl carryeth a sting as hard as any horn, this haunteth only the deepest part of the Sea, yet is it sometime taken by the Fisher-men, and then they cut off the tail, and eat the residue of the body. Yet I will not expresly define whether this may be called a Sea-Serpent, or a Serpentine-fish; it may be it is the same that is a Fork-fish, or Ray, which by reason of the tayl thereof, it might give occasion to *Albertus* to call it a Serpent of the Sea.

    There be also Snakes or *Hyders* in the Sea, for although all Water-serpents, as well of the fresh, salt, and sweet waters may be called *Hyders*, or Snakes, yet there be some peculiar Snakes, such are those in the *Indian* Sea, where they have broad tayls, and they harm more by biting with the sharpnesse of their teeth, then by any venom that is contained in them; and therefore in this they somewhat resemble the Snakes of the earth. And *Pliny* writeth, that once before *Persis*, upon the coasts of certain Islands, there were seen of these Sea-hyders very many, of the length of twenty cubits, wherewithall a whole Navy or fleet of ships were mightily affrighted. And the like is reported of three other Islands, lying betwixt the promontory of *Carmania* and *Arabia*; and such were those also in the *African* Sea, who are said by *Aristotle* not to be afraid of a Gally, but will set upon the men therein, and over-turn it. And he himself saw many bones of great wilde Oxen, who had been destroyed by these kinde of Sea-snakes or *Hyders*.

The greatest River that falleth into the red Sea, is called *Sinthus*, the fall whereof afar off, seemeth to the beholders to be like winding Snakes, as though they were coming against the passengers, to stay them from entrance into that Land; and there is not only a sight of resemblance of Serpents there, but also the very truth of them, for all the Sea-men know when they are upon these coasts, by the multitude of Serpents that meet them. And so do the Serpents called *Grae* about *Persis*. And the Coast of *Barace* hath the same noysome premonstration, by occurrence of many odious, black, and very great Sea-serpents. But about *Barygaza* they are lesse, and of yellow earthy colour; their eyes bloody, or fiery red, and their heads like Dragons. *Keranides* writeth of a Sea-Dragon, in this manner, saying: The Dragon of the Sea is a fish without scales, and when this is grown to a great and large proportion, whereby it doth great harm to other creatures, the winds or clouds take him up suddenly into the air, and there by violent agitation, shake his body to pieces: the parcels whereof so mangled and torn asunder, have been often found in the tops of the Mountains. And if this be true (as it may well be) I cannot tell whether there be in the world a more noble part of Divine providence, and sign of the love of God to his creatures, who armeth the clouds of heaven to take vengeance of their destroyers. The tongue of this Sea-Dragon (saith he) is like a Horses tayl, two foot in length; the which tongue preserved in Oyl, and carried about by a man, safeguardeth him from languishing in infirmities, and the fat thereof, with the herb Dragon annoynted on the head or sick parts, cureth the headache, and driveth away the Leprosie, and all kinde of scabs in the skin.

JOHN GWILLIM: from *A Display of Heraldrie* (1611).

Fishes are borne after diuers manner, viz. *Directly, Vpright, Imbowed, Extended, Endorsed, Respecting each other, Surmounting one another, Fretted, and Triranguled,* etc. All *Fishes* (saith *Leigh*) that are borne *feeding* shall bee termed in *blazon devouring,* because they doe swallow all *whole* without *mastication* or *chewing*: and you must tell whereon they feede. All *Fishes* raised directly *upright*, and having *Finnes*, shall be termed in *Blazon, Hauriant*; ab *Hauriendo*, signifying to *draw* or *sucke*, because *Fishes* doe oftentimes put their *heads* in such sort above the *waters*, to refresh themselves with the coole and temperate *Aire*, but especially when the *waters* doe so rage and boile in the depth of the *Seas* against some tempestuous storme, that they cannot endure the unwonted *heate* thereof. All *Fishes* being borne *Transuerse* the *Escocheon* must in blazon be termed *Naiant*, of the word *Nato*, to *swimme*; for in such manner doe they beare themselves in the *waters* when they *swimme*.

WILLIAM BROWNE: from *Britannia's Pastorals* (1613).

Now as an *Angler* melancholy standing
Upon the greene bancke yeelding roome for landing,
A wrigling yealow worme thrust on his hooke,
Now in the midst he throwes, then in a nooke:
Here puls his line, there throwes it in againe,
Mendeth his Corke and Baite, but all in vaine,
He long stands viewing of the curled streame.
At last a hungry *Pike*, or well-growne *Breame*
Snatch at the worme, and hasting fast away,
He knowing it, a Fish of stubborne sway,
Puls up his rod, but soft: (as having skill)
Wherewith the hooke fast holds the Fishes gill.
Then all his line he freely yeeldeth him,
Whilst furiously all up and downe doth swimme
Th' insnared Fish, here on the top doth scud,
There underneath the banckes, then in the mud;
And with his franticke fits so scares the shole,
That each one takes his *hyde*, or starting hole:
By this the *Pike* cleane wearied, underneath

A *Willow* lyes, and pants (if Fishes breath)
Wherewith the *Angler* gently puls him to him,
And least his hast might happen to undoe him,
Layes downe his rod, then takes his line in hand,
And by degrees getting the Fish to land,
Walkes to another Poole: at length is winner
Of such a dish as serves him for his dinner.

WILLIAM D'AVENANT: from *Brittania Triumphans* (1613).

Imposture

Yes! and this moral magistrate; your strict
O'er solemn friend, that in such comely phrase
Disputes for active virtue, and declares
Himself the mark of all unrighteous opposites.
His magnanimity shall yield at last,
Straight take my angle in his hand, then bait
The hook with gilded flies, to fish in troubled seas:
For all the world is such, and, in a storm,
Where the philosopher, that still swims in
Profoundest depths, will, Sir, as easily
Be snapt, as fools that float on shallow streams,
And taken with a line no stronger, Sir, than what
Will tear a little gudgeon's jaws.

Squire

This day, a day as fair as heart could wish,
This giant stood on shore of sea to fish,
For angling rod he took a sturdy oak,
For line a cable that in storm ne'er broke;
His hook was such as heads the end of pole,
To pluck down house ere fire consumes it whole.
This hook was bated with a dragon's tail;
And there on rock he stood to bob for whale,
Which straight he caught and nimbly home did pack

With ten cart load of dinner on his back:
Thus homward bent, his eye too rude and cunning
Spies knight and lady by an hedge a sunning.
That modicum of meat he down did lay,
For it was all he eat on fasting day.

JOHN DENNYS: from *The Secrets of Angling* (1613).

Obiection

Some youthfull *Gallant* here perhaps will say
This is no pastime for a gentleman.
It were more fit at cards and dice to play,
To use both fence and dauncing now and than,
Or walke the streets in nice and strange Aray,
Or with coy phrases court his Mistris fan,
    A poore delight with toyle and painfull watch,
    With losse of time a silly Fish to catch.

What pleasure can it be to walke about,
The fields and meades in heat or pinching cold?
And stand all day to catch a silly *Trout*,
This is not worth a teaster to be sold,
And peraduenture sometimes goe without,
Besides the toles and troubles manifold,
    And to be washt with many a showre of rayne,
    Before he can returne from thence again?

More ease it were, and more delight I trow,
In some sweet house to passe the time away,
Amongst the best, with braue and gallant show,
And with faire dames to daunce, to sport and play,
And on the board, the nimble dice to throw,
That brings in gaine, and helps the shot to pay,
    And with good wine and store of dainty fare,
    To feede at will and take but little care.

The Answere

I meane not here mens errours to reproue,
Nor do enuie their seeming happy state;
But rather meruaile why they doe not loue
An honest sport that is without debate;
Since their abused pastimes often moue
Their mindes to anger and to mortall hate:
    And as in bad delights their time they spend,
    So oft it brings them to no better end.

Indeed it is a life of lesser paine,
To sit at play fron noone till it be night:
And then from night till it be noone againe,
With damned oathes, pronounced in despight,
For little cause and euery trifle vaine,
To curse, to brawle, to quarrell, and to fight,
    To packe the Cardes, and with some cozning tricke,
    His fellowes Purse of all his coyne to picke.

Or to beguile another of his Wife,
As did *Æghistus Agamemnon* serue:
Or as that Roman monarch* led a life
To spoil and spend, while others pine and sterue,
And to compell their friends with follish strife,
To take more drinke then will their health preserue:
    And to conclude, for debt or just desart,
    In baser tune to sing the *Counter*-part.

O let me rather on the pleasant Brinke
Of *Tyne* and *Trent* possesse some dwelling-place;
Where I may see my Quill and Corke downe sinke,
With eager bit of *Barbill, Bleike,* or *Dace*:
And on the World and his Creator thinke,
While they proud *Thais* painted sheat imbrace.
    And with the fume of strong *Tobacco's* smoke,
    All quaffing round are ready for a choke.

Let them that list these pastimes then pursue,
And on their pleasing fancies feede their fill;

*Nero.

So I the Fields and Meadowes greene may view,
And by the Riuers fresh may walke at will,
Among the *Dayzes* and the *Violets* blew:
Red *Hyacinth* and yellow *Daffadill,*
  Purple *Narcissus*, like the morning rayes,
  Pale *Ganderglas* and azour *Culuerkayes.*

I count it better pleasure to behold
The goodly compasse of the loftie Skye,
And in the midst thereof like burning gold
The flaming Chariot of the worlds great eye;
The watry cloudes that in the ayre vprold
With sundry kindes of painted collours flie:
  And faye *Aurora* lifting vp her head,
  And blushing rise from old *Thitonus* bed.

The hills and Mountaines raised from the Plaines,
The plaines extended leuell with the ground,
The ground deuided into sundry vaines,
The vaines inclos'd with running riuers rounde,
The riuers making way through natures chaine,
With headlong course into the sea profounde:
  The surging sea beneath the valleys low,
  The valleys sweet, and lakes that louely flowe.

The lofty woods the forrests wide and long,
Adornd with leaues and branches fresh and greene,
In whose coole bow'rs the birds with chaunting song,
Doe welcome with thin quire the *Summers* Queene,
The meadowes faire where *Flora's* guifts among,
Are intermixt the verdant grasse between,
  The siluer skaled fish that softlie swimme,
  Within the brookes and Cristall watry brimme.

All these and many more of his creation,
That made the heauens, the *Angler* oft doth see,
And takes therein no little delectation,
To think how strange and wonderfull they be,
Framing thereof an inward contemplation,
To set his thoughts from other fancies free,
  And whiles hee lookes on these with joyfull eye,
  His minde is rapt aboue the starry skye.

GERVASE MARKHAM: from *The Pleasures of Princes, or Goodmen's Recreations* (1614).

Now for the inward qualities of the minde, albe some Writers reduce them into twelve heads, which indeed whosoever injoyeth cannot chuse but be very compleat in much perfection, yet I must draw them into many moe branches. The first, and most especiall whereof, is that a skilfull Angler ought to be a generall Scholler, and lerne in all the liberall Sciences, as a Gramarian, to know how eyther to Write or discourse of his Art in true termes, eyther without affectation or rudenesse. Hee should have sweetnesse of speech, to perswade and intice other to delight in an exercise so much laudable. He should have strength of arguments, to defend and maintaine his profession against envy or slaunder. Hee should have knowledge in the Sunne, Moone, and Starres, that by their aspects he may guesse the seasonablenesse or unseasonablenesse of the weather, the breeding of stormes, and from what coastes the Windes are ever delivered. Hee should be a good knower of Countryes, and well bred to high wayes, that by taking the readiest pathes to every Lake, Brooke, or River, his journeyes may be more certaine, and lesse wearisome. Hee should have knowledge in proportions of all sorts, whether Circular, square, or Diametricall, that when he shall be questioned of his diurnall progresses, he may give a Graphicall discription of the Angles and Channels of Rivers, how they fall from their heads, and what compasses they fetch in their severall windings. Hee must also have the perfect Art of Numbring, that in the counting of Lakes, or Rivers, hee may know how many foot or inches each severally containeth, and by adding, subtracting, or multiplying the same, hee may yeeld the reason of every Rivers, swift or slow current. Hee would not be unskilfull in Musique, that whensoever eyther melancholy, heaviness of thought, or the perturbations of his owne fancies stirreth up sadnesse in him, he may remoove the same with some godly Hymne or Antheme, of which David gives him ample examples. Hee must be of a well setled and constant beliefe, to injoy the benefit of his expectation, for then to dispayre it were better never to put in practise: and hee must ever think where the waters are pleasant and likely, that there the Creator of all things hath stored up much of his plenty: and though your satisfaction be not as ready as your wishes, yet you must hope still, that with perseverance you shall reape the fulnesse of your Harvest: then he must be full of love, both to his pleasure and to his neighbour: to his pleasure, which otherwise

would be irkesome and tedious, and to his neighbour that he neither
give offence in any particular, nor be guilty of any generall destruction:
then hee must be exceeding patient, and neither bete nor excruciate
himselfe with losses or mischances, as in loosing the pray when it is
almost in the hand, or by breaking his Tooles by ignorance or neg-
ligence, but with a pleased sufferance amend errours, and thinke
mischances instructions to better carefulnesse. Hee must then be full
of humble thoughts, not disdayning when occasion commands to
kneele, lye downe, or wet his feet or fingers as oft as there is any
advantage given thereby, to the gaining the end of his labour. Then he
must be strong and valiant, neither to be amased with stormes, nor
affrighted with Thunder, but to holde them according to their naturall
causes, and the pleasure of the highest: neither must he, like the Foxe
which prayeth upon Lambes, imploy all his labour against the smaller
frye, but like the Lyon that ceazeth Elephants, thinke the greatest fish
which swimmeth, a reward little enough for the paines which he
endureth. Then must he be liberall, and not working onely for his
owne belly, as if it could never be satisfied: hee must with much
cheerefulnesse bestow the fruits of his skill amongst his honest neighbours who being partners of his gaine, will doubly renowne his
tryumph, and that is ever a pleasing reward to vertue. Then must hee
be prudent, that apprehending the reasons why the fish will not bite,
and all other casuall impediments which hinder his sport, and knowing
the remedies for the same, hee may direct his labours to be without
troublesomnes: then he must have a moderate contentation of minde,
to be satisfied with indifferent things, and not out of an avaricious
greediness thinke every thing too little, be it never so abundant: then
must he be of a thankefull nature, praising the Author of all goodnesse,
and shewing a large gratefulnesse for the least satisfaction: then must
hee be of a perfect memory, quicke, and prompt to call into his minde
all the needfull things which are any way in his exercise to be
employed, least by omission of any, he frustrate his hopes, and make
his labour effectlesse. Lastly, he must be of a strong constitution of
body, able to endure much fasting, and not of a gnawing stomacke,
observing houres, in which if it be unsatisfied, it troubleth both the
minde and body, and looseth that delight which maketh the pastime
onely pleasing.

BEN JONSON: from *To Penshurst*. From *The Forest* (1616).

> And if the high-swoll'n Medway fail thy dish,
>   Thou hast thy ponds that pay thee tribute fish:
> Fat, aged carps, that run into thy net;
>   And pikes, now weary their own kind to eat,
> As loath the second draught or cast to stay,
>   Officiously, at first, themselves betray;
> Bright eels, that emulate them, and leap on land
>   Before the fisher, or into his hand.
> Then hath thy orchard fruit, thy garden flowers,
>   Fresh as the air and new as are the hours:
> The early cherry, with the later plum,
>   Fig, grape and quince, each in his time doth come;
> The blushing apricot and woolly peach
>   Hang on thy walls, that every child may reach.

ROBERT BURTON: from *The Anatomy of Melancholy* (1621).

Fishing is a kind of hunting by water, be it with nets, weeles, baits, angling, or otherwise, and yields all out as much pleasure to some men as dogs or hawks; 'When they draw their fish upon the bank,' saith Nic. Henselius Silesiographiae, *cap.* 3. speaking of that extraordinary delight his countrymen took in fishing, and in making of pools. James Dubravius that Moravian, in his book *de pisc.* telleth, how travelling by the highway side in Silesia, he found a nobleman, 'booted up to the groins', wading himself, pulling the nets, and labouring as much as any fisherman of them all: and when some belike objected to him the baseness of his office, he excused himself, 'that if other men might hunt hares, why should not he hunt carps?' Many gentlemen in like sort with us will wade up to the arm-holes upon such occasions, and voluntarily undertake that to satisfy their pleasure, which a poor man for a good stipend would scarce be hired to undergo. Plutarch, in his book *de soler. animal.* speaks against all fishing, 'as a filthy, base, illiberal employment, having neither wit nor perspicacity in it, nor worth the labour'. But he that shall consider the variety of baits for all seasons, and pretty devices which our anglers have invented, peculiar lines, false flies, several sleights, etc, will say, that it deserves like commendation, requires as much study and perspicacity as the rest, and is to be preferred before many of them. Because hawking and hunting are very laborious, much riding, and many dangers accompany them; but this is still and quiet: and if so be the angler catch no fish, yet he hath a wholesome walk to the brookside, pleasant shade by the sweet silver streams; he hath good air, and sweet smells of fine fresh meadow flowers, he hears the melodious harmony of birds, he sees the swans, herons, ducks, water-horns, coots, etc. and many other fowl, with their brood, which he thinketh better than the noise of hounds, or blast of horns, and all the sport that they can make.

MICHAEL DRAYTON: from *Poly-Olbion* (1612–22).

When as the salmon seekes a fresher streame to find
(Which hither from the sea comes yeerely by his kind,
As he in season growes) and stems the watry tract
Where Tivy falling downe, doth make a cataract,
Forc't by the rising rocks that there her course oppose,
As though within their bounds they meant her to inclose;
Heere, when the labouring fish doth at the foote arrive,
And finds that by his strength but vainlie he doth strive,
His taile takes in his teeth: and bending like a bowe,
That's to the compasse drawne, aloft himself doth throwe:
Then springing at his height, as doth a little wand,
That bended end to end, and flerted from the hand,
Farre off it selfe doth cast; so doth the salmon vaut.
And if at first he faile, his second summersaut
Hee instantlie assaies; and from his nimble ring.
Still yarking, never leaves, untill himself he fling
Above the streame full top of the surrounded heape.

ANON: from *Vox Piscis: or, The Book-Fish* (1626).

On Midsummer Eue last past 1626 a Codfish being brought to the Fish-market of Cambridge and there cut up, as usually others are for sale, in the depth of the mawe of this fish was found wrapped in a piece of Canvase, a booke *in decimo sexto,* containing in it three treatises bound up in one; and severally new reprinted, and here published upon that occasion.

The place, where this Fish was among others caught, being about the Coasts of Lin, is called *Lin Deeps*, from whence usually such fish are brought into that market. The Fisherman that caught it *William Skinner* of Lin, by whose partners this fish, amongst others of the same kinde, was brought to *Cambridge* Market, where *Iaccomy Brand* (the wife of *William Brand* one of those partners) selling that fish, did cut off the head, and tooke out the Garbidge: which when shee had throwne by, another woman, casually standing by, espyed in the maw of the fish a peece of canvasse, and taking it up found the Booke wrapped up in it, being much soyled, and defaced, and couered ouer with a kinde of slime and congealed matter. This Booke was then and there beheld by many with admiration, and by *Beniamin Prime* the Batchelors Beadle (who also was present at the opening of the fish) was presently carried to the Vice-chancellor of the Vniversity who tooke speciall notice thereof, and examined the Truth of the particulars before mentioned. Whereupon by *Daniel Boys* a Book-binder, the leaues of the Booke were carefully washed and cleansed, being shewed unto many both before and after the cleansing thereof. Whereupon diuers letters were written by Scolars of the Vniversitie to their friends abroad, relating the particulars of this accident whereof themselves were eye-witnesses. And thus much for the fact it selfe.

JOHN DONNE: from his *Sermon on Matthew 4:18–20* (preached December 1619, revised 1630).

So the world is a Sea. It is a Sea, if we consider the Inhabitants. In the Sea, the greater fish devoure the lesse; and so doe the men of this world too. And as fish, when they mud themselves, have no hands to make themselves cleane, but the current of the waters must worke that; So have the men of this world no means to cleanse themselves from those sinnes which they have contracted in the world, of themselves, till a new flood, waters of repentance, drawne up, and sanctified by the Holy Ghost, worke that blessed effect in them.

All these wayes the world is a Sea, but especially it is a Sea in this respect, that the Sea is no place of habitation, but a passage to our habitations. So the Apostle expresses the world, *Here we have no continuing City, but we seeke one to come;* we seeke it not here, but we seeke it whilst we are here, els we shall never finde it. Those are the two great works which we are to doe in this world; first to know, that this world is not our home, and then to provide us another home, whilst we are in this world. Therefore the Prophet sayes, *Arise, and depart, for this is not your rest.* Worldly men, that have no farther prospect, promise themselves some rest in this world, (*Soule, thou hast much goods laid up for many yeares, take thine ease, eate, drinke, and be merry,* sayes the rich man) but this is not your rest; indeed no rest; at least not yours. You must depart, depart by death, before yee come to that rest; but then you must arise, before you depart; for except yee have a resurrection to grace here, before you depart, you shall have no resurrection to glory in the life to come, when you are departed.

Now, in this Sea, every ship that sayles must necessarily have some part of the ship under water; Every man that lives in this world, must necessarily have some of his life, some of his thoughts, some of his labours spent upon this world; but that part of the ship, by which he sayls, is above water; Those meditations, and those endevours which must bring us to heaven, are removed from this world, and fixed entirely upon God. And in this Sea, are we made fishers of men: Of men in generall; not of rich men, to profit by them, nor of poore men, to pierce them the more sharply, because affliction hath opened a way into them; Not of learned men, to be over-glad of their approbation of our labours, Nor of ignorant men, to affect them with an astonishment, or admiration of our gifts: But we are fishers of men, of all men, of that which makes them men, their soules. And for this fishing in this Sea, this Gospel is our net.

Eloquence is not our net; Traditions of men are not our nets; onely the Gospel is. The Devill angles with hooks and bayts; he deceives, and he wounds in the catching; for every sin hath his sting.

MICHAEL DRAYTON: *The Fisherman.* From *The Muses' Elysium* (1630).

The crystal current streams continually I keep,
Where every pearl-pav'd ford and every blue-ey'd deep,
With me familiar are; when in my boat being set,
My oars I take in hand, my angle and my net
About me, like a prince myself in state I steer,
Now up, now down the stream, now am I here, now there,
The pilot and the fraught myself; and at my ease
Can land me when I list, or in what place I please;
The silver-scaled shoals, about me in the streams,
As thick as ye discern the atoms in the beams,
Near to the shady bank where slender sallies grow,
And willows their shagg'd tops down towards the waters bow,
I shove in with my boat to shield me from the heat,
Where, choosing from my bag some prov'd especial bait,
The goodly, well-grown trout I with my angle strike,
And with my bearded wire I take the ravenous pike,
Of whom when I have hold, he seldom breaks away,
Though at my line's length so long I let him play,
Till by my hand I find him well-near weari'd be,
When softly by degrees I draw him up to me.
The lusty salmon too, I oft with angling take,
Which me above the rest most lordly sport doth make,
Who, feeling he is caught, such frisks and bounds doth fetch,
And by his very strength my line so far doth stretch,
As draws my floating cork down to the very ground,
And, wresting of my rod, doth make my boat turn round.
I never idle am; sometimes I bait my weels,
With which by night I take the dainty silver eels;
And with my draught-net then I sweep the streaming flood,
And to my trammel next and cast-net from the mud
I beat the scaly brood; no hours I idly spend,
But wearied with my work I bring the day to end.

CONRAD HERESBACH: *Entreating of Angling.* From *The Whole Art of Husbandry.*
Translated from the Latin by Gervase Markham, 1631.

I will not enter here into any large Encomiums, touching the praise of this art of Angling. It shall suffice me that all men know it, that few good men but love it, and a world of pore men live by it; neither will I stand upon the use and vertue thereof, because it is eyther for profit or recreation; nor upon the Antiquitie, because no man living knew the beginning; nor upon any thing that is linked unto it by the Curious. I will onely rest myself upon the Art it selfe and fully as the shortnesse of the time and the slownesse of my Speech will give me leave, deliver unto you what I know therein.

The Art of Angling or the art of deceiving Fish, consisteth in these few principles. First the man, the instruments, the Bayts, and the Seasons good or ill for the purpose.

Touching the man, howsoever some would sire upon him twelve vertues, some twenty, some more, some lesse, yet I must contract them and say, if he be Tullie's honest man, he is then the Anglers sufficient man: there is required in him much patience and constancy, the one will take from him Anguish, the other error; he must love the sport earnestly, for No Love, no Lucke; he must have humble Thoughts and humble Gestures, for he must not disdaine to kneele, to lye groveling, to stand barehead, nay to do any humble action to attain his purpose: he must be of a strong constitution, for he is like to undergoe the worst terrors of Tempests. Lastly for his apparrell it must be warme and wholsome not garish or glistering, the one is wholesome for his Body, the other is much offensive for his sport. For as the Fish is of a most pure sight, so they are of a most nice conceit, and where they once take offence, no flatterie can reconcile them: therefore his apparrell must be sad and deepe coloured like the water, plaine and close to his Bodie, and indeede so like a Shadow that it will give no shaddow.

JOHN DONNE: *The Baite.* From *Songs and Sonets* (1633).

Come live with mee, and bee my love,
And wee will some new pleasures prove
Of golden sands, and christall brookes,
With silken lines, and silver hookes.

There will the river whispering runne
Warm'd by thy eyes, more then the Sunne.
And there the 'inamor'd fish will stay,
Begging themselves they may betray.

When thou wilt swimme in that live bath,
Each fish, which every channell hath,
Will amorously to thee swimme,
Gladder to catch thee, then thou him.

If thou, to be so seene, beest loath,
By Sunne, or Moone, thou darknest both,
And if my selfe have leave to see,
I need not their light, having thee.

Let others freeze with angling reeds,
And cut their legges, with shells and weeds,
Or treacherously poore fish beset,
With strangling snare, or windowie net:

Let coarse bold hands, from slimy nest
The bedded fish in banks out-wrest,
Or curious traitors, sleavesilke flies
Bewitch poore fishes wandring eyes.

For thee, thou needst no such deceit,
For thou thy selfe art thine owne bait;
That fish, that is not catch'd thereby,
Alas, is wiser farre then I.

PHINEAS FLETCHER: from *Piscatory Eclogues, Eclogue V* (1633).

> Algon, oft hast thou fish'd, but sped not straight;
>   With hook and net thou beat'st the water round:
> Oft-times the place thou changest oft the bait;
> And, catching nothing, still and still dost wait:
>   Learn by thy trade to cure thee: time hath found
>   In desp'rate cures a salve for ev'ry wound.
> The fish, long playing with the baited hook,
> At last is caught: thus many a nymph is took;
> Mocking the strokes of love, is with her striking strook.

ANON: from *A Strange Metamorphosis of Man, Transformed into a Wildernesse* (1634).

The pike is the pirate of the lake, that roves and preyes upon the little fishermen of that sea, who is so covetous and cruell, that he gives no quarter to any; when hee takes his prize hee goes not to the shore to make his market, but greedily devoures it himselfe; yea, is such a cormorant, that he will not stay the dressing of it. He is called the wolfe of the water, but is indeed a monster of nature; for the wolfe spares his kinde, but hee will devoure his own nephewes ere they come to full growth. He is very gallant in apparell, and seemes to affect to go rather in silver than in gold, wherein he spares for no cost; for his habit is all layd with silver plate downe to the foot in scallop wise. Hee is a right man of warre, and is so slender built, and drawes so little water, as hee will land at pleasure, and take his prey where he list; no shallop* shall follow where hee will lead. The pikes themselves are the taller ships, the pickerels of a middle sort, and the Jacks, the pinnaces amongst them, which are all armed according to their burden. The master or pilot sits at the prore, yet hath he the rudder so at command, that hee can winde and turne the vessell which way he will in the twinkling of an eye. He sets up but little sayles, because he would not bee discovered who he is, yea, many times no sail at all, but he trusts to the finnes, his oares. The youthfuller sort of pikes, whom through familiarity they call Jacks, are notable laddes indeed, and to their strength and bigness will

*Dingy.

fish as their fathers will. In a word, a man would easily bee mistaken in him in beholding him so handsome and gentle a creature, and never imagin him to be half so ravenous as he is; but *fronti nulla fides*.

MILDMAY FANE, Second Earl of Westmorland: from *To N.B. an Angler.* From *Otia Sacra* (1648).

Thou that dost cast into the Silver brook
        Thy worm-fed Hook,
The greedier Fishes so to cheat
        Seeking for meat,
Remember that Times wheel will bring
        Thy deeds to censuring;
And then as thou through wile
Those Creatures didst beguile,
So caught thou'lt be for thy deceit,
And made the food for thine own bait.

T. VENNER: *Of Fish.* From *Via Recta ad Vitam Longam* (1650).

Carp is of sweet exquisite taste, but the nourishment doth not answer to the taste; if it were, it would be numbered amongst fishes of the primest note. It giveth slimy, phlegmatic, excremental nourishment, and quickly satiateth the stomach. Let all who are of weak stomach eschew it. The head and spawn of the carp are the pleasantest and wholesomest; to be preferred before the rest of the fish.

   The barbell is soft and moist, of easy concoction, and very pleasant taste; of good nourishment, but somewhat muddy and excremental. The greater excel the lesser for meat, because their superfluous moisture is amended by age. The spawn of them is to be objected to as most offensive to the belly and stomach.

   The tench is unwholesome. Hard of concoction, unpleasant of taste, noisome to the stomach, and filleth the body with gross slimey humour. Notwithstanding, it is meat fit for labouring men.

ANDREW MARVELL: from *Upon Appleton House* (c. 1650–3).

But, where the floods did lately drown,
There at the evening stake me down;
For now the waves are fallen and dried,
And now the meadows fresher dyed,
Whose grass, with moisture colour dashed,
Seems as green silks but newly washed.
No serpent new, nor crocodile,
Remains behind our little Nile;
Unless itself you will mistake
Among these meads the only snake.
See in what wanton harmless folds
It everywhere thc meadow holds,
And its yet muddy back doth lick,
Till as a crystal mirror slick,
Where all things gaze themselves, and doubt
If they be in it, or without;
And for his shade which therein shines,
Narcissus-like, the sun too pines.
Oh what a pleasure 'tis to hedge
My temples here with heavy sedge;
Abandoning my lazy side,
Stretched as a bank unto the tide;
Or to suspend my sliding foot
On the osier's undermined root,
And in its branches tough to hang,
While at my lines the fishes twang!
But now away my hooks, my quills,
And angles, idle utensils!
The young MARIA walks to-night:
Hide, trifling youth, thy pleasures slight;
'Twere shame that such judicious eyes
Should with such toys a man surprise:

         *   *   *

And now the salmon-fishers moist
Their leathern boats begin to hoist;
And, like Antipodes in shoes,
Have shod their heads in their canoes.
How tortoise-like, but not so slow,

These rational amphibii go!
Let's in: for the dark hemisphere
Does now like one of them appear.

ANON: *Death's Trade* (17th century).

Death is a fisherman, the world we see
His fish-pond is, and we the fishes be.
He, sometimes, angler-like, doth with us play,
And slily takes us one by one away;
Diseases are the murdering hooks, which he
Doth catch us with, the bait mortality,
Which we poor silly fish devour, till strook,
At last, too late, we feel the bitter hook.

At other times he brings his net, and then
At once sweeps up whole cities-full of men,
Drawing up thousands at a draught, and saves
Only some few, to make the others' graves,
His net some raging pestilence; now he
Is not so kind as other fishers be;
For if they take one of the smaller fry,
They throw him in again, he shall not die:
    But death is sure to kill all he can get,
    And all is fish with him that comes to net.

HENRY WOTTON: *On a Bank as I Sate A-fishing.*
    From *Reliquiae Wottonianae* (1651).

This day Dame Nature seem'd in love:
The lusty-sap began to move;
Fresh juice did stir th' embracing vines,
And birds had drawn their valentines.
The jealous trout that low did lie,
Rose at a well-dissembled flie;
There stood my friend, with patient skill,
Attending of his trembling quill.

Already were the eaves possest
With the swift Pilgrim's daubèd nest;
The groves already did rejoice
In Philomel's triumphing voice,
The showers were short, the weather mild,
The morning fresh, the evening smiled.

Joan takes her neat-rubb'd pail, and now
She trips to milk the sand-red cow,–
Where, for some sturdy foot-ball swain,
Joan strokes a syllabub or twain,
The fields and garden were beset
With tulips, crocus, violet:
And now, though late, the modest rose
Did more than half a blush disclose.
Thus all looks gay, and full of cheer,
To welcome the new livery'd year.

WILLIAM BASSE: from *Pastorals* (1653). Also quoted in
The Compleat Angler.

As inward love breeds outward talk,
The hound some praise, and some, the hawk;
Some, better pleased with private sport,
Use tennis; some, a mistress court:
  But these delights I neither wish,
  Nor envy, while I freely fish.

Who hunts, doth oft in danger ride;
Who hawks, lures oft both far and wide;
Who uses games shall often prove
A loser: but who falls in love
  Is fettered in fond Cupid's snare:
  My angle breeds me no such care.

Of recreation there is none
So free as fishing is alone;
All other pastimes do no less

Than mind and body both possess:
    My hand alone my work can do,
    So I can fish and study too.

I care not, I, to fish in seas;
Fresh rivers best my mind do please,
Whose sweet calm course I contemplate,
And seek in life to imitate;
    In civil bounds I fain would keep,
    And for my past offences weep.

And when the timorous trout I wait
To take, and he devours my bait,
How poor a thing, sometimes I find,
Will captivate a greedy mind;
    And when none bite, I praise the wise
    Whom vain allurements ne'er surprise.

But yet, though while I fish I fast,
I make good fortune my repast,
And thereunto my friend invite,
In whom I more than that delight,
    Who is more welcome to my dish,
    Than to my angle was my fish.

As well content no prize to take,
As use of taken prize to make;
For so our Lord was pleased, when
He fishers made fishers of men:
    Where (which is in no other game)
    A man may fish and praise His name.

The first men that our Saviour dear
Did choose to wait upon Him here,
Blest fishers were; and fish the last
Food was that He on earth did taste:
    I therefore strive to follow those
    Whom He to follow Him hath chose.

IZAAK WALTON: from *The Compleat Angler* (1653).

Viator: But Master, first let me tell you that that very hour which you were absent from me, I sate down under a Willow tree by the water side, and considered what you had told me of the owner of that pleasant Meadow in which you then left me, that he had a plentiful estate, and not a heart to think so; that he had at this time many Law Suites depending, and that they both damp'd his mirth and took up so much of his time and thoughts, that he himself had not leisure to take the sweet content that I, who pretended no title, took in his fields; for I could there sit quietly, and looking on the water, see fishes leaping at Fries of several shapes and colours; looking on the Hils, could behold them spotted with Woods and Groves, looking down the Meadows, could see here a Boy gathering *Lillies* and *Ladysmocks*, and there a Girle cropping *Culverkeys* and *Cowslips*, all to make Garlands sutable to this pleasant Month of *May*; these and many other Field-flowers so per-fum'd the air, that I thought this Meadow like the field in *Sicily* (of which *Diodorus* speaks) where the perfumes arising from the place, makes all dogs that hunt in it, to fall off, and to lose their hottest sent. I say, as I thus sate joying in mine own happy condition, and pittying that rich mans that ought this, and many other pleasant Groves and Meadows about me, I did thankfully remember what my Saviour said, that *the meek posses the earth*; for indeed they are free from those high, those restless thoughts and contentions which corrode the sweets of life. For they, and they only, can say as the Poet has happily exprest it.

> Hail blest estate of poverty!
> Happy enjoyment of such minds,
> As rich in low contentedness,
> Can, like the reeds in roughest winds,
>   By yeelding make that blow but smal
>   At which proud Oaks and Cedars fal.

JOHN FLOUD: *To my dear Brother Izaak Walton, Upon his Compleat Angler.* From *The Compleat Angler* (1655).

> Erasmus in his learned colloquies
> Has mixt some toys, that by varieties
> He might entice all readers: for in him
> Each child may wade, or tallest giant swim.
> And such is this Discourse: there's none so low
> Or highly learn'd, to whom hence may not flow
> Pleasure and information; both which are
> Taught us with so much art, that I might swear,
> Safely, the choicest critic cannot tell
> Whether your matchless judgment most excell
> In angling or its praise: where commendation
> First charms, then makes an art a recreation.
> 　'Twas so to me: who saw the cheerful spring
> Pictur'd in every meadow, heard birds sing
> Sonnets in every grove, saw fishes play
> In the cool crystal springs, like lambs in May;
> And they may play, till anglers read this book;
> But after, 'tis a wise fish, 'scapes a hook.

THOMAS BARKER: from *Barker's Delight, or, The Art of Angling, etc.* (1657–9).

To the
RIGHT HONORABLE
EDVVARD Lord Montague,
Generall of the Navy, and one of
the Lords Commissioners
of the Treasury.

Noble Lord,

I do present this my book as I have named it *Barker's delight*, to your Honour. I pray God send you safe home to your good Lady and sweet Babes. *Amen, Amen.* If you shall find anything delightfull in the reading of it, I shall heartily rejoyce, for I know you are one who takes delight in that pleasure, and have good judgement and experience, as many noble persons and Gentlem. of true piety and honour do and have. The favour that I have found from you, and a great many more that did and do love that pleasure, shall never be bury'd in oblivion by me. I am now grown old, and am willing to enlarge my little book. I have written no more but my own exerience and practise, and have set forth the true ground of Angling, which I have been gathering these threescore yeares, having spent many pounds in the gaining of it, as is well known in the place where I was born and educated, which is *Bracemeale* in the Liberty of *Salop*, being a Freeman and Burgesse of the same City. If any noble or gentle Angler, of what degree soever he be, have a mind to discourse of any of these wayes and experiments, I live in *Henry* the 7th's Gifts, the next doore to the Gatehouse in *Westm*. my name is *Barker*, where I shall be ready, as long as please God, to satisfie them, and maintain my art, during life, which is not like to be long; that the younger fry may have my experiments at a smaller charge than I had them, for, it would be too heavy for every one that loveth that exercise to be at that charge as I was at first in my youth, the losse of my time, with great expences. Therefore I took it in consideration, and thought fit to let it be understood, and to take pains to let forth the true grounds and wayes that I have found by experience both for fitting of the rods and tackles both for ground-baits and flyes, with directions for the making thereof, with observations for times and seasons, for the ground-baits and flyes, both for day and night, with the dressing, wherein I take as much delight as in the taking of them, and to shew how I can perform it, to furnish any Lords table, onely with trouts, as it is furnished with flesh, for sixteen or twenty dishes. And I have a desire to preserve their health (with help of God) to go dry in their boots and shooes in angling, for age taketh the pleasure from me. My Lord, I am

Your Honours most humble
Servant,

Thomas Barker.

* * *

The best dish of stewed fish that ever I heard commended of the English, was dressed this way: First they were broiled on a charcole fire, being cut on the side as fried Trouts, then the stew pan was taken and set on a chaffing-dish of coles, there was put into the stew-pan half a pound of sweet butter, one penniworth of beaten cinnamon, a little vinegar; when all was melted the fish was put into the pan, and covered with a covering plate, so kept stewing half an hour, being turned, then taken out of the stew-pan and dished, be sure to beat your sauce before you put it on your fish, then squeeze a lemmon on your fish: it was the best dish of fish that ever I heard commended by Noblemen and Gentlemen. This is our English fashion.

There are divers wayes of stewing, this which I set down last was the English way: But note this, that your stewed trouts must be cut on the side: you may make a dish of stewed trouts out of your boyling kettle, stewing of them with the same materialls as I did the broiled trouts, I dare warrant them good meat, and to be very well liked.

The Italian he stews upon a chaffing-dish of coles, with whitewine, cloves and mace, nutmegs sliced, a little ginger; you must understand when this fish is stewed, the same liquor that the fish is stewed in must be beaten with some sweet butter and juice of a lemmon, before it is dished for the service. The French doth adde to this a slice or two of bacon, Though I have been no traveller I may speak it, for I have been admitted into the most Ambassadors Kitchins that have come into England this forty years, and do wait on them still at the Lord Protector's charge, and I am paid duly for it: sometimes I see slovenly scullions abuse good fish most grosly.

*   *   *

I have a willing mind with Gods help to preserve all those that love this recreation, to goe dry in their boots and shooes, to preserve their healths, which one receit is worth much more than this book will cost.

First, they must take a pint of Linseed oyle, with half a pound of mutton suet, six or eight ounces of bees wax, and half a penniworth of rosin, boyle all this in a pipkin together, so let it coole untill it be milk warm, then take a little hair brush and lay it on your new boots; but its best that this stuff be laid on before the boot-maker makes the boots, then brush them once over after they come from him; as for old boots you must lay it on when your boots be dry.

If you want good Tackles of all sorts, you must go to Mr *Oliver Flecher* at the west end of *Pauls*, at the sign of the three Trouts.

If you would have the best Hooks of all sorts, go to *Charles Kirby*, who lives in shooe lane in Harp alley, in Mill-yard.

If you would have a rod to beare and to fit neatly, you must go to *John Hobs* who liveth at the sign of the George behind the Mews by Charing-crosse.

HENRY VAUGHAN: *With a gift of a Salmon, sent to that famous and best of men, my dear friend, Dr Thomas Powell* (? 1660).
Translated from the Latin by A. B. Grosart.

Accept the Salmon that with this I send.
To you renown'd and best-belovèd friend;
Caught 'neath the Fall, where mid the whirling foam
O' the quick-darting Usk, he just had come.
Twas thus in brief: the treach'rous colour'd fly
For a meal, guil'd his unprophetic eye,
So catching at it, he himself was caught:
Swallowing it down, this evil fate he wrought,
– His only purpose being then to dine –
Lo! to be swallow'd, swiftly he was mine:
Misled by his gay-painted fly astray,
Of angler's rod he is the welcome prey.
Benign retirement! (Full reward to me
For all my life's thick-coming misery:)
How safe this salmon – and long years have seen –
If he content in the still pools had been:
But soon as for the thund'ring Fall he craves,
To bound and flash amidst its tossing waves,
He leaps to seize what seems a noble prize,
And gulps the hidden hook whereon he dies.
Often are little things the types of great:
Look thee around, and with all this thoul't meet.
The foamy Fall the world is, man the fish;
The plum'd hook, sin guis'd in some lordly dish.

ALEXANDER BROME: *On a Fisherman.* From *Songs and Other Poems* (1661).

A fisher, while he angled in a brook,
A dead mans skull by chance hung on his hook;
The pious man in pitty did it take,
To bury it, a grave with's hand did make;
And as he digg'd found gold. Thus to good men,
    Good turnes with good turnes are repay'd agen.

THOMAS FULLER, D. D.: from *The History of the Worthies of England* (1662).

Barke-shire. Naturall Commodities. Trouts.

This is a pleasant and wholesome Fish, as whose feeding is pure and cleanly, in the swiftest streams, and on the hardest gravell. Good and great of his kind are found in the River of *Kennet* nigh *Hungerford*, though not so big as that which *Gesner* affirmes taken in the *Leman-lake*, being three cubits in length. They are in their perfection in the moneth of *May*, and yearly decline with the Buck. Being come to his full growth, he decays in goodness, not greatness, and thrives in his head till his death. Note by the way, that an *hog-back* and *little-head*, is a sign that any fish is in season.

Lincolne-shire. Natural Commodities. Pikes

A *Cub-Foxe*, drinking out of the River *Arnus* in *Italy*, had his head seized on by a mighty *Pike*, so that neither could free themselves, but were ingrapled together. In this contest a young man runs into the water, takes them both out alive, and carrieth them to the Duke of *Florence*; whose palace was hard by. The Porter would not admit him, without promising of sharing his full half in what the Duke should give him. To which he (hopelesse otherwise of Entrance) condescended. The Duke highly affected with the Rarity, was in giving him a good reward, which the other refused, desiring his Highnesse would appoint one of his Guard, to give him an hundred Lashes, that so his Porter might have fifty, according to his composition.

ROBERT VENABLES: from *The Prefatory Address* from *The Experienced Angler: or Angling Improved, etc.* (1662).

The minds of anglers being usually more calm and composed than many others, especially hunters and falconers, who too frequently lose their delight in their passion, and too often bring home more of melancholy and discontent than satisfaction in their thoughts; but the angler, when he hath the worst success, loseth but a hook or line, or perhaps, what he never possessed, a fish; and suppose he should take nothing, yet he enjoyeth a delightful walk by pleasant rivers in sweet pastures, amongst odoriferous flowers, which gratify his senses and delight his mind; which contentments induce many, who affect not angling, to choose those places of pleasure for their Summer's recreation and health.

But, peradventure, some may alledge that this art is mean, melancholy, and insipid; I suppose the old answer, *de gustibus non est disputandum*, will hold as firmly in recreations as palates, many have supposed Angling void of delight, having never tried it, yet have afterwards experimented it so full of content, that they have quitted all other recreations, at least in its season, to pursue it; and I do pursuade myself, that whosoever shall associate himself with some honest expert angler, who will freely and candidly communicate his skill unto him, will in short time be convinced that *Ars non habet inimicum nisi ignorantem*; and the more any experiment its harmless delight, not subject to passion or expence, he will probably be induced to relinquish those pleasures which being obnoxious to choler or contention so discompose the thoughts, that nothing during that unsettlement can relish or delight the mind; to pursue that recreation which composeth the soul to that calmness and serenity, which gives a man the fullest possession and fruition of himself and all his enjoyments; this clearness and equanimity of spirit being a matter of so high a concern and value in the judgments of many profound Philosophers, as any one may see that will bestow the pains to read, *de Tranquilitate Animi*, and *Petrarch de Utriusque Conditionis Statu:* Certainly he that lives *Sibi et Deo*, leads the most happy life; and if this art do not dispose and incline the mind of man to a quiet calm sedateness, I am confident it doth not, as many other delights; cast blocks and rubs before him to make his way more difficult and less pleasant. The cheapness of the recreation abates not its pleasure, but with rational persons heightens it; and if it be delightful the charge of melancholy falls upon that score, and if example, which is the best proof, may sway any thing, I know no sort of men less subject to melancholy than anglers; many have cast off other recreations and embraced it, but I never knew any angler wholly cast off, though occasions might interrupt, their affections to their beloved recreation; and if this art may prove a *Noble brave rest* to thy mind, it will be satisfaction to his, who is thy well-wishing Friend.

ROBERT BOYLE: from *Occasional Reflections, Fourth Section, Which Treats of Angling Improved to Spiritual Uses, Discourse III: Upon Fishing with a Counterfeit Fly* (1665).

Being at length come to the river side, we quickly began to fall to the sport for which we came thither, and *Eugenius* finding the fish forward enough to bite, thought fit to spare his flies, till he might have more need of them, and therefore ty'd to his line a hook furnished with one of those counterfeit flies which in some neighbouring countries are much used, and which being made of the feathers of wild-fowl, are not subject to be drench'd by the water, whereon those birds are wont to swim. This fly being for a pretty while scarce any oftener thrown in, than the hook it hid was drawn up again with a fish fasten'd to it, *Eugenius* looking on us with a smiling countenance, seemed to be very proud of his success; which *Eusebius* taking notice of, whilst (says he) we smile to see how easily you beguile these silly fishes that you catch so fast with this false bait, possibly we are not much less unwary ourselves; and the world's treacherous pleasures do little less delude me and you. For *Eugenius*, (continues he) as the Apostles were fishers of men in a good sense, so their and our grand adversary is a skilful fisher of men in a bad sense, and too often in his attempts to cheat fond mortals, meets with a success as great and as easy, as you now find yours. Certainly that tempter, as the Scripture calls him, does sadly delude us, even when we rise at his best baits, and as it were his true flies: for alas! the best things he can give are very worthless, most of them in their own nature, and all of them in comparison of what they must cost us to enjoy them. But however riches, power, and the delights of the senses are real goods in their kind, though they be not of the best kind: yet alas! many of us are so fitted for deceits, that we do not put this subtle angler to make use of his true baits to catch us! We suffer him to abuse us much more grossly, and to cheat us with empty titles of honor, or the ensnaring smiles of great ones, or disquieting drudgeries disguis'd with the specious names of great employments: and though these, when they must be obtained by sin, or are proposed as the recompenses for it, be, as I was going to say, but the devil's counterfeit flies; yet, as if we were fond of being deceiv'd, we greedily swallow the hooks for flies that do but look like such; so dim-sighted are we, as well to what vice shews, as to what it hides. Let us not then, (concludes *Eusebius*,) rise at baits whereby we may be sure to be either grossly, or at least exceedingly deceiv'd; for whoever ventures to commit a sin to taste the sweets that the fruition of it seems to promise, certainly is so far deceiv'd, as to swallow a true hook for a bait, which either proves but a counterfeit fly, or hides *that* under its alluring shew, which makes it not need to be a counterfeit one to deceive him.

SAMUEL PEPYS: from *The Diarys* (18 March 1667).

At night home to supper and so to bed. My father's letter this day doth tell me of his own continued illness, and that my mother grows so much worse that he fears she cannot long continue – which troubles me very much. This day Mr Caesar told me a pretty experiment of his, of Angling with a Minikin, a gut-string varnished over, which keeps it from swelling and is beyond any hair for strength and smallness – the secret I like mightily.

ABRAHAM COWLEY: from *Bathing in the River*. From *Works of Mr Abraham Cowley* (1668).

> The *fish* around her crowded, as they do
> To the false light that treach'rous fishers shew,
> And all with as much ease might taken be,
>   As she at first took me.
>   For ne'ere did *Light* so clear
>   Among the *waves* appear,
> Though ev'ery night the Sun himself set there.
>
> Why to *Mute Fish* should'st thou thy self discover,
> And not to me thy no less *silent* Lover?
> As some from *Men* their buried *Gold* commit
>   To *Ghosts* that have no use of it!
>   Half their rich treasures so
>   *Maids* bury; and for ought we know
> (Poor *Ignorants*) they're *Mermaids* all below.

NICHOLAS COX: from *The Gentleman's Recreation* (1674).

And now a word or two concerning Fish: *Pliny* saith, That Nature's great and wonderful power is more demonstrated in the Sea than on the Land: and this may appear by those numerous and various Creatures which inhabit in and about that Element; which will appear more at large, if you will read their History written either by *Rondeletius*, *Gesner*, *Johnstonus*, or *Aldrovandus*. The number and the various shapes of these Fishes are not more strange, than their different Natures, Inclinations and Actions. Give me leave to speak a little hereof.

There is a fish called the *Cuttle-fish*, which will cast a long Gut out of her Throat, with which she angles: for lying obscurely in the Mud, she permits small fish to nibble at it, and by that means draws them near her by little and little, till coming within her reach, she leaps upon them and devours them: hence she is called the *Sea-Angler*.

The *Hermit* is a Fish that when she grows old will seek out a dead Fish's shell, fit for her purpose, and there dwell secluded from all company, studying nothing more than how to defend her self against the injuries of Wind and Weather.

The *Sargus* is a Fish so lascivious (as *Du-Bartas* expresseth it rarely well) that when he cannot finde change of Mates enough in the Sea, he will get ashore and Cuckold a Goat.

> Goes courting She-Goats on the grassie Shore,
> Horning their Husbands that had Horns before.

Whereas it is reported that the *Mullet* is so chaste, that when she is deprived of her Mate, she will follow him to the shore and die.

The *Torpedo*, or *Cramp-fish*, is a Fish of so baneful and poysonous a nature, that all the other Fish that come within her reach are immediately stupified and without motion, so that they easily become her prey; nay, she will so suddenly convey her Poyson up the Rod and Line of the Angler, when she feels her self entangled, that his Hands and Arms immediately losing their strength, become nummed and senseless.

The *Scolopendra* hath as rare and strange a way of defending her self from the Anglers subtilty, as any Fish whatever, if we may credit the relation of *Du-Bartas*, whose words are these:

> But if the *Scolopendra* have suckt in
> The sowre-sweet morsel with the barbed pin,
> She hath as rare a Trick to rid her from it;

For instantly she all her Guts will vomit;
And having clear'd them from the danger, then
She fair and softly sups them in again,
So that not one of them within her Womb
Changeth his Office or his wanted room.

The *Remora* is a Fish of so strange and secret a property (and for that reason is often used for a Metaphor) that as the same *Du Bartas* saith,

Let all the Winds in one Wind gather them,
And (seconded with *Neptune's* strongest stream)
Let all at once blow all their stiffest gales,
Astern a Galley under all her sails;
Let her be holpen with an hundred Oars,
Each lively handled by five lusty Rowers;
The *Remora* fixing her feeble Horn
Into the Tempest-beaten Vessels Stern,
Stays her stone still.

In the year of our Lord 1180, near *Orford* in *Suffolk*, there was a Fish taken in the perfect shape of a Man; he was kept by *Bartholomew de Glanvile* in the Castle of *Orford* above half a year; but at length, not being carefully looked to, he stole to the Sea, and was never seen after. He never spake, but would eat any Meat that was given him, especially raw Fish, when he had squeezed out the juice: He was often had to Church, but never shewed any signe of Adoration.

WILLIAM GILBERT: from *Gilbert's Delight* (1676).

To Make Paste Bait

Then go to Mother Gilberts, at the Flower de Luce, at Clapton, near Hackney, and whilst you are drinking a Pot of Ale, bid the Maid make you two or three pennyworth of Ground Bait and some Paste (which they do very neatly, and well); and observing them, you will know how to make it yourself for any other Place; which is too tedious here to Insert.

Essential Equipment

Whenever you go out to Fish, faill not to have with you, viz. A good Coat for all Weathers. An Apron to put your Ground-Bait, Stones, and Paste in. A Basket to put your Fish in. A neat Rod of about four Foot long, in several pieces, one with another. Two or three Lines fitted up, of all Sorts. Spare Hooks, Links, Floats, Silk, Wax, Plummetts, Caps, and a Landing Nett, etc. And if you have a boy to go along with you, a good Neats-Tongue, and a Bottle of Canary should not be wanting.

IZAAK WALTON and CHARLES COTTON: from *The Compleat Angler* (1676).

Piscator: The water is more productive than the earth. Nay, the earth hath no fruitfulness without showers or dews; for all the herbs, and flowers, and fruit, are produced and thrive by the water; and the very minerals are fed by streams that run under ground, whose natural course carries them to the tops of many high mountains, as we see by several springs breaking forth on the tops of the highest hills; and this is also witnessed by the daily trial and testimony of several miners.

Nay, the increase of those creatures that are bred and fed in the water are not only more and more miraculous, but more advantageous to man, not only for the lengthening of his life, but for the preventing of sickness; for it is observed by the most learned physicians, that the casting off of Lent, and other fish days, which hath not only given the lie to so many learned, pious, wise founders of colleges, for which we should be ashamed, hath doubtless been the chief cause of those many putrid, shaking intermitting agues, unto which this nation of ours is now more subject, than those wiser countries that feed on herbs, salads, and plenty of fish; of which it is observed in story, that the greatest part of the world now do. And it may be fit to remember that Moses appointed fish to be the chief diet for the best commonwealth that ever yet was.

And it is observable, not only that there are fish, as namely the Whale, three times as big as the mighty Elephant, that is so fierce in battle, but that the mightiest feasts have been of fish. The Romans, in the height of their glory, have made fish the mistress of all their entertainment; they have had musick to usher in their Sturgeons, Lampreys, and Mullets, which they would purchase at rates rather to be wondered at than believed. He that shall view the writings of Macrobius, or Varro, may be confirmed and informed of this, and of the incredible value of their fish and fish-ponds.

* * *

Piscator: O Sir, doubt not but that *Angling* is an Art; is it not an Art to deceive a *Trout* with an artificial Flie? a *Trout*! that is more sharp sighted than any Hawk you have nam'd, and more watchful and timorous than your high mettled *Marlin* is bold? and yet, I doubt not to catch a brace or two tomorrow, for a friend's breakfast: doubt not therefore, Sir, but that *Angling* is an Art, and an Art worth your learning: the Question is rather, whether you be capable of learning it? for *Angling* is somewhat like *Poetry*, men are to be born so: I mean, with inclinations to it, though both may be heightned by discourse and practice, but he that hopes to be a good *Angler* must not only bring an inquiring, searching, observing wit; but he must bring a large measure of hope and patience, and a love and propensity to the Art it self; but having once got and practis'd it, then doubt not but *Angling* will prove to be so pleasant, that it will prove to be like Vertue, *a reward to it self.*

* * *

Piscator: The Tench, the physician of fishes, is observed to love ponds better than rivers, and to love pits better than either: yet Camden observes, there is a river in Dorsetshire that abounds with Tenches, but doubtless they retire to the most deep and quiet places in it.

This fish hath very large fins, very small and smooth scales, a red circle about his eyes, which are big and of a gold colour, and from either angle of his mouth there hangs down a little barb. In every Tench's head there are two little stones which foreign physicians make great use of, but he is not commended for wholesome meat, though there be very much use made of them for outward applications. Rondeletius says, that at his being at Rome, he saw a great cure done by applying a Tench to the feet of a very sick man. This, he says, was done after an unusual manner, by certain Jews. And it is observed that many of these people have many secrets yet unknown to Christians; secrets that have never yet been written, but have been since the days of their Solomon, who knew the nature of all things, even from the cedar to the shrub, delivered by tradition, from the father to the son, and so from generation to generation without writing; or, unless it were casually, without the least communicating them to any other nation or tribe; for to do that they account a profanation. And, yet it is thought they they, or some spirit worse than they, first told us, that lice, swallowed alive, were a certain cure for the yellow-jaundice. This and many other medicines, were discovered by them, or by revelation; for doubtless, we attained them not by study.

Well, this fish besides his eating, is very useful, both dead and alive, for the good of mankind. But I will meddle no more with that, my honest humble art teaches no such boldness: there are too many foolish meddlers in physick and divinity that think themselves fit to meddle with hidden secrets, and so bring destruction to their followers. But I'll not meddle with them any farther than to wish them wiser; and shall tell you next, for I hope I may be so bold, that the Tench is the physician of fishes, for the Pike especially, and that the Pike being either sick or hurt, is cured by the Touch of the Tench. And it is observed that the tyrant Pike will not be a wolf to his Physician but forbears to devour him though he be never so hungry.

This fish, that carries a natural balsam in him to cure both himself and others, loves yet to feed in very foul water, and amongst weeds. And yet, I am sure, he eats pleasantly, and, doubtless, you will think so too, if you taste him and I shall therefore proceed to give you some few, and but a few, directions how to catch this Tench, of which I have given you these observations.

He will bite at a paste made of brown bread and honey, or at a March-worm or a lob-worm; he inclines very much to any paste with which tar is mixt, and he will bite also a smaller worm with his head nipped off, and a cod-worm put on the hook before that worm. And I doubt not but that he will also, in the three hot months, for in the nine colder he stirs not much, bite at a flagworm or at a green gentle: but can positively say no more of the Tench, he being a fish I have not often angled for; but I wish my honest scholar may, and be ever fortunate when he fishes.

* * *

There is also a *Bleak*, or fresh-water-Sprat, a Fish that is ever in motion, and therefore called by some the *River-Swallow*; for just as you shall observe the *Swallow* to be most evenings in Summer ever in motion, making short and quick turns when he flies to catch Flies in the air (by which he lives) so does the *Bleak* at the top of the water. *Ausonius* would have him called *Bleak* from his whitish colour: his back is of a pleasant sad or Sea-water-green, his belly white and shining as the Mountain-snow: and doubtless though he have the fortune (which vertue has in poor people) to be neglected, yet the *Bleak* ought to be much valued, though we want *Allamot* salt, and the skill that the *Italians* have to turn them into Anchovis. This fish may be caught with a *Pater-noster* line, that is, six or eight very small hooks tyed along the line one half a foot above the other: I have seen five caught thus at one time, and the bait has been Gentles, than which none is better.

Or this fish may be caught with a fine small artificial flie, which is to be of a very sad, brown colour, and very small, and the hook answerable. There is no better sport than whipping for *Bleaks* in a boat, or on a bank in the swift water in a Summers evening, with a Hazle top about five or six foot long, and a line twice the length of the Rod. I have heard Sir *Henry Wotton* say, that there be many that in *Italy* will catch *Swallows* so, or especially *Martins* (this *Bird-angler* standing on the top of a Steeple to do it, and with a line twice so long as I have spoken of): And let me tell you, Scholar, that both *Martins* and *Bleaks* be most excellent meat.

And let me tell you, that I have known a *Hern* that did constantly frequent one place, caught with a hook baited with a big Minnow or a small *Gudgion*. The line and hook must be strong, and tied to some loose staff so big as she cannot flie away with it, a line not exceeding two Yards.

* * *

Venator: Well, Master, these verses be worthy to keep a room in every man's memory. I thank you for them; and I thank you for your many instructions, which, God willing, I will not forget. And as St Austin, in his *Confessions*, commemorates the kindness of his friend Verecundus, for lending him and his companion a country house, because there they rested and enjoyed themselves, free from the troubles of the world, so, having had the like advantage, both by your conversation and the art you have taught me, I ought ever to do the like; for, indeed your company and discourse have been so useful and pleasant, that, I may truly say, I have only lived since I enjoyed them and turned angler, and not before. Nevertheless, here I must part with you; here in this now sad place, where I was so happy as first to meet you: but I shall long for the ninth of May; for then I hope again to enjoy your beloved company, at the appointed time and place. And now I wish for some somniferous potion, that might force me to sleep away the intermitted time, which will pass away with me as tediously as it does with men in sorrow; nevertheless I will make it as short as I can, by my hopes and wishes: and, my good Master, I will not forget the doctrine which you told me Socrates taught his scholars, that they should not think to be honoured so much for being philosphers, as to honour philosophy by their virtuous lives. You advised me to the like concerning Angling, and I will endeavour to do so; and to live like those many worthy men, of which you made mention in the former past of your discourse. This is my firm resolution. And as a pious man advised his friend, that, to beget mortification, he should frequent churches, and view monuments, and charnel-houses, and then and there consider how many dead bodies time had piled up at the gates of death, so when I would beget content, and increase confidence in the power, and wisdom and providence of Almighty God, I will walk the meadows, by some gliding stream, and there contemplate the lilies that take no care, and those very many other various little living creatures that are not only created, but fed, man knows not how, by the goodness of the God of Nature, and therefore trust in him. This is my purpose; and so, let everything that hath breath praise the Lord: and let the blessing of St Peter's Master be with mine.

Piscator: And upon all that are lovers of virtue; and dare trust in his providence; and be quiet; and go a Angling.

'Study to be quiet.'

JOHN EVELYN: from *The Diary* (18 March 1680).

18 At the *Ro: Society* was a letter from *Surenam* of a certaine small Eele that being taken with hooke and line at 100 foote length, did so benumb, and stupifie the limbs of the Fisher, that had not the line suddainly beene cutt, by one of the Hand (who was acquainted with its effects) the poore man had immediately died: There is a certaine wood growing in the Country, which put into a *Waire* or *Eele-pot*, dos as much intoxicate the fish as *Nux Vomica* dos other fish, by which this *mortiferous Torpedo* is not onley caught, but becomes both harmelesse, and excellent meate.

EDMUND WALLER (1606–87): *Upon a Lady's Fishing with an Angle.*

See where the fair Clorinda sits, and seems
Like new-born Venus risen from the streams;
In vain the beauties of the neighbouring field,
    In vain the painted flowers' pride
    With their faint colours strive to hide
That flower to which Flora herself would yield.
    Each object's pleasant to the sight,
    The streams, the meadows yield delight,
But nothing fair as her you can espy
Unless i' th' brook (her looking-glass) you chance to cast your
   eye.

See how she makes the trembling angle shake,
Touched by those hands that would make all men quake.
See how the numerous fishes of the brook
    (For now the armour of their scales
    Nothing against her charms prevails)
Willingly hang themselves upon her hook;
    See how they crowd and thronging wait
    Greedy to catch the proffered bait;
In her more bright and smoother hands content
Rather to die, than live in their own watery element.

With how composed a look and cheerful air,
(Calm as the stream and as the season fair)
With careful eyes she views the dancing float,
    Longing to have it disappear,
    That she its head may higher rear,
And make it swim i' th' air above the moat;
    She sits as silent as the fish,
    Seems burdened with no other wish,
So well she's masked under this fair pretence,
An infidel would swear she's made of perfect innocence.

But ah! Clorinda's is a cruel game,
As she with water sports, she sports with flame,
She innocently angles here, but then
    Thousands of charming baits she lays,

A thousand other several ways;
Her beauteous eyes ensnare whole shoals of men,
Each golden hair's a fishing line,
Able to catch such hearts as mine,
And he that once views her bewitching eyes,
To her victorious charms (like me) must ever be a prize.

JAMES CHETHAM: from *The Angler's Vade Mecum* (1681).

Oyntments to Alure Fish to the Bait.

Take Mans Fat and Cats Fat, of each half an Ounce, Mummy finely poudred three Drams, Cummin-seed finely poudred, one Dram, distilled Oyl of Annise and Spike, of each six Drops, Civet two Grains, and Camphir four Grains, make an Oyntment according to Art, and when you Angle, anoint eight Inches of the Line next the Hook therewith, and keep it in a pewter Box, made something taper, and when you use this Oyntment, never Angle with less than three hairs next Hook, because if you Angle but with one hair, it will not stick on . . . Take the Bones or Scull of a Dead-man, at the opening of a Grave, and beat the same into pouder, and put of this pouder in the Moss wherein you keep your Worms, but others like Grave Earth as well.

Night-Angling

In the night usually the best Trouts bite, and will rise ordinarily in the still deeps, but not so well in the Streams; and although the best and largest Trouts bite in the night (being afraid to stir in the day time) yet I account this way of Angling both unwholsom, unpleasant and very ungentile, and to be used by none but idle poaching fellows; therefore I shall say nothing of it, only describe how to lay night-hooks, which if you live close by a River side, or have a large Moat or Pond at your house, will not be unpleasant sometimes to practice; but as for damming, groping, spearing, hanging, twitchling, firing by night, and netting, I will purposely omit them, and them esteem to be used only by disorderly Fellows; for whom this little Treatise is not in the least intended.

The Best Way to boyl a Carp

Take a Carp (alive if possible) scour him and rub him clean with Water and Salt, but scale him not, then open him, and put him with his Blood and his Liver (which you must save when you open him) into a small Pot or Kettle: then take sweet Marjoram, Time and Parsly, of each a handful, a sprig of Rosemary and another of Savory, bind them into two or three small bundles, and put them to your Carp, with four or five whole Onyons, twenty pickled Oysters, and three Anchovies, then pour upon your Carp, as much Claret Wine as will cover him; and season the Claret well with Salt, Cloves, bruised Mace, slic'd Nutmeg, and the rinds of Oranges and Lemons, that done, cover the Pot, and set it on a quick fire, till it be sufficiently boyled, then take out the Carp and lay it with the broth in the Dish, and pour upon it a quarter of a pound of good fresh Butter, melted and beaten with half a dozen spoonfuls of the Broth, the Yealks of two or three Eggs, and some of the Herbs shred; Garnish the Dish with Lemons and so serve it up.

ROBERT NOBBS: *Of the Parts and Lineaments of a Pike.* From *The Complete Troller* (1682).

As to the shape and proportion of this great devourer, the figure of his body is very long, his back broad, and almost square; altogether equal to the lower fins: his head is lean and very bony, which bones in his head some have resembled to things of mysterious consequence: one of which they commonly compare to the cross, another to the spear, three others to those bloody nails which were instruments of our Saviour's passion: If those comparisons smell any thing of superstition, yet as to physical use, those bones may be profitable. For the jaw-bone beaten to powder, may be helpful for *pleurisies* and the sharpness of *urine*; some do approve of it as a remedy for a pain in the heart and stomach; others affirm that the small bones pulverized, may be fitly used to dry up sores, and many the like medicinal qualities are attributed to the pike's head. An ancient author writing of the nature of things, does discover a stone in the brain of a pike, much like unto a chrystal: Gesner himself, the great naturalist, testifies that he found in the head of a little pike two white stones. As to the shape of his head, his snout is long, which some have compared to the bill or beak of a goose. His lower jaw is far longer than his upper; and in it are placed many teeth, not orderly disposed, but of divers ranks and orders; his eyes are of a golden colour, and very quick sighted, as are all sorts of fish; his belly is always white, but his back and sides are of a black and speckled yellow; his ventricle is very large and capacious, and his throat short, as we may see by his prey which he hath newly taken and not digested; part of it will come up into his mouth, but this is when he seizes upon a great prize. A credible author affirms that he saw a pike of that wonderful bigness that had another within him considerably great, and that within had a water-rat in its belly; so that the ventricle of the great one must needs be exceeding large and extensive. Gesner likewise observes that his heart and gall is very medicinal to cure *agues*, abate *fevers*, etc. and that his biting is venemous and hard to be cured.

HANNAH WOOLLEY: *Terms for Carving all sort of Meat at Table.*
From *The Gentlewoman's Companion; or a Guide to the Female Sex*
(1682).

For *Fish*; *Chine* that *Salmon*, *String* that *Lampry*, *Splat* that *Pike*, *Sauce* that *Plaice*, and *Sauce* that *Tench*, *Splay* that *Bream*, *Side* that *Haddock*, *Tusk* that *Barbel*, *Culpon* that *Trout*, *Transon* that *Eel*, *Tranch* that *Sturgeon*, *Tame* that *Crab*, *Barbe* that *Lobster*.

JOHN BUNYAN: *The Author's Apology.*
From *The Pilgrim's Progress* (1684).

You see the ways the Fisher-man doth take
To catch the fish; what engines doth he make?
Behold how he engageth all his wits;
Also his snares, lines, angles, hooks, and nets.
Yet fish there be, that neither hook, nor line,
Nor snare, nor net, nor engine can make thine;
They must be grop'd for, and be tickled too,
Or they will not be catch'd, whate'er you do.

JOHN EVELYN: from *The Diary* (22 October 1685).

Hence we went to Swallow-fild the house is after the antient building of honourable gent: houses where they kept up the antient hospitality: but the Gardens and Waters as elegant as 'tis possible to make a flat, with art and Industrie and no meane Expenses, my Lady being so extraordinarily skilld in the flowry part: and the dilligence of my Lord in the planting: so that I have hardly seene a seate which shews more toakens of it, then what is here to be found, not onely in the delicious and rarest fruits of a Garden, but in those innumerable and plentifull furniture of the grounds about the seate of timber trees to the incredible ornament and benefit of the place: There is one Ortchard of a 1000 Golden and other cider Pepins: Walks and groves of Elms, Limes, Oake: and other trees: and the Garden so beset with all manner of sweete shrubbs, as perfumes the aire marvelously: The distribution also of the Quarters, Walks, Parterre, etc. is excellent: The Nurseries, Kitchin-garden, full of the most desireable plants; two very noble Orangeries well furnish'd; but above all, The Canale, and fishponds, the one fed with a white, the other with a black-running water, fed by a swift and quick river: so well and plentifully stor'd with fish, that for Pike, Carp, Breame, and Tench; I had never seene anything approaching it: We had Carps and Pike, etc, of size fit for the table of a Prince, every meale, and what added to the delight, the seeing hundreds taken in the drag, out of which the Cooke standing by, we pointed what we had most mind to, and had Carps every meale, that had ben worth at London twenty shill a piece: The Waters are all flag'd about with Calamus arromaticus; of which my lady has hung a Closset, that retaines the smell very perfectly: Also a certain sweete willow and other exotics: There is to this a very fine bowling-green; Meadow, pasture, Wood, in a word all that can render a Country seate delightfull.

ROBERT PLOT: *The Pike.* From *The Natural History of Stafford-shire* (1686).

Nor doth this *fresh-water Wolf* only seize *Froggs* and fish, but upon *fowle*, and other *Animals* not of that Element. Thus in the moat at *Himley*, the *Jacks* are so bold with the young *Ducks*, that as the Reverend Mr *Paston Rector* of the place seriously inform'd me, a whole brood of young *ducks* had been destroyed there by them in a *days* time; and this the larger *Jacks* will doe, even when these *ducks* are grown near as bigg as the old ones: whereof one was catch't (having taken in such a duck the wrong way) that could not gorge it so farr, but that the *Ducks* head hung out of his *mouth*; in which posture both *Jack* and *Duck*, were hung up in the *Hall* of *Himley* house, to be admired, as long as the stench would permit. Which very well agrees with what *Gesner* affirms (though it come not quite up to it) that a *Polish* Gentleman of *Cracow* did faithfull assure Him, that He had seen two young *Geese* at one time in the belly of a *Jack*. Nay of so bold and greedy a devouring disposition is this *Tyrant* of the *Rivers*, when He is in the height of his hunger, that as Mr *Walton* acquaints us, there have been instances of it, that a large *Pike* has bit at, and devoured a *dogg*, that has been swimming in the water.

CHARLES COTTON: *The Retirement.* From *Poems on Several Occasions* (1689).

Farewell, thou busy World! and may
  We never meet again:
Here can I eat, and sleep, and pray
And do more good in one short day,
Than he, who his whole age out-wears
Upon the most conspicuous theatres
  Where nought but vanity and vice appears.

Good God! how sweet are all things here!
How beautiful the fields appear!
  How cleanly do we feed and lie!
Lord! what good hours do we keep!
How quietly we sleep!
  What peace! what unanimity!
How innocent from the lewd fashion
Is all our business, all our recreation!

How calm and quiet a delight
  It is alone
To read, and meditate, and write,
  By none offended and offending none!

To walk, ride, sit, or sleep at one's own ease
And pleasing a man's self, none other to displease!

O my belov'd nymph! fair Dove;
Princess of rivers, how I love
   Upon thy flowery banks to lie
And view thy silver stream,
When gilded by a summer's beam.
   And in it all thy wanton fry
   Playing at liberty,
And with my angle upon them,
   The all of treachery
   I ever learnt, industriously to try!

Lord! would men let me alone,
What an over-happy one
   Should I think myself to be,
Might I in this desert place,
Which most men in discourse disgrace,
   Live but undisturb'd and free!
Here, in this despis'd recess
   Would I, maugre winter's cold,
And the summer's worst excess,
   Try to live out to sixty full years old!
And, all the while,
   Without an envious eye
On any thriving under Fortune's smile
   Contented live, and then contented die.

RICHARD FRANCK: from *Northern Memoirs* (1694).

Arnoldus: However, Isaac Walton (late author of the *Compleat Angler*) has imposed upon the world this monthly novelty, which he understood not himself; but stuffs his book with morals from Dubravius and others, not giving us one precedent of his own practical experiments, except otherwise where he prefers the trencher before the troling-rod; who lays the stress of his arguments upon other men's observations, wherewith he stuffs his indigested octavo; so brings himself under the angler's censure, and the common calamity of a plagiary, to be pitied (poor man) for his loss of time, in scribling and transcribing other men's notions. These are the drones that rob the hive, yet flatter the bees they bring them honey.

Theophilus: I remember the book, but you inculcate his *erratas*; however, it may pass muster among common mudlers.

Arnoldus: No, I think not; for I remember in Stafford, I urged his own argument upon him, that pickerel weed of it self breeds pickerel. Which question was no sooner stated, but he transmits himself to his authority, viz. Gesner, Dubravius, and Androvanus. Which I readily opposed, and offered my reasons to prove the contrary; asserting, that pickerels have been fished out of pools and ponds where that weed (for ought I knew) never grew since the nonage of time, nor pickerel ever known to have shed their spawn there. This I propounded from a rational conjecture of the heronshaw, who to commode her self with the fry of fish, because in a great measure part of her maintenance, probably might lap some spawn about her legs, in regard adhering to the segs and bull-rushes, near the shallows, where the fish shed their spawn, as my self and others without curiosity have observed. And this slimy substance adhering to her legs, and she mounting the air for another station, in probability mounts with her. Where note, the next pond she happily arrives at, possibly she may leave the spawn behind her, which my Compleat Angler no sooner deliberated, but drop'd his argument, and leaves Gesner to defend it; so huff'd away: which rendred him rather a formal opinionist, than a reform'd and practical artist, because to celebrate such antiquated records, whereby to maintain such an improbable assertion.

Theophilus: This was to the point, I confess; pray, go on.

Arnoldus: In his book, intituled the *Compleat Angler*, you may read there of various and diversified colours, as also the forms and proportions of flies. Where, poor man, he perplexes himself to rally and scrape together such a parcel of fragments, which he fancies arguments convincing enough to instruct the adult and minority of youth, into the slender margin of his uncultivated art, never made practicable by himself I'm convinc'd. Where note, the true character of an industrious angler, more deservedly falls upon Merril and Faulkner, or rather upon Isaac Owldham, a man that fish'd salmon but with three hairs at hook, whose collections and experiments were lost with himself.

Theophilus: That was pity.

JEAN DE LA FONTAINE: *The Fishes and the Flute-player.* From
Fables, Book X (1694).
Translated from the French by Edward Marsh, 1933.

The Shepherd Thyrsis wooed Annette
With music of his flute and voice
So beautiful that hearing it
The souls in Hades might rejoice.
One day he sang beside a stream that flowed
Where Zephyr in the flowery meads abode,
The Maiden fishing at his side;
But past her quill the victims glide,
No booty crowns her wishes.
The Swain, who by his tuneful art
Had melted the ungentlest heart,
Thought, but thought wrong, 'twould captivate the fishes.
'O citizens of this pure wave,' sang he,
'Come, leave your Naiad in her watery grot,
And hail a goddess lovelier far than she.
Fear not within her prisons to be barred:
Towards men alone her heart is hard:
Her gentle care shall be your lot.
Against your life she harbours no design:
A pool awaits you, clear as crystal fine:
And ev'n though two or three should die,
In Anne's white arms one moment they would lie,
And I should wish their doom were mine.'
        The plea was eloquent in form and matter,
But nothing could have fallen flatter:
The audience was deaf as it was dumb,
The stream undimpled lay, untwitched the line,
And not a single fish would come;
So when his music on the winds had faded,
The Shepherd cast a net – a happier thought!
For in a trice the fish were caught,
And at the damsel's feet paraded.

Shepherds, whose flocks instead of sheep are men!
Ye Kings, who by persuasion think to gain
The loyalty of alien races!
That never was, nor will be, how to set
About the business – try a net!
'Tis Power alone will keep them in their places.

EDMUND GIBSON: from *Lancashire.* From *Camden's Britannia,
newly translated into English with large Additions and Improvements* (1695).
Translated from the Latin.

Near Sefton, *Alt*, a little river runs into the sea, leaving its name to
Altmouth, a small village, which it passes by, and runs a little distance
from *Ferneby*, where in the mossy grounds belonging to it, they cast up
Turves, which serve the Inhabitants both for fire and candle. Under the
Turf there lyes a blackish dead water, which has a kind of I know not
what oily fat substance floating upon it, and little fishes swimming in it,
which are took by those that dig the Turves here; so that we may say,
we have fish dug out of the ground here, as well as they have about
Heraclea and *Tius* in Pontus. Nor is this strange, when in watry places
of this nature, the fish by following the water often swim underground, and men there fish for them with spades. But that in
Paphlagonia many fish are dug up, and those good ones too, in places
not at all watery, has somewhat of a peculiar and more hidden cause to
it. That of Seneca was pleasantly said, *What reason is there why fish
should not travel the Land, if we traverse the Sea.*

JOHN WORLIDGE: from *Of Fishing.* From *Systema Agriculturae; the
Mystery of Husbandry Discovered* (fourth edition 1697).

In the Isle of Wight, and other places Westward, in the Rocks on the
Seashore, are great numbers of Cormorants bred, being a large Fowl,
and live only by preying on Fish; and are so dextrous at it, that in the
open Seas they will dive, and swiftly pursue their Game, and take and
carry them to their Nests; that the Inhabitants near adjacent do often
go to these Rocks, and furnish themselves with Fish brought thither by

them at their breeding-times. These Birds may be so brought up tame, that they will in our ordinary clear Rivers dive, and take you as many Trouts or other Fish, as you please, or the place affords, putting but a small collar over the Neck of the Fowl that the Fish may not pass into her Stomock. When you intend for your Game, you must carry her out Fasting: put on her Loop or Collar, and let her go into the Water, she will Dive, and streightly pursue the Fish she hath most mind to, forward and backward; and when she hath caught her Game, she gives a toss into the Air, and receives it endwise into her Mouth; which will stretch like the Head of a Snake, and admit of a large Fish into her Throat, which will stop at the Collar. Then hold out an Eel to her (which you must carry alive or dead with you to that purpose) and she will come to your hand, and will by your assistance disgorge her prey immediately, and to her Sport again; and will so continue, till she hath furnish you with as much as you can desire. By this means may you take more than any other way whatsoever, and exceeds any of the Sports of Hawking or Hunting.

'The finny race'

The Eighteenth Century

Frontispiece by William Hogarth to *Dr Brook Taylor's Method of Perspective Made Easy* (1754).

THOMAS D'URFEY: *The Fisherman's Song*, first sung in *The Famous History of the Rise and Fall of Massaniello* (1700). From *Wit and Mirth: or Pills to Purge Melancholy* (1719).

Of all the World's Enjoyments,
    That ever valu'd were;
There's none of your Employments,
    With Fishing can Compare:
        Some Preach, some Write,
        Some Swear, some Fight,
All Golden Lucre courting,
    But Fishing still bears off the Bell;
For Profit or for Sporting.
    Then who a Jolly Fisherman, a Fisherman will be?
      His Throat must wet,
      Just like his Net,
    To keep out Cold at Sea.

The Country Squire loves Running,
    A Pack of well-mouth'd Hounds;
Another fancies Gunning
    For wild Ducks in his Grounds:

This Hunts, that Fowls,
This Hawks, *Dick* Bowls,
No greater Pleasure wishing,
    But *Tom* that tells what Sport excells,
Gives all the Praise to Fishing.
    Then who, etc.

A good *Westphalia Gammon*,
    Is counted dainty Fare;
But what is't to a *Salmon*,
    Just taken from the Ware:
        Wheat Ears and *Quailes*,
        Cocks, Snipes, and *Rayles*;
Are priz'd while Season's lasting,
    But all must stoop to Crawfish Soop,
Or I've no skill in tasting.
    Then who, etc.

Keen Hunters always take too
    Their prey with too much pains;
Nay often break a Neck too,
    A Pennance for no Brains:
        They Run, they Leap,
        Now high, now deep,
Whilst he that Fishing chooses;
    With ease may do't, nay more to boot,
May entertain the Muses.
    Then who, etc.

And tho' some envious wranglers,
    To jeer us will make bold;
And Laugh at Patient Anglers,
    Who stand so long i' th' Cold:
        They wait on Miss,
        We wait on this,
And think it easier Labour;
    And if you'd know, Fish profits too,
Consult our *Holland* Neighbour.
    Then who, etc.

JOHN WHITNEY: from *The Dedication* to *The Genteel Recreation: Or, the Pleasure of Angling, A Poem. With a Dialogue between Piscator and Corydon (1700).*

To My Honoured Friend John Hyde, Esq;

Sir,

The *Liberty* you gave me this last *Summer* to Angle in your great pond at Winckhurst, emboldens me in gratitude to present you with this little treatise on the pleasure of *Angling*; the observations are my own, and some of the Pleasure I received in your good company when *Angling* at *Heaver*, and since in the Company of Capt. *Comer*, and an other Gentleman at *Winckhurst*; where in one Day we caught about twenty brace of extraordinary large *Carps* with very sweet *Eeles* and *Tench*; I believe I shall hardly forget the *Pearch* of eighteen Inches long, caught by Capt. *Comer*, nor the Old Gentleman's resolution, while we were drinking a Dram of the Bottle, a Fish run with his rod, which he being unwilling to loose, stript off his Cloaths and leapt in, and in swimming proved too nimble for the Fish, for I assure you, he brought them both out with much content to regain his Rod.

Sir, the Capt. assures me, there be larger Pearch in the Pond tho I never saw a braver, should I commend the Fish some may think I flatter, but of all the Ponds I ever Angled in I never received so much delight in so little time, nor ever eat of sweeter or larger *Carps*, for all we caught that did not exceed sixteen or eighteen Inches, we turn'd into the water again, thinking it pity to kill them before they came to their full growth, which commonly exceeds twenty.

Sir, I know you Love to Fish and Angling, and how to your great cost, you have caused to be dig'd a large square Pond in your great Yard before your dwelling place at *Sundridge*, and storing it with brave *Carps* and other Fish, which Pond contains in length three hundred foot, and two hundred and ten foot in breadth, all dug out of the side of a Hill, to the depth of fourteen Foot, and wharfing it ninety foot against the Highway side, with extraordinary good Plancks of Oak, the Trees being fell'd in your own ground that made them, and then in the middle of the Pond, a most delightful *Summer* House to go to by Boat, twelve long and ten foot broad, with a Fountain in the middle, where the water plays in sundry Figures; besides the Rails and Ballisters that compass it round, there's a Platform of lead on the top, with Rails and Ballisters to walk and Angle upon.

But that which gives the greater grace, in my Opinion, is the *Summer House* standing upon a Fish House, which beside the Fish there kept, is stored all round with Nests for Ducks, where they breed in abundance, and under the Eves of the uppermost Platform, there is an Ingenious contrivance for Coves, wherein the Pidgeons encrease extraordinary; It's no easy matter for a Simon Suck-egg to Rob either of their Nests, unless he'll adventure at one time both Drowning and Hanging; 'Tis very pleasant walking round the pond, where a Man hath six or seven foot of Earth over his head on the one side for a shelter, while the other side defends him from the water by a shade of Osiers.

I have also seen your round Fountain in your delightful best Garden, and the stock of Fish therein kept to be always at hand to pleasure your Friends, which is continually stored with *Trouts* and *Carps* of the largest size; I remember also the Oval Fountain in the Kitchen Garden, which is a good Nursery for the younger fry, but above all, I admire your Ingenuity in contriving that Square Pond on the top of your House, which contains good *Carps* and other Fish, and is an excellent divertisement when you are pleased to disport your self and friends with your fine Water Works, I admired once how the water ascended to that Height, to be always full of sweet and fresh water, till you were pleased to shew me how you performed it by help of an Engine.

If there be delights any where, I think you have them all at home, for a Man to see Fish swimming on the top of your House and the Fowls of Heaven to live and breed under the water, will be strange to those whose faith is too weak to believe, or capacity to understand your Ingenuity, how you have made Coves for Pidgeons under the Pond where they breed, that a Man may justly say, that only Lead keeps the two elements asunder.

ROBERT HOWLETT: from *The Angler's Sure Guide: or Angling Improved* (1706).

Of the Grayling, or Umber. His Names, Nature, Vertue, Growth, and Season

The Grayling is called in Latin *Thymalus*, a *Thymo* having a scent like the Flowers of Thyme. The Grayling and Umber are both one and the same Fish, differing in Name only, as the Pike and Luce, according to Age and Bigness; and is called an Umber, ex *Umbra*, a Shadow, for the swiftness of his motion. He's much of the nature of a Trout, both as to his Food and

Flesh; calvers like a Trout, and eats as firm as a Trout; but differs from a Trout in Taste: And as we say of Smelts, when first taken out of the Water, they smell like Violets, so the Grayling at his first taking smells of Water-thyme; which has led some to think it's a great part of his Food; and *St Ambrose* calls him the Flower of Fishes.

Of the Pike. His Names, Nature, Size, Age and Vertue

The Pike is a melancholy Fish, swims by himself and lives alone. His Flesh is very Midicinal: The Croslike bone in his Head is given against the Falling-sickness; and his Flesh is so harmless and excellent, that it may be given to a sick Person. His Spawn and Row provoke both to Vomit and Stool, and are used for that Purpose; the Jaws calcin'd helps the Stone, cleanses and dries up Ulcers, old Sores and Hemorrhoids; the Teeth in Powder gives Ease in the Pleurisie; the Grease takes away Coughs in Children, by anointing the Feet therewith; the Gall taken inwardly, cures Agues; outwardly helps Spots and Dimness of the Eyes; the Heart eaten cures Fevers.

Signs of Rain

If Sheep bleat, or skip and play wantonly.
If Swine carry Hay, Straw, etc. to hide it.
If Dogs guts rumble.
If Moles cast up Earth more than ordinary, and the Earth they cast be small and dry.
If Frogs croak more commonly than they do.
If Toads make from their Holes in the Evening.
If Worms come quite out of the Earth, more than they use to do.
If Pismires or Ants run often to their Nests.
If Flies or Fleas bite or sting worse than they wont.

LOUIS LIGER: from *Amusements de la Campagne, ou Nouvelles Ruses Innocentes, Volume 2* (1710).
Translated from the French by David Profumo, 1984.

Fishing for frogs is extremely entertaining, and the method most widely practised in the country; one fishes for them by night with a flame: this is the way.

You take some straw torches, and in the company of several others
you proceed to the spot which frogs are known to frequent: it is
necessary for one or two of the Fishermen to strip off and immerse
themselves in the water, and everyone takes a bag, which is held
between the legs, to secure the Frogs that will be found within reach.

Once these Fishermen are positioned in the water in this fashion,
the others in the party need to take a straw-torch each, or else a
flaming brand, partly in order to light up the Fishermen as they collect
the Frogs which will be surrounding them in a throng on all sides, and
partly to entice these creatures to run towards the glimmering of the
flame, which they mistake for sunlight.

It is all the easier to catch these Frogs if they don't budge at all: but
with that in mind, one must be careful to make no noise, because as
soon as the least sound strikes them, they immediately retreat, and you
won't catch any more.

The darker the conditions, the better the Fishing will be; and it
could be said that this procedure for catching Frogs is so infallible, that
one had only to take the bags, and you will be certain to bring them
back stuffed full.

The person who is in the water ought to have a cloth bag and put
this between his legs, in such a way that the bottom of it is hanging
down, or so it is attached to his person so he can make use of it when
he wants to put in it the Frogs he catches.

ALEXANDER POPE: from *Windsor Forest* (1713).

> In genial spring, beneath the quivering shade,
> When cooling vapours breath along the mead,
> The patient fisher takes his silent stand,
> Intent, his angle trembling in his hand:
> With looks unmov'd, he hopes the scaly breed,
> And eyes the dancing cork and bending reed.
> Our plenteous streams a various race supply,
> The bright-eyed perch with fins of Tyrian dye;
> The silver eel, in shining volumes roll'd;
> The yellow carp, in scales bedropp'd with gold;
> Swift trouts, diversified with crimson stains;
> And pikes, the tyrants of the watery plains.

CAPTAIN ALEXANDER SMITH: from *The School of Venus, Or, Cupid restor'd to Sight; Being a History of Cuckolds and Cuckold Makers* (1716).

No sooner was it break of Day but the King having a Resolution to go to *Hampton Court,* and to take the Prince of *Newberg* along with him, in order to Divert him there with a Ball, every thing was presently got in readiness to carry the Court thither by Water. Then having taken their respective Places in the Barges, which were cover'd with *Persian* Carpets, the ground Work of Gold, and hung with Silk Brocaded Tapestries of a Rose Colour, and at the same time the Air resounding with a most agreeable Sympathy of Trumpets, Kettle-Drums, Flutes, Violins, Voices, Theorbes, and Cymbals; *Nell Gwin,* who was also among 'em, had found out Matter of Divertisement for the Gentlemen and Ladies; and among the rest, one which occasion'd a great deal of Mirth. She desir'd to stop upon the Water, the better to enjoy the Fair Season, and the Melodious Harmony of Musick. She then caus'd to be brought forth some Angling Rods, with silk Lines, and Hooks of Gold. The King went to Angling with several others, but could catch nothing, whereat the Ladies Laugh'd very heartily, and the King told 'em he would Angle no longer; and so pulling up his Line, found half a Dozen of Fry'd Smelts ty'd to the Hook with a silk Thread. He fell a Laughing aloud, and so did every Body else. *Nelly* told him, *That so great a King should have something peculiar above the rest; that poor Fishermen caught Fish alive, but his were ready Drest.* The Prince of *Newberg* told 'em, *That six being not enough, he would try whether he could take two or three more, to add to the King's Fish.* He threw his Line, and feeling it weighty, *O! Sir,* said he, *we shall live Merrily;* and so pulling it up, found a Purse ty'd to the Hook, which being open'd, there was in it a golden Case, set with Stones, and the Picture of a certain Lady within it, whom the Prince lov'd. This occasion'd a general Mirth, and the King, who knew now that *Nelly* had order'd the Divers to tie the Fish and Picture to the Hooks, was above all the rest extreamely delighted with it. *Cleopatra* (said he to *Nell*) *caus'd a* Sardine *to be ty'd to* Mark Anthony's *Hook, but you exceed her in your Contrivance, for you bestow Pictures, which are more acceptable. These are Presents,* said the Lady, *whom the Picture represented, which Cost her nothing. She sent Yesterday to my House, to tell me, that she being inclin'd to have her Picture drawn, she desir'd I would send her mine, because she would take a View of the Drapery; you see, Sir, to what Use she has put it. Nothing could happen more agreeable to me,* said the Prince; and then Addressing himself to

Nelly, quoth he, *I know not how to pay you my Respects sufficiently. I should be very glad* (answer'd she) *to Merit your Acknowledgements; but you thank me for a good Office I had no hand in: I believe it were the Naiades of the* Thames, *who perform'd this Act of Gallantry, on purpose to Oblige you, and this fair Lady, whom you entirely Love, I believe, with unfeigned Sincerity.*

JOHN GAY: from *Rural Sports, A Georgic, To Mr Pope.*
From *Poems* (1720).

As in successive course the seasons roll,
So circling pleasures recreate the soul.
When genial spring a living warmth bestows,
And o'er the year her verdant mantle throws,
Now swelling inundation hides the grounds,
But crystal currents glide within their bounds;
The finny brood their wonted haunts forsake,
Float in the sun, and skim along the lake,
With frequent leap they range the shallow streams,
Their silver coats reflect the dazzling beams.
Now let the fisherman his toils prepare,
And arm himself with ev'ry wat'ry snare;
His hooks, his lines peruse with careful eye,
Increase his tackle, and his rod re-tie.

When floating clouds their spongy fleeces drain,
Troubling the streams with swift-descending rain,
And water, tumbling down the mountain's side,
Bear the loose soil into the swelling tide;
Then, soon as vernal gales begin to rise,
And drive the liquid burthen thro' the skies,
The fisher to the neighbouring current speeds,
Whose rapid surface purls, unknown to weeds;
Upon a rising border of the brook
He sits him down, and ties the treach'rous hook;
Now expectation cheers his eager thought
His bosom glows with treasure yet uncaught,
Before his eyes a banquet seems to stand,
Where ev'ry guest applauds his skilful hand.
*

When a brisk gale against the current blows,
And all the wat'ry plain in wrinkles flows,
Then let the fisherman his art repeat,
Where bubbling eddies favour the deceit.
If an enormous salmon chance to spy
The wanton errors of the floating fly,
He lifts his silver gills above the flood,
And greedily sucks in th' unfaithful food;
Then downward plunges with the fraudful prey,
And bears with joy the little spoil away;
Soon in smart pain he feels the dire mistake,
Lashes the wave, and beats the foamy lake,
With sudden rage he now aloft appears,
And in his eye convulsive anguish bears;
And now again, impatient of the wound,
He rolls and wreathes his shining body round;
Then headlong shoots beneath the dashing tide,
The trembling fins the boiling wave divide;
Now hope exalts the fisher's beating heart,
Now he turns pale, and fears his dubious art;
He views the tumbling fish with longing eyes,
While the line stretches with th' unwieldy prize;
Each motion humours with his steady hands,
And one slight hair the mighty bulk commands:
Till tired at last, despoil'd of all his strength,
The game athwart the stream unfolds his length.
He now, with pleasure, views the gasping prize
Gnash his sharp teeth, and roll his blood-shot eyes;
Then draws him to the shore, with artful care,
And lifts his nostrils in the sick'ning air:
Upon the burthen'd stream he floating lies,
Stretching his quivering fins, and gasping dies.

JOHN GAY: *To a Young Lady with Some Lampreys.*
From *Poems* (1720).

With lovers 'twas of old the fashion
By presents to convey their passion:
No matter what the gift they sent,
The lady saw that love was meant.
Fair Atalanta, as a favour,
Took the boar's head her hero gave her;
Nor could the bristly thing affront her,
'Twas a fit present from a hunter.
When squires send woodcocks to the dame,
It serves to show their absent flame:
Some by a snip of woven hair,
In posied lockets bribe the fair;
How many mercenary matches
Have sprung from di'mond-rings and watches!
But hold – a ring, a watch, a locket,
Would drain at once a poet's pocket;
He should send songs that cost him nought,
Nor even be prodigal of thought.

Why then send lampreys? fie, for shame!
'Twill set a virgin's blood on flame.
This to fifteen a proper gift!
It might lend sixty-five a lift.

I know your maiden aunt will scold,
And think my present somewhat bold.
I see her lift her hands and eyes.

'What, eat it, niece; eat Spanish flies!
Lamprey's a most immodest diet:
You'll neither wake nor sleep in quiet.
Should I to-night eat sago-cream,
'Twould make me blush to tell my dream;
If I eat lobster, 'tis so warming,
That ev'ry man I see looks charming;
Wherefore had not the filthy fellow

Laid Rochester upon your pillow?
I vow and swear, I think the present
Had been as modest and as decent.

'Who has her virtue in her power?
Each day has its unguarded hour;
Always in danger of undoing,
A prawn, a shrimp may prove our ruin!

'The shepherdess, who lives on salad,
To cool her youth, controls her palate;
Should Dian's maids turn liqu'rish livers,
And of huge lampreys rob the rivers,
Then all beside each glade and visto,
You'd see nymphs lying like Calisto.

'The man who meant to heat your blood,
Needs not himself such vicious food—'

In this, I own, your aunt is clear,
I sent you what I well might spare:
For when I see you (without joking),
Your eyes, lips, breasts are so provoking,
They set my heart more cock-a-hoop,
Than could whole seas of craw-fish soup.

DANIEL DEFOE: from *A Tour Thro' the Whole Island of Great Britain:
Letter 3* (1724).

About twenty-two miles from Excester we go to Totness, on the river
Dart. This is a very good town; of some trade, but has more gentlemen
in it than tradesmen of note; they have a very fine stone-bridge here
over the river, which being within seven or eight miles of the sea, is
very large, and the tide flows ten or twelve foot at the bridge. Here was
had the diversion of seeing them catch fish, with the assistance of a
dog. The case is this, on the south side of the river, and on a slip, or
narrow cut or channel made on purpose for a mill, there stands a
corn-mill; the mill tail, or floor for the water below the wheels is

wharfed up on either side with stone, above high-water mark, and for above twenty or thirty foot in length below it, on that part of the river towards the sea; at the end of this wharfing is a grating of wood, the cross-bars of which stand bearing inward, sharp at the end, and pointing inward towards one another, as the wires of a mouse-trap.

When the tide flows up, the fish can with ease go in between the points of these cross-bars, but the mill being shut down they can go no farther upwards; and when the water ebbs again, they are left behind, not being able to pass the points of the grating, as above, outwards; which like a mouse-trap keeps them in, so that they are left at the bottom with about a foot, or a foot and half water. We were carried hither at low water, where was saw about fifty or sixty small salmon, about seventeen to twenty inches long, which the country people call salmon peal, and to catch these, the person who went with us, who was our landlord at a great inn next the bridge, put in a net on a hoop at the end of a pole, the pole going cross the hoop, which we call in this country a shove net: the net being fixed at one end of the place they put in a dog, who was taught his trade before hand, at the other end of the place, and he drives all the fish into the net, so that only holding the net still in its place, the man took up two or three and thirty salmon peal at the first time.

JAMES SAUNDERS: *Of the Angler.* From *The Compleat Fisherman* (1724).

The Angler or Person thus employ'd in catching the Fish, is a Person under some eminent Circumstances, which allows a perfect Description of him; for he is a very particular Person indeed, nor is every Man qualified for the Work, Or, as it is justly call'd not a Work but a SPORT.

1 He is one that does not angle as a Trade or Employment, or for his Bread, but for SPORT; and therefore as above, *I do not call it a Work*, tho' otherwise it is really a thing that is to be manag'd with a great Application and Diligence: But I suppose 'tis a thing that no body ever follow'd for his Bread, or to get Money, and this is the justest Claim the *Angler* has to call himself a Gentleman, or *Gentleman Angler*. I shall leave the Dispute as I find it, he that has nothing else to show for his being a Gentleman, will find it hard to make his Title good in the

Herald' Book; yet he that being before a Gentleman, and delights in or applies himself to Angling, will find his Quality and Honour not at all impaired by his Application to so innocent and so pleasing a Diversion.

2 He is however, or is to be suppos'd to be a Man of Leisure, for he who being a Man of Business neglects that Business and spends the Hours on the Banks of a River catching a Gudgeon, which should be employ'd behind his Compter or in his Counting House, in order to get his Family Bread, makes the Sport become a Vice in his Morals; his Angling is a Crime, and he spends that time in his Sport, which is not his own; and which he ought to reckon among the mispent Hours, that he must account for hereafter. Such I would be far from encouraging in this Work, either by recommending the Sport to them, or instructing them in the artful part of it.

3 Some have said that an Angler must be a Man of no thinking, because say they, he is constantly busy on such Trifles, as that of catching a Trout, and can spend a whole Day, or perhaps a Day and Night, nay many Days and Nights, on so mean an Affair, and they would therefore compare him to the Lord *Rochester's* Countreyman, who

> Whistled as he went for want of Thought.

On the other Hand, I take it to be rather a Token of a thinking retir'd Disposition, or else a meer want of Employment; and they might then more justly apply it to those who the same Lord *Rochester* represents as profess'd Thinkers,

> Who
> Retire to think because they've nought to do.

It must be allow'd that as it is a kind of *still Life*, (as the Painters call it) it is most suitable to retir'd Minds; 'tis a pleasing kind of Diversion to a Person who loves to be alone, and yet I do not think it is at all of kin to any thing of what they call Melancholy; for 'tis a Mistake when we think that a truly melancholy Man, can apply himself with such Calmness and such a sedate Mind, as is requir'd to make Angling a Sport; for the mind of a melancholy Man is far from being in Repose, on the contrary, there is nothing farther from it; a melancholy Man has his Spirits always in Agitation, and in a Hurry; and therefore you find him the most easy of any Man in the World to be put in a Passion, and to fly out in the most dangerous Extreams of it upon every trifling Occasion; such a Man is not fit to be an Angler, nay is not fit to be trusted by the

River side with an Angle Rod in his Hand. On the contrary, he that angles, must have all his Passions at his Command, he must govern his Temper with an absolute Sway, and be able to sustain his Mind under the greatest Disappointments.

Alas the Sport of Angling is liable to the greatest Vicissitudes, and to the most provoking Incidents; *Job's* Loss of his Children by the Fall of the House, was a very great Trial indeed, but what is all that to a Man having taken a charming Trout, or a large Pike, and brought him with the utmost Dexterity to the very Landing Net, or perhaps just to the River's Bank, and at one Spring have him get from him and recover the River again, when he was as it were in his Hands; if the Angler does not stamp and stare, swear an Hundred Oaths, or pull the Hair off his Head, nay if he does not throw himself into the very River after it, he must be allow'd to be a Man of great Temper, and have the Command of himself to a Wonder.

Whereas on the contrary, the true Angler takes all this as calmly and quietly as if it had been nothing; but goes, and new fits his Tackle, new baits his Hook, and throws it into the River again, with as much Calmness, as if nothing had happen'd; only *by the way*, he does not throw his Hook again in the same Place, for Reasons we shall see, as we go on.

Nor are two or three, or many such Disappointments in a Day, able to move him, provided he is assured that he was not defective in the Art; that every thing was as it should be, and that nothing but unforeseen and unavoidable Circumstances in the Case, made the Fish escape him.

JAMES THOMSON: from *Spring* (1728).
From *The Seasons*.

When with his lively ray the potent sun
Has pierced the streams, and roused the finny-race,
Then, issuing cheerful, to thy sport repair;
Chief should the western breezes curling play,
And light o'er ether bear the shadowy clouds,
High to their fount, this day, amid the hills,
And woodlands warbling round, trace up the brooks;
The next, pursue their rocky-channel'd maze,
Down to the river, in whose ample wave

Their little naiads love to sport at large.
Just in the dubious point, where with the pool
Is mix'd the trembling stream, or where it boils
Around the stone, or from the hollow'd bank
Reverted plays in undulating flow,
There throw, nice-judging, the delusive fly;
And as you lead it round in artful curve,
With eye attentive mark the springing game.
Straight as above the surface of the flood
They wanton rise, or urged by hunger leap,
Then fix, with gentle twitch, the barbed hook:
Some lightly tossing to the grassy bank,
And to the shelving shore slow dragging some,
With various hand proportion'd to their force.
If yet too young, and easily deceived,
A worthless prey scarce bends your pliant rod,
Him, piteous of his youth and the short space
He has enjoy'd the vital light of Heaven,
Soft disengage, and back into the stream
The speckled captive throw. But should you lure
From his dark haunt, beneath the tangled roots
Of pendant trees, the monarch of the brook,
Behoves you then to ply your finest art.
Long time he, following cautious, scans the fly;
And oft attempts to seize it, but as oft
The dimpled water speaks his jealous fear.
At last, while haply o'er the shaded sun
Passes a cloud, he desperate takes the death,
With sullen plunge. At once he darts along,
Deep-struck, and runs out all the lengthened line;
Then seeks the farthest ooze, the sheltering weed,
The cavern'd bank, his old secure abode;
And flies aloft, and flounces round the pool,
Indignant of the guile. With yielding hand,
That feels him still, yet to his furious course
Gives way, you, now retiring, following now
Across the stream, exhaust his idle rage:
Till floating broad upon his breathless side,
And to his fate abandon'd, to the shore
You gaily drag your unresisting prize.

JONATHAN SWIFT: from a letter to Viscount Bolingbroke and
Alexander Pope, Dublin, 5 April 1729.

I am sorry for Lady Bolingbroke's ill health; but I protest I never knew
a very deserving person of that sex, who had not too much reason to
complain of ill health. I never wake without finding life a more
insignificant thing than it was the day before: which is one great
advantage I get by living in this country, where there is nothing I shall
be sorry to lose; but my greatest misery is recollecting the scene of
twenty years past, and then all on a sudden dropping into the present. I
remember when I was a little boy, I felt a great fish at the end of my
line which I drew up almost on the ground, but it dropt in, and the
disappointment vexeth me to this very day, and I believe it was the type
of all my future disappointments. I should be ashamed to say this to
you, if you had not a spirit fitter to bear your own misfortunes, than I
have to think of them. Is there patience left to reflect by what qualities
wealth and greatness are got, and by what qualities they are lost?

JACQUES VANIÈRE: from *Praedium Rusticum, Book XV* (1730).
Translated from the Latin by John Duncombe, 1809.

> When I both see and hear
> The various arts of fishers, and survey
> How they the fish deceitfully betray,
> Reflect I must with equal grief and truth;
> That the same arts deceive unwary youth,
> The snares, of old for fish alone design'd,
> Are now employ'd to captivate mankind;
> Man catches man, and by the bait betrays
> With proffer'd kindness, or, still cunning, lays
> Nets to entrap th' unwary, and embroils
> Cities and towns to profit from the spoils.
> For you, dear youths, soft pleasure lies in wait,
> And hides her hook beneath a honey'd bait,
> But all her treach'rous gifts will only gain
> For a short joy a lasting load of pain.
> Here when the bait allures the fish to taste
> The transient pleasure of a sweet repast,

You see for this how dearly he must pay;
Life is the purchase, and himself the prey.
Thus soft allurements serve to varnish o'er
The frauds of pleasure, unperceiv'd before;
But if a youth is once inspir'd, he'll find
He cannot void the poison from his mind;
No more than could the fish when snar'd withdraw
The crooked steel from his tormented jaw;
While lasting grief for short delights he gains,
Still rues his transient joys with ever-during pains.

SAMUEL RICHARDSON: from *Pamela* (1740).

I am but just come off from a walk in the garden, and have deposited my letter; we took a turn in the garden to angle, as Mrs Jewkes had promised me. She baited the hook, I held it, and soon hooked a lovely carp. 'Play it, play it,' said she. I did, and brought it to the bank. A sad thought just then came into my head; and I threw it in again. What pleasure it seemed to have, to flounce, when at liberty! 'Why throw it in?' said she. 'O Mrs Jewkes!' said I, 'I was thinking this poor carp was the unhappy Pamela. I was comparing you and myself to my naughty master. As we hooked and deceived the poor carp, so was I betrayed by false baits; and when you said, 'Play it, play it', it went to my heart to think I should sport with the destruction of the poor fish I had betrayed; I could not but fling it in again: and did you not see the joy with which the happy carp flounced from us? O,' said I, 'may some good merciful body procure me my liberty in the same manner; for I think my danger equal!'

'Lord bless thee!' said she, 'what a thought is there!' – 'I can angle no more,' added I. 'I'll try *my* fortune,' said she, and took the rod. 'Do,' answered I; 'and I will plant life, if I can, while you are destroying it. I have some horse-beans, and will go and stick them in one of the borders, to see how long they will be coming; and I will call them my garden.'

WILLIAM THOMPSON: from *Hymn to May* (?1740).

Let us our steps direct where Father Thames
In silver windings draws his humid train,
And pours, where'er he rolls his naval stream,
Pomp on the city, plenty o'er the plain.
Or by the banks of Isis shall we stray,
Ah why so long from Isis' banks away?
Where thousand damsels dance, and thousand shepherds play.

Or choose you rather Theron's calm retreat,
Embosom'd, Surry, in thy verdant vale,
At once the muses' and the graces' seat;
There gently listen to my faithful tale.
Along the dew-bright parterres let us rove,
Or taste the odours of the mazy grove;
Hark how the turtles coo: I languish too with love.

Amid the pleasaunce of Arcadian scenes,
Love steals his silent arrows on my breast;
Nor falls of water, nor enamell'd greens,
Can sooth my anguish, or invite to rest.
You, dear Ianthe, you alone impart
Balm to my wounds, and cordial to my smart:
The apple of my eye, the life-blood of my heart.

With line of silk, with hook of barbed steel,
Beneath the broken umbrage let us lay,
And from the water's crystal bosom steal
Upon the grassy bank the finny prey:
The perch, with purple speckled manifold;
The eel, in silver labyrinth self-roll'd,
And carp, all-burnish'd o'er with drops of scaly gold.

JOHN WILLIAMSON: from *The British Angler* (1740).

What a delightful Scene, says a late Author, is a soft murmuring
Stream! Whether we reflect on the gentle Motion of its Waters, or on

the various Benefits and Advantages arising from it, or use our Endeavours to trace it to its Head; we are charmed with its gliding in such beautiful Meanders: The numberless Accommodations it affords us, fill us with the most grateful Acknowledgements, and our Curiosity is excited, to the last Degree, by the Obscurity of its Original.

Let us consider it in its gradual Progression and Increase. It is at first nothing more than a Vein of Water, issuing from some Hill, upon a Bed of Sand or Clay. The little Stones that are dispersed round about, are sufficient to interrupt its Current. It turns and winds, and murmurs as it rolls along. At last it clears its Way, falls in a Torrent down upon the Plains, and swells, by being united with some other Streams. It hollows the Ground by the Rapidity of its Fall, and throws up the Earth on each Side of it. It insensibly forces it way thro' every Thing that obstructs its Passage, and digs a Bed or Channel for itself. The Overflowing of the adjacent Ponds, the Snow that melts, and trickles down the Hills, and the additional Supplies of various Brooks and Rills that fall into it, fortify and enrich it. Then it assumes a Name, and steers its Course along the Sides of flowry Meads: It takes a Tour all round the Hills, and graces, as its turns and winds, the spacious Plains.

'Tis the general Rendezvous of almost all Kind of living Creatures. A Thousand little parti-coloured Birds, of various Notes, divert themselves upon its sandy Banks, skim o'er its Surface, dip their Wings in its refreshing Streams, and sometimes plunge to the Bottom in pursuit of Game. This is their favourite Place all Day; and when the Approach of Night compels them to withdraw, they quit it with Reluctance. The numerous Herds forsake their Pastures twice a Day to pay their visit to the Streams, in which they quench their Thirst, or seek some cool Retreat. In a Word, the River is as delightful to Man, as it is to the Birds and Beasts: We generally reject the Hills and Woods, and fix our Habitations on its Banks.

It enriches the Fishermen with a Profusion of its Stores, and refreshes the Farmer's thirsty Soil. It adorns the pompous Seats of the Nobility with the most delightful Prospects, and makes the Country every way agreeable: It pays a Visit to those large Towns that are indebted to its friendly Streams for all their Wealth and Commerce: There it majestically rolls along between two Rows of costly Buildings, which not only adorn, but are adorned by it. The incessant Concourse of People, the Multitude of Carriages of all Sorts, that are for ever passing over its Bridges; the infinite Number of Boats, and other

Vessels, that are constantly floating on its Surface; in short, those agreeable, but confused Sounds that are heard, not only over its Waters, but all along its Kays, give us at once the Idea of Trade and Opulence.

The principal Aim of Divine Providence in the Formation of Rivers, was, no doubt, to Furnish both Man and Beast with one of the most necessary Ornaments of Life; one that will either refresh us when we are faint and thirsty, keep our Habitations as well as our Bodies clean and wholesome, and not only dress our daily Provisions, but adorn our Table with the most delicate Part of them. Passing over the Golden Sands, that in some Countries roll down their Streams, we may always apply to our rivers for this other Kind of Treasure, which we shall find with more Certainty, and procure with greater Ease. Tho' the infinite Variety of Fish with which the Sea abounds for our Refreshment and Delight, seems a perfect Prodigy; yet those which our Rivers nourish and support are still more surprising. And if the Fishes did not, by Instinct, put in Practice a Thousand artful Stratagems for the Preservation of their Species, which contribute at the same Time as much to our Advantage and Pleasure, as their own Safety, they would never be able, in so small a Compass of Water, to avoid the numberless Snares and Engines that are every where planted, in order to surprise them. But of these Engines, which are most of them unfair, and highly prejudicial to the Gentleman Angler, I shall take no other Notice than to condemn the Use of them.

THOMAS GRAY: *Ode on the Death of a Favourite Cat, Drowned in a Tub of Gold Fishes* (written 1747).

'Twas on a lofty Vase's side,
Where China's gayest Art had dyed
   The azure Flowers, that blow:
Demurest of the Tabby Kind,
The pensive Selima reclined
   Gazed on the Lake below.

Her conscious Tail her Joy declared.
The fair round Face, the snowy Beard,
   The Velvet of her Paws,

Her Coat that with the Tortoise vyes,
Her Ears of Jett, and Emerald Eyes
   She saw, and purr'd Applause.

Still had she gazed; but midst the Tide
Two angel-Forms were seen to glide,
   The Genii of the Stream:
Their scaly Armour's Tyrian Hue
Thro' richest Purple to the View
   Betray'd a golden Gleam.

The Hapless Nymph with Wonder saw
A Whisker first and then a Claw,
   With many an ardent Wish,
She stretch'd in vain to reach the Prize.
What female Heart can Gold despise?
   What Cat's averse to Fish?

Presumptuous Maid! with Looks intent
Again she stretch'd, again she bent
   Nor knew the Gulph between.
Malignant Fate sate by and smil'd
The slippery Verge her Feet beguiled:
   She tumbled headlong in.

Eight Times emerging from the Flood
She mew'd to every watry God,
   Some speedy Aid to send.
No Dolphin came, no Nereïd stirr'd;
No cruel Tom, nor Susan heard.
   A Fav'rite has no Friend!

From hence, ye Beauties, undeceiv'd
Know, one false step is ne'er retrieved,
   And be with Caution bold.
Not all that tempts your wand'ring Eyes
And heedless Hearts is lawful Prize,
   Nor all that glisters, Gold.

SAMUEL JOHNSON: from *The Rambler* (Number thirty-six, 21 July 1750).

There are however two defects in the piscatory eclogue, which perhaps cannot be supplied. The sea, though in hot countries it is considered by those who live, like Sannazarius, upon the coast, as a place of pleasure and diversion, has notwithstanding much less variety than the land, and therefore will be sooner exhausted by a descriptive writer. When he has once shewn the sun rising or setting upon it, curled its waters with the vernal breeze, rolled the waves in gentle succession to the shore, and enumerated the fish sporting in the shallows, he has nothing remaining but what is common to all other poetry, the complaint of a nymph for a drowned lover, or the indignation of a fisher that his oysters are refused, and Mycon's accepted.

Another obstacle to the general reception of this kind of poetry, is the ignorance of maritime pleasures, in which the greater part of mankind must always live. To all the inland inhabitants of every region, the sea is only known as an immense diffusion of waters, over which men pass from one country to another, and in which life is frequently lost. They have, therefore, no opportunity of tracing, in their own thoughts, the descriptions of winding shores, and calm bays, nor can look on the poem in which they are mentioned, with other sensations, than on a sea-chart, or the metrical geography of Dionysius.

This defect Sannazarius was hindered from perceiving, by writing in a learned language to readers generally acquainted with the works of nature; but if he had made his attempt in any vulgar tongue, he would soon have discovered how vainly he had endeavoured to make that loved, which was not understood.

JAMES THOMSON: from *On a Country Life*. From *Poems on Several Occasions* (1750).

> How sweet and innocent are country sports,
> And, as men's tempers, various are their sorts.
>   You, on the banks of soft meandering Tweed,
> May in your toils ensnare the watery breed,
> And nicely lead the artificial flee,
> Which, when the nimble, watchful trout does see,

He at the bearded hook will briskly spring;
Then in that instant twitch your hairy string,
And, when he's hook'd, you, with a constant hand,
May draw him struggling to the fatal land.
    Then at fit seasons you may clothe your hook,
With a sweet bait, dress'd by a faithless cook;
The greedy pike darts to't with eager haste,
And being struck, in vain he flies at last;
He rages, storms, and flounces through the stream,
But all, alas! his life cannot redeem.

RICHARD BOWLKER: from *The Art of Angling* (c. 1758).

My Father catcht a Pike in Barn Meer (a large standing Water in Cheshire) was an Ell long, and weigh'd thirty-five pounds, which he brought to Lord Cholmondley; His Lordship ordered it to be turn'd into a Canal in the Garden, wherein were abundance of several Sorts of Fish; about twelve months after his Lordship draw'd the Canal and found that this overgrown Pike had devour'd all the Fish, except one large Carp that weighed between nine and ten Pounds, and that was bitten in several places; the Pike was then put into the Canal again together with abundance of Fish with him to feed upon, all which he devoured in less than a Year's time, and was observ'd by the Gardiner and Workmen there to take the Ducks and other Water-fowl under Water; whereupon they shot Magpies and Crows and throw'd them into the Canal, which the Pike took before their Eyes; of this they acquainted their Lord, who thereupon order'd the Slaughter-man to fling Calf's-bellies, Chickens-guts, and such like Garbage to him to prey upon, but being soon after neglected he dyed, as suppos'd from want of Food.

DR THOMAS SCOTT (attrib.): from *The Angler's Eight Dialogues in Verse, Dialogue VII* (1758).

Axylus: The Pike's my joy, of all the scaly shoal;
And of all fishing instruments, the Trowl.
My bounding heart against my bosom beats,

Now while my tongue the glorious strife repeats.
O when he feels my jerking hook, with pow'r
And rage he bounces from his weedy bow'r:
He traverses the stream with strong career,
With straiten'd string his madding course I steer,
He springs above the waves, at length o'ercome
This Ev'ning he shall feast my cheerful home.
Grant me your presence, each my honour'd guest,
To good Serena we entrust the rest.
Musaeus: Serena, knowing in all household art,
Graces, in ev'ry scene, each changing part.
Your table she improves, her curious care
Bestows the sapor delicate and rare.
Yet, unoffending be my tale; the dish
By various recipes may please our wish.
'Twas where the Stour, with his broad humid train,
Severs your hills from lowly Stratford's plain,
My fishing Æra with a Luce began,
Drest by the jolly mistress of the Swan.
With dext'rous knife she stript his silver mail,
And bath'd the carkass in her cleanly pail.
Then, like Embalmer of the Memphian Race,
With critic Eye she mark'd th'incisions place
Just under the late-heaving gills, and drew
His blood-warm entrails reeking from their stew.
In the disbowell'd void, she, next, convey'd
Sweet-breathing Marj'ram, and the spicy blade,
Fragrance of Thyme, aquatic Sav'ry's spoil,
And the churn's golden lumps of clodded oil:
The pickled Oyster, in due order, pass'd,
All-seas'ning salt, and rich Anchovy last.
With laths and fillet on his axle bound,
By culinary laws he wheels his Round.
His liquor'd sides emit luxuriant steam
Of Claret, Spanish sprats, and recent cream.
Now, smoking in the dish, he swims once more
In a hot bath (the pan's unwasted store)
With juice from Seville's piquant Orange prest,
Such supper thee, Apicius, would have blest.

CHRISTOPHER SMART: from *Jubilate Agno* (1759–63. First published 1939. Edited by W. F. Stead).

Let Matthan rejoice with the Shark, who is supported by multitudes of small value.

Let Jacob rejoice with the Gold Fish, who is an eye-trap.

Let Jairus rejoice with the Silver Fish, who is bright and lively.

Let Lazarus rejoice with Torpedo, who chills the life of the assailant through his staff.

Let Mary Magdalen rejoice with the Place, whose goodness and purity are of the Lord's making.

Let Simon the leper rejoice with the Eel-pout, who is a rarity on account of his subtlety.

Let Alpheus rejoice with the Whiting, whom God hath blessed in multitudes and his days are as the days of PURIM.

Let Onesimus rejoice with the Cod – blessed be the name of the Lord Jesus for a miraculous draught of men.

Let Joses rejoice with the Sturgeon, who saw his maker in the body and obtained grace.

Let Theophilus rejoice with the Folio, who hath teeth, like the teeth of a saw.

Let Bartimeus rejoice with the Quaviver – God be gracious to the eyes of him, who prayeth for the blind.

Let CHRISTOPHER, who is Simon of Cyrene, rejoice with the Rough – God be gracious to the CAM and to DAVID CAM and his seed for ever.

Let Timeus rejoice with the Ling – God keep the English Sailors clear of French bribery.

Let Salome rejoice with the Mermaid, who hath the countenance and a portion of human reason.

Let Zacharias rejoice with the Gudgeon, who improves in his growth till he is mistaken.

Let Campanus rejoice with the Lobster – God be gracious to all the CAMPBELLS especially John.

Let Martha rejoice with the Skallop – the Lord revive the exercise and excellence of the Needle.

Let Mary rejoice with the Carp – the ponds of Fairlawn and the garden bless for the master.

Let Zebedee rejoice with the Tench – God accept the good Son for his parents also.

Let Joseph of Arimathea rejoice with the Barbel – a good coffin and a tomb-stone without grudging?

Let Elizabeth rejoice with the Crab – it is good, at times, to go back.

Let Simeon rejoice with the Oyster, who hath the life without locomotion.

Let Jona rejoice with the Wilk – Wilks, Wilkie, and Wilkinson bless the name of the Lord Jesus.

Let Nicodemus rejoice with the Muscle, for so he hath provided for the poor.

Let Gamaliel rejoice with the Cockle – I will rejoice in the remembrance of mercy.

Let Agabus rejoice with the Smelt – The Lord make me serviceable to the HOWARDS.

Let Rhoda rejoice with the Sea-Cat, who is pleasantry and purity.

Let Elmodam rejoice with the Chubb, who is wary of the bait and thrives in his circumspection.

Let Jorim rejoice with the Roach – God bless my throat and keep me from things stranggled.

Let Addi rejoice with the Dace – It is good to angle with meditation.

Let Luke rejoice with the Trout – Blessed be Jesus in Aa, in Dee and in Isis.

Let Cosam rejoice with the Perch, who is a little tyrant, because he is not liable to that, which he inflicts.

Let Levi rejoice with the Pike – God be merciful to all dumb creatures in respect of pain.

Let Melchi rejoice with the Char, who cheweth the cud.

CHARLES BOWLKER: from *The Art of Angling* (1774).

Take nettles and cinque-foil, chop them small; then mix the juice of house-leek with them; rub your hands therewith, then throw it into the water, and keep your hands in it; the fish will come to them. Or take heartwort, and lime, mingle them together and throw them into a standing water, which will fox them; and then they are easily taken. But the best method is to take *coculus indicus*, which is a poisonous narcotic, called also *baccæ piscatoriæ* – fisher's berries – and pound them in a mortar, then make balls of the paste, which will be produced, about the size of a pea, and throw them into the standing water; the fish that taste of it will be very soon intoxicated, and will rise, and lie on the surface of the water; put your landing-net under them directly, and take them out, for they will soon recover. It is not necessary to know these secrets, as I am sure no true lover of angling will ever make use of them; only, by being acquainted with them, they will enable him to detect poachers.

Take goats blood, barley meal, and lees of sweet white wine, mix them with the lungs of a goat, boiled and pounded fine; make the whole into pills, which throw into ponds or pits, and you may soon catch the fish, who will prove intoxicated. . . . *This, however, as well as all other unfair practices, is seldom resorted to by a generous Angler.*

OLIVER GOLDSMITH: from *A History of the Earth and Animated Nature* (1774).

In short, as we cannot describe the alembic by which the rattlesnake distils its malignity, nor the process by which the scorpion, that lives among roses, converts their sweets to venom, so we cannot discover the manner by which fishes become thus dangerous: and it is well for us of Europe that we can thus wonder in security. It is certain that with us, if fishes, such as carp or tench, acquire any disagreeable flavour from the lakes in which they have been bred, this can be removed, by their being kept some time in finer and better water: there they soon clear away all those disagreeable qualities their flesh had contracted, and become as delicate as if they had been always fed in the most cleanly manner. But this expedient is with us rather the precaution of luxury than the effect of fear: we have nothing to dread from the noxious qualities of our fish; for all the animals our waters furnish are wholesome.

Happy England! where the sea furnishes an abundant and luxurious repast, and the fresh waters an innocent and harmless pastime: where the angler, in cheerful solitude, strolls by the edge of the stream, and fears neither the coiled snake, nor the lurking crocodile; where he can retire at night, with his few trouts (to borrow the pretty description of old Walton) to some friendly cottage, where the landlady is good, and the daughter innocent and beautiful; where the room is cleanly, with lavender in the sheets, and twenty ballads stuck about the wall! There he can enjoy the company of a talkative brother sportsman, have his trouts dressed for supper, tell tales, sing old tunes, or make a catch.

There he can talk of the wonders of nature with learned admiration, or find some harmless sport to content him, and pass away a little time, without offence to God, or injury to man!

JAMES ADAIR: from *The History of the American Indians* (1775).

They have a surprising method of fishing under the edges of rocks, that stand over deep places of a river. There, they pull off their red breeches, or their long slip of stroud cloth, and wrapping it round their arm, so as to reach to the lower part of the palm of their right hand, they dive under the rock where the large cat-fish lie to shelter themselves from the scorching beams of the sun, and to watch for prey: as soon as those fierce aquatic animals see that tempting bait, they immediately seize it with the greatest violence, in order to swallow it. This is the time for the diver to improve the favourable opportunity: he accordingly opens his hand, seizes the voracious fish by his tender parts, hath a sharp struggle with it against the crevices of the rock, and at last brings it safe ashore. Except the Choktah, all our Indians, both male and female, above the state of infancy, are in the watery element nearly equal to amphibious animals, by practice: and from the experiments necessity has forced them to, it seems as if few were endued with such strong natural abilities, – very few can equal them in their wild situation of life.

WILLIAM COWPER: *To the Immortal Memory of the Halibut on which I dined this day, Monday, April 26, 1784.* From his *Correspondence* (1784).

Where hast thou floated, in what seas pursued
Thy pastime? when wast thou an egg new spawn'd,
Lost in th'immensity of ocean's waste?
Roar as they might, the overbearing winds
That rock'd the deep, thy cradle, thou wast safe –
And in thy minikin and embryo state,
Attach'd to the firm leaf of some salt weed,
Didst outlive tempests, such as wrung and rack'd

The joints of many a stout and gallant bark,
And whelm'd them in the unexplored abyss.
Indebted to no magnet and no chart,
Nor under guidance of the polar fire,
Thou wast a voyager on many coasts,
Grazing at large in meadows submarine,
Where flat Batavia, just emerging, peeps
Above the brine – where Caledonia's rocks
Beat back the surge – and where Hibernia shoots
Her wondrous causeway far into the main.
– Wherever thou hast fed, thou little thought'st,
And I not more, that I should feed on thee.
Peace, therefore, and good health, and much good fish
To him who sent thee! and success, as oft
As it descends into the billowy gulf,
To the same drag that caught thee! – Fare thee well!
Thy lot thy brethren of the slimy fin
Would envy, could they know that thou wast doom'd
To feed a bard, and to be praised in verse.

THOMAS BEST: from *A Concise Treatise on the Art of Angling, etc.*
(1787).

A thousand foes the finny people chace,
Nor are they safe from their own kindred race:
The Pike, fell tyrant of the liquid plain,
With rav'nous waste devours his fellow-train;
Yet, howsoe'er with raging famine pin'd,
The Tench he spares, a salutary kind.
Hence too the Perch, a like voracious brood,
Forbears to make this gen'rous race his food;
Tho' on the common drove no bound he finds,
But spreads unmeasur'd waste o'er all the kinds,
Nor less the greedy Trout and gutless Eel,
Incessant woes, and dire destruction deal.
The lurking Water-rat in caverns preys;
And in the weeds the wily Otter slays.
The ghastly Newt, in muddy streams annoys;

And in swift floods the felly Snake destroys;
Toads, for the shoaling fry, forsake the lawn;
And croaking Frogs devour the tender spawn.
Neither the 'habitants of land nor air,
(So sure their doom) the fishy numbers spare!
The Swan, fair regent of the silver tide,
Their ranks destroys and spreads their ruin wide:
The Duck her offspring to the river leads,
And on the destin'd fry insatiate feeds:
On fatal wings the pouncing Bittern soars,
And wafts her prey from the defenceless shores;
The watchful Halcyons to the reeds repair,
And from their haunts the scaly captives bear:
Sharp Herns and Corm'rants too their tribes oppress,
A harrass'd race peculiar in distress;
Nor can the Muse enumerate their foes,
Such is their fate, so various are their woes!

Signs of the Change of Weather from the Animal Creation.

So long as the swallows fly aloft after their prey, we think ourselves
sure of a serene sky; but when they skim along near the ground, or the
surface of the water, we judge the rain is not far off, and the observation will seldom fail: in the year 1775, a drought of three months
continuance broke up at the summer solstice: the day before the rain
came upon us, the swallows flew very near the ground, which they had
never done in the fine weather.

In the mountainous country of Derbyshire, which goes by the name
of *the Peak*, the inhabitants observe, that if the sheep wind up the hills
in the morning to their pasture, and feed near the tops, the weather,
though cloudy and drizzling, which is very frequently the case in those
parts, will clear away by degrees, and terminate in a fine day; but if they
feed in the bottoms, the rains will continue and increase.

Dogs grow sleepy and stupid before rain, and shew that their
stomachs are out of order, refusing their food, and eating grass, that
sort which is hence called *dog's grass*: this they cast up again soon
afterwards, and with it the foulness that offended their stomachs.
Water-foul dive and wash themselves more than ordinary; and even
the fish in rivers are affected, because all anglers agree, that they never
bite freely when rain is depending ... Flies, on the contrary, are

particularly troublesome, and seem to be more hungry than usual; and toads are seen in the evening, crawling across the road or beaten path, where they seldom appear but when they are restless with an approaching change.

Before any considerable quantity of rain is to fall, most living creatures are affected in such sort, as to render them some way sensible of its approach, and of the access of something new to the surface of the earth, and of the atmosphere. Moles work harder than ordinary, they throw up more earth, and sometimes comes forth: the worms do so too; ants are observed to stir about, and bustle more than usually for some time, and then retire to their burrows before the rain falls. All sorts of insects and flies are more stirring and busy than ordinary. Bees are ever on this occasion in fullest employ; but betake themselves all to their hives, if not too far for them to reach before the storm arises. The common flesh-flies are more bold and greedy: snails, frogs, and toads, appear disturbed and uneasy. Fishes are sullen, and made qualmish by the water, now more turbid than before. Birds of all sorts are in action: crows are more earnest after their prey, as are also swallows and other small birds, and therefore they fall lower, and fly nearer to the earth in search of insects and other such things as they feed upon. When the mountains of the north begin to be capped with fogs, the moor-cocks and other birds quit them, fly off in flocks, and betake themselves to the lower lands for the time. Swine discover great uneasiness; as do likewise sheep, cows, and oxen, appearing more solicitous and eager in pasture than usual. Even mankind themselves are not exempt from some sense of a change in their bodies.

BARON MUNCHAUSEN (pseudonym of Rudolf Erich Raspe):
from *Gulliver Revived* (1787).

In a voyage which I made to the East Indies with Captain Hamilton, I took a favourite pointer with me; he was, to use a common phrase, worth his weight in gold, for he never deceived me. One day, when we were, by the best observations we could make, at least three hundred leagues from land, my dog pointed; I observed him for near an hour with astonishment, and mentioned the circumstance to the Captain, and every officer on board, asserting, that we must be near land, for my dog smelt game; this occasioned a general laugh; but that did not alter in the least the good opinion I had of my dog. After much conversation pro and con, I boldly told the Captain I placed more confidence in TRAY'S nose than I did in the eyes of every seaman on board, and therefore boldly proposed laying the sum I had agreed to pay for my passage (viz. one hundred guineas) that we should find game within half an hour; the Captain (a good hearty fellow) laughed again, desired Mr Crawford, the Surgeon, who was present, to feel my pulse; he did so, and reported me in perfect health: the following dialogue between them took place; I overheard it, though spoken low, and at some distance.

Captain: His brain is turned; I cannot with honour accept his wager.
Surgeon: I am of a different opinion; he is quite sane, and depends more upon the scent of his dog than he will upon the judgement of all the officers on board; he will certainly lose, and he richly merits it.
Captain: Such a wager cannot be fair on my side; however, I'll take him up, if I return his money afterwards.

During the above conversation, Tray continued in the same situation, and confirmed me still more in my former opinion. I proposed the wager a second time; it was then accepted.

Done and Done were scarcely said on both sides, when some sailors, who were fishing in the long-boat, which was made fast to the stern of the ship, harpooned an exceeding large shark, which they brought on board, and began to cut up for the purpose of barelling the oil, when, behold, they found no less than *six brace of live partridges* in this animal's stomach!

They had been so long in that situation, that one of the hens was sitting upon four eggs, and a fifth was hatching when the shark was opened!!!

THOMAS YOUNG: from *An Essay on Humanity to Animals* (1788).

I have often wondered that Thomson, who was distinguished by his humanity during life, and is yet distinguished by it in his poetry, did not altogether condemn fishing for amusement. He even speaks of it with complacency and approbation, in his description of angling; which seems to follow somewhat awkwardly after the lines immediately preceding, in which he had 'touch'd light on the numbers of the Samian sage', and had gone so far as to condemn the killing of animals even for food. He could not, however, help condemning the cruellest sort of fishing, viz. with the worm:

> But let not on thy hook the tortur'd worm,
> Convulsive, twist in agonizing folds;
> Which, by rapacious hunger swallow'd deep,
> Gives, as you tear it from the bleeding breast
> Of the weak, helpless, uncomplaining wretch,
> Harsh pain and horror to the tender hand.
> *Spring — 385*

It must be observed, that fishing with any *living* bait, is to be condemned for the same reason as fishing with the worm: in all such instances we torture *two* animals *at once* for our amusement; in others, only one.

GILBERT WHITE: from *The Natural History and Antiquities of Selborne* (1789).

To the Honourable Daines Barrington
Letter LIV

Dear Sir,

When I happen to visit a family where *gold* and *silver fishes* are kept in a glass bowl, I am always pleased with the occurrence, because it offers me an opportunity of observing the actions and propensities of those beings with whom we can be little acquainted in their natural state. Not long since I spent a fortnight at the house of a friend where there was such a *vivary*, to which I paid no small attention, taking every occasion to remark what passed within its narrow limits. It was here that I first observed the manner in which fishes die. As soon as the creature sickens, the head sinks lower and lower, and it stands as it were on its head; till, getting weaker, and losing all poise, the tail turns over, and at last it floats on the surface of the water with its belly uppermost. The reason why fishes, when dead, swim in that manner is very obvious; because, when the body is no longer balanced by the fins of the belly, the broad muscular back preponderates by its own gravity, and turns the belly uppermost, as lighter from its being a cavity, and because it contains the swimming-bladders, which contribute to render it buoyant. Some that delight in *gold* and *silver fishes* have adopted a notion that they need no aliment. True it is that they will subsist for a long time without any apparent food but what they can collect from pure water frequently changed; yet they must draw some support from animalcula, and other nourishment supplied by the water; because, though they seem to eat nothing, yet the consequences of eating often drop from them. That they are best pleased with such *jejune* diet may easily be confuted, since if you toss them crumbs they will seize them with great readiness, not to say greediness: however, bread should be given sparingly, lest, turning sour, it corrupt the water. They will also feed on the water-plant called *lemma* (*duck's meat*), and also on small fry.

When they want to move a little they gently protrude themselves with their *pinnæ pectorales* [pectoral fins]; but it is with their strong muscular tails only that they and all fishes shoot along with such inconceivable rapidity. It has been said that the eyes of fishes are immoveable: but these apparently turn them forward or backward in their sockets as their occasions require. They take little notice of a lighted candle, though applied close to their heads, but flounce and seem much frightened by a sudden stroke of the hand against the support whereon the bowl is hung; especially when they have been motionless, and are perhaps asleep. As fishes have no eyelids, it is not easy to discern when they are sleeping or not, because their eyes are always open.

Nothing can be more amusing than a glass bowl containing such fishes: the double refractions of the glass and water represent them, when moving, in a shifting and changeable variety of dimensions, shades, and colours; while the two mediums, assisted by the concavo-convex shape of the vessel, magnify and distort them vastly; not to mention that the introduction of another element and its inhabitants into our parlours engages the fancy in a very agreeable manner.

Gold and *silver fishes*, though originally natives of *China* and *Japan*, yet are become so well reconciled to our climate as to thrive and multiply very fast in our ponds and stews. *Linnæus* ranks this species of fish under the genus of *cyprinus*, or *carp*, and calls it *cyprinus auratus* [golden carp].

Some people exhibit this sort of fish in a very fanciful way; for they cause a glass bowl to be blown with a large hollow space within, that does not communicate with it. In this cavity they put a bird occasionally; so that you may see a goldfinch or a linnet hopping as it were in the midst of the water, and the fishes swimming in a circle around it. The simple exhibition of the fishes is agreeable and pleasant; but in so complicated a way becomes whimsical and unnatural, and liable to the objection due to him,

> Qui variare cupit rem prodigialiter unam.
> [Who delights in extravagantly varying a theme.]

I am, etc.

ANDREW BURNABY: from *Travels Through North America* (1798).

There is a society of sixteen ladies, and as many gentlemen, called the fishing company, who meet once a fortnight upon the Schuilkill. They have a very pleasant room erected in a romantic situation upon the banks of that river, where they generally dine and drink tea. There are several pretty walks about it, and some wild and rugged rocks, which, together with the water and fine groves that adorn the banks, form a most beautiful and picturesque scene. There are boats and fishing tackle of all sorts, and the company divert themselves with walking, fishing, going up the water, dancing, singing, conversing, or just as they please. The ladies wear an uniform, and appear with great ease and advantage from the neatness and simplicity of it. The first and most distinguished people of the colony are of this society; and it is very advantageous to a stranger to be introduced to it, as he hereby gets acquainted with the best and most respectable company in Philadelphia.

'A most glorious nibble'

The Early Nineteenth Century

BEGINNING EARLY by Sir Francis Chantrey. Frontispiece to *Maxims and Hints for an Angler and Miseries of Fishing* by Richard Penn (1839 edition).

ANON: *The Jolly Fisherman* (c. 1800).

I am a jolly fisherman,
   I catch what I can get,
Still going on my betters plan,
   all's fish that comes to net.

Chorus
Then praise the jolly fisherman,
   who takes what he can get,
Still going on his betters plan,
   all's fish that comes to net.

Fish just like men I've often caught,
   crabs, gudgeons, poor John, cod fish,
And many a time to market brought,
   a devilish sight of odd fish.

Thus all are fishermen through life,
   with weary pains and labour,
This baits with gold and that a wife,
   and all to catch his neighbour.

The pike to catch the little fry,
   extends his greedy jaw,

For all the world as you and I,
    have seen your man of law.

He who to laziness devotes
    his time is sure a numb fish,
And members who give silent votes,
    may fairly be called dumb fish.

False friends to eels we may compare,
    the roach resembles true ones,
Like gold fish we find old ones rare,
    plenty as herrings new ones.

Like fish then mortals are a trade,
    and trap'd, and sold, and bought,
The old wife and the tender maid,
    are both with tickling caught.

Indeed the fair are caught, 'tis said,
    if you but throw the line in,
With maggots, flies, or something red,
    or any thing that's shining.

With small fish you must lie in wait
    for those of high condition,
But it is alone a golden bait,
    can catch a learn'd physician.

CHARLES LAMB: from a letter to Robert Lloyd, 7 February 1801.

I shall expect you to bring me a brimful account of the pleasure which
Walton has given you, when you come to town. It must square with your
mind. The delightful innocence and healthfulness of the Angler's mind
will have blown upon yours like a Zephyr. Don't you already feel your
spirit *filled* with the scene – the banks of rivers – the cowslip-beds – the
pastoral scenes – the neat ale-houses – and hostesses and milkmaids as
far exceeding Virgil and Pope as the *Holy Living* is beyond Thomas à
Kempis. Are not the eating and drinking joys painted to the Life? Do
they not inspire you with an immoral hunger? Are you not ambitious of
being made an Angler?

REV. WILLIAM DANIEL: from *Rural Sports* (1801–2).

The late DR FRANKLIN observed, that of all the amusements, which the ingenuity of Man had devised, none required the exercise of *Patience* so much as *Angling*; and he enforced his remark by reciting the following: – that setting out from Philadelphia, at six o'clock on a summer's morning, to go about fifteen miles, he passed a brook where a Gentleman was angling; he enquired what sport, and was told none; but, added the Gentleman, I have only been here *two hours*. The Doctor continued his journey, and on his return in the evening, found the Angler at the same spot, and repeated his enquiry; very good sport was the reply: the query was naturally resumed, by asking how many fish he had caught? None at all, answered the Gentleman, but about the middle of the day I had a *most glorious nibble*.

* * *

Carp is one of the naturalized fish of this country, being supposed to have been brought by *Leonard Mascal*, a Sussex Gentleman (in which county, perhaps, this fish abounds more than any other), about the year 1514; and it is remarked in an old *distich*, enumerating the good things of which this Island was destitute, prior to this period, that

Turkies, *Carps*, Hops, Pickerell, and Beer,
Came into England *all* in one year.

This, however, is erroneous, for in the *Boke of St Albans*, printed at Westminster by *Wynkyn de Worde*, in 1496, the *Carp* was mentioned as a *dayntous fisshe*, although scarce. Turkies were unknown until 1524; in the same year *Hops* were introduced; before this, *Wormwood* and other *bitter* plants were used to preserve *Beer*; and the Parliament, in 1528, petitioned against *Hops*, as a *wicked weed*. *Pike* are related to have been first known in 1537, although in the above book, they are mentioned as not being a *scarce* fish, as was the case with the *Carp*: numbers of *Pike* are recorded to have been dressed at the great feast given in 1466 by GEORGE NEVIL, Archbishop of *York*. Beer was known in *England* in 1492, in which year a licence was granted by *Henry VII* to a *Fleming*, to *export fifty tons*; and we read of an Excise on *Beer* in 1284.

* * *

A piece of water, at Thornville Royal, Yorkshire, which had been ordered to be filled up, and wherein wood, rubbish, etc. had been thrown for years, was in November 1801, directed to be cleared out.

Persons were accordingly employed, and almost choaked up by weeds and mud, so little water remained, that no person expected to see any fish, except a few Eels; yet nearly two hundred brace of Tench, of all sizes, and as many Perch, were found. After the pond was thought to be quite free, under some roots there seemed to be an animal, which was conjectured to be an otter; the place was surrounded, and on opening an entrance among the roots, a *Tench* was found of most singular form, having literally assumed the shape of the hole, in which he had of course for many years been confined. His *length*, from fork to eye, was *two feet nine inches*; his circumference, almost to the tail, was *two feet three inches*; his *weight, eleven pounds nine ounces and a quarter*; the colour was also singular, his belly being that of a Charr, or a vermilion. This extraordinary fish, after having been inspected by many Gentlemen, was carefully put into a pond; but either from confinement, age, or bulk, it at first merely floated, and at last, with difficulty, swam gently away. It is now alive and well.

To this account some *Sceptics* have demurred, and have expressed their doubts, in *prose* and *verse*, as follows:

The *yellow-bellied* TENCH of *Thornville House*, in Yorkshire, which is *supposed* to have lain so many *centuries*, and lived under the *roots* of some ancient *trees*, without *water*, is to be dressed at that celebrated mansion, as soon as an instrument is procured in which a proper *kettle of fish* may be made of this *amphibious* animal: it is to be served up with *sauce piquant*, at a kind of *Arthur's Round Table*, to a select corps of *Knights of the Long-bow*!

The TENCH of THORNVILLE HOUSE:

A TRUE STORY!!!

O' the marvellous,
At *Thornville House*,
We read of feats in plenty,
Where with *long bow*
They hit, I trow,
Full nineteen shots in twenty!

Their fame to fix,
'Midst other tricks,
In which they so delight, Sir,

These blades, pray know,
The *hatchet throw*,
Till it is out of sight, Sir!

Of beast and bird
Enough we've heard,
By *cracks* as loud as thunder;
So now they dish
A monster *Fish*,
For those who *bite at wonders*!

The scullion wench
Did catch a *Tench*,
Fatter than Berkshire hogs, Sir,
Which, pretty soul,
Had made his hole
Snug shelter'd by some logs, Sir!

Sans *water* he
Had liv'd, d'ye see,
Beneath those roots of wood, Sir!
And there, alack,
Flat on his back,
Had lain since NOAH's flood, Sir!

Now he's in stew,
For public *goût*,
And fed with lettuce-cosse, Sir;
In hopes the Town
Will gulp him down,
With good *humbugging* sauce, Sir!

But, notwithstanding the *squibs* and *witticisms* of incredulity, the account is authentic.

WILLIAM PRIEST: from *Travels in the United States of America*
(1802).

Fishing parties among the farmers, and in small towns in some parts of America, are very agreeably arranged: twelve or fourteen neighbours form themselves into a sort of club, and agree to fish one day in the week during the summer; previous to which they fix on a romantic situation on the side of a wood commanding the intended scene of action. Under some of the large trees they erect a sort of hut, forming a dining-room and kitchen.

When the time is fixed to begin fishing, the steward for the day sends down a negro cook, with bread, butter, wine, liquors, culinary utensils, etc. About ten in the morning the fishermen arrive, and follow the sport in boats, canoes, or from the shore, either with angles or nets; but they seldom make use of the latter, except when they are disappointed in angling: they are then determined the fish, though not in a humour to bite, shall not deprive them of their dinner. At one they all meet at the place of general rendezvous, where all hands are employed in preparing the fish for the cook; by which means the dinner is soon on the table. – When over, and a few glasses have circulated, those who do not choose to remain drinking, take a nap during the heat of the day, which in this country is from two to four in the afternoon. At five the ladies arrive, and the company amuse themselves in catching fish for supper, walking in the woods, swinging, singing, playing on some musical instrument, etc. I have often been on these parties, and never spent my time more to my satisfaction.

WILLIAM TAPLIN: from *The Sporting Dictionary* (1803).

Upon the subject of ANGLING, it may not be inapplicable to term it a most *unfortunate* attachment with those classes of society who have no property but their *trades*, and to whom *time* alone must be considered a kind of freehold estate: such time lost by a river side, in the frivolous and uncertain pursuit of a paltry plate of fish, instead of being employed in business, has reduced more men *to want*, and their families to *a workhouse*, than any species of sport whatever. Racing, hunting, shooting, coursing, and cocking (destructive as the latter has been) have never produced so long a list of *beggars* as the sublime *art of angling*; in confirmation of which fact, the eye of observation need only turn to any of those small country towns near which there happens to run a *fishing stream*, when the profitable part of the pleasure may be instantly perceived by the poverty of the inhabitants.

COLONEL THOMAS THORNTON: from *A Sporting Tour Through the Northern Parts of England and Great Parts of the Highlands of Scotland* (1804).

As soon as we had recovered from the consternation this accident occasioned, I ordered the boat to cruise about, for the chance of his taking me again, which I have known frequently to happen with pike, who are wonderfully bold and voracious: on the second trip, I saw a very large fish come at me, and, collecting my line, I felt I had him fairly hooked; but I feared he had run himself tight round some root, his weight seemed so dead: we rowed up, therefore, to the spot, when he soon convinced me he was at liberty, by running me so far into the lake, that I had not one inch of line more to give him. The servants, foreseeing the consequences of my situation, rowed, with great expedition, towards the fish, which now rose about seventy yards from us, an absolute wonder! I relied on my tackle, which I knew was in every respect excellent, as I had, in consequence of the large pike killed the day before, put on hooks and gimp, adjusted with great care; a precaution which would have been thought superfluous in London, as it certainly was for most lakes, though here, barely equal to my fish. After playing him for some time, I gave the rod to Captain Waller, that he might have the honour of landing him; for I thought him quite exhausted, when, to our surprise, we were again constrained to follow the monster nearly across this great lake, having the wind too much against us. The whole party were now in high blood, and the delightful *Ville de Paris* quite manageable; frequently he flew out of the water to such a height, that though I knew the uncommon strength of my tackle, I dreaded losing such an extraordinary fish, and the anxiety of our little crew was equal to mine. After about an hour and a quarter's play, however, we thought we might safely attempt to land him, which was done in the following manner: Newmarket, a lad so called from the place of his nativity, who had now come to assist, I ordered, with another servant, to strip and wade in as far as possible, which they readily did. In the meantime I took the landing-net, while Captain Waller, judiciously ascending the hill above, drew him gently towards us. He approached the shore very quietly, and we thought him quite safe, when, seeing himself surrounded by his enemies, he in an instant made a last desperate effort, shot into the deep again, and, in the exertion, threw one of the men on his back. His immense size was now very apparent; we proceeded with all due caution, and, being once more drawn towards land, I tried to get his head into the net, upon effecting which, the servants were ordered to seize his tail, and slide him on shore; I took all imaginable pains to accomplish this, but in vain, and began to think myself strangely awkward, when, at length, having got his snout in, I discovered that the hoop of the net, though adapted to very large pike, would admit no more than that part. He was, however, completely spent, and, in a few moments we landed him, a perfect monster! He was stabbed by my directions in the spinal marrow, with a large knife, which appeared to be the most humane manner of killing him, and I then ordered all the signals with the *sky-scrapers* to be hoisted; and the whoop re-echoed through the whole range of the Grampians. On opening his jaws to endeavour to take the hooks from him, which were both fast in his gorge, so dreadful a forest of teeth, or tusks, I think I never beheld: if I had not had a double link of gimp, with two swivels, the depth between his stomach and mouth would have made the former quite useless. His measurement, accurately taken, was *five feet four inches*, from eye to fork*.

*Col. Thornton later estimates the weight of the pike, caught in Loch Alvie, as between forty-seven and forty-eight pounds.

WILLIAM WORDSWORTH: from *Excursion on the Banks of Ullswater* (1805). From *A Guide Through the District of the Lakes.*

Friday, November 9 – Rain, as yesterday, till ten o'clock, when we took a boat to row down the lake. The day improved, – clouds and sunny gleams on the mountains. In the large bay under Place Fell, three fishermen were dragging a net, – a picturesque group beneath the high and bare crags! A raven was seen aloft; not hovering like the kite, for that is not the habit of the bird, but passing on with a straightforward perseverance, and timing the motion of its wings to its own croaking. The water were agitated; and the iron tone of the raven's voice, which strikes upon the ear at all times as the more dolorous form its regularity, was in fine keeping with the wild scene before our eyes. This carnivorous fowl is a great enemy to the lambs of these solitudes; I recollect frequently seeing, when a boy, bunches of unfledged ravens suspended from the churchyard gates of H—, for which a reward of *so* much a head was given to the adventurous destroyer. – The fishermen drew their net ashore, and hundreds of fish were leaping in the prison. They were all of the kind called skellies, a sort of fresh-water herring, shoals of which may sometimes be seen dimpling or rippling the surface of the lake in calm weather. This species is not found, I believe, in any other of these lakes; nor, as far as I know, is the chevin, that *spiritless* fish (though I am loth to call it so, for it was a prime favourite with Isaac Walton), which must frequent Ullswater, as I have seen a large shoal passing into the lake from the river Eamont. *Here* are no pike, and the char are smaller than those of the other lakes, and of inferior quality; but the grey trout attains a very large size, sometimes weighing above twenty pounds. This lordly creature seems to know that 'retiredness is a piece of majesty'; for it scarcely ever caught, or even seen, except when it quits the depths of the lake in the spawning season, and runs up into the streams, where it is too often destroyed in disregard of the law of the land and of Nature.

GEORGE CRABBE: from *The Borough,*
Letter XXII: The Poor of the Borough: Peter Grimes (1810).

> Alone he was, the same dull scenes in view,
> And still more gloomy in his sight they grew:
> Though man he hated, yet employ'd alone
> At bootless labour, he would sweat and groan,
> Cursing the shoals that glided by the spot,
> And gulls that caught them when his arts could not.
>   Cold nervous tremblings shook his sturdy frame,
> And strange disease – he couldn't say the name;
> Wild were his dreams, and oft he rose in fright,
> Waked by his view of horrors in the night, –
> Horrors that would the sternest minds amaze,
> Horrors that demons might be proud to raise:
> And though he felt forsaken, grieved at heart,
> To think he lived from all mankind apart;
> Yet, if a man approach'd, in terrors he would start.
>   A winter pass'd since Peter saw the town,
> And summer-lodgers were again come down;
> These, idly curious, with their glasses spied
> The ships in bay as anchor'd for the tide, –

The river's craft, – the bustle of the quay, –
And sea-port views, which landmen love to see.
   One, up the river, had a man and boat
Seen day by day, now anchor'd, now afloat;
Fisher he seem'd, yet used no net nor hook;
Of sea-fowl swimming by no heed he took,
But on the gliding waves still fix'd his lazy look;
At certain stations he would view the stream,
As if he stood bewilder'd in a dream,
Or that some power had chain'd him for a time,
To feel a curse or meditate on crime.

REV. WILLIAM DANIEL: from *The Supplement to Rural Sports*
(1813).

The WORLD's a great Ocean, in which all Men *Fish*,
   They catch what they can, and they keep what they get;
The LAWYER in general gets a large Dish,
   For *every* thing's *Fish* that come into his Net!

The LADIES, all lovely, from Head to the Heels,
   Catch Lovers by *dozens*, as Children catch Flies;
But there's no catching *them*, for they're slippery as *Eels*,
   Whilst they angle away, and all bait with their *Eyes*.

The POET for Fame and for Food often *trolls*,
   The DOCTORS all fish for a *Fee*, oft, and big;
   'Tis the Care of the PARSON to angle for Souls,
   And he baits with a Sermon, and hooks a *Tithe pig*.

The wise POLITICIAN, to mend matters wishes,
   And *pro bono Publico* offers his Pelf*:
But he's only watching the *Loaves* and the *Fishes*,
   To shove others out, and to get in *himself*.

*Loot.

COLONEL PETER HAWKER: from *The Diary* (entries for 1813).

May 30th – I left London and arrived this evening at Longparish.

My reason for being so anxious to leave town was, that my little child had been at the point of death, and when given over by Sir E. Home I saved his life by strong port wine negus and nutmeg.

June 9th – Notwithstanding my little infant (Richard Hawker) had completely recovered his health and appetite, he was this evening suddenly seized with another relapse, and died between nine and ten o'clock at night.

12th – Longparish House. My wound having got so much better as to admit of my walking (with a stick) I went fly fishing, and killed (yesterday and to-day) fourteen trout.

WILLIAM WORDSWORTH: from *The Excursion* (1814).

'A blessed lot is yours!'
He said, and with that exclamation breathed
A tender sigh; – but, suddenly the door
Opening, with eager haste two lusty Boys
Appeared – confusion checking their delight.
– Not Brothers they in feature or attire;
But fond Companions, so I guessed, in field.
And by the river-side – from which they come,
A pair of Anglers, laden with their spoil.
One bears a willow-pannier on his back,
The Boy of plainer garb, and more abashed
In countenance, – more distant and retired.
Twin might the Other be to that fair Girl
Who bounded tow'rds us from the garden mount.
Triumphant entry this to him! – for see,
Between his hands he holds a smooth blue stone,
On whose capacious surface is outspread
Large store of gleaming crimson-spotted trouts;
Ranged side by side, in regular ascent,
One after one, still lessening by degree
Up to the dwarf that tops the pinnacle.
Upon the Board he lays the sky-blue stone

With its rich spoil; – their number he proclaims;
Tells from what pool the noblest had been dragged;
And where the very monarch of the brook,
After long struggle, had escaped at last –
Stealing alternately at them and us
(As doth his Comrade too) a look of pride.
And, verily, the silent Creatures made
A splendid sight together thus exposed;
Dead – but not sullied or deformed by Death,
That seemed to pity what he could not spare.
   But oh! the animation in the mien
Of those two Boys! Yea in the very words
With which the young Narrator was inspired,
When, as our questions led, he told at large
Of that day's prowess! Him might I compare,
His look, tones, gestures, eager eloquence,
To a bold Brook which splits for better speed,
And, at the self-same moment, works its way
Through many channels, ever and anon
Parted and reunited: his Compeer
To the still Lake, whose stillness is to the eye
As beautiful, as grateful to the mind.

T. F. SALTER: from *Treatment of Drowned Persons*. From *The Angler's Guide, Being a New, Plain and Complete Practical Treatise on the Art of Angling for Sea, River and Pond Fish* (1815).

A bellows should be applied to one nostril, whilst the other nostril and the mouth are kept closed, and the lower end of the prominent part of the wind-pipe is pressed backward. The bellows is to be worked in this situation; and when the breast is swelled by it, the bellows should stop, and an assistant should press the belly upward to force the air out. The bellows should then be applied as before, and the belly again pressed; this process should be repeated twenty to thirty times in a minute, so as to imitate natural breathing as nearly as possible, as the trachea is always open through the glottis; air conveyed through the mouth, the nostrils being closed, would necessarily pass into the lungs. If the cartilages of the larynx (throat) be pressed against the vertebrae (bones of the neck) so as to close the aesophagus (gullet) and prevent the passage of air into the stomach, and at the same time the mouth and left nostril be closed, and the pipe of the bellows inserted into the right nostril be closed, the air will pass into the lungs through the wind-pipe, because that is the only opening through which it can pass; its passage into the oesophagus, or its egress through the mouth or left nostril being prevented in the manner above described.

If there be any signs of returning life, such as sighing, gasping, twitching, or any convulsive motions, beating of the heart, the return of the natural colour and warmth, opening a vein in the arm or external jugular of the neck, may prove beneficial; but the quantity of blood taken away should not be large. The throat should be tickled with a feather, in order to excite the propensity to vomit, and the nostrils also with a feather, snuff, or any other stimulant, so to provoke sneezing. A tea-spoonful of warm water may be administered now and then, in order to learn whether the power of swallowing be returned; and if it be, a table spoonful of warm wine, or brandy and water may be given with advantage; and not before, as the liquor might pass into the trachea before the power of swallowing returns. The other methods should be continued with ardour and perseverance for two hours or upwards, although there should not be the least symptom of life.

In the application of stimulants, electricity has been recommended; and when it can be easily procured, its exciting effects might be tried in aid of the means already recommended; but the electrical strokes should be given in a low degree, and gradually as well as cautiously increased.

G. C. BAINBRIDGE: from *The Fly-fisher's Guide* (1816).

Without referring to the antiquity of the art, as a recommendation, or enumerating the catalogue of virtuous qualities, such as patience, perseverance, etc., of which an Angler is supposed to be possessed, it is simply necessary to observe, that many very eminent and learned characters have devoted much of their leisure time to this agreeable recreation; and it is a fact worthy of notice, that although many persons have quitted other sports for the amusement of *Fly Fishing*, yet the memory of the writer does not furnish a single instance of a Fly Fisher deserting his occupation, and transferring his preference to any other of the list of Rural Sports: this observation is very general, and is certainly a strong argument in favour of the superior pleasure which Angling affords.

The peculiar and almost immediate relief which this innocent pursuit yields to the distressed or uneasy mind, by calming the perturbations which misfortunes or other vexatious circumstances may have excited, is to be ranked amongst the first of its recommendations. But as this relief is also experienced in *some* degree by the practiser of *other* modes of Angling, it may not be considered precisely correct to class it amongst the advantages of *Fly Fishing*. To proceed therefore to those observations, upon which the claim of unfavourable weather might otherwise hang heavy, and by not being agreeably occupied lead to the introduction of that most disagreeable companion – ENNUI.

CHEAPNESS has been always urged in favour of Angling; and certain it is, that no other amusement can be procured at such an easy rate; for it is within the reach of the humblest individual.

In addition to the foregoing advantages, that of CLEANLINESS must not be omitted. How greatly preferable is the simple formation of an artificial fly of feathers and fur, to the unpleasantness attendant upon baiting a hook with worm, maggot or paste. The one will last during the diversion of a whole day, and with care much longer; whilst the other requires adjusting or renewing, after every trifling nibble; to say nothing of the cruelty which attaches to the introduction of a hook into the worm whilst living, or the extraction of a gorged hook from the entrails of a ravenous fish.

PETER PINDAR (pseudonym of John Wolcot):
Ballad To a Fish of the Brooke. From *Works* (1816).

> Why flyest thou away, with fear?
> Trust me, there's nought of danger near,
>   I have no wicked hooke,
> All cover'd with a snaring bait,
> Alas! to tempt thee to thy fate,
>   And dragge thee from the brooke.

O harmless tenant of the flood
I do not wish to spill thy blood;
   For Nature unto thee
Perchance hath given a tender wife
And children dear to charme thy life
   As she hath done for me.

Enjoy thy streame, O harmless fish;
And when an angler, for his dish,
   Through Gluttony's vile sin,
Attempts, a wretch, to pull thee *out*,
God give thee strength, O gentle trout,
   To pull the raskall *in*!

JOHN KEATS: from *I stood tip-toe upon a little hill.*
   From *Poems* (1817).

Linger awhile upon some bending planks
That lean against a streamlet's rushy banks,
And watch intently Nature's gentle doings:
They will be found softer than ring-dove's cooings.
How silent comes the water round that bend;
Not the minutest whisper does it send
To the o'erhanging sallows: blades of grass
Slowly across the chequer'd shadows pass.
Why, you might read two sonnets, ere they reach
To where the hurrying freshnesses aye preach
A natural sermon o'er their pebbly beds;
Where swarms of minnows show their little heads,
Staying their wavy bodies 'gainst the streams,
To taste the luxury of sunny beams
Temper'd with coolness. How they ever wrestle
With their own sweet delight, and ever nestle
Their silver bellies on the pebbly sand.
If you but scantily hold out the hand,
That very instant not one will remain;
But turn your eye, and they are there again.

PISCATOR (pseudonym of T. P. Lathy):
from *The Angler; a Poem, in Ten Cantos* (1819).

As he grows weak, more daring gets my hand,
Cautious, though bold, I pull towards the land;
Elate with hope I see his scaly side,
A full grown Salmon, and the river's pride.
But, ah! he bursts away, and hope's delayed; –
Again my utmost skill must be display'd.
Repeated trials foil'd, he yields at length,
And in the landing-net spends his last strength;
Beauteous his spots, as now on land he lies,
Which growing fainter, vanish as he dies.
And now, of sport sufficient for the day,
For use, not waste, Man is allowed to slay;
Nor will I, like the miser, wish for more,
Having already a superfluous store:
But tir'd of luck, and wearied out with toil,
Trudge toward home deep-laden with my spoil;
And heart no less with gratitude replete,
To HIM, who gave the charter – 'KILL AND EAT'.

WASHINGTON IRVING: from *The Sketch Book of Geoffrey Crayon,
Gent.* (1819–20).

For my part I was always a bungler at all kinds of sport that required
either patience or adroitness, and had not angled above half an hour
before I had completely 'satisfied the sentiment', and convinced
myself of the truth of Izaak Walton's opinion, that angling is something like poetry – a man must be born to it. I hooked myself instead
of the fish; tangled my line in every tree; lost my bait; broke my rod;
until I gave up the attempt in despair, and passed the day under the
trees, reading old Izaak: satisfied that it was his fascinating vein of
honest simplicity and rural feeling that had bewitched me, and not
the passion for angling. My companions, however, were more per-

severing in their delusion. I have them at this moment before my eyes, stealing along the border of the brook, where it lay open to the day, or was merely fringed by shrubs and bushes. I see the bittern rising with hollow scream as they break in upon his rarely-invaded haunt; the kingfisher watching them suspiciously from his dry tree that overhangs the deep black mill-pond, in the gorge of the hills; the tortoise letting himself slip sideways from the stone or log on which he is sunning himself; and the panic-struck frog plumping in headlong as they approach, and spreading an alarm throughout the watery world around.

I recollect also, that, after toiling and watching and creeping about for the greater part of a day, with scarcely any success, in spite of all our admirable apparatus, a lubberly country urchin came down from the hills with a rod made from a branch of a tree, a few yards of twine, and, as Heaven shall help me! I believe, a crooked pin for a hook, baited with a vile earthworm – and in half an hour caught more fish than we had nibbles throughout the day!

But, above all, I recollect, the 'good, honest, wholesome, hungry' repast, which we made under a beech-tree, just by a spring of pure sweet water that stole out of the side of a hill; and how, when it was over, one of the party read old Izaak Walton's scene with the milkmaid, while I lay on the grass and built castles in a bright pile of clouds, until I fell asleep.

* * *

There is certainly something in angling, if we could forget, which anglers are apt to do, the cruelties and tortures inflicted on worms and insects, that tends to produce a gentleness of spirit, and a pure serenity of mind. As the English are methodical even in their recreations, and are the most scientific of sportsmen, it has been reduced among them to perfect rule and system. Indeed, it is an amusement peculiarly adapted to the mild and highly-cultivated scenery of England, where every roughness has been softened away from the landscape. It is delightful to saunter along those limpid streams which wander, like veins of silver, through the bosom of this beautiful country: leading one through a diversity of small home scenery; sometimes winding through ornamented grounds; sometimes brimming along through rich pasturage, where the fresh green is mingled with sweet-smelling flowers; sometimes venturing in sight of villages and hamlets, and then running capriciously away into shady retirements. The sweetness and serenity of nature, and the quiet watchfulness of the sport, gradually bring on pleasant fits of musing; which are now and then agreeably interrupted by the song of a bird, the distant whistle of the peasant, or perhaps the vagary of some fish, leaping out of the still water, and skimming transiently about its glassy surface. 'When I would beget content,' says Izaak Walton, 'and increase confidence in the power and wisdom, and providence of Almighty God, I will walk the meadows by some gliding stream, and there contemplate the lilies that take no care, and those very many other little living creatures that are not only created, but fed (man knows not how) by the goodness of the God of nature, and therefore trust in Him.'

SIR WALTER SCOTT: *On Ettrick Forest's Mountains Dun.*
From *Miscellaneous Poems* (1820).

On Ettrick Forest's mountains dun,
'Tis blithe to hear the sportsman's gun,
And seek the heath-frequenting brood
Far through the noonday solitude;
By many a cairn and trenched mound,
Where chiefs of yore sleep lone and sound,
And springs, where grey-hair'd shepherds tell
That still the fairies love to dwell.

Along the silver streams of Tweed,
'Tis blithe the mimic fly to lead,
When to the hook the salmon springs,
And the line whistles through the rings;
The boiling eddy see him try,
Then dashing from the current high,
Till watchful eye and cautious hand
Have led his wasted strength to land.

'Tis blithe along the midnight tide,
With stalwart arm the boat to guide;
On high the dazzling blaze to rear,
And heedful plunge the barbed spear;
Rock, wood, and scaur, emerging bright,

Fling on the stream their ruddy light,
And from the bank our band appears
Like Genii, arm'd with fiery spears.

'Tis blithe at eve to tell the tale,
How we succeed, and how we fail,
Whether at Alwyn's lordly meal,
Or lowlier board of Ashestiel;
While the gay tapers cheerly shine,
Bickers the fire, and flows the wine –
Days free from thought, and nights from care,
My blessing on the Forest fair!

JOHN CLARE: *Rustic Fishing*. From *The Village Minstrel* (1821).

On Sunday mornings, freed from hard employ,
How oft I mark the mischievous young boy
With anxious haste his pole and lines provide,
For makeshifts oft crook'd pins to thread were tied;
And delve his knife with wishes ever warm
In rotten dunghills for the grub and worm,
The harmless treachery of his hooks to bait;
Tracking the dewy grass with many a mate,
To seek the brook that down the meadows glides,
Where the grey willow shadows by its sides,
Where flag and reed in wild disorder spread,
And bending bulrush bows its taper head;
And, just above the surface of the floods,
Where water-lilies mount their snowy buds,
On whose broad swimming leaves of glossy green
The shining dragon-fly is often seen;
Where hanging thorns, with roots wash'd bare, appear,
That shield the moor-hen's nest from year to year;
While crowding osiers mingling wild among
Prove snug asylums to her brood when young,
Who, when surpris'd by foes approaching near,
Plunge 'neath the weeping boughs and disappear.
There far from terrors that the parson brings,

Or church bell hearing when its summons rings,
Half hid in meadow-sweet and keck's high flowers,
In lonely sport they spend the Sunday hours.
Though ill supplied for fishing seems the brook,
That breaks the mead in many a stinted crook,
Oft chok'd in weeds, and foil'd to find a road,
The choice retirement of the snake and toad,
Then lost in shallows dimpling restlessly,
In fluttering struggles murmuring to be free –
O'er gravel stones its depth can scarcely hide
It runs the remnant of its broken tide,
Till, seemly weary of each chok'd control,
It rests collected in some gulled hole
Scoop'd by the sudden floods when winter's snow
Melts in confusion by a hasty thaw;
There bent in hopeful musings on the brink
They watch their floating corks that seldom sink,
Save when a wary roach or silver bream
Nibbles the worm as passing up the stream,
Just urging expectation's hopes to stay
To view the dodging cork, then slink away;
Still hopes keep burning with untir'd delight,
Still wobbling curves keep wavering like a bite:
If but the breezy wind their floats should spring,
And move the water with a troubling ring,
A captive fish still fills the anxious eyes
And willow-wicks lie ready for the prize;
Till evening gales awaken damp and chill,
And nip the hopes that morning suns instil,
And resting flies have tired their gauzy wing,
Nor longer tempt the watching fish to spring,
Who at the worm no nibbles more repeat,
But lunge from night in sheltering flag-retreat.
Then disappointed in their day's employ,
They seek amusement in a feebler joy.
Short is the sigh for fancies prov'd untrue:
With humbler hopes still pleasure they pursue
Where the rude oak-bridge scales the narrow pass,
Half hid in rustling reeds and scrambling grass,
Or stepping-stones stride o'er the narrow sloughs

Which maidens daily cross to milk their cows;
There they in artless glee for minnows run,
And wade and dabble past the setting sun,
Chasing the struttle o'er the shallow tide,
And flat stones turning up where gudgeons hide.
All former hopes their ill success delay'd,
In this new change they fancy well repaid.
And this they wade, and chatter o'er their joys
Till night, unlook'd-for, young success destroys,
Drives home the sons of solitude and streams,
And stops uncloy'd hope's ever-fresh'ning dreams.
They then, like schoolboys that at truant play,
In gloomy fear lounge on their homeward way,
And inly tremble, as they gain the town,
Where chastisement awaits with many a frown,
And hazel twigs, in readiness prepar'd,
For their long absence bring a meet reward.

LORD BYRON: from *Don Juan, Canto XIII*, with Byron's note
(1819–24).

    And angling, too, that solitary vice,
    Whatever Izaak Walton sings or says;
    The quaint, old, cruel coxcomb, in his gullet
    Should have a hook, and a small trout to pull it.

It would have taught him humanity at least. This sentimental savage, whom it is a mode to quote (amongst novelists) to show their sympathy for innocent sports and old songs, teaches how to sew up frogs, and break their legs by way of experiment, in addition to the art of angling, the cruelest, the coldest, and the stupidest of pretended sports. They may talk about the beauties of Nature, but the angler merely thinks about his dish of fish; he has no leisure to take his eyes from off the streams, and a single *bite* is worth to him more than all the scenery around. Besides, some fish bite best on a rainy day. The whale, the shark, and the tunny fishery have somewhat of noble and perilous in them; even net fishing, trawling, etc., are more humane and useful. But angling! No angler can be a good man.

JOHN CLARE: from a letter to James Hessey, 27 February 1825.
(First published in *The Prose of John Clare*, edited by J. W. and Anne
Tibble, 1951).

At the end of a little common when I was a boy called Parkers Moor
there was a little spring of beautiful soft water which was never dry it
used to flow from under a hedding at the end of a land out of a little
hole about as deep and round as a cutten* – it used then to dubble its
way thro the grass in a little ripple of its own making no bigger than a
grip or a cart rut – in this little springhead there used to be hundreds of
the little fish called minnows not so big as the struttle† and these used
to be found in that hole every year but how they came there I could not
tell some years a quantity of struttle were found and often a few
gudgeons – when a boy we used to go on a sunday in harvest and leck it
out with a dish and string the fish on rushes – and thereby thinking
ourselves great fishers from the number we had caught not heeding the
size.

*A furrow in the corner of a field.
†Stickleback.

THOMAS DOUBLEDAY and ROBERT ROXBY: from *A Collection
of Right Merrie Garlands for North Country Anglers* (edited by Joseph
Crawhall, 1864): Garland for 1825: *The Auld Fisher's Farewell to
Coquet*.

> Come bring to me my limber gad
>   I've fish'd wi' mony a year,
> An' let me hae my weel-worn creel,
>   An' a' my fishing gear;
> The sunbeams glint on *Linden-Ha'*,
>   The breeze comes frae the west,
> An' lovely looks the gowden morn
>   On the streams that I like best.
>
> I've thrawn the *flee* thae sixty year,
>   Ay, sixty year an' mair,
> An' monie a speckled Troutie kill'd
>   Wi' *heckle*, heuk an' hair;

An' now I'm auld an' feeble grown,
    My locks are like the snaw,
But I'll gang again to Coquet-side,
    An' take a fareweel thraw.

O Coquet! in my youthfu' days
    Thy river sweetly ran,
An' sweetly down the woody braes
    The bonnie birdies sang;
But streams may rin, an' birds may sing,
    Sma' joy they bring to me,
The blithesome strains I dimly hear,
    The streams I dimly see.

But, ance again, the weel-kenn'd sounds
    My minutes hall beguile,
An' glistering in the airly sun
    I'll see thy waters smile;
An' sorrow shall forget his sigh,
    An' Age forget his pain,
An' ance mair, by sweet Coquet-side,
    My heart be young again.

Ance mair I'll touch wi' gleesome foot
    Thy waters clear and cold,
Ance mair I'll cheat the gleg-e'ed trout,
    An' wile him frae his hold;
Ance mair, at *Weldon's* frien'ly door,
    I'll wind my tackle up,
An' drink 'Success to Coquet-side',
    Though a tear fa' in the cup.

An' then fareweel, dear Coquet-side!
    Aye gaily may thou rin,
An' lead thy waters sparkling on,
    An' dash frae linn to linn;
Blithe be the music o' thy streams
    An' banks through after-days,
An' blithe be every fisher's heart
    Shall ever tread thy Braes!

SIR JONAH BARRINGTON: from *Personal Sketches of His Own Times* (1827).

In the year 1800, a labourer dwelling near the town of Athy, County Kildare, (where some of my family then resided) was walking with his comrade up the banks of the Barrow to the farm of a Mr Richardson, on whose meadows they were employed to mow; each, in the usual Irish way, having his scythe loosely wagging over his shoulder, and lazily lounging close to the bank of the river, they espied a salmon partly hid under the bank. It is the nature of this fish that, when his *head* is concealed, he fancies no one can see his *tail* (there are many wise-acres, besides the salmon, of the same way of thinking). On the present occasion the body of the fish was visible.

'Oh Ned – Ned dear!' said one of the mowers, 'Look at that big fellow there– isn't it a pity we ha'nt no spear?'

'May be,' said Ned, 'we could be after picking the lad with the scythe-handle.'

'True for you!' said Dennis: 'the spike of yeer handle is longer nor mine; give the fellow a dig with it at any rate.'

'Ay, will I,' returned the other: 'I'll give the lad a prod he'll never forget any how.'

The spike and their sport was all they thought of: but the *blade* of the scythe, which hung over Ned's shoulders, never came into the contemplation of either of them. Ned cautiously looked over the bank; the unconscious salmon lay snug, little imagining the conspiracy that had been formed against his tail.

'Now hit the lad smart!' said Dennis: 'there now – there! rise your fist: now you have the boy! now Ned – success!'

Ned struck at the salmon with all his might and main, and that was not trifling. But whether 'the boy' was picked or not never appeared: for poor Ned, bending his neck as he struck at the salmon, placed the vertebrae in the most convenient position for unfurnishing his shoulders: and his head came tumbling splash into the Barrow, to the utter astonishment of his comrade, who could not conceive *how* it could *drop off* so suddenly. But the next minute he had the consolation of seeing the head attended by *one of his own ears*, which had been most dexterously sliced off by the same blow which beheaded his comrade.

The head and ear rolled down the river in company, and were

picked up with extreme horror at the mill-dam, near Mr Richardson's, by one of the miller's men.

'Who the devil does this head belong to' exclaimed the miller.

'Whoever owned it,' said the man, 'had three ears, at any rate.'

PROFESSOR JOHN WILSON: from *Noctes Ambrosianae*. (A series of imaginary conversations contributed to Blackwood's Magazine 1822–35.)

June 1827

Tickler: I fear, Colonel, since you lost your arm, that you are no longer a sportsman.

C. Cyril Thornton: I have given up shooting, although Joe Manton constructed a light piece for me, with which I generally contrived to hit and miss time about; but I am a devout disciple of Izaak, and was grievously disappointed on my arrival t'other day in Kelso, to find another occupier in Walton-hall; but my friend, Mr Alexander Ball-antyne, and I, proceed to Peebles on the 1st of June, to decide our bet of a rump and dozen, he with the spinning minnow, and I with Phin's delight.

Shepherd: Watty Ritchie'll beat you baith with the May-flee, if it be on, or ony length aneath the stanes.

North: You will be all sorry to hear that our worthy friend Watty is laid up with a bad rheumatism, and can no longer fish the Megget Water and the lochs, and return to Peebles in the same day.

Shepherd: That's what a' your waders comes to at last. Had it no been, Mr North, for your plowterin in a' the rivers and lochs o' Scotland, baith saut water and fresh, like a Newfoundland dog, or rather a seal or an otter, you needna had that crutch aneath your oxter. Corrnall Cyril, saw ye him ever a fishin?

C. Cyril Thornton: Never but once, for want of better ground, in the Crinan Canal, out of a coal-barge, for braises, when I was a red-gowned student at Glasgow.

Shepherd: Oh! but you should have seen him in Loch Owe, or the Spey. In he used to gang, out, out, and ever sae far out frae the pint o' a promontory, sinkin aye furder and furder down, first to the waistband o' his breeks, then up to the middle button o' his waistcoat, then to the verra breast, then to the oxters, then to the neck, and then to the verra chin o' him, sae that you wunnered how he could fling the flee, till last o' a' he would plump richt out o' sight, till the Highlander on Ben Cruachan thocht him drooned; but he wasna born to be drooned – no he, indeed – sae he taks to the soomin, and strikes awa wi' ae arm, like yoursel, sir – for the tither had haud o' the rod – and, could ye believ't, though it's as true as Scriptur, fishing a' the time, that no a moment o' the cloudy day micht be lost; settles at an island a quarter o' a mile aff, wi' trees, and an old ruin o' a religious house, wherein beads used to be coonted, and wafers eaten, and mass muttered hundreds o' years ago; and gettin footin on the yellow sand or the green sward, he but gies himsel a shake, and ere the sun looks out o' the clud, has hyucket a four-pounder, whom in four minutes (for it's a multiplying pirn the cretur uses), he lands gasping through the giant gills, and glitterin wi' a thousan' spots, streaks, and stars, on the shore. That's a pictur o' North's fishing in days o' yore. But look at him noo – only look at him noo – wi' that auld-farrant face o' his, no unlike a pike's, crunkled up in his chair, his chin no that unwullin to tak a rest on his collar-bane – the hauns o' him a' covered wi' chalk-stanes – his legs like winnle-straes – and his knees but knobbs, sae that he canna cross the room, far less soom ower Loch Owe, without a crutch; and wunna you join wi' me, Cornall Cyril, in hauding up baith your hauns – I aux your pardon, in hauding up your richt haun – and comparing the past wi' the present, exclaim, amaist sobbin, and in tears, 'Vanity o' vanities! all is vanity'!

North (*suddenly hitting the Shepherd over the sconce with his crutch*): Take that, blasphemer!

ANON: from *The Quarterly Review* (October 1828).

The author of Salmonia mentions Nelson's fondness for fly-fishing, and expresses a wish to see it noticed in the next edition of 'that most exquisite and touching life of our Hero by the Laureate, an immortal monument raised by genius to valour'. We believe neither Halieus nor the Laureate will be displeased with the following little anecdote, from a letter of a gentleman now at the head of the medical profession, with which he favoured us shortly after perusing Salmonia. 'I was [says our friend] at the Naval Hospital at Yarmouth, on the morning when

Nelson, after the battle of Copenhagen (having sent the wounded before him), arrived at the Roads and landed on the jutty. 'The populace soon surrounded him, and the military were drawn up in the market-place ready to receive him; but, making his way through the crowd, and the dust, and the clamour, he went straight to the hospital. I went round the wards with him, and was much interested in observing his demeanour to the sailors; he stopped at every bed, and to every man he had something kind and cheering to say. At length, he stopped opposite a bed on which a sailor was lying, who had lost his right arm close to the shoulder-joint, and the following short dialogue passed between them: *Nelson* "Well, Jack, what's the matter with you?" *Sailor.* "Lost my right arm, your honour." Nelson paused, looked down at his own empty sleeve, then at the sailor, and said playfully, "Well Jack, then you and I are spoiled for fishermen – cheer up, my brave fellow." And he passed briskly on to the next bed; but these few words had a magical effect upon the poor fellow, for I saw his eyes sparkle with delight as Nelson turned away and pursued his course through the wards. As this was the only occasion on which I saw Nelson, I may, possibly, overrate the value of the incident.'

SIR HUMPHRY DAVY: from *Salmonia, or Days of Fly-Fishing in a Series of Conversations with Some Account of the Habit of Fishes belonging to the Salmo Genus* (1828).

Halieus: Nay, I can find authorities of all kinds, statesmen, heroes, and philosophers; I can go back to Trajan, who was fond of angling. Nelson was a good fly-fisher*, and as a proof of his passion for it, continued the pursuit even with his left hand. Dr Paley was ardently attached to this amusement; so much so, that when the Bishop of Durham enquired of him when one of his most important works would be finished, he said, with great simplicity and good humour, 'My Lord, I shall work steadily at it when the fly-fishing season is over', as if this were a business of his life. And I am rather reserved in introducing living characters, or I could give a list of the highest names of Britain, belonging to modern times, in science, letters, arts, and arms, who are

*I have known a person who fished with him at Merton, in the Wandle.

ornaments of this fraternity, to use the expression borrowed from the free-masonry of our forefathers.

Physicus: I do not find much difficult in understanding why warriors, and even statesmen, fishers of men, many of whom I have known particularly fond of hunting and shooting, should likewise be attached to angling; but I own I am at a loss to find reasons for a love of this pursuit amongst philosphers and poets.

Halieus: The search after food is an instinct belonging to our nature; and from the savage in his rudest and most primitive state, who destroys a piece of game, or a fish with a club or spear, to man in the most cultivated state of society, who employs artifice, machinery, and the resources of various other animals, to secure his object, the origin of the pleasure is similar, and its object the same: but that kind of it requiring most art may be said to characterise man in his highest or intellectual state: and the fisher for salmon and trout with the fly employs not only machinery to assist his physical powers, but applies sagacity to conquer difficulties; and the pleasure derived from ingenious resources and devices, as well as from active pursuit, belongs to this amusement. Then as to its philosophical tendency; it is a pursuit of moral discipline, requiring patience, forbearance, and command of temper. As connected with natural science, it may be vaunted as demanding a knowledge of the habits of a considerable tribe of created beings – fishes, and the animals that they prey upon, and an acquaintance with the signs and tokens of the weather and its changes, the nature of waters, and of the atmosphere. As to its poetical relations, it carries us into the most wild and beautiful scenery of nature: amongst the mountain lakes, and the clear and lovely streams that gush from the higher ranges of elevated hills, or that make their way through the cavities of calcareous strata. How delightful in the early spring, after the dull and tedious time of winter, when the frosts disappear, and the sunshine warms the earth and waters, to wander forth by some clear stream, to see the leaf bursting from the purple bud, to scent the odours of the bank perfumed by the violet, and enamelled, as it were, with the primrose and the daisy; to wander upon the fresh turf below the shade of trees, whose bright blossoms are filled with the music of the bee; and on the surface of the waters to view the gaudy flies sparkling like animated gems in the sunbeams, whilst the bright and beautiful trout is watching them from below; to hear the twittering of the water-birds, who, alarmed at your approach, rapidly hide themselves beneath the flowers and leaves of the water-lily; and as the season advances, to find all these objects changed for others of the same kind, but better and brighter, till the swallow and the trout contend as it were for the gaudy May-fly, and till, in pursuing your amusement in the calm and balmy evening, you are serenaded by the songs of the cheerful thrush and melodious nightingale, performing the offices of paternal love, in thickets ornamented with the rose and woodbine!

Physicus: All these enjoyments might be obtained without the necessity of torturing and destroying an unfortunate animal, that the true lover of nature would wish to see happy in a scene of loveliness.

EDWARD BULWER, Lord Lytton: from *Eugene Aram* (1832).

Thus meditating, he arrived at the banks of the little brooklet, and was awakened from his reverie by the sound of his own name. He started, and saw the old corporal seated on the stump of a tree, and busily employed in fixing to his line the mimic likeness of what anglers, and, for aught we know, the rest of the world, call the 'violet fly'.

'Ha, master! – at my day's work, you see; fit for nothing else now. When a musket's half worn-out, schoolboys buy it; pop it at sparrows. I be like the musket; but never mind – have not seen the world for nothing. We get reconciled to all things: that's my way – augh! Now, sir, you shall watch me catch the finest trout you have seen this summer; know where he lies – under the bush yonder. Whi-sh, sir, whi-sh!'

The corporal now gave his warrior soul up to the due guidance of the violet fly. Now he whipped it lightly on the wave; now he slid it coquettishly along the surface; now it floated, like an unconscious beauty, carelessly with the tide; and now, like an artful prude, it affected to loiter by the way, or to steal into designing obscurity under the shade of some overhanging bank. But none of these manoeuvres captivated the wary old trout on whose acquisition the corporal had set his heart; and, what was especially provoking, the angler could see distinctly the dark outline of the intended victim as it lay at the bottom, like some well-regulated bachelor who eyes from afar the charms he has discreetly resolved to neglect.

The corporal waited till he could no longer blind himself to the displeasing fact that the violet fly was wholly inefficacious; he then drew up his line, and replaced the contemned beauty of the violet fly with the novel attractions of the yellow-dun.

'Now, sir!' whispered he, lifting up his finger, and nodding sagaciously to Walter. Softly dropped the yellow-dun upon the water, and swiftly did it glide before the gaze of the latent trout; and now the trout seemed aroused from his apathy – behold, he moved forward, balancing himself on his fins; now he slowly ascended towards the surface – you might see all the speckles of his coat. The corporal's heart stood still – he is now at a convenient distance from the yellow-dun: lo! he surveys it steadfastly; he ponders, he see-saws himself to and fro. The yellow-dun sails away in affected indifference; that indifference whets the appetite of the hesitating gazer – he darts forward, he is opposite the yellow-dun, he pushes his nose against it with an eager rudeness, he – no, he does not bite; he recoils, gazes again with surprise and suspicion on the little charmer; he fades back slowly into the deeper water, and then suddenly turning his tail towards the disappointed bait, he makes off as fast as he can – yonder – yonder, and disappears! No, that's he leaping yonder from the wave. Jupiter! what a noble fellow! What leaps he at? A real fly.

'D——his eyes!' growled the corporal.

'You might have caught him with a minnow,' said Walter, speaking for the first time.

'Minnow! repeated the corporal, gruffly; 'ask your honour's pardon. Minnow! – I have fished with the yellow-dun these twenty years, and never knew it fail before. Minnow! – baugh! But ask pardon; your honour is very welcome to fish with a minnow if you please it.'

'Thank you, Bunting. And pray what sport have you had to-day!'

'Oh – good, good!' quoth the corporal, snatching up his basket and closing the cover, lest the young Squire should pry into it. No man is more tenacious of his secrets than your true angler. 'Sent the best home two hours ago; one weighed three pounds, on the faith of a man; indeed, I'm satisfied now; time to give up;' and the corporal began to disjoint his rod.

'Ah, sir!' said he, with a half sigh, 'a pretty river this, don't mean to say it is not; but the river Lea for my money. You know the Lea? – not a morning's walk from Lunnun. Mary Gibson, my first sweetheart, lived by the bridge – caught such a trout there, by-the-bye! – had beautiful eyes – black, round as a cherry – five feet eight without shoes – might have 'listed in the forty-second.'

'Who, Bunting?' said Walter, smiling. 'the lady or the trout?'

CHARLES DARWIN: from *A Naturalist's Voyage Round the World* (1839). Entry for 12 October 1833.

Owing to bad weather we remained two days at our moorings. Our only amusement was catching fish for our dinner; there were several kinds and all good eating. A fish called the 'armado' (a Silurus) is remarkable from a harsh grating noise which it makes when caught by hook and line, and which can be distinctly heard when the fish is beneath the water. This same fish has the power of firmly catching hold of any object, such as the blade of an oar or the fishing line, with the strong spine both of its pectoral and dorsal fin. In the evening the weather was quite tropical, the thermometer standing at 79°. Numbers of fireflies were hovering about, and the musquitoes were very troublesome. I exposed my hand for five minutes and it was soon black with them: I do not suppose there could have been less than fifty, all busy sucking.

PROFESSOR JOHN WILSON: from *Twaddle on Tweedside* (1833). From *Anglimania* (collected pieces on angling and angling literature).

Twenty years ago, at two o'clock of a summer morning we left the school-house at Dalmally, where we were lodging, and walked up Glenorchy – fourteen miles long – to Inveruren. On the banks of that fishy loch we stood, eyeing the sunshine beautifully warming the breezy dark moss-water. We unscrewed the brass head of our walking-cane, to convert it into a rod: when, lo! the hollow was full of emptiness! We had disembowelled it the evening before, and left all the pieces on the chest of drawers in our bedroom! This was as bad as being without our Book. The dizziness in our head was as if the earth had dwindled down to the size of the mere spot on which we stood, but still kept moving as before at the same rate, on its own axis, and round the sun. On recovering our stationary equilibrium, we put our pocket-pistol to our head, and blew out its brains into our mouth – in the liquid character of Glenlivet. Then down the glen we bounded like a deer belling in his season, and by half-past seven were in the school-house. We said nothing – not that we were either sullen or sulky; but stern resolution compressed our lips, which opened but to swallow a few small loaves and fishes – and having performed twenty-eight miles, we started again for the Loch. At eleven – for we took our swing easily and steadily – our five flies were on the water. By sunset we had killed twenty dozen – none above a pound – and by far the greater number about a quarter – but the *tout ensemble* was imposing – and the weight could not have been short of five stone. We filled both creels (one used for salmon), bag, and pillow-slip, and all the pockets about our person – and at first peep of the evening star went our ways again, down the glen towards Dalmally. We reached the school-house 'ae wee short hour ayont the twal', having been on our legs almost all the four-and-twenty hours, and for eight up to the waist in water – distance walked, fifty-six miles – trouts killed, twenty dozen and odds – and weight carried

> At the close of the day when the hamlet was still,
> And mortals the sweets of forgetfulness proved,

certainly seventy pounds for fourteen miles; and if the tale be not true, may May-day miss Maga.

And, now, alas! we could not hobble for our book from the holms of Ashiestiel to Clovenford!

THOMAS MEDWIN: from *The Angler in Wales, or Days and Nights of Sportsmen* (1834).

There are four inns at Bow solely supported by the angle, thanks to Izaac. I chose the sign of 'The Pike', and was bowed into *the* parlour, an odd-shaped, many-sided place, in every corner of which stood huge cupboards – no, they had no porcelain in them, and I should say buffets, (for I like to be correct in my phraseology,) and round the polygon hung sundry coloured and uncoloured drawings of fishes. I examined them attentively, and perceived that they were *ex-voto's* made by the pious (I doubt that word) devotees of the rod in commemoration of their triumphs over divers jacks, (a jack is a pike before he comes to years of discretion,) chubs, tenches, and perches; and at the bottom of each marvel of art and nature was neatly inscribed in a printing hand, after the date, first the admeasurement of the fish and his weight, next a minute description of the bait, float, hook, rod, and line instrumental in the exploit, and lastly, in characters of gold, the name of the too happy and thus immortalized victor.

Among the *lares* of the place, and doubtless worshipped as such, (at least, they ought to have been by the host,) I observed – strange I should not have done so at first – a gilt frame (the others were black) suspended over the chimney-piece, inclosing a silver-leaf paper in the shape of that malacostomous, bull-headed, cow-dung-eating, finned animal, a chub. It was a monster (*horrendum informe*) of the species, and must have weighed, from its length, if Sir H. Davy's rule is a good one (which *query?* because fishes are not always in good season or well fed), at least four pounds. I was surprised to find no name, date, or history, attached to this, I have no doubt, faithful model, and was puzzling my brains to account for this, as I thought, invidious *exceptio regulae*, when I was struck by the sudden apparition of a consequential personage.

He went about four feet and a half high, very well set upon his pins, though on the wrong side of sixty, and had on one of those classical wigs (his was a black one) that I am sorry to see getting out of fashion, yclept bobs, *ie* smooth at the top and pole of the head, and ornamented with two rows behind, and one in front, of curls, which the Greeks, from their size and shape and resemblance to the bells of the flower, called hyacinthine. Tastes change – I am sorry for it – out upon 'em! He was habited in a drab fustian jacket with very ample pockets, indescribable pantaloons to match, and Hessian boots without tassels, that came up to the calf – by the by, I remember a college-friend of mine writing to Hoby to make him a pair for a *large calf*, and such seemed to me the punchy little gentleman, who accosted me with, 'Sir, you are looking at that 'ere picture, (frame, he meant; but fine frames and pictures were probably synonymous with him): sir, I'm proud to say, sir, that, sir, I caught, sir, that chub, sir.'

'I congratulate you. What a noble fish!'

'Yes, sir. I've never been man enough to get sich another, sir. It is the biggest fish, sir, that has been seen in the Lee ever since, sir; and that is ten years ago, sir! I will show you the hook with which I hooked him, sir.'

With that, he opened one of the aforesaid closets, and then unlocked a compartment in it, about five feet high. It was, I found, his *sanctum sanctorum*. On the shelf were lying, in the nicest order, some portentous black pocket-books, enclosing cases that, I found, contained, on bamboo frames, twelve lines in each, of hair and Indian hurl, alternately, like the flats and sharps of a piano, and galore of shots, from number one downwards, in as many divisions of the sliding centre-bit; and side by side lay floats of all sizes, some green and red, some red and green, some yellow and red, and some red and yellow; together with sundry and divers plumbing machines, kill-devils, minnow-tackle, spring snap-hooks, nets, and kettles for live baits, fishing-panniers, landing-nets, worm-bags, and boxes for gentles and other uses.

He thought he had now produced the desired effect, and said – 'Now, sir, I will show you, sir, the hook, sir.' He opened a shagreen-cased snap-box, and produced the trophy with the air of a hero, and that self-consciousness of superiority that deeds of fame and glory justify. I was astonished to see no rods among his implements of slaughter, but had observed some sticks, of three feet long, standing erect, each in its receptacle, arranged in gradation like the tubes of a Pan-pipe, and, by way of climax, at the extreme end, a portable stool, of the same material of which they were composed – 'These, sir,' said he, 'I find the best rods, sir; they are all of bamboo, sir, and the joints slide into one another, sir; and when I am tired with my day's sport, sir – for I never misses walking down, sir, to the Lee, sir, for the Sunday, sir, – I always takes one for a stick, sir.'

As he was speaking, several persons, armed with rods of a similar description to that of the little old gentleman, bustled in, and showed by their deference how much they appreciated the high 'eminence' to which 'merit' had raised him; and in a short time the house swarmed with fishers. He seemed perfectly known to them all; and in fact, it was easy to see that he was the Apollo, the *arbiter ludorum*, the oracle of the temple.

STEPHEN OLIVER: from *Scenes and Recollections of Fly-fishing in Northumberland, Cumberland and Westmoreland* (1834).

Small retailers of second-hand wit are fond of laughing at their own humour, in reminding the angler of what Doctor Johnson is reported to have said of fly-fishing: 'a rod and a line, with a fly at one end and a fool at the other'. This piece of pleasantry may be readily excused, and may pass with other witty sayings ascribed to Doctor Johnson for as much as it is worth. There is no profession, however honourable and useful, of which much more bitter things have not been said; and a jest may always be allowed on that which is only followed as a recreation, though sometimes a trifler may be met with who talks about it as if it were the serious business of his life. The Doctor's imperfect sight would always be a hindrance to his becoming an expert angler, even had he felt an inclination to the sport; and this defect of vision, his insensibility to melody – for he could scarcely distingusish one tune from another – and his confirmed habits of town life, rendered him indifferent and insensible to the charms of the country, which have so powerful an influence on the angler's pleasures. Conversation and argument, in which he excelled, the sharp encounter of wits, the discussion of principles of criticism and morals, were his delight; and while he drank his dozen dishes of tea, to display his stores of knowledge or confute an opponent, was to him the summit of earthly enjoyment. It is not however likely that Doctor Johnson in reality thought meanly of angling as an amusement, for it was at his instigation that the Rev. Moses Brown published, in 1750, an edition of Walton and Cotton's *Complete Angler*, which had been many years out of print.

* * *

The angler's coat and trowsers should be of cloth, not too thick and heavy, for if they be the sooner wet they will be the sooner dry. Water-proof velveteens, fustians, and mole-skins – rat-catcher's costume – ought never to be worn by the angler; for if he should have to swim a mile or two on any occasion – when overtaken by the tide on Duddon sands, for instance, or across Bassenthwaite or Ullswater, to save going six miles about – he would find them a serious weight when once thoroughly saturated with water; and should he have a stone of fish in his creel, it would be safest not to make the attempt. An elderly gentleman of the Kitchiner school, now sitting at my elbow, who knows the 'Peptic Precepts' better than he does his catechism – which he has long since forgotten, except a phrase or two which he sometimes quotes as St Paul, in religious company – suggests the propriety of anglers wearing *cork* jackets, which if strapped under the shoulders, would enable the wearer to visit any part of a lake, where, in warm weather, with an umbrella over his head, he might enjoy his sport, cool and comfortable, as if in a 'sunny pleasure dome with caves of ice'. The same gentleman thinks that a bottle of Reading sauce, a box of 'peptic pills', and a portable frying-pan ought to form part of every angler's travelling equipage. Having merely noticed these recommendations of the worthy member of the 'Eating-made-easy' club, I leave it to those who may feel so inclined, to avail themselves of the above hints.

THOMAS TOD STODDART: from *The Art of Angling, As Practised in Scotland* (1835).

LOCHS! – we love the word LOCHS, as applied to those hill-girdled expanses which decorate our native land. Lake is too tame a designation – a shallow epithet. It has nothing to do with mountains and precipices, heaths and forests. Beautiful it may be, very beautiful! Windermere is very beautiful; Derwent water is very beautiful; Buttermere, Ullswater, and Coniston, are very beautiful; nay, in truth, they are of a higher nature than beautiful; for these all lie among hills – but not Scottish hills; not the unplanted places – dwellings of the storm and the eagle.

What is of all things on earth the most changeable appears so the least – we mean water, taken in a wide sense, as the sea, or a loch. There is no mountain in the land which we can certify as presenting the same aspect it did five centuries ago. Forests then grew where the bare turf lies, and what is not wooded may have been naked and desert. So with valleys: the ploughshare hath altered Nature, and mansions occupy the lair of the brute and the resort of the robber; but waters, seas, lochs, and many rivers, are still the same. Our forefathers saw them, calm or agitated, as we behold them. The olden names are as appropriate as ever. Looking on them, we see histories verified, legends enhanced; we descry the fording of armies, the flight of queens, the adventures of forsaken princes, hunted like wolves in their own shackled realm – a price on their anointed heads –.

> The sleuths of fate unbound
> To track their solitary flight
> O'er the disastrous ground!

Loch Lomond! Loch Awe! Loch Laggan! Loch Ericht! Loch Rannoch! Loch Tay! Loch Earn! Loch Lubnaig! Loch Achray! Loch Ketturin! – why need we name more? – and yet hundreds there are, wild and magnificent as these, which we love as well, wherein all day long we have angled, with an angler's hope and patience, with a poet's thoughts expanding within us, fearless of the world's contempt, and speaking of Nature as we speak not to men, but guilelessly, having no distrust, and eloquently, dreading no rebuke.

*   *   *

Song – The Taking of the Salmon

A birr! a whirr! a salmon's on,
    A goodly fish! a thumper!
Bring up, bring up the ready gaff,
And if we land him, we shall quaff
    Another glorious bumper!
    Hark! 'tis the music of the reel,
        The strong, the quick, the steady;
    The line darts from the active wheel –
        Have all things right and ready.

A birr! a whirr! the salmon's out,
    Far on the rushing river;
Onward he holds with sudden leap,
Or plunges through the whirlpool deep,
    A desperate endeavour!
    Hark to the music of the reel!
        The fitful and the grating:
    It pants along the breathless wheel,
        Now hurried – now abating.

A birr! a whirr! the salmon's off! –
    No, no, we still have got him;
The wily fish is sullen grown,
And, like a bright imbedded stone,
    Lies gleaming at the bottom.
    Hark to the music of the reel!
        'Tis hush'd, it hath forsaken;
    With care we'll guard the magic wheel,
        Until its notes rewaken.

A birr! a whirr! the salmon's up,
    Give line, give line and measure:
But now he turns! keep down ahead,
And lead him as a child is led,
    And land him at your leisure.
    Hark to the music of the reel!
        'Tis welcome, it is glorious;
    It wanders through the winding wheel,
        Returning and victorious.

A birr! a whirr! the salmon's in,
   Upon the bank extended;
The princely fish is gasping slow,
His brilliant colours come and go,
   All beautifully blended.
Hark to the music of the reel,
   It murmurs and it closes:
Silence is on the conquering wheel,
   Its wearied line reposes.

No birr! no whirr! the salmon's ours,
   The noble fish, the thumper:
Strike through his gill the ready gaff,
And bending homewards, we shall quaff
   Another glorious bumper!
Hark to the music of the reel,
   We listen with devotion;
There's something in that circling wheel
   That wakes the heart's emotion!

*   *   *

And here we would advise, among other things, always to give the precedence to him who seems determined to take it from you, by his rapid advances towards the pools you are engaged on; for, be assured, he is at once vulgar, ignorant, selfish, and upstart, and demands only your silent contempt. Even rustic anglers respect the rights of those before them, and consider it unlucky to pass each other, unless from necessity, or mutual understanding. Never refuse to show another the contents of your creel, should he ask you; but do not blazon them abroad to every one you meet, for vaunters gain no respect by their readiness to chagrin others. If you can help a brother angler in a difficulty, do it, whether by the gift of a few hooks, which cost you almost nothing, or by assisting to mend his rod when broken. Any such small service you will generally find well repaid. Do not grudge a mouthful of what was intended for your own refreshment, to one, although a stranger, who seems to require it as well as yourself. Be more civil to the gamekeeper than the squire, if caught in a trespass, but always put on a good-humoured fare in order to get easily out of the scrape. When attacked by a watch-dog, give him across the head with the butt of your rod, and send a stone after him to keep him company to his kennel. Should a bull attack you, trust to your heels, or, if too late, stand steady, and jerk yourself out of the way the moment he lowers his horns; he will rush on several yards, as if blindfold, and take a couple of minutes before he repeats his charge; use these to your advantage. Never carry another man's fish, nor part with your own to adorn an empty creel; in the one case you are tempted to bounce, and in the other you act the tempter. Should you hook a large fish and lose him, there is no need to publish your misfortune; sympathy in such a case is out of the question; and if you gain credit, you do more than you deserve. When engaged to compete with another angler, set about it silently; a boast on your part is an advantage to him, which you may understand the better on the close of the contest. When crowed over by a very indifferent angler, take it good humouredly; it is easier to depreciate skill than to possess it. Beware of tackle-puffers, and of such especially, of whom there is at least one in Edinburgh, who can afford to sell real Limericks at one-fourth of the cost at which they can be fabricated in Ireland. Had King Solomon been an angler, he would have added another chapter to his book of Proverbs, and Dr Johnson, out of respect for the wise man, would have spared his ill-judged sarcasm. The greatest losses an angler can sustain are those of his patience and good temper; they are worth a cart-load of salmon. While crossing a rapid ford, expose as little of yourself as possible to the force of the water; keep the legs close, your side towards the stream, and one calf covering the other; should you feel yourself losing ground, plant the butt end of your rod firmly above you, but do not rest a single second in any one position without protection from the strength of the current. When angling, always keep one eye upon Nature, and the other upon your hooks, and ponder while you proceed. Never fall in love with one you meet by the waterside; there are situations when every woman looks an angel. And, last of all, keep up the fraternity of the craft. Anglers are a more gifted and higher order of men than others, in spite of the sneers of pompous critics, or the trumpery dixit of a paradoxical poet. In their histories, there are glimpses snatched out of heaven – immortal moments dropping from Eternity upon the forehead of Time. As a gift of his calling, poetry mingles in the angler's being: yet he entreats for no memorial of his high imaginings – he compounds not with capricious Fame for her perishing honours – he breaks not the absorbing enchantment by any outcry of his, but is content to remain 'a mute, inglorious Milton', secretly perusing the epic fiction of his own heart.

EDWARD JESSE: from *An Angler's Rambles* (1836).

The Thames trout are taken of a large size, some of them having been caught, and that lately, weighing as much as sixteen pounds. Trout from eight to twelve pounds are by no means uncommon, and they afford excellent sport to the angler. When caught, and if in season, there is no fish in the world perhaps, which can equal them in flavour and goodness. The high price which is given for them is one proof of this, and I never yet met with a *real* epicure who would not give them the preference to any other fish. I will state an instance of this.

Two old friends, whose names I do not feel myself justified in mentioning, but who will be recognized by many who have partaken of the hospitality of their table, were in the habit of coming to our pretty village of Hampton, not only to fish (they were punters) but also to regale themselves with Thames trout. They were so alive to the merits of these fish, that on leaving Hampton they enjoined the worthy host of the Red Lion, at whose house they had taken up their quarters, to send them in London the first fine trout he could procure. He was desired not to mind the expense, but to dispatch the fish in a post-chaise, so that it might arrive in time for dinner. The host had soon afterwards an opportunity of procuring a remarkably large and beautiful trout, which was duly sent in a post-chaise to Mr W—'s house in Spring Gardens. It arrived at five o'clock, and was immediately taken to his sitting-room. After admiring it for a short time, he sent an invitation to his friend Mr T— to come and partake of it at six o'clock, and described the appearance and beauty of the fish. He received an answer from his friend, acquainting him that he was dying from a sudden attack of gout, but that it would be a great satisfaction to him if he could *see* the fish, provided it would not be injured by being conveyed to his house for that purpose. The trout was accordingly sent – Mr T— feasted his eyes upon it, and soon afterwards closed them for ever.

THOMAS TOD STODDART: from *Angling Reminiscences* (1837).

Ah! I shall never visit Yarrow any more, because its breed of yellow fins is now extinct – and well might they be so – for the waters of that stream have been harrowed without mercy, sifted and ransacked by every species of ingenuity, down from Douglas-burn-foot to the bridge at Broadmeadows, and farther perhaps: but farther was never angled, although often, from Newark Tower to that of the wizard Sir Michael Scott at Oakwood, have we trodden, along the birchen braes of the silvery river. Its yellow-fins are indeed departed! – the huge, thick-shaped, golden-flanked fellows, that were wont to be caught in the May month, during glints of the sun on a warm rainy morning. They loved best the clear, shining minnow, or sometimes a yellow-bodied fly, with a rough red hackle twisted round it; but of these, the minnow was the more captivating lure; it brought out the daintiest fish from their retreats, and spun so enchantingly down the primest streams that, troutless as one knew many of these to be, there was still a delight, difficult to forego, in playing among them its tiny form. The Yarrow yellow-fins were ever famous, and an unfrequent specimen may to this day be taken, but only one, out of some scores of grey, lean, loch trout, or of the big-bellied variety found in Tweed. It was, in truth, a lovely fish, ornate with a rare sprinkling of stars, darker than crimson, and these on a light amber ground, which shaded off towards the belly, became gradually like mother-of-pearl. The head was small, the back curved, and the fins yellow, as a newly minted guinea.

WILLIAM SHIPLEY: from *A True Treatise on the Art of Fly-fishing* (1838).

Nothing ever hurled against angling has alarmed anglers more than the following lines from, in our opinion, the best written, the most popular, and the most dangerously-immoral poem of our time:

> And angling too, that solitary vice,
>   Whatever Isaak Walton sings or says:
> The quaint old cruel coxcomb in his gullet
> Should have a hook and a small trout to pull it.
>   *Byron's* Don Juan, canto XII, stanza 16

Not only do these four verses contain severe and chosen epithets of abuse launched against the common father of anglers, but they convey a strong censure against the art itself – the whole art of angling – calling it 'a solitary vice', that is, a vice of the very worst sort, since it must be founded on self and unparticipated enjoyment. For our parts we have always smiled at the noble poet's indignation against the cruelty of anglers, and the more so, since that indignation is expressed in a work, the hero of which is a model of refined cruelty – one of those lax, yet interesting young gentlemen, who think less of breaking a woman's heart – be she maid, wife, or widow – than poor quiet old Isaak would of paining a grasshopper. Angling a 'solitary vice'! Gambling, dog-fighting, boxing, intrigues, both with married and with single, are certainly not 'solitary' vices; but that is the only negative praise that can attach to them; and he who has been known to indulge in and to patronize them, must have been in rather a maudlin mood when he spun the above verses. Captain Medwin, in his *Angler in Wales*, who knew Lord Byron, says of the noble poet, that 'he was always straining at some paradox to startle with. I believe he never threw a fly in his life, or, except at Newstead, in some dull pond, ever wetted a line, or used any other bait than a worm'. There can be but little doubt, that Lord Byron did not mean his censure to apply to fly-fishers; but, as the text stands, it is directed against anglers in general, and for that reason we have noticed it.

THOMAS HOOD: *The Supper Superstition.* From *Hood's Own: or, Laughter from Year to Year* (1839).

'Oh flesh, flesh, how art thou fishified!'

'Twas twelve o'clock by Chelsea chimes,
   When all in hungry trim,
Good Mister Jupp sat down to sup
   With wife, and Kate, and Jim.

Said he, 'Upon this dainty cod
   How bravely I shall sup' –
When, whiter than the tablecloth,
   A GHOST came rising up!

'O father dear, O mother dear,
   Dear Kate, and brother Jim –
You know when some one went to sea –
   Don't cry – but I am him!

'You hope some day with fond embrace
　　To greet your absent Jack,
But oh, I am come here to say
　　I'm never coming back!

'From Alexandria we set sail,
　　With corn, and oil, and figs,
But steering "too much Sow", we struck
　　Upon the Sow and Pigs!

'The ship we pumped till we could see
　　Old England from the tops;
When down she went with all our hands,
　　Right in the Channel's Chops.

'Just give a look at Norey's chart,
　　The very place it tells;
I think it says twelve fathoms deep,
　　Clay bottom, mixed with shells.

'Well, there we are till "hands aloft",
　　We have at last a call;
The pug I had for brother Jim,
　　Kate's parrot too, and all.

'But oh, my spirit cannot rest
　　In Davy Jones's sod,
Till I've appeared to you and said –
　　Don't sup on that 'ere cod!

'You live on land, and little think
　　What passes in the sea;
Last Sunday week, at 2 p.m.
　　That cod was picking me!

'Those oysters, too, that look so plump,
　　And seem so nicely done,
They put my corpse in many shells,
　　Instead of only one.

'Oh, do not eat those oysters then,
　　And do not touch the shrimps;
When I was in my briny grave,
　　They sucked my blood like imps!

'Don't eat what brutes would never eat,
　　The brutes I used to pat,
They'll know the smell they used to smell,
　　Just try the dog and cat!'

The spirit fled – they wept his fate.
　　And cried, alack, alack!
At last up started brother Jim,
　　'Let's try if Jack was Jack!'

They called the dog, they called the cat,
　　And little kitten too,
And down they put the cod and sauce,
　　To see what brutes would do.

Old Tray licked all the oysters up,
　　Puss never stood at crimps,
But munched the cod – and little kit
　　Quite feasted on the shrimps!

The thing was odd, and minus cod
　　And sauce, they stood like posts;
Oh, prudent folks, for fear of hoax,
　　Put no belief in Ghosts!

RICHARD PENN: from *Maxims and Hints for an Angler and Miseries of
Fishing* (1833, enlarged 1839).

XXVIII

When you see a large fish rising so greedily in the middle of a sharp
stream, that you feel almost sure of his instantly taking your May-fly, I
would advise you to make an accurate survey of all obstructions in the

immediate neighbourhood of your feet – of any ditch which may be close behind you – or of any narrow plank, amidst high rushes, which you may shortly have to walk over in a hurry. If you should hook the fish, a knowledge of these interesting localities will be very useful to you.

XXX

Never mind what they of the old school say about 'playing him till he is tired'. Much valuable time and many a good fish may be lost by this antiquated proceeding. Put him into your basket *as soon as you can.* Everything depends on the manner in which you commence your acquaintance with him. If you can at first prevail upon him to go a little way down the stream with you, you will have no difficulty afterwards in persuading him to let you have the pleasure of seeing him at dinner.

XXXV

Lastly – when you have got hold of a good fish, which is not very tractable, if you are married, gentle reader, think of your wife, who, like the fish, is united to you by very tender ties, which can only end with her death, or her going into weeds. If you are single, the loss of the fish, when you thought the prize your own, may remind you of some more serious disappointment.

Postscript

Mr Jackson and Mr Thompson went last week to the house of Mr Jenkins, for a few days' fishing. They were received with the utmost kindness and hospitality by Mr and Mrs Jenkins, and on the following morning after breakfast, the gardener (who was on that day called the fisherman) was desired to attend them to the river. Thompson, who had a landing-net of his own, begged to have a boy to carry it. Jack was immediately sent for, and he appeared in *top* boots, with a livery hat and waistcoat.

Arrived at the water-side, Thompson gave his gnat-basket to the boy, and told him to go on the other side of the river, and look on the grass for a few May-flies. Jack said that he did not exactly know what May-flies were, and that the river could not be crossed without going over a bridge a mile off. Thompson is a patient man, so he began to

fish with his landing net for a few May-flies, and after he had necessarily frightened away many fish, he succeeded in catching six or
seven May-flies.

Working one of them with the blowing-line much to his own satisfaction, and thinking to extract a compliment from his attendant, he
said, 'They do not often fish here in this way – do they?' 'No,' said
the boy, 'they drags wi' a net; they did zo the day afore yesterday.'

Our angler, after much patient fishing, hooked a fine trout; and
having brought him carefully to the bank, he said, 'Now, my lad,
don't be in a hurry, but get him out as soon as you can.' Jack ran to
the water's edge, threw down the net, and seizing the line with both
hands, of course broke it immediately.

Nothing daunted, Thompson now mended his tackle and went on
fishing; and when he thought, 'good easy man', that the very moment
for hooking another trout was arrived, there was a great splash just
above his fly; – and the boy exclaiming, 'Damn un, I miss'd un',
instantly threw a second brick-bat at a rat which was crossing the
river.

Mine host, in order to accommodate his friends, dined early; and
when they went after dinner to enjoy the evening fishing, they found
that the miller had turned off the water, and that the river was nearly
dry, – so they went back to tea.

JAMES HENRY LEIGH HUNT: from *The Indicator and The
Companion; a Miscellany for the Fields and the Fireside* (1840).

The anglers are a race of men who puzzle us. We do not mean for
their patience, which is laudable, nor for the infinite non-success of
some of them, which is desirable. Neither do we agree with the good
old joke attributed to Swift, that angling is always to be considered as
'a stick and a string, with a fly at one end and a fool at the other'.
Nay, if he had books with him, and a pleasant day, we can account
for the joyousness of that prince of punters, who, having been seen in
the same spot one morning and evening, and asked whether he had
had any success, said No, but in the course of the day he had had 'a
glorious nibble'.

But the anglers boast of the innocence of their pastime; yet it puts
fellow-creatures to the torture. They pique themselves on their

meditative faculties; and yet their only excuse is a want of thought. It is this that puzzles us. Old Isaac Walton, their patriarch, speaking of his inquisitorial abstractions on the banks of a river, says,

> Here we may
> Think and pray,
> Before death
> Stops our breath.
> Other joys
> Are but toys,
> And to be lamented.

So saying, he 'stops the breath' of a trout, by plucking him up into an element too thin to respire, with a hook and a tortured worm in his jaws –

> Other joys
> Are but toys.

If you ride, walk, or skate, or play at cricket, or at rackets, or enjoy a ball or a concert, it is 'to be lamented'. To put pleasure into the faces of half a dozen agreeable women, is a toy unworthy of the manliness of a worm-sticker. But to put a hook into the gills of a carp – there you attain the end of a reasonable being; there you show yourself truly a lord of the creation. To plant your feet occasionally in the mud, is also a pleasing step. So is cutting your ancles with weeds and stones –

> Other joys
> Are but toys.

The book of Isaac Walton upon angling is a delightful performance in some respects. It smells of the country air, and of the flowers in cottage windows. Its pictures of rural scenery, its simplicity, its snatches of old songs, are all good and refreshing; and his prodigious relish of a dressed fish would not be grudged him, if he had killed it a little more decently. He really seems to have a respect for a piece of salmon; to approach it, like the grace, with his hat off. But what are we to think of a man, who in the midst of his tortures of other animals, is always valuing himself on his harmlessness; and who actually follows up one of his most complacent passages of this kind, with an injunction to impale a certain worm twice upon the hook, because it is lively, and might get off! All that can he said of such an extraordinary inconsistency is, that having been bred up in an opinion of the innocence of his amusement, and possessing a healthy power of exercising voluntary thoughts (as far as he had any), he must have dozed over the opposite side of the question, so as to become almost, perhaps quite, insensible to it. And angling does indeed seem the next thing to dreaming. It dispenses with locomotion, reconciles contradictions, and renders the very countenance null and void. A friend of ours, who is an admirer of Walton, was struck, just as we were, with the likeness of the old angler's face to a fish. It is hard, angular, and of no expression. It seems to have been 'subdued to what it worked in'; to have become native to the watery element. One might have said to Walton, 'Oh flesh, how art thou fishified!' He looks like a pike, dressed in broadcloth instead of butter.

The face of his pupil and follower, or, as he fondly called himself, son, Charles Cotton, a poet and a man of wit, is more good-natured and uneasy. Cotton's pleasures had not been confined to fishing. His sympathies indeed had been a little superabundant, and left him perhaps, not so great a power of thinking as he pleased. Accordingly, we find in his writings more symptoms of scrupulousness upon the subject, than in those of his father.

Walton says, that an angler does no hurt but to fish; and this he counts as nothing. Cotton argues, that the slaughter of them is not to be 'repented'; and he says to his father (which looks as if the old gentleman sometimes thought upon the subject too)

> There whilst behind some bush we wait
>   The scaly people to betray,
> We'll *prove it just*, with treacherous bait,
>   To make the preying trout our prey.

This argument, and another about fish's being made for 'man's pleasure and diet', are all that anglers have to say for the innocence of their sport. But they are both as rank sophistications as can be; sheer beggings of the question. To kill fish outright is a different matter. Death is common to all; and a trout, speedily killed by a man, may suffer no worse fate than from the jaws of a pike. It is the mode, the lingering cat-like cruelty of the angler's sport, that renders it unworthy. If fish were made to be so treated, then men were also made to be racked and throttled by inquisitors. Indeed among other advantages of angling, Cotton reckons up a tame, fishlike acquiescence to whatever the powerful choose to inflict.

> We scratch not our pates,
> Nor repine at the rates
> Our superiors impose on our living;
> But do frankly submit,
> Knowing they have more wit
> In demanding, than we have in giving.
>
> Whilst quiet we sit,
> We conclude all things fit,
> Acquiescing with hearty submission, etc.

And this was no pastoral fiction. The anglers of those times, whose skill became famous from the celebrity of their names, chiefly in divinity, were great fallers-in with passive obedience. They seemed to think (whatever they found it necessary to say now and then upon that point) that the great had as much right to prey upon men, as the small had upon fishes; only the men luckily had not hooks put into their jaws, and the sides of their cheeks torn to pieces. The two most famous anglers in history are Antony and Cleopatra. These extremes of the angling character are very edifying.

We should like to know what these grave divines would have said to the heavenly maxim of 'Do as you would be done by'. Let us imagine ourselves, for instance, a sort of human fish. Air is but a rarer fluid; and at present, in this November weather, a supernatural being who should look down upon us from a higher atmosphere, would have some reason to regard us as a kind of pedestrian carp. Now fancy a Genius fishing for us. Fancy him baiting a great hook with pickled salmon, and twitching up old Isaac Walton from the banks of the river Lee, with the hook through his ear. How he would go up, roaring and screaming, and thinking the devil had got him!

> Other joys
> Are but toys.

We repeat, that if fish were made to be so treated, then we were just as much made to be racked and suffocated; and a footpad might have argued that old Isaac was made to have his pocket picked, and be tumbled into the river. There is no end of these idle and selfish beggings of the question, which at last argue quite as much against us as for us. And granting them, for the sake of argument, it is still obvious, on the very same ground, that men were also made to be taught better. We do not say, that all anglers are of a cruel nature; many of them, doubtless, are amiable men in other matters. They have only never thought perhaps on that side of the question, or been accustomed from childhood to blink at it. But once thinking, their amiableness and their practice become incompatible; and if they should wish, on that account, never to have thought upon the subject, they would only show that they cared for their own exemption from suffering, and not for its diminution in general*.

*Perhaps the best thing to be said finally about angling is, that not being able to determine whether fish feel it very sensibly or otherwise, we ought to give them the benefit rather than the disadvantage of the doubt, where we can help it; and our feelings the benefit, where we cannot.

G. P. R. PULMAN: from *Rustic Rhymes* (1841).

A happy life ez pass'd by we
Who in th' fiel's da like to be,
An' by th' stream to strake about
Wi' rod an' line, a' ketchin trout.
We don't want carpet-rooms, ner halls,
Ner dandy-music, dancing balls,
Ner nit no coaches painted fine,
Wi' liv'ry sarvan's up behine.

While we can treyde the grass an' vish,
An' hev th' luck to ketch a dish,
An' hear th' birds all zing za gay,
An' zee th' gurt fat bullicks play
(Then think what famous beef they'd make,
An' how we'd eyte a gurdl'd steak);
In eyv'nin zit our furn's among,
An' tull our tale, and zing our zong,
An' blow a cloud, an' drink a pot –
We'll envy no man what 'e 've got.

JOHN BOWRING: from *Memoirs of Jeremy Bentham* (1842).

If the teachings of the University were not very instructive, so neither were its amusements very interesting. Fishing was one of them. Bentham sometimes went to fish, as a relief from the weary monotony of existence. It brought some new ideas, and new occupations. At that time, a bubble on the water's surface was a variety, and had a charm; and to catch a minnow was an interruption to the dulness of the day. But even the fishing sports partook of the system of neglect with which all education was conducted. Generally a poacher was hired to go with a casting-net. He caught the fish; and the youths went and got it dressed at a neighbouring inn. A few practised fly-fishing, who had skill and strenth. Bentham had neither the one nor the other.

WILLIAM SCROPE: from *Days and Nights of Salmon-Fishing in the Tweed* (1843).

But to business. The rod was hastily put together; a beautiful new azure line passed through the rings; a casting line, made like the waist of Prior's Emma, appended, with two trout flies attached to it of the manufacture even of me, Harry Otter. An eager throw to begin with: round came the flies intact. Three, four, five, six throws – a dozen: no better result. The fish were stern and contemptuous. At length some favourable change took place in the clouds, or atmosphere, and I caught sundry small trout; and finally, in the cheek of a boiler, I fairly hauled out a two-pounder. A jewel of a fish he was – quite a treasure all over. After I had performed the satisfactory office of bagging him, I came to a part of the river which, being contracted, rushed forward in a heap, rolling with great impetuosity. Here, after a little flogging, I hooked a lusty fellow, strong as an elephant, and swift as a thunderbolt. How I was agitated say ye who best can tell, ye fellow tyros! Every moment did I expect my trout tackle, for such it was, to part company. At length, after various runs of dubious result, the caitiff began to yield; and at the expiration of about half an hour, I wooed him to the shore. What a sight then struck my optics! A fair five-pounder at the least; not fisherman's weight, mark me, but such as would pass muster with the most conscientious lord mayor of London during the high price of bread. Long did I gaze on him, not without self-applause. All too large he was for my basket; I therefore laid the darling at full length on the ground, under a birch tree, and covered over the precious deposit with some wet bracken, that it might not suffer from the sunbeam.

I had not long completed this immortal achievement ere I saw a native approaching, armed with a prodigious fishing rod of simple construction guiltless of colour or varnish. He had a belt round his waist, to which was fastened a large wooden reel or pirn, and the line passed from it through the rings of his rod: a sort of Wat Tinlinn he was to look at. The whole affair seemed so primitive – there was such an absolute indigence of ornament, and poverty of conception, that I felt somewhat fastidious about it. I could not, however, let a brother of the craft pass unnoticed, albeit somewhat rude in his attire; so, 'What sport,' said I, 'my good friend?'

'I canna say that I hae had muckle deversion; for she is quite fallen in, and there wull be no good fishing till there comes a spate.'

Now, after this remark, I waxed more proud of my success; but I did not come down upon him at once with it, but said somewhat slyly, and with mock modesty –

'Then you think there is not much chance for any one, and least of all for a stranger like myself.'

'I dinna think the like o' ye can do muckle; though I will no say but ye may light on a wee bit trout, or may be on a happening fish. That's a bonny little wand you've got; and she shimmers so with varnish, that I'm thinking that when she is in the eye o' the sun the fish will come aneath her, as they do to the blaze in the water.'

Sandy was evidently lampooning my Higginbotham. I therefore replied, that she certainly had more shining qualities than were often met with on the northern side of the Tweed. At this personality, my pleasant friend took out a large mull from his pocket, and, applying a copious quantity of its contents to his nose, very politely responded –

'Ye needna fash yoursel to observe aboot the like o' her; she is no worth this pinch o' snuff.'

He then very courteously handed his mull to me.

'Well,' said I, still modestly, 'she will do well enough for a bungler like me.' I was trolling for a compliment.

'Ah, that will she,' said he.

Though a little mortified, I was not sorry to get him to this point; for I knew I could overwhelm him with facts, and the more diffidently I conducted myself the more complete would be my triumph. So laying down my pet rod on the channel, I very deliberately took out my two-pounder, as a feeler. He looked particularly well; for I had tied up his mouth, that he might keep his shape, and moistened him, as I before said, with soaked fern to preserve his colour. I fear I looked a little elate on the occasion; assuredly I felt so.

'There's a fine fish now – a perfect beauty!'

'Houte-toute! that's no fish ava.'

'No fish, man! What the deuce is it, then? Is it a rabbit, or a wild duck, or a water-rat?'

'Ye are joost gin daft. Do ye no ken a troot when ye see it?'

I could make nothing of this answer, for I thought that a trout was a fish*; but it seems I was mistaken. However, I saw the envy of the man; so I determined to inflict him with a settler at once. For this purpose I inveigled him to where my five-pounder was deposited; then kneeling down, and proudly removing the bracken I had placed over him, there lay the monster most manifest, extended in all his glory. The light – the eye of the landscape – before whose brilliant sides Runjeet Sing's diamond, called 'the mountain of light', would sink into the deep obscure; dazzled with the magnificent sight, I chuckled in the plenitude of victory. This was unbecoming in me, I own, for I should have borne my faculties meekly; but I was young and sanguine; so (*horresco referens*) I gave a smart turn of my body, and, placing an arm akimbo, said, in an exulting tone, and with a scrutinizing look, 'There, what do you think of that?' I did not see the astonishment in Sandy's face that I had anticipated, neither did he seem to regard me with the least degree of veneration; but, giving my pet a shove with his nasty iron-shod shoes, he simply said,

'Houte! that's a wee bit gilse.'

This was laconic. I could hold no longer, for I hate a detractor; so I roundly told him that I did not think he had ever caught so large a fish in all his life.

'Did you, now? – own.'

'I suppose I have.'

'Suppose! But don't you know?'

'I suppose I have.'

'Speak decidedly, yes or no. That is no answer.'

'Well, then, I suppose† I have.'

---

*Salmon, salmon trout, and bull trout alone, are called fish in the Tweed. If a Scotchman means to try for trout, he does not say 'I am going a *fishing*,' but 'I am going a *trouting*.'

†*Suppose*, in Scotch, does not imply a doubt, but denotes a certainty.

And this was the sum total of what I could extract from this *nil admirari* fellow.

A third person now joined us, whom I afterwards discovered to be the renter of that part of the river. He had a rod and tackle of the selfsame fashion with the apathetic man. He touched his bonnet to me; and if he did not eye me with approval, at least he did not look envious or sarcastic.

'Well, Sandy,' said he to his piscatorial friend, my new acquaintance, 'what luck the morn?'

'I canna speecify that I hae had muckle; for they hae bin at the sheep-washing up bye, and she is foul, ye ken. But I hae ta'en twa saumon – ane wi' Nancy, and the ither wi' a Toppy – baith in Faldon-side Burn fut.'

And twisting round a coarse linen bag which was slung at his back, and which I had supposed to contain some common lumber, he drew forth by the tail a never-ending monster of a salmon, dazzling and lusty to the view; and then a second, fit consort to the first. Could you believe it? One proved to be fifteeen pounds, and the other twelve! At the sudden appearance of these whales I was shivered to atoms: dumb-foundered I was, like the Laird of Cockpen when Mrs Jean refused the honour of his hand. I felt as small as Flimnap the treasurer in the presence of Gulliver.

*   *   *

A friend of mine (sacred be his name!) of great repute for his dexterity with the rod, and celebrated for his agreeable and amiable qualities, as well as for his intelligence and various accomplishments, had this poetical facility of seeing what did not really exist in substance. A curious instance of this popular talent occurred at a friend's house in the country with whom he was staying. There was a fine piece of water in the park, well stored with fish, where he used to spend most part of the morning, rod in hand; so that his perseverance excited considerable admiration from the host, as well as from his guests. Not having been very successful, his ardour at length began to flag. It was a pity, for it is a pleasant thing to be excited. What was to be done? You shall see. A report was raised that there was an enormous pike seen in the water, about the length of a decent-sized alligator. He was said to have maimed a full-grown swan, and destroyed two cygnets, besides sundry ducks. At first he was no more believed in than the great sea snake, which encloses at least half the world in his folds. But after the lapse of a few days, the keeper came to the private ear of my friend, and told him that a *mortal* large pike was basking amongst some weeds, and could be seen plainly. 'You are sure to cotch en, sir.' He was rewarded for this intelligence, and exhorted to keep the important secret from the other visitors at the mansion.

When piscator, cunning fellow! thought that all were out of the way, employed in hunting, shooting, or some other occupation, he and John Barnes the keeper glided down secretly to the awful spot, and they there described the semblance of a fish so enormous that it was doubted if any thing less than a small rope could hold him. The sportsman was astounded – the keeper was not; for the said awful animal was nothing more than a large painted piece of wood, carved deftly by himself into the shape of a pike, painted according to order, and stuck in the natural position by means of a vertical prop, which could not be discovered amongst the weeds. It was too bad, really a great deal too bad; but tolerably ingenious, and beautifully deceptive. The gentleman approached with tact and caution, and the eyes of the fish glared upon him; as well they might, for they were very large and dazzling, being made of glass, and originally designed to be inserted in a great horned owl which the keeper had stuffed.

'What a prodigious fish, John!'

'Very perdigious indeed, sir.'

'What eyes he has!'

'So he has, sir.'

'I'll try him with a roach. There – it went in beautifully, and he did not move.'

'No, he won't take it no how. Give him a frog; he seems a difficult fish.'

Piscator did tender him a very lively one in vain; in short, he offered every bait he could possibly think of, running through all the devices and temptations he was master of. Cautious in his approaches, that the supposed fish might not see him, he always advanced to make his cast upon his knees, to the no small merriment of his friends, who were looking at him through a telescope from the windows of the mansion.

Well, thus he spent the whole morning; waiting, however, at times, for a cloud to intercept the sun-beams, and a breath of air to ruffle the surface of the water. When these came, he would set to work again with renovated hopes; till at last, tired and discomfited, he bent his steps homewards. On his arrival there, he was accosted on the very threshold by some of the guests.

'Oh! you have been fishing all the morning, I see; but what could make you stay out so long, and get away so cunningly with the keeper?'

'Why, to tell you the truth, Barnes (you know what a good creature he is) told me of an immense pike that was lying amongst the weeds at the end of the lake; he must be the same that swallowed the cygnets. I never saw so enormous a monster in fresh water.'

Omnes: Well, where is he – where is he? let us look at him.

Host: John, tell the cook we will have him for dinner to-day. Dutch sauce, remember.

Piscator: You need not be in such a hurry to send to the cook, for I am sorry to say I did not catch him.

Host: Not catch him – not catch him! Impossible, with all your skill, armed as you are to the teeth, with roach, bleak, minnows, frogs, kill-devils, and the deuce knows what. Not catch him! Come, you're joking.

Piscator: Serious, I assure you. I never was so beat before, and yet I never fished better; but though I did not absolutely hook him, *he ran at me several times.*

*   *   *

When you get hold of a *monstrum horrendum ingens* of a fish, say of some five and forty pounds, you must anticipate a very long and severe battle. If, therefore, you have a disposable Gilly with you, despatch him instantly for some skilful fisherman, as well to assist you when you are exhausted with fatigue, as to bring your dinner and supper; not forgetting a dark lantern, that you may not be beaten by the shades of night – a circumstance by no means improbable. At the first onset you will probably be obliged to keep your arms and rod aloft, in order to steer clear of the rocks. This action, with a heavy rod and large fish on your line, is very distressing, if continued even for a short time; and it will be necessary to repeat it often, if the channel is not very favourable; and in that case your muscles will ache insupportably, if they at all resemble those of other men. The easiest position, when it is safe to use it, is to place the butt of your rod against the stomach as a rest, and to bring the upper part of the arm and the elbow in close contact with the sides, putting on at the same time an air of determination.

If your leviathan should be superlatively boisterous, no one knows what may happen. For instance, should you be in a boat, and he should shoot away down the river, you must follow rapidly; then, when he again turns upwards, what a clever fellow your fisherman must be, to stop a boat that has been going down a rapid stream at the rate of eight miles an hour, and bring it round all of a sudden in time to keep company with the fish, who has taken an upward direction! And what a clever fellow a piscator must be, if he can prevent twenty yards of his line, or more, from hanging loose in the stream! These sort of things will happen, and they are ticklish concerns. All I can do is to recommend caution and patience; and the better to encourage you in the exercise of these virtues, I will recount what happened to Duncan Grant in days of yore.

First, you must understand that what is called 'preserving the river' was formerly unknown, and every one who chose to take a cast did so without let or hindrance.

In pursuance of this custom, in the month of July, some thirty years ago, one Duncan Grant, a shoemaker by profession, who was more addicted to fishing than to his craft, went up the way from the village of Aberlour, in the north, to take a cast in some of the pools above Elchies Water. He had no great choice of tackle, as may be conceived; nothing, in fact, but what was useful, and scant supply of that.

Duncan tried one or two pools without success, till he arrived at a very deep and rapid stream, facetiously termed *the Mountebank*: here he paused, as if meditating whether he should throw his line or not. 'She is very big,' said he to himself, 'but I'll try her; if I grip him he'll be worth the hauding.' He then fished it, a step and a throw, about half way down, when a heavy splash proclaimed that he had raised him, though he missed the fly. Going back a few paces, he came over him again, and hooked him. The first tug verified to Duncan his prognostication, that if he was there 'he would be worth the hauding'; but his tackle had thirty plies of hair next the fly, and he held fast, nothing daunted. Give and take went on with dubious advantage, the fish occasionally sulking. The thing at length became serious; and, after a succession of the same tactics, Duncan found himself at the Boat of Aberlour, seven hours after he had hooked his fish, the said fish fast under a stone, and himself completely tired. He had some thoughts of breaking his tackle and giving the thing up; but he finally hit upon an expedient to rest himself, and at the same time to guard against the surprise and consequence of a sudden movement of the fish.

He laid himself down comfortably on the banks, the butt end of his rod in front; and most ingeniously drew out part of his line, which he held in his teeth. 'If he tugs when I'm sleeping,' said he, 'I think I'll find him noo.' And no doubt it is probable that he would. Accordingly, after a comfortable nap of three or four hours, Duncan was awoke by a most unceremonious tug at his jaws. In a moment he was on his feet, his rod well up, and the fish swattering down the stream. He followed as best he could, and was beginning to think of the rock at Craigel-lachie, when he found to his great relief that he could 'get a pull on him'. He had now comparatively easy work; and exactly twelve hours after hooking him, he cleicked him at the head of Lord Fife's water: he weighed fifty-four pounds, Dutch, and had the tide lice upon him.

Thus Duncan Grant has instructed us how to manage a large Salmon. Let us now see how a large Salmon may manage us.

In the year 1815, Robert Kerse hooked a clean Salmon of about forty pounds in the Makerstoun Water, the largest, he says, he ever encountered: sair work he had with him for some hours; till at last Rob, to use his own expression, was 'clean dune out'. He landed the fish, however, in the end, and laid him on the channel; astonished, and rejoicing at his prodigious size, he called out to a man on the opposite bank of the river, who had been watching him for some time.

'Hey, mon, sic a fish!'

He then went for a stone to fell him with; but as soon as his back was turned, the fish began to wamble towards the water, and Kerse turned, and jumped upon it; over they both tumbled, and they, line, hook, and all went into the Tweed. The fish was too much for Rob, having broke the line, which got twisted round his leg, and made his escape, to his great disappointment and loss, for at the price clean salmon were then selling, he could have got five pounds for it.

Thus you see how a large fish may manage us.

EDWARD LEAR: from *A Book of Nonsense* (1846).

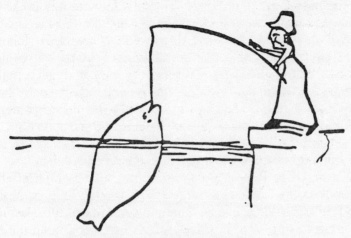

There was Young Lady of Wales,
Who caught a large fish without scales;
When she lifted her hook, she exclaimed, 'Only look!'
The extatic Young Lady of Wales.

CHARLES LANMAN: from *Adventures of an Angler in Canada, Nova Scotia and the United States* (1848).

But the most unique and interesting of my fishing adventures remains to be described. I had heard a great deal about the good fishing afforded by the lake* already mentioned, and I desired to visit it, and spend a night upon its shore. Having spoken to my friend Hummel, and invited a neighbour to accompany us, whom the people have named 'White Yankee', the noontide hour of a pleasant day found us on our winding march; and such a grotesque appearance as we made, was exceedingly amusing. The group was mostly animated when climbing the steep and rocky ravines which we were compelled to pass through. There was Peter, 'long, lank and lean', and wild in his attire and countenance as an eagle of the wilderness, with an axe in his hand, and a huge knapsack on his back, containing our provisions and

*In the Catskill Mountains.

utensils for cooking. Next to him followed White Yankee, with three blankets lashed upon his back, a slouched white hat on his head, and nearly a half pound of tobacco in his mouth. Crooked-legged withal, and somewhat sickly was this individual, and being wholly unaccustomed to this kind of business, he went along groaning, grunting, and fuming, as if he was 'sent for, and *didn't want* to come'. In the rear trotted along your humble friend, with a gun upon his shoulder, a powder-horn and shot-pouch at his side, cow-hide boots on his feet, and a cap on his head – his beard half an inch long, and his flowing hair streaming in the wind.

We reached our place of destination about five o'clock, and halted under a large impending rock, which was to be our sleeping place. We were emphatically under the 'shadow of a rock, in a weary land'. Our first business was to build a fire, which we did with about one cord of green and dry wood. Eighty poles were then cut, to which we fastened our lines. The old canoe in the lake was bailed out, and having baited our hooks with the minnows we had brought with us, we planted the poles in about seven feet of water, all around the lake shore. We then prepared and ate our supper, and awaited the coming on of night. During this interval, I learned the following particulars concerning the lake. It was originally discovered by a hunter, named Shew. It is estimated to cover about fifty acres, and in the centre, to be more than two hundred feet in depth. For my part, however, I do not believe it contains over five acres, though the mountains which tower on every side but one, are calculated to deceive the eye; but, as to its depth, I could easily fancy it to be bottomless, for the water is remarkably dark. To the number of trout in this lake there seems to be no end. It is supposed they reach it, when small, through Sweetwater Brook, when they increase in size, and multiply. It also abounds in green and scarlet lizards, which are a serious drawback to the pleasures of the fastidious angler. I asked Peter many questions concerning his adventures about the lake, and he told me that the number of 'harmless murders' he had committed here was about three hundred. In one day, he shot three deer; at another time, a dozen turkeys; at another, twenty ducks; one night, an old bear; and again, half a dozen coons; and, on one occasion, annihilated a den of thirty-seven rattlesnakes.

At nine o'clock, we lighted a torch and went to examine our lines; and it was my good fortune to haul out not less than forty-one trout, weighing from one to two pounds a-piece. These, we put into a spring of very cold water, which bubbled from the earth a few paces from our camping place, and then retired to repose. Branches of hemlock constituted our couch, and my station was between Peter and White Yankee. Little did I dream, when I first saw these two bipeds, that I should ever have them for my bed-fellows; but who can tell what shall be on the morrow? My friends were in the land of Nod in less than a dozen minutes after we had retired; but it was hard for me to go to sleep in the midst of the wild scene which surrounded me. There I lay, flat on my back, a stone and my cap for a pillow, and wrapt in a blanket, with my nose exposed to the chilly night air. And what pictures did my fancy conjure up, as I looked upon the army of trunks around me, glistening in the fire-light! One moment they were a troop of Indians from the spirit-land, come to revisit again the hunting grounds of their fathers, and weeping because the white man had desecrated their soil; and again, I fancied them to be a congress of wild animals, assembled to try, execute, and devour us, for the depredations our fellows had committted upon their kind during the last one hundred years. By and by, a star peered upon me from between the branches of a tree, and my thoughts ascended heavenward. And now, my eyes twinkled and blinked in sympathy with the star, and I was a dreamer.

HENRY DAVID THOREAU: from *The Union Magazine* (1848).

As we poled up a swift rapid for half a mile above Aboljacarmegus Falls, some of the party read their own marks on the huge logs which lay piled up high and dry on the rocks on either hand, the relics probably of a jam which had taken place here in the Great Freshet in the spring. Many of these would have to wait for another great freshet, perchance, if they lasted so long, before they could be got off. It was singular enough to meet with property of theirs which they had never seen, and where they had never been before, thus detained by freshets and rocks when on its way to them. Methinks that must be where all my property lies, cast up on the rocks on some distant and unexplored stream, and waiting for an unheard-of freshet to fetch it down. O make haste, ye gods, with your winds and rains, and start the jam before it rots!

The last half mile carried us to the Sowadnehunk dead-water, so called from the stream of the same name, signifying 'running between mountains', an important tributary which comes in a mile above. Here we decided to camp, about twenty miles from the Dam, at the mouth of

Murch Brook and the Aboljacknagesic, mountain streams, broad off from Ktaadn, and about a dozen miles from its summit, having made fifteen miles this day.

We had been told by McCauslin that we should here find trout enough; so, while some prepared the camp, the rest fell to fishing. Seizing the birch poles which some party of Indians, or white hunters, had left on the shore, and baiting our hooks with pork, and with trout, as soon as they were caught we cast our lines into the mouth of the Aboljacknagesic, a clear, swift, shallow stream, which came in from Ktaadn. Instantly a shoal of white chivin (*Leucisci pulchelli*), silvery roaches, cousin-trout, or what not, large and small, prowling thereabouts, fell upon our bait, and one after another were landed amidst the bushes. Anon their cousins, the true trout, took their turn, and alternately the speckled trout, and the silvery roaches, swallowed the bait as fast as we could throw in; and the finest specimens of both that I have even seen, the largest one weighing three pounds, were heaved upon the shore, though at first in vain, to wriggle down into the water again, for we stood in the boat; but soon we learned to remedy this evil; for one, who had lost his hook, stood on shore to catch them as they fell in a perfect shower around him – sometimes, wet and slippery, full in his face and bosom, as his arms were outstretched to receive them. While yet alive, before their tints had faded, they glistened like the fairest flowers, the product of primitive rivers; and he could hardly trust his senses, as he stood over them, that these jewels should have swam away in that Aboljacknagesic water for so long, so many dark ages – these bright fluviatile flowers, seen of Indians only, made beautiful, the Lord only knows why, to swim there! I could understand better for this, the truth of mythology, the fables of Proteus, and all those beautiful sea-monsters – how all history, indeed, put to a terrestrial use, is mere history; but put to a celestial, is mythology always.

But there is the rough voice of Uncle George, who commands at the frying-pan, to send over what you've got, and then you may stay till morning. The pork sizzles and cries for fish. Luckily for the foolish race, and this particularly foolish generation of trout, the night shut down at last, not a little deepened by the dark side of Ktaadn, which, like a permanent shadow, reared itself from the eastern bank. Lescarbot, writing in 1609, tells us that the Sieur Champdoré, who, with one of the people of the Sieur de Monts, acscended some fifty leagues up the St John in 1608, found the fish so plenty, 'qu'en mettant la chaudière sur le feu ils en avoient pris suffisamment pour eux disner avant que l'eau fust chaude'. Their descendants here are no less numerous. So we accompanied Tom into the woods to cut cedar-twigs for our bed. While he went ahead with the axe and lopped off the smallest twigs of the flat-leaved, cedar, the arbor-vitæ of the gardens, we gathered them up, and returned with them to the boat, until it was loaded. Our bed was made with as much care and skill as a roof is shingled; beginning at the foot, and laying the twig end of the cedar upward, we advanced to the head, a course at a time, thus successively covering the stub-ends, and producing a soft and level bed. For us six it was about ten feet long by six in breadth. This time we lay under our tent, having pitched it more prudently with reference to the wind and the flame, and the usual huge fire blazed in front. Supper was eaten off a large log, which some freshet had thrown up. This night we had a dish of arbor-vitæ, or cedar-tea, which the lumberer sometimes uses when other herbs fail –

> A quart of arbor-vitæ,
> To make him strong and mighty,

but I had no wish to repeat the experiment. It had too medicinal a taste for my palate. There was the skeleton of a moose here, whose bones some Indian hunters had picked on this very spot.

In the night I dreamed of trout-fishing; and, when at length I awoke, it seemed a fable that this painted fish swam there so near my couch, and rose to our hooks the last evening, and I doubted if I had not dreamed it all. So I arose before dawn to test its truth, while my companions were still sleeping. There stood Ktaadn with distinct and cloudless outline in the moonlight; and the rippling of the rapids was the only sound to break the stillness. Standing on the shore, I once more cast my line into the stream, and found the dream to be real and the fable true. The speckled trout and silvery roach, like flying-fish, sped swiftly through the moonlight air, describing bright arcs on the dark side of Ktaadn, until moonlight, now fading into daylight, brought satiety to my mind, and the minds of my companions, who had joined me.

SERGEI AKSAKOV, (1791–1859): *The Fisherman Growing Old.*
Translated from the Russian by Arthur Ransome, from *Rod and Line,*
1929.

'Almost all young fish, especially of the smaller kinds, are so beautiful,
or, to be more precise, so pretty, active and clean, that the people of the
south of Russia use the word *ruibka* (little fish) as a word of affection
and tenderness in praise of maidenly beauty and charm'. . . . He
quotes from his favourite Gogol the passage in which the young
Cossack begs his love, 'Heart of mine, my little fish, my jewel! Look at
me! Put out through the lattice if only thy little white hand!. . .' He
goes on: 'For the peasant of Great Russia that is too delicate; but he
too loves to watch every kind of fish, sparkling merrily on the surface of
the water, flashing its silver or golden scales, its rainbow stripes;
sometimes swimming quietly, secretly, sometimes still and motionless
on the bottom of the river! Not a peasant, old or young, will pass by
river or pond without looking to see "how the free fishes play" and often
a peasant travelling on foot hurrying somewhere on necessary business, forgets for a time his working life and, leaning over a dark blue
pool looks earnestly into the shadowy depths, admiring the quick
movements of the fish, especially when it is playing and splashing,
when, coming to the top, suddenly with a sharp turn and a blow of its
tail it goes down again, leaving a swirling circle on the surface, the
margins of which, gradually spreading, do not at once efface themselves in the quiet smoothness of the water; or when, with only its back
fin cutting the surface, the fish flies like an arrow in some one direction
and in pursuit of it there runs a long wave which, dividing into two,
offers the strange figure of a widening triangle . . . Is there need to say
after this that the fisherman watches every kind of fish with a still
greater and special love and sees a large or unusual fish with ecstasy
and a joyful throbbing of the heart? These expressions, perhaps, may
seem laughable to non-fishermen – I shall not be offended; I am
talking to fishermen and they will understand me! Each one of them,
growing old, finds pleasure in remembering the lively feeling that
inspired him in youth when, rod in hand, forgetting sleep and tired-
ness, he gave himself up passionately to his beloved sport. Each one of
them, surely, remembers with satisfaction that golden time . . . And I
too remember it as a long ago, sweet, and not quite clear dream. I
remember the sultry noons, the banks overgrown with tall, scented
herbs and flowers, the shadow of the alder tree quivering on the water,

the deep pool of the river, and the young fisherman clinging to an overhanging bough, his hair hanging down, motionlessly gazing with charmed eyes into the dark blue but clear depths . . . And how many fish were crowded there . . . What orfe, what chub, what perch!. . . And how the heart of the boy stood still and his breath caught . . . Long ago it was, very long ago. But even now young fishermen are tasting the same experience and God grant them long to preserve that lively innocent feeling of the passionate fisherman.'

'A very good quality in a man'

The Later Nineteenth Century

BLACK BASS FISHING IN THE ADIRONDACKS, STATE OF NEW YORK. From a woodcut after R. F. Zogbaum (1884). From *Angling in British Art* by Walter Shaw Sparrow (1923).

GEORGE BORROW: from *Lavengro* (1851).

And there I sat upon the bank, at the bottom of the hill which slopes down from 'the Earl's Home'; my float was on the waters, and my back was towards the old hall. I drew up many fish, small and great, which I took from off the hook mechanically, and flung upon the bank, for I was almost unconscious of what I was about, for my mind was not with my fish. I was thinking of my earlier years – of the Scottish crags and the heaths of Ireland – and sometimes my mind would dwell on my studies – on the sonorous stanzas of Dante, rising and falling like the waves of the sea – or would strive to remember a couplet or two of poor Monsieur Boileau.

'Canst thout answer to thy conscience for pulling all those fish out of the water and leaving them to gasp in the sun?' said a voice, clear and sonorous as a bell.

I started, and looked round. Close behind me stood the tall figure of a man, dressed in raiment of quaint and singular fashion, but of goodly materials. He was in the prime and vigour of manhood; his features handsome and noble, but full of calmness and benevolence; at least I thought so, though they were somewhat shaded by a hat of finest beaver, with broad drooping eaves.

'Surely that is a very cruel diversion in which thou indulgest, my young friend? he continued.

'I am sorry for it, if it be, sir,' said I, rising; 'but I do not think it cruel to fish.'

'What are thy reasons for thinking so?'

'Fishing is mentioned frequently in Scripture. Simon Peter was a fisherman.'

'True; and Andrew his brother. But thou forgettest; they did not follow fishing as a diversion, as I fear thou doest. – Thou readest the Scriptures?'

'Sometimes.'

'Sometimes? – not daily? – that is to be regretted. What profession dost thou make? – I mean to what religious denomination dost thou belong, my young friend?'

'Church.'

'It is a very good profession – there is much of Scripture contained in its liturgy. Dost thou read aught beside the Scriptures?'

'Sometimes.'

'What dost thou read besides?'

'Greek, and Dante.'

'Indeed! then thou hast the advantage over myself; I can only read the former. Well, I am rejoiced to find that thou hast other pursuits beside thy fishing. Dost thou know Hebrew?'

'No.'

'Thou shouldest study it. Why dost thou not undertake the study?'

'I have no books.'

'I will lend thee books, if thou wish to undertake the study. I live yonder at the hall, as perhaps thou knowest. I have a library there, in which are many curious books, both in Greek and Hebrew, which I will show to thee, whenever thou mayest find it convenient to come and see me. Farewell! I am glad to find that thou hast pursuits more satisfactory than thy cruel fishing.'

And the man of peace departed, and left me on the bank of the stream. Whether from the effect of his words or from want of inclination to the sport, I know not, but from that day I became less and less a practitioner of that 'cruel fishing'.

CHARLES KINGSLEY: from *Yeast: A Problem* (1851).

Lancelot sat and tried to catch perch, but Tregarva's words haunted him. He lighted his cigar, and tried to think earnestly over the matter, but he had got into the wrong place for thinking. All his thoughts, all his sympathies, were drowned in the rush and whirl of the water. He forgot everything else in the mere animal enjoyment of sight and sound. Like many young men at his crisis of life, he had given himself up to the mere contemplation of Nature till he had become her slave; and now a luscious scene, a singing bird, were enough to allure his mind away from the most earnest and awful thoughts. He tried to think, but the river would not let him. It thundered and spouted out behind him from the hatches, and leapt madly past him, and caught his eyes in spite of him, and swept them away down its dancing waves, and let them go again only to seep them down again and again, till his brain felt a delicious dizziness from the everlasting rush and the everlasting roar. And then below, how it spread, and writhed, and whirled into transparent fans, hissing and twining snakes, polished glass-wreaths, huge crystal bells, which boiled up from the bottom, and dived again beneath long threads of creamy foam, and swung round posts and roots, and rushed blackening under dark weed-fringed boughs, and gnawed at the marly banks, and shook the ever-restless bulrushes, till it was swept away and down over the white pebbles and olive weeds, in one broad rippling sheet of molten silver, towards the distant sea. Downwards it fleeted ever, and bore his thoughts floating on its oily stream; and the great trout, with their yellow sides and peacock backs, lounged among the eddies, and the silver grayling dimpled and wandered upon the shallows, and the may flies flickered and rustled round him like water fairies, with their green gauzy wings; the coot clanked musically among the reeds; the frogs hummed their ceaseless vesper-monotone; the kingfisher darted from his hole in the bank like a blue spark of electric light; the swallows' bills snapped as they twined and hawked above the pool; the swift's wings whirred like musket-balls, as they rushed screaming past his head; and ever the river fleeted by, bearing his eyes away down the current, till its wild eddies began to glow with crimson beneath the setting sun. The complex harmony of sights and sounds slid softly over his soul, and he sank away into a still daydream, too passive for imagination, too deep for meditation, and

'Beauty born of murmuring sound,
  Did pass into his face.'

Blame him not. There are more things in a man's heart than ever get in through his thoughts.

HERMAN MELVILLE: from *Moby Dick or The Whale* (1851).

Once more. Say, you are in the country; in some high land of lakes. Take almost any path you please, and ten to one it carries you down in a dale, and leaves you there by a pool in the stream. There is a magic in it. Let the most absent-minded of men be plunged in his deepest reveries – stand that man on his legs, set his feet a-going, and he will infallibly lead you to water, if water there be in all that region. Should you ever be athirst in the great American desert, try this experiment, if your caravan happen to be supplied with a metaphysical professor. Yes, as every one knows, meditation and water are wedded for ever.

But here is an artist. He desires to paint you the dreamiest, shadiest, quietest, most enchanting bit of romantic landscape in all the valley of the Saco. What is the chief element he employs? There stand his trees, each with a hollow trunk, as if a hermit and a crucifix were within; and here sleeps his meadow, and there sleep his cattle; and up from yonder cottage goes a sleepy smoke. Deep into distant woodlands winds a mazy way, reaching to overlapping spurs of mountains bathed in their hillside blue. But though the picture lies thus tranced, and though his pine-tree shakes down its sighs like leaves upon this shepherd's head, yet all were vain, unless the shepherd's eye were fixed upon the magic stream before him. Go visit the Prairies in June, when for scores on scores of miles you wade knee-deep among Tiger-lilies – what is the one charm wanting? – Water – there is not a drop of water there! Were Niagara but a cataract of sand, would you travel your thousand miles to see it? Why did the poor poet of Tennessee, upon suddenly receiving two handfuls of silver, deliberate whether to buy him a coat, which he sadly needed, or invest his money in a pedestrian trip to Rockaway Beach? Why is almost every robust healthy boy with a robust healthy soul in him, at some time or other crazy to go to sea? Why upon your first voyage as a passenger, did you yourself feel such a mystical vibration, when first told that you and your ship were now out of sight of land? Why did the old Persians hold the sea holy? Why did the Greeks give it a separate deity, and own brother of Jove? Surely all this is not without meaning. And still deeper the meaning of that story of Narcissus, who, because he could not grasp the tormenting, mild image he saw in the fountain, plunged into it and was drowned. But that same image, we ourselves see in all rivers and oceans. It is the image of the ungraspable phantom of life; and this is the key to it all.

REV. C. DAVID BADHAM: *Rana, or Fishing Frog.*
From *Prose Halieutics: or Ancient and Modern Fish Tattle* (1854).

Turpis in littore Rana. – Mart.

Our ideas of fish generally are of a pleasing kind; and whether they be seen sporting in water, struggling in a net, or laid out for sale in a market-place, the exhibition is one which seldom fails to gratify the eye. Those tribes that are beautifully striped, banded, spotted, or marbled, or which blaze in the rich hues of gems and humming-birds, make lively demands on our admiration; and even those that have not such brilliant colouring nor characteristic markings to set off the skin, frequently glisten in the sheen of silvery scales, and are as fair and attractive in their attire as some young bride at the altar! Nor are colour and shining scales the only attractions these creatures can boast: their figure also is generally graceful, and suggestive of agile and rapid movement; while other kinds that are deficient in this so usual elegance of shape, often please from some peculiar quaintness of contour, or from some evident adaptation of their organization to meet a particular exigency. Even the repugnance excited by the shark does not proceed from his personal, but moral deformity; not because he is ugly to look at, but an ugly customer to have to do with. As every rule, however, has its exception, so are Sea-frogs the exception to that of the prepossessing appearance of fish in general, and Nature, elsewhere lavish of beauty and grace, has bestowed upon them nothing but deformity and disgrace; they are the bugbears and scape-goats of the deep, from which most monsters, the terror of young and the delight of grown-up children, have been constructed. No one could doubt the paternity of those open-mouthed chimeras of national nurseries – the Old Bones, Spring Devils, Befanos, Croc-Mitaines, Bric-à-Bracs, etc – who had seen a sea-frog as prepared by the Neapolitan boatmen for a show, the inside thoroughly cleared out and eviscerated, with the mouth set wide open, and a lantern in the interior, shining through the pellucid skin: all these are in fact but tame copies of this incarnate fright. From the same fertile source also painters and poets famed for their grotesque or horrific representations – the Ariostos and the Brughels – have largely, though it may be at the moment unwittingly, drawn. Too ugly for any associate, and claiming no natural kin with any, the lopheus swims about in bloated self-sufficiency, alone, without congener or any one legitimate family tie; wholly unlike in person, except in possessing a cartilaginous skeleton, any other member of the Chondropterygian group; the female moreover, as Aristotle has well observed, does not bring forth her brood hatched in pouches, but from eggs. Another essential difference, too, between these sea-frogs and the sharks and rays, with which they used to be associated, is the different position of the fins. In other cartilaginous fish, these are placed far back, and serve as legs; but in the lopheus they are situated immediately under the throat, and act as *hands* for prehension and for burrowing in the sand. Nor is the position assigned by Cuvier to this fish among the Gobidae, founded on the above peculiarity, less unsatisfactory or forced, since all other connecting links are as deficient here as in the older arrangement. Most members of the division into which this fish is now foisted are eatable; but though the Greeks (nasty fellows!) have registered the sea-frog among their prime viands, and considered the liver, especially, equal to that of the narke, and the flesh of the *belly* worthy to be served up any banquet, –

Βάτραχον ’ένθ’ ΐδης καὶ γάστριον αὐτοῦ σκεύασον,—

the rank and flabby carcase has found few partisans elsewhere, and Belon says its only value 'lies in whatever undigested food may be found in its insides – ‘C’est un poisson moult laid à veoir, duquel on ne tient gran compte de manger si ce n’est pour esventrer et luy tirer les poissons qu’il ha encor touts en dudedans le corps’. Let the reader for a moment imagine a gigantic tadpole blow out to the size of a porpoise (sometimes indeed much larger, for Pontoppidan mentions one of twelve feet long, and several authors speak of individuals of seven feet and upwards), with an immense head, and a mouth extending on either side far beyond the width of the body, opening to view a capacious den, shagged throughout with hooked and mobile teeth, a triple tier in the upper and an equal number in the lower jaw, the palate, tongue, fauces, pharynx, and far down the throat, glistening with a like display of ivory fangs; unfishy orbs resembling those of the ‘star-gazer’, planted high in the forehead; a scaleless skin, which is reeking, cold, and clammy; its surface from near the tail to the corners of the mouth as crawling with long, wriggling, carunculated appendages, like so many worms in agony; the flesh ‘boggy’ to the touch, save where it is padded out with an enormously distended liver, or just over the branchial cavity, a pantry constantly replenished with provisions; add to all this a large pair of Caliban hand-like fins planted close under the throat; a fierce, malevolent aspect, and an ungainly mode of wallowing rather than swimming through the brine – and it will be apparent, even from this very imperfect sketch, that such a fish-scarecrow could not fail to arrest attention, even had there been no other claim to regard than his portentous ugliness.

HENRY DAVID THOREAU: from *Walden, or Life in the Woods* (1854).

Early in the morning, while all things are crisp with frost, men come with fishing reels and slender lunch, and let down their fine lines through the snowy field (the frozen lake) to take pickerel and perch; wild men, who instinctively follow other fashions and trust other authorities than their townsmen, and by their goings and comings stitch towns together in parts where else they would be ripped. They sit and eat their luncheon in stout fear-naughts on the dry oak leaves on the shore, as wise in natural lore as the citizen is artificial. They never consulted with books and know and can tell much less than they have done. The things which they practise are said not to be known. Here is one fishing for pickerel with grown perch for bait. You look into his pail with wonder as into a summer pond, as if he kept summer locked up at home, or knew where she had retreated. How, pray did he get these in mid-winter? Oh, he got the worms out of rotten logs since the ground froze, and so he caught them. His life itself passes deeper into Nature than the studies of the naturalist penetrate, himself a subject for the naturalist.

The latter raises the moss and bark gently with his knife in search of insects; the former lays open logs to their core with his axe, and moss and bark fly far and wide. He gets his living by barking trees. Such a man has some right to fish, and I love to see Nature carried out in him. The perch swallows the grub worm, the pickerel swallows the perch, and the fisherman swallows the pickerel and so all the chinks in the scale are filled.

When I strolled around the pond in misty weather I was sometimes amused by the primitive mode which some ruder fisherman adopted. He would perhaps have placed alder branches over the narrow hole in the ice, which were four or five rods apart, and equal distances from the shore, and having fastened the end of his line to a stick to prevent its being pulled through, having passed the slack line over a twig of the alder, a foot or more above the ice, and tied a dry oak leaf to it, which being pulled down, would show when he had a bite. These alders loomed through the mist at regular intervals as you walked round the pond.

Ah! those pickerel of Walden! When I see them lying on the ice or in the well which the fishermen cuts in the ice, making a little hole to admit the water, I am always surprised at their rare beauty, as if they were fabulous fishes, they are so foreign to the streets, even to the woods, foreign as Arabia to our Concord life. They possess a quite dazzling and transcendent beauty, which separates them by a wide interval from the cadaverous cod and haddock whose fame is trumpeted in our streets. They are not green, like the pines, nor grey like the stones, nor blue like the sky, but they have, to my eyes, if possible, yet rarer colours, like flowers and precious stones, as if they were pearls, the animalized *nuclei* or crystals of the Walden water. They, of course, *are* Walden all over and all through; are themselves small Waldens in the animal kingdom of Waldenses. It is surprising that they are caught here – that in this deep and capacious spring, far beneath the rattling teams and chaises and tinkling sleighs that travel the Walden road, this great gold and emerald fish swims. I never chanced to see its kind in any market; it would be the cynosure of all eyes there. Easily with a few convulsive quirks, they give up their watery ghosts, like a mortal translated before his time to the thin air of heaven. . .

HENRY WADSWORTH LONGFELLOW: from *Hiawatha's Fishing.*
From *The Song of Hiawatha, Canto VIII* (1855).

> Forth upon the Gitche Gumee,
> On the shining Big-Sea-Water,
> With his fishing-line of cedar,
> Of the twisted bark of cedar,
> Forth to catch the sturgeon Nahma,
> Mishe-Nahma, King of Fishes,
> In his birch-canoe exulting
> All alone went Hiawatha.
>   Through the clear, transparent water
> He could see the fishes swimming
> Far down in the depths below him;
> See the yellow perch, the Sahwa,

Like a sunbeam in the water,
See the Shawgashee, the crawfish,
Like a spider on the bottom,
On the white and sandy bottom.
　At the stern sat Hiawatha,
With his fishing-line of cedar;
In his plumes the breeze of morning
Played as in the hemlock branches;
On the bows, with tail erected,
Sat the squirrel, Adjidaumo;
In his fur the breeze of morning
Played as in the prairie grasses.
　On the white sand of the bottom.
Lay the monster Mishe-Nahma,
Lay the sturgeon, King of Fishes;
Through his gills he breathed the water,
With his fins he fanned and winnowed,
With his tail he swept the sand-floor.
　There he lay in all his armour;
On each side a shield to guard him,
Plates of bone upon his forehead,
Down his sides and back and shoulders
Plates of bone with spines projecting.
Painted was he with his war-paints,
Stripes of yellow, red, and azure.
Spots of brown and spots of sable;
And he lay there on the bottom,
Fanning with his fins of purple,
As above him Hiawatha
In his birch-canoe came sailing,
With his fishing-line of cedar.
　'Take my bait,' cried Hiawatha,
Down into the depths beneath him,
'Take my bait, O Sturgeon, Nahma!
Come up from below the water,
Let us see which is the stronger!'
And he dropped his line of cedar
Through the clear, transparent water,
Waited vainly for an answer,
Long sat waiting for an answer,

And repeating loud and louder,
'Take my bait, O King of Fishes!'
    Quiet lay the sturgeon, Nahma,
Fanning slowly in the water,
Looking up at Hiawatha,
Listening to his call and clamour,
His unnecessary tumult,
Till he wearied of the shouting;
And he said to the Kenozha,
To the pike, the Maskenozha,
'Take the bait of this rude fellow,
Break the line of Hiawatha!'
    In his fingers Hiawatha
Felt the loose line jerk and tighten;
As he drew it in, it tugged so
That the birch-canoe stood endwise,
Like a birch-log in the water,
With the squirrel, Adjidaumo,
Perched and frisking on the summit.
    Full of scorn was Hiawatha
When he saw the fish rise upward,
Saw the pike, the Maskenozha,
Coming nearer, nearer to him,
And he shouted through the water,
'Esa! esa! shame upon you!
You are but the pike, Kenozha,
You are not the fish I wanted,
You are not the King of Fishes!'
    Reeling downward to the bottom
Sank the pike in great confusion,
And the mighty sturgeon, Nahma,
Said to Ugudwash, the sun-fish,
To the bream, with scales of crimson,
'Take the bait of this great boaster,
Break the line of Hiawatha!'
    Slowly upward, wavering, gleaming,
Rose the Ugudwash, the sun-fish,
Seized the line of Hiawatha,
Swung with all his weight upon it,
Made a whirlpool in the water,

Whirled the birch-canoe in circles,
Round and round in gurgling eddies,
Till the circles in the water
Reached the far-off sandy beaches,
Till the water-flags and rushes
Nodded on the distant margins.
    But when Hiawatha saw him
Slowly rising through the water,
Lifting up his disc refulgent,
Loud he shouted in derision,
'Esa! esa! shame upon you!
You are Ugudwash, the sun-fish,
You are not the fish I wanted,
You are not the King of Fishes!'
    Slowly downward, wavering, gleaming,
Sank the Ugudwash, the sun-fish,
And again the sturgeon, Nahma,
Heard the shout of Hiawatha,
Heard his challenge of defiance,
The unnecessary tumult,
Ringing far across the water.
    From the white sand of the bottom
Up he rose with angry gesture,
Quivering in each nerve and fibre,
Clashing all his plates of armour,
Gleaming bright with all his war-paint;
In his wrath he darted upward,
Flashing leaped into the sunshine,
Opened his great jaws, and swallowed
Both canoe and Hiawatha.

THE O'GORMAN: from *The Practice of Angling* (1855).

I will now conclude this long chapter by a cursory notice of anglers, as
men; and I do assert, that I have almost invariably found them persons
of good and charitable dispositions, possessing mild, though firm
tempers, sharp and intellectual minds; incapable of committing base
and ungenerous actions; much inclined to the heavenly passion of love;

free from the debasing vice of avarice; lively and light-hearted; agreeable and intelligent. The very pursuit, while it demands the possession of intellect, must sharpen it. Were I to select the professions among the members of which I have met the best men, and the most skilful anglers, I would certainly name the army and the law. I mean the highest branch of the latter; as for the attorneys, with many honourable exceptions, they are an incorrigible race. Indeed, I have rarely seen any of them who could angle at all, perhaps only one; and he was a sinister biped (left-handed). They are, for the most part, devoted to worldly gain; and, as Giles Daxon used to say, will never give a direct answer to a question.

Few merchants are good anglers. I have met but two or three: one a near relation of my own, who now, however, thinks such a practice beneath his crown and dignity. Let us charitably hope that is, because he has not time.

CHARLES KINGSLEY: from *Chalk Stream Studies, by a Minute Philosopher.* From *Fraser's Magazine* (1858).

Come, then, you who want pleasant fishing days without the waste of time and trouble and expense involved in two hundred miles of railway journey, and perhaps fifty more of highland road, and try what you can see and do among the fish not fifty miles from town. Come to pleasant country inns, where you can always get a good dinner; or, better still, to pleasant country houses, where you can always get good society; to rivers which will always fish, brimfull in the longest droughts of summer, instead of being, as those mountain ones are, very like a turnpike-road for three weeks, and then like bottled porter for three days; to streams on which you have strong south-west breezes for a week together on a clear fishing water, instead of having, as on those mountain ones, foul rain 'spate' as long as the wind is south-west, and clearing water when the wind chops up to the north, and the chill blast of 'Clarus Aquilo' sends all the fish shivering to the bottom; streams, in a word, where you may kill fish (and large ones) four days out of five from April to October, instead of having, as you will most probably in the mountain, just one day's sport in the whole of your month's holiday. Deluded friend, who suffered in Scotland last year a month of Tantalus his torments, furnished by art and nature with rods, flies, whisky, scenery, keepers, salmon innumerable, and all that man can want, except water to fish in; and who returned, having hooked accidentally by the tail one salmon – which broke all and went to sea – why did you not stay at home and take your two-pounders and three-pounders out of the quiet chalk brook which never sank an inch through all that drought, so deep in the caverns of the hills are hidden its mysterious wells? Truly, wise men bide at home, with George Riddler, while 'a fool's eyes are in the ends of the earth'.

Repent, then; and come with me, at least in fancy, at six o'clock upon some breezy morning in the end of June, not by roaring railway nor by smoking steamer, but in the cosy four-wheel, along brown heather moors, down into green clay woodlands, over white chalk downs, past Roman camps and scattered blocks of Sarsden stone, till we descend into the long green vale where, among groves of poplar and abele, winds silver Whit. Come and breakfast at the neat white inn, of yore a posting-house of fame. The stables are now turned into cottages; and instead of a dozen spruce ostlers and helpers, the last of the post-boys totters sadly about the yard and looks up eagerly at the rare sight of a horse to feed. But the house keeps up enough of its ancient virtue to give us a breakfast worthy of Pantagruel's self; and after it, while we are looking out our flies, you can go and chat with the old post-boy, and hear his tales, told with a sort of chivalrous pride, of the noble lords and fair ladies before whom he has ridden in the good old times gone by – even, so he darkly hints, before 'His Royal Highness the Prince' himself. Poor old fellow, he recollects not, and he need not recollect, that these great posting houses were centres of corruption, from whence the newest vices of the metropolis were poured into the too-willing ears of village lads and lasses, and that not even the New Poor-Law itself has done more for the morality of the South of England than the substitution of the rail for coaches.

* * *

Every still spot in a chalk stream becomes so choked with weed as to require mowing at least thrice a year, to supply the mills with water. Grass, milfoil, water crowfoot, hornwort, starwort, horsetail, and a dozen other delicate plants, form one tangled forest, denser than those of the Amazon, and more densely peopled likewise*.

---

*To this list will soon be added our Transatlantic curse, *Babingtonia diabolica*, alias *Anacharis alsinastrum*. It has already ascended the Thames as high as Reading; and a few

Do you doubt it? Then come, for the sun burns bright, and fishing is impossible. Lie down upon the bank above this stop. There is a camp-shutting (a boarding in English) on which you can put your elbows. Lie down on your face, and look down through two or three feet of water clear as air, into the water forest where the great trout feed.

Here; look into this opening in the milfoil and crowfoot bed. Do you see a grey film around that sprig? Look at it through the pocket lens. It is a forest of glass bells, on branching stalks. They are Vorticellæ; and every one of those bells, by the ciliary current on its rim, is scavenging the water – till a tadpole comes by and scavenges it. How many millions of living creatures are there on that one sprig? Look here! – a brown polype, with long waving arms – a gigantic monster, actually a full half-inch long. He is *Hydra fusca*, most famous, and earliest described (I think by Trembley). Ere we go home, I may show you perhaps *Hydra viridis*, with long pea-green arms, and *Rosea*, most beautiful in form and colour of all the strange family. You see that lump, just where his stalk joins his bell-head? That is a budding baby. Ignorant of the joys and cares of wedlock, he increases by gemmation. See! here is another, with a full-sized young one growing on his back. You may tear it off, if you will – he cares not. You may cut him into a dozen pieces, they say, and each one will grow, as a potato does. I suppose, however, that he also sends out of his mouth little free ova – medusoids – call them what you will, swimming by ciliæ, which afterwards, unless the water beetles stop them on the way, will settle down as stalked polypes, and in their turn practise some mystery of Owenian parthenogenesis, or Steenstruppian alternation of generations, in which all traditional distinctions of plant and animal, male and female, are laughed to scorn by the magnificent fecundity of the Divine imaginations.

That dusty cloud which shakes off in the water as you move the weed, under the microscope would be one mass of exquisite forms: *Desmidiæ* and *Diatomaceæ* – and what not? Instead of running over long names, take home a little in a bottle, put it under your microscope, and if you think good, verify the species from Hassall, Ehrenberg, or other wise book; but without doing that, one glance through the lens will show you why the chalk trout grow fat.

---

years more, owing to the present aqua-vivarium mania, will see it filling every mill-head in England, to the torment of all millers. Young ladies are assured that the only plant for their vivariums is a sprig of anacharis for which they pay sixpence – the market value being that of a wasp, flea, or other scourge of the human race; and when the vivarium fails, its contents, anacharis and all, are tost into the nearest ditch; for which the said young lady ought to be fined five pounds; and would be, if Governments governed. What an 'if'!

ADVERTISING POSTER (c. 1859).

The Talking and Performing Fish! This unparalleled *Lusus Naturae* will be exhibited at 191 Piccadilly (between St James's Church and the Egyptian Hall) on Thursday, May 5th and Every Day from 10 to 10.

This amphibious creature was caught with much trouble, and at great personal hazard, by Signor CAVANA and Crew, off the Coast of Africa, on the 5th of May, 1854. It measures 12 feet in length, weighs 8 cwt. and is the only individual of the species hitherto publicly exhibited.

In offering this curious animal to public view, the Proprietor begs to inform his visitors that they are not to confound it with the Marine Wolf, as it is quite of a different species. The female which he has the honour to present to the public, and which weighs 8 cwt., obeys the word of command, and executes various performances which have caused great admiration to the first naturalists of England, France, and Portugal.

The creature, notwithstanding its great ferocity, has with difficulty been tamed and, in a sense, domesticated. Such is its present docility and obedience, that it has left its locality at night in search of its keeper, and has laid down to sleep by his side. It is of enormous bulk, has two rows of teeth, and is covered with fine hair. It only feeds on fish, of which it daily eats the immense quantity of 45 lbs. It is ferocious and dangerous to its enemy, but docile to its keeper, whose orders and expressions it comprehends, and whose face and hands it kisses. Its intelligence is so acute that it pronounces several words distinctly.

WILLIAM YARRELL: from *A History of British Fishes* (1836–60).

M. Valenciennes has entered into a critical examination of the legends respecting an enormously large and aged German Pike, which have been repeated in different ways by many writers on European ichthyology, but which he clearly shows to be either in part or wholly apocryphal. Marquard Freher says that the Pike was taken at Kaiserlautern, in a lake still called the Kaiserwag, and that a gilt brazen collar which it bore had an inscription, stating that it was put into the lake by the hand of the Emperor Frederick the Second, in the year 1230. It was taken out, and carried to Heidelberg in 1497, and it had therefore lived in the lake 267 years. Its picture was seen in the palace of Heidelberg by Maynard, and a black line, drawn on the wall, purporting to be the measure of its length, was seventeen feet long. Gesner, who lived nearer the time at which this fish was said to have been taken, says that it was captured in a lake near Heilbronn in Suabia, and that the inscription on the ring was in the Greek language, but to the same purport as that quoted by Maynard; and Lehman reports that in 1592 its portrait and also a sketch of the ring were preserved in a castle erected on the road leading from Heilbronn to Spires. Other conjectures and versions of the story are mentioned by M. Valenciennes.

As a testimony to the truth of the legend, the skeleton of the Emperor's monstrous Pike was long shown in the Cathedral of Manheim, but an eminent German anatomist found, from the number of its vertebræ, that the bones of more than one fish had been used in its composition. It is to be observed, however, that it was customary in those ages to put rings in the gill-covers of fishes, and Bock states that in 1610 a Pike was taken in the Meuse, bearing a copper ring, on which was graven the name of the city of Stavern and the date of 1448.

* * *

The following anecdote is copied from a little book entitled *Friendly Contributions for the Benefit of the Royal Schools of Industry*:

> The late Mr Baron Thompson was very curious in all matters of and concerning eating; and was, moreover, somewhat selfish and uncommunicative when he had made any gastronomic discovery, to the pursuit of which he frequently made his summer and spring circuits subservient: and it was known that he often jockeyed his less eager brethren out of the Oxford circuit that he might get the best sausages and brawn at Oxford, and eat the first stewed and potted lampreys at Worcester, and finish with Simnel cake at Shrewsbury.
>
> One day, looking over the bridge at Carlisle, he saw a man fishing with what he fancied was a new bait (boiled cheese); and as the judge was in a logical mood, he considered that the using of a new bait was all in favour of catching a new fish. He smoothed down his wig; and, as well as he could, smoothed the wrinkles of his face into a smile, and asked the man what he was fishing for? – 'Allmacks!' was the answer: the judge was right; new baits caught new fish; he had never before heard of a piscine Allmacks. His curiosity and his generosity were at once excited, and slipping into the fisher's hand a retaining fee of half-a-crown, bound him over to bring up the bodies of all the Allmacks caught that day before him at his inn, in time then and there to be dressed for dinner; in fact, a sort of piscatory *habeas*

corpus was issued. The judge trotted nimbly home; prepared for court – first, however, imparting to his marshal that he should dine alone, and confiding to him that a certain man would bring a certain new kind of fish, which he desired should be carefully dressed in three different ways – plain boiled, fried, and broiled. The court rose: it is not pretended that any justice was done, neither did the guilty escape, nor were the innocent convicted, that the judge might dine; but those who were accustomed to the judge's manner, saw that as the hour of dinner crept round a slight cloud of impatience passed over his brow, and there was less sifting of the evidence, and less subtlety of logic than usual. The judge got back to his lodging; the dinner came up; the judge, with his mouth watering, was all impatience: the master led the way with a small dish, in which were four fried Gudgeons, two Miller's Thumbs, and a Bream; and the next two dishes contained a boiled Perch, a boiled Eel, and a Samlet. The judge stared; and then, to his mortification, first learned that Allmacks meant *all sorts** – *what one can catch*.

*Allmacks – all sorts – Brockett's Glossary of North-country Words, p.131.

JOHN YOUNGER: from *On River Angling for Salmon and Trout* (1840, revised 1860).

It seems to have been an early practice with anglers, which is yet much followed in books written on the Art of Angling, to face up the subject with pretensions of its being an amusement above all others conducive to religious contemplation. This is silly, either as a notion or a pretence; and on the other hand it is equally pitiful to read the frivolous sarcasms by which this pursuit is in turn assailed.

Dr Johnson and Lord Byron, these famed fondlings of their age, have said some smart things to render angling ridiculous as a pastime. Having acquired no taste for it themselves, they wished to make believe that they stigmatized it from a moral sentiment; and this, not so much perhaps from an inclination to

Compound for sins they were inclined to
By damning those they had no mind to,

as from an opposition to the whimsicalities of early writers on the subject; such as old Isaac Walton, and the religious sportswoman of 1496, Dame Juliana Barnes, who mixed up their descantations with pretences of its being favourable to holy meditations, from the rural quietude of the pursuit. This must have been alleged by these early anglers and writers through a sort of mental defence against a superstitious suspicion, that it was not perhaps the most Christian way of spending the sweet summer days of a brief probationary term of an eternal existence. Hence the struggle to the present hour of a hundred-and-nine scribblers on the subject to maintain a point, of the propriety of which they are by no means thoroughly convinced: only, finding the pastime a kind of exercise agreeable to their propensities – like that of cats to hunt mice, and lords foxes – they make a specious pretence of considering its gratification, not only as no sin, but rather in the light of a duty. Now the truth lies in this as in many disputed points, midway between the two extremes. No one who inclines to go a-fishing can reasonably suppose the pursuit any way very particular in point of morality – let him allege what he may, we believe that the angler foregoes such considerations. We view the matter simply in this way, that every man is so much of a boy (which may often be the best part of his character) that he goes out a-fishing because he had got into an early habit of so going, and finds amusement in it preferable to walking, or even to riding, should he be master of a horse; or else he pursues it, fain to find recreation in that in which he perceives his neighbour so well pleased, just as he would go a-quoiting, a-cricketing, or a-curling. To talk of following it on a principle of love or admiration of field scenery, the wood-skirted grandeur of cliff or stream, is surely either a pretence or an illusion of his own mind; because every staunch angler may be said to leave his admiration of the picturesque, the beautiful, and romantic in nature, as something to be particularly kept in mind, returned to and enjoyed 'at a more convenient season' – as governor Felix did his taste for the most sublime doctrines of Christianity. I have felt that I could admire the beautiful in landscape as much as my neighbours, perhaps any of them, yet never could find either taste or time for the disposition of sentiment while sallying out on a fishing excursion; and however romantically beautiful the branch overhung its shadow in the water, I no sooner hanked my hooks on it than, if within reach, crash down it came, whilst a wish hurried over my mind that all river-skirting trees were removed. I would hardly except the bordering willows of Dryburgh, or those skirting the rivers of Babylon, where the Israelites hung their harps in the days of their captivity.

By no poetical feeling whatever should the free swing of line be ever interrupted. Let sketchers put imaginary trees in their landscapes as they please, yet such are ever the true angler's real feelings, disguise them as he may: *Keep tree, rock, and ivy full line-swing from the margin of lake and stream.* One truth is worth fifty of these fishing authors' sickly *preachments.* If our tractates on the subject should never sell, let us not heap disgrace on our own poor head by feigning sanctity we never feel. Such would be worse than prevalent superstition or common hypocrisy. I can see no more sentimentality in angling for fish than in the rural sports of Fox or Otter hunting. The excitement is kept up by the solicitude of success, and this is the same in fishing for reputation in the sport, as in fishing for a dinner; the true angler being always intent in the pursuit, however passive he may appear.

The fertility of Isaac's imagination, and the ingenuity of his mind, would have made him to excel in whatever his hand might have found to do. A mind too versatile to have been confined within the critical rules of any age or art had excited him to write out his mixed thoughts, feelings, conceits, songs, and sermons, on all favourite subjects, just as they occurred to his fancy – hence all are found pouched up together like his fish baits. Had he not fallen madly fond of angling pursuits, I have no doubt but he might have been one of the greatest devotees of his superstitious age. Or had he turned to 'the breeding of the fighting-cock', like several of his angling predecessors, he would likely have *crossed on* till he had produced midden fowls to have beaked it with eagles; but luckily he had not the cock-fighting propensity. And what, after all, was fishing in the *Dove* and *Stowr*, with paddock baits, for geds and gudgeons, to the run of a salmon in the silver Tweed? I wonder how he would have looked if he had been brought here by rail, and set down below our *Hare Crag* with a twenty feet rod in hand, and seen and felt a twenty pound salmon snap down his fly to the bottom, and there hold it as firmly as if it had been fixed to the rock in the deep, with only a little tremulous indication of life at both ends: and then, again, when the sudden bolt up the strong current took place, with the dash out at the top, showing the broad, silvery, and glancing side to the light of day! To imagine the odds between old Isaac and Dr Johnson, brought perforce into that particular position is ludicrous enough, and can only be exceeded by the next supposed image of seeing both snug at supper in their Inn, with the same salmon presented in his next glorious altitude, well-dressed, and set round with sprigs of parsley and piggins of sauce. Who of the two would have said the grace? I think that duty would have devolved on old Isaac of necessity, as the doctor's mouth-watering would have prevented articulation. The doctor, on returning thanks, would assuredly have acknowledged the blessing as sent by God's merciful providence to his maw, by whatever method of stick and string it had been captured.

WALTER THORNBURY: from *The Life of J. M. W. Turner, R. A.*
(1861).

Turner, as we have seen, was very fond of fishing. He seldom went to visit a country friend without binding up a rod with his pilgrim's staff and the inevitable umbrella. He was an intensely persevering fisherman too; no bad weather could drive him from his post, or ill-luck exhaust his patience. Even here we discern the elevation of his character. The bodily frame that endured the long day's rain was animated by the soul that wrestled manfully for fame. The hand that for hours without repining held the unlucky rod was the hand that for years continued to paint pictures, though they would not sell. At Petworth he pursued his angling with systematic ardour; and, when he went to revisit the scenes of his childhood at Brentford, or walked over from his house at Twickenham to call upon his friend Mr Trimmer at Heston, he invariably appeared carrying his rod. One of Mr Trimmer's sons, still living, well remembers seeing Turner sit on the lawn at Brentford, fishing in a pond for carp. It was a raging wet, dreary day; but the indomitable sportsman mitigated its severities by adopting a kitchen chair for his seat and a board for resting his feet on; and, thus equipped, with one hand he held his huge umbrella, and with the other his rod. The weather was as undesirable as it possibly could be; but there he sat till the dinner bell rang, with the quiet fortitude of a hero, not to be lightly turned from his piscatorial purpose.

It is highly probable that the melancholy monotony of sport under such uninviting conditions was relieved to Turner by the sense of being amid Nature; and it is not unlikely that even on that wet day he carefully noted its special features – the ripples, reflections, and eddies of the water, the gleams of green weed and the silvery glances of the sullen fish. All these, it may be, were garnered up in that vast and tenacious memory which no note-taking habits could weaken.

DAVID CAIRNCROSS: from *The Origin of the Silver Eel, with Remarks on Bait and Fly-fishing* (1862).

The reader may at once be informed that the progenitor of the silver eel is a small beetle. The study of its nature and habits has occupied my attention for the period above mentioned*. That it truly is the progenitor of the silver eel I feel fully satisfied in my own mind, from a rigid and extensive comparison of its structure and habits with those of other insects. This will be the reader's opinion too, I feel assured, after he has fairly weighed the array of facts brought before him, and tested the conclusions naturally flowing from them by actual experiment. As my own mind is now fully made up on the subject, I have at last yielded to the solicitation of my scientific friends, and fearless of the result I send it forth to the world.

*Sixty years.

* * *

Two farmers were the first to credit my statements concerning the origin of the silver eel; one of them had some land lying near a marsh whose water ran over a projecting rock from thirty to forty feet high, and falling over it with such force as in no part of its descent to touch the rock. They drained this marsh by digging an open ditch through the centre of it. As the work of draining proceeded they came upon quantities of silver eels, for whose presence in that spot they could in no way account. Hearing of my discovery, they applied to me for information. Going up the drain one day with them, I captured a few beetles, and informed them that these insects were the parents of the eels; they believed me, and rejoiced in the solution of the mystery.

JONATHAN COUCH: from *A History of British Fishes* (1865).

The Pike has been long popularly known as characterized by an eager and almost indiscriminate appetite, accompanied with great boldness in all that relates to the satisfying of its cravings; and numerous stories illustrative of this are recorded in books of Natural History. We will quote a few of these, from writers that are less accessible to readers in general, in order to shew this predominant disposition of what has been termed the tyrant of the lake and stream; and in which its voracity equals, if it does not exceed, even that of the generality of Sharks; although from its more limited powers and opportunities it does not usually display them on the higher animals or man. The naturalist Jonston quotes Rondeletius as saying (what I do not find in my copy of that author, 1554 AD) that a friend of his had stopped on the border of the Rhone that his mule might drink, when a Pike seized the animal by the lower lip, and held it so fast, that as the animal started backward the fish was lifted out of the water and secured. Another of these fishes was known to have seized the foot of a young woman as she held it naked in a pond.

A more modern instance of similar ferocity is given from Mr Pennell's *Angler Naturalist*, as quoted in the *Athenæum*; and the half-starved condition of the fish in this case will help us to understand the influence which was at work in the other instances, to drive these fishes to the remarkable manifestations of boldness reported of them: A young gentleman, 'aged fifteen, went with three other boys to bathe in Inglemere Pond, near Ascot race course, in June, 1856: he walked gently into the water to about the depth of four feet, when he spread out his hands to attempt to swim; instantly a large fish came up and took his hand into his mouth as far as the wrist, but finding he could not swallow it, relinquished his hold, and the boy turning round, prepared for a hasty retreat out of the pond; his companions who saw it also scrambled out as fast as possible'. He 'had scarcely turned himself round when the fish came up behind him, and immediately seized his other hand crosswise, inflicting some very deep wounds on the back of it; the boy raised his first bitten and still bleeding arm, and struck the monster a hard blow on the head, when the fish disappeared'. Seven wounds were dressed on one hand, 'and so great was the pain the next day, that the lad fainted twice; the little finger was bitten through the nail, and it was more than six weeks before it was well. The nail came off, and the scar remains to this day. A few days after this occurrence one of the woodmen was walking by the side of the pond, when he saw something white floating'. It was found to be a large Pike in a dying state, and he brought it to the shore, 'and the boy at once recognised his antagonist. The fish appeared to have been a long time in the agonies of death, and the body was very lean and curved like a bow. It measured forty-one inches, and died the next day. There can be no doubt the fish was in a state of complete starvation. If well fed it is probable it might have weighed from thirty to forty pounds'. In Dr Crull's *Present State of Muscovy* (1698), mention is made of a Pike that when taken was found to have an infant child in its stomach.

*   *   *

But although delayed by a muddled or nauseous condition of the water, Eels are not to be hindered by mechanical difficulties; and it is amusing to trace the means to which they have recourse in passing over barriers that might seem inaccessible to their efforts. It was at a time when a moderate but rapid stream had from dry weather become a small cascade, that the only way of ascent was up the declivity of a perpendicular rock, from which on one side hung some moss and herbage into the water below. When these Eels in succession came to this place they moved about rapidly near where the stream fell down from above, and presently disappeared; when looking more closely it was seen that on one side of the projecting rock they had crept among the fibres of the moss that hung downward, and were moving upwards with wriggling motion, like worms; but resting at times and taking care to keep at a safe distance from the falling current. At last they reached the top and settled into rest, with the head a little stretched out into the river; but after a time, seizing a favourable moment of recovered energy, they put out their renewed strength and moved upward in the stream. Those of them, however, which had taken the other side of the rock were differently situated, and their task was to thrust themselves over a sloping surface by dint of their unaided exertions; in accomplishing which some quitted the water altogether; but they still kept on a moist portion of the ascent, up which by a slow and laboriously serpentine action they contrived to urge their way to reach at last some moss, the support of which they hastily made use of to secure success. It was amusing to observe that it would sometimes happen that a head would be thrust out into the current, where observation shewed that it ran by too strong to be encountered, and then it was withdrawn to seek a more favourable spot; while others venturing thus too far were washed down the current, and had the labour to go over again. On one occasion while watching this continued succession of Eels, a Flounder made two attempts to stem this downward current, but these efforts were without success.

Similar to the extended notice of this migration that we have given is one by Mr Arderon, in the *Transactions of the Royal Society, Volume xliv*, who saw them as they passed up the floodgates of the water-works at Norwich, of the height of six feet, in order to reach the water above; and we close our account of this interesting subject of the influence of instinct, with an extract bearing on the same, from Jesse's second series of *Gleanings in Natural History*, where, referring to the Thames, he says, 'At the locks at Teddington and Hampton the young Eels have

been seen to ascend the large posts of the floodgates, in order to make
their way when the gates have been shut longer than usual. Those which
die stick to the posts; others, which get a little higher, meet the same fate,
until at last a sufficient layer of them is formed to enable the rest to
overcome the difficulty of the passage. A curious instance of the means
which young Eels will have recourse to in order to accomplish their
migrations, is annually proved in the neighbourhood of Bristol. Near
that city there is a large pond, immediately adjoining which is a stream.
On the bank between these two waters a large tree grows, the branches
of which hang into the pond. By means of these branches the young Eels
climb up into the tree, and from thence let themselves drop into the
stream below, thus migrating to far-distant waters, where they increase
in size, and become useful and beneficial to man. A friend of mine, who
was a casual witness of this circumstance, informed me that the tree
appeared to be quite alive with those little animals. The rapid and
unsteady motion of the boughs did not appear to impede their progress'.

H. CHOLMONDELEY PENNELL (ed.): from *Dum Capimus
Capimur*. From *Fishing Gossip, or Stray Leaves from the Note-books of
Several Anglers* (1866).

Gudgeon – Hurley – Julia – Nothing particularly exceptional or con-
gruous surely in these three substantives that they should insist upon
presenting themselves to my mental camera in such pertinacious juxta-
position? Nice, silky, euphemistic words they are, no doubt – words
naturally suggestive of gurgling water, whispering willows, and what
Barney Maguire calls the 'laste taste in life' of *dilettante* sentimentalism –
but is that any reason for their ringing the changes in a sort of 'grand
chain' through my head all night, and taking me a regular slap in the face
this morning the moment I opened my eyes upon the quadrangle of old
Trinity Hall? Heigh-ho! who'd have thought that a week's gudgeon-
fishing would have produced such psychological manifestations? And
am I not lying, too, in saying that 'gudgeon' is a euphemistic word?
Distinctly: one more *un*-euphonious it would perhaps be a puzzler to
name; and so evidently thought Izaak Walton's poet, Jo Chalkill, when
he was driven to find a rhyme for it in *sturgeon*. Poor Jo! 'gudgeon' was
evidently altogether too much for him. Elsewhere he tries his hand at it
again with even worse success:

> Roach or dace
> We do chase,
> Bleak or gudgeon
> Without *grudging*.

Awful! He might at least have improved upon this, by adopting the spelling of Davors:

> And thou, sweet Boyd, that with thy watery sway
>   Dost wash the cliffes of Deighton and of Week . . .
> In whose fair streams the speckled trout doth play,
>   The roach, the dace, the *gudging*, and the bleike.

How much more neatly 'John Williamson, gent, temp. 1740', manages the matter:

> Tho' little art the gudgeon may suffice,
> His sport is good, and with the greatest vies;
> Few lessons will the angler's use supply
> Where he's so ready of himself to die!

Well, be the difficulty great or small, there certainly *is* a peculiar fascination in catching, if not in poetising, gudgeon. Doesn't Salter tell us of an angling curate who was engaged to be married to a bishop's daughter, lingering so long over his twelve-dozenth fish as to arrive too late for the ceremony, whereupon his lady declined to be wedded to a man who preferred his basket to his bride?

Wasn't Sir Isaac Newton, like his great piscatorial namesake, master of the art of catching gudgeon? as well as Bacon, Gay, Cecil, Hollinshed, and a host of other celebrities? Why, even our neighbours over the Channel take naturally to it. Moule's *Fish Heraldry* tells us that it was the cognisance of John Goujon, one of the first French sculptors of the sixteenth century; and old Salter says that in the waters round Ghent 'it is the general practice to angle for it with a bit of raw sheep's liver'. (How a Thames gudgeon would turn up his nose at such a plebeian bait!)

In a gastronomic point of view, *gobio* gives precedence to none: a fry of fat gudgeon, eaten piping hot, with a squeeze of lemon-juice, is a dish 'to set before a king', and as superior to anything that Greenwich or Blackwall can produce, as Mouet's champagne is to gooseberry pop. John Williamson, gent, aforesaid, who seems to have had a keen eye to the good things of this life, commends the gudgeon 'for a fish of an excellent nourishment, easy of digestion, *and increasing good blood'*. Nay, even as a cure for desperate diseases, the gudgeon is not without his encomiasts; for Dr Brookes says, in his *History of Fishes*, that he 'is thought good for a consumption, *and by many swallowed alive'*; though it is to be presumed that the fish so disposed of were not of the same size as the four from Uxbridge, to which the doctor refers immediately afterwards as 'weighing a pound' each.

Dr Brookes' remedy reminds one of Madame de Genlis' prescription for a less serious attack. On being charged by her companions, one day when out fishing, with being a 'fine Paris lady', she suddenly snatched up a fresh-caught gudgeon, and exclaiming, 'This will show whether I am a fine Paris lady!' swallowed it alive, to the utter discomfiture of her tormentors, who declined to follow her in so vivisectional a test of fashion.

Galloway, the fisherman at Chertsey, tells, I remember, a good story of two old gentlemen, 'mighty gudgeon-fishers', who were in the habit of betting heavily on their respective 'takes'; till at last the old fellow who almost always won was discovered with a *silk casting-net* stowed away under the boards of his punt! Almost as great a sell that, as the parson losing his wife! This piscatorial clergyman, by the way, lived at Hampton; and if any Cockney wishes to remember the best gudgeon grounds, let him not forget his *H*'s. Curious how many there are of them scattered up and down the Thames – Hampton, Halliford, Harleyford, Hurley, Henley all beginning with the eighth letter of the alphabet, and all redolent of gudgeon-fishing. Gudgeon-fishing! which I maintain to be, *par excellence*, the sport of the poet and the philosopher.

JOHN RUSKIN: from *The Crown of Wild Olive* (1866).

Twenty years ago, there was no lovelier piece of lowland scenery in South England, nor any more pathetic, in the world, by its expression of sweet human character and life, than that immediately bordering on the sources of the Wandel, and including the low moors of Addington, and the villages of Beddington and Carshalton, with all their pools and streams. No clearer or diviner waters ever sang with constant lips of the hand which 'giveth rain from heaven'; no pastures ever lightened in spring-time with more passionate blossoming; no sweeter homes ever

hallowed the heart of the passer-by with their pride of peaceful glad-
ness, – fain-hidden – yet full-confessed. The place remains (1870)
nearly unchanged in its larger features; but with deliberate mind I say,
that I have never seen anything so ghastly in its inner tragic meaning, –
not in Pisan Maremma, – not by Campagna tomb, – not by the
sand-isles of the Torcellan shore, – as the slow stealing of aspects of
reckless, indolent, animal neglect, over the delicate sweetness of that
English scene: nor is any blasphemy or impiety, any frantic saying, or
godless thought, more appalling to me, using the best power of judgment I have to discern its sense and scope, than the insolent defiling of
those springs by the human herds that drink of them. Just where the
welling of stainless water, trembling and pure, like a body of light,
enters the pool of Carshalton, cutting itself a radiant channel down to
the gravel, through warp of feathery weeds, all waving, which it traverses with its deep threads of clearness, like the chalcedony in moss-
agate, starred here and there with the white grenouillette; just in the
very rush and murmur of the first spreading currents, the human
wretches of the place cast their street and house foulness; heaps of
dust and slime, and broken shreds of old metal, and rags of putrid
clothes; which, having neither energy to cart away, nor decency
enough to dig into the ground, they thus shed into the stream, to
diffuse what venom of it will float and melt, far away, in all places
where God meant those waters to bring joy and health. And, in a little
pool behind some houses farther in the village, where another spring
rises, the shattered stones of the well, and of the little fretted channel
which was long ago built and traced for it by gentler hands, lie
scattered, each from each, under a ragged bank of mortar, and scoria,
and bricklayer's refuse, on one side, which the clean water nevertheless chastises to purity; but it cannot conquer the dead earth beyond:
and there, circled and coiled under festering scum, the stagnant edge
of the pool effaces itself into a slope of black slime, the accumulation of
indolent years. Half-a-dozen men, with one day's work could cleanse
those pools, and trim the flowers about their banks, and make every
breath of summer air above them rich with cool balm; and every
glittering wave medicinal, as if it ran, troubled only of angels, from the
porch of Bethesda. But that day's work is never given, nor, I suppose,
will be; nor will any joy be possible to heart of man, for evermore,
about those wells of English waters.

SIR SAMUEL W. BAKER: from *The Nile Tributaries of Abyssinia*
(1867).

In the afternoon I arranged my tackle, and strolled down to the pool to
fish. There was a difficulty in procuring bait; a worm was never heard
of in the burning deserts of Nubia, neither had I a net to catch small
fish; I was therefore obliged to bait with pieces of hippopotamus.
Fishing in such a pool as that of the Atbara was sufficiently exciting, as
it was impossible to speculate upon what creature might accept the
invitation; but the Arabs who accompanied me were particular in
guarding me against the position I had taken under a willow-bush
close to the water, as they explained, that most probably a crocodile
would take me instead of the bait; they declared that accidents had
frequently happened when people had sat upon the bank either to
drink with their hands, or even while watching their goats. I accordingly fished at a few feet distant from the margin, and presently I had a
bite: I landed a species of perch about two pounds' weight; this was the
'boulti', one of the best Nile fish mentioned by the traveller Bruce. In a
short time I had caught a respectable dish of fish, but hitherto no
monster had paid me the slightest attention; accordingly I changed my
bait, and upon a powerful hook, fitted upon treble-twisted wire, I
fastened an enticing strip of a boulti. The bait was about four ounces,
and glistened like silver; the water was tolerably clear, but not too
bright, and with such an attraction I expected something heavy. My
float was a large-sized pike-float for live bait, and this civilized sign had
been only a few minutes in the wild waters of the Atbara, when, bob!
and away it went! I had a very large reel, with nearly three hundred
yards of line that had been specially made for monsters; down went the
top of my rod, as though a grindstone was suspended on it, and, as I
recovered its position, away went the line, and the reel revolved, not
with the sudden dash of a spirited fish, but with the steady determined
pull of a trotting horse. What on earth have I got hold of? In a few
minutes about a hundred yards of line were out, and as the creature
was steadily but slowly travelling down the centre of the channel, I
determined to cry 'halt!' if possible, as my tackle was extremely strong,
and my rod was a single bamboo. Accordingly, I put on a power strain,
which was replied to by a sullen tug, a shake, and again my rod was
pulled suddenly down to the water's edge. At length, after the roughest
handling, I began to reel in slack line, as my unknown friend had
doubled in upon me; and upon once more putting severe pressure

upon him or her, as it might be, I perceived a great swirl in the water about twenty yards from the rod. The tackle would bear anything and I strained so heavily upon my adversary, that I soon reduced our distance; but the water was exceedingly deep, the bank precipitous, and he was still invisible. At length, after much tugging and counter-tugging, he began to show; eagerly I gazed into the water to examine my new acquaintance, when I made out something below, in shape between a coach-wheel and a sponging-bath; in a few moments more I brought to the surface an enormous turtle, well hooked. I felt like the old lady who won an elephant in a lottery: that I had him was certain, but what was I to do with my prize? It was at the least a hundred pounds' weight, and the bank was steep and covered with bushes; thus it was impossible to land the monster, that now tugged and dived with the determination of the grindstone that his first pull had suggested. Once I attempted the gaff, but the trusty weapon that had landed many a fish in Scotland broke in the hard shell of the turtle, and I was helpless. My Arab now came to my assistance, and at once terminated the struggle. Seizing the line with both hands, utterly regardless of all remonstrance (which, being in English, he did not understand), he quickly hauled our turtle to the surface, and held it, struggling and gnashing its jaws, close to the steep bank. In a few moments the line slackened, and the turtle disappeared. The fight was over! The sharp horny jaws had bitten through treble-twisted brass wire as clean as though cut by shears. My visions of turtle soup had faded.

GEORGE ROOPER: from *The Autobiography of the Late Salmo Salar, Esq. comprising a narrative of the Life, Personal Adventures and Death of a Tweed Salmon* (1867).

'The sea-lice which had clung to our scales, unable to exist in the fresh water, had dropped off, and no care or trouble was present. A restless feeling had, indeed, arisen within me, and I was on the point of suggesting to my companions a movement higher and still higher up the stream, when my attention was attracted by what appeared to me a familiar object – a shrimp or prawn, or some other small object of the ocean so lately quitted, and which had furnished me with many a beautiful meal. It floated gently over my head, not over bright in colour, but showy, and its hues, which were dispersed uniformly over its body, blended together, and formed one harmonious whole. Its movements were short and rapid, such as are those of the insects – "Crustaceæ", I think, is the proper term – I have referred to, and it seemed to be striving, with doubtful result, to stem the somewhat rapid stream. What induced me I cannot say: I was not hungry; indeed, I had felt no desire to eat since I entered the fresh water; I was hardly in the mood for play, for I felt that the serious business of life was before me; but, impelled by some unaccountable impulse, I rose from my resting-place, and attempted to seize it in my mouth. The motion was rapid, but still too slow to be effectual; the creature vanished ere my lips could close on it. Whilst turning slowly round to seek my former station – somewhat sulkily, too, for the object I had failed to attain had, in consequence, acquired a value it had not previously possessed – I heard a voice say, –

'"Ay, but that was a bonny grilse! Ay, but it was a grand rise he made, too! Ye were ower quick in striking."

'"I think I was," was the reply, "but we'll try again."

'"Bide a wee, sir; bide a wee; give him time to return to his old station before you show him the flee again."

'Utterly unconscious of the meaning of these words, and in no respect connecting them with myself or my doings, I saw with some surprise, not unmixed with pleasure, the little jerking figure again passing within three feet of my nose. There was a band of silver round its throat that excited my cupidity, and I was, moreover, somewhat nettled at the failure of my previous attempt to seize it. Without a moment's pause, I dashed at it, and, seizing the bright wings between my lips, was prepared, at least, to carry it down with me, to be swallowed or not, as might happen; when, to my amazement and alarm, ere I could as much as turn away, after my spring, the creature snatched itself from out my very jaws, and vanished as it had previously done. Sulky and annoyed, I sought again my resting-place, and again I heard the same voice which had before spoken, –

'"Deed, sir, ye were just ower hasty again; ye dinna let the fash tak' a grip of the flee before you snatch it out of his mouth."

'"Never mind, Sandy; we'll try again."

'"A'm thinking I'll just change the flee; mebbe he's seen ower muckle of this ane."

'Read from the light of after-experience, these words were plain enough; but, young and inexperienced as I was, they conveyed no meaning, no warning, and it can hardly be wondered at that, tantalized as I had been, no sooner did I see a creature similar in form and habit to the other, but somewhat larger and brighter, apparently striving to stem the stream a little above me, than, again dashing at it, I seized it firmly in my teeth, and, turning round, was going back to my lair, when I felt a sharp, smarting pain, a convulsive shock shook my frame, and I found myself madly struggling against some great, unknown, invisible power, which controlled my will, and, for a time at least, rendered me helpless, almost hopeless.

'Willing to realize the worst, and anxious to learn something certain respecting my condition, I rushed upwards, and, jumping high in the air, saw two men standing on the bank, with whose movements, with reference to my own position, I had no difficulty in tracing the connexion. The one with a long rod in his hand, the line from which restrained and controlled me, stood motionless; whilst the other, with a horrible hook attached to the end of a stick in his hand, seemed to be aiding and advising him.

'"Canny, lad," I heard him say; "canny, noo; he is but light heukit; I ken by his jumping. Canny, noo; he's just a fresh-run grilse, an' his mouth unco saft."

'I had heard enough; and by this time my terror had somewhat abated, and my natural energy returned in aid of the strength with which I was gifted. No longer coursing about the pool with aimless rapidity, or wasting my strength in fruitless jumps, I dropped back gradually into the deep pool behind, and, sinking to the bottom, lay motionless behind the big rock I had so lately quitted. My companion kept ever beside me, and, though she could render no assistance, her presence was an aid and consolation to me, and I felt cooler and stronger for her sympathy. Aided by the weight of water above me, I defied the power still exercised by my persecutor to move me. I felt but little pain, and, but for the choking sensation occasioned by the interference of the free passage of water through my gills, little annoyance; and it was only on observing a huge stone thrown for the purpose of dislodging me, descending directly upon my head, that I started from my lair. Rushing wildly away, my escape was brought about by the very means intended for my destruction. Impeded by the line, my movement was slow, and the stone, barely missing me, fell upon the line itself, released the hook from the slight hold it had in my mouth, and I felt that I was free! Joyous, exulting in my deliverance, I again sought the surface, and, as I jumped two or three times out of the water, I had the satisfaction of observing visible marks of disappointment and regret on the countenances of my friends on shore. The one stood with his rod straight upwards, his line floating down the stream, himself in the precise attitude in which he had maintained that dead, strong pull against me, which, by exhausting my strength, had so nearly proved fatal; the other was apparently solacing himself with a pinch of snuff, and the only words I heard him utter were, –

'"Ay, but that was a bonny grilse! Deil tak' the stane!"'

JAMES GREENWOOD: from *The Purgatory of Peter the Cruel* (1868).

There could no longer be a doubt as to what his fate was. 'He don't appear very lively,' remarked one of the young gentlemen as he took Peter between his forefinger and thumb. It would have been astonishing if he had, unless the liveliness he displayed were that of madness and despair. Now indeed was the purport of that mysterious conversation made clear to him! He was to wriggle and kick on a fish-hook, and the fish were the hungry savages who where to come and bite at him. It was singular that he should have remained in ignorance so long, since, as a boy, he had, when fishing for small fry, impaled a fly on a hook, ay, and on a crooked brass pin, for that matter, many and many a time.

'The proper way is to stick the barb right through him, is it not?' enquired the young monster who had the custody of Peter, and who, as he spoke, held the point of the cold, cruel hook within an inch of the victim's eyes. They were evidently inexperienced fishermen.

'Not right through the body where his heart and that is, would you?' replied the other dubiously.

'Why not? Are you afraid I shall hurt him?'

'Oh no. Because the more you hurt him the more he'll wriggle and kick, and the better sport we shall have; but you see, if you don't mind how you fix him he'll die directly, and that would be a pity. Suppose you stick it through his wings?'

'Stay a moment! I know a better way than either. Let us tie a bit of our fine silk round his body, and so fasten him to the hook. He may serve for more than one cast then, if we are lucky.'

Fainting in terror as he was when he heard these words, Peter feebly opened one eye and cast a look of gratitude on the person who had uttered them. Anything, anything rather than that either of the previous suggestions should be adopted.

And so they fastened him. It was a painful and tedious operation, and when it was completed Peter felt as though the encircling silk must cut him in halves, but the recollection of what he had escaped fortified him, and presently he was swung out, and fell souse into the stream.

This however, though for the moment startling, was, as far as it went, a change for the better. The cool, sparkling water comforted his cramped and aching limbs, and, presently venturing to sip a little of it, he felt quite refreshed. Not that his were prospects the enjoyment of which demanded the full and unimpaired use of one's faculties. Nothing but death was before him, and it was therefore rather an advantage to have a foot or two over the cold threshold, since his whole body must inevitably follow presently.

Peter found it not at all difficult to sustain himself in the water, although he was burdened by the weight of the tiny hook, and was rather inclined to lie still on the surface, knowing that to wriggle and kick would be exactly the way to rouse some spiky-toothed monster lurking beneath a weed or stone, and so hasten his own destruction. But he was not allowed to remain passive. It was expected of him that he should kick and wriggle, and since he did not choose to do so voluntarily, his persecutors compelled him by moving the line gently up and down.

'He is a lazy beggar!' he heard a voice on the bank exclaim.

'You had better have hung him on the hook, I think; suppose you untie him and stick him on now?'

'Hush! Don't make a noise! There's a fine fellow rising at him now; he looks hungry, and as though he meant mischief.'

Hearing this, Peter was so alarmed that he made an upward jump, and instantly the 'fine fellow' rose and marked him. Had Peter been in his human shape he would have observed nothing more remarkable about the fish except that it was of the stickleback breed, and that it was large and very handsome in colour; but regarding it through his tiny bluebottle eyes it presented a very different appearance. Its sides were armed with horny plates similar to those that protect the rhinoceros; along its back were three upreared spikes, each formidable to impale a bluebottle; its glaring eyes were set in rigid bony sockets, and its jaws ever open and shutting disclosed a double row of teeth, compared with which, as to sharpness, the point of a needle was blunt as a pin's head. As the fish's eyes and Peter's met, the former set back his grisly lips and opened his mouth snarling like a cat, so that the affrighted bluebottle could see into it as far down as its gullet. Then the stickleback made a sudden rush forward, and Peter closed his eyes, making sure that it was all over.

GEORGE ELIOT: from *Middlemarch* (1871).

'I hear what you are talking about,' said the wife. 'But you will make no impression on Humphrey. As long as the fish rise to his bait, everybody is what he ought to be. Bless you, Casaubon has got a trout-stream, and does not care about fishing in it himself: could there be a better fellow?'

  'Well, there is something in that,' said the Rector, with his quiet inward laugh. 'It is a very good quality in a man to have a trout-stream.'

REV. FRANCIS KILVERT: from *The Diary* (Monday, 4 July 1872).

We came to a bank above the Wye where a group of men were standing looking across the river. A man was standing near the further shore up to his knees in water salmon fishing. A gentleman was on the bank close by watching him. We stopped to look and the men told us that the man fishing was the keeper of Mr Bulten of Llangoed and the gentleman watching him was Mr Bulten himself. The keeper had been fishing about ten minutes when we saw the top of the long rod suddenly bend and at the same moment heard the sharp clicking of the reel as the line flew out. A salmon was hooked and as the keeper drew him in, we saw the fish leap shining in the air, plunge heavily, and lash the water fiercely with his tail. Again he rushed out and again he was wound up rolling over in the water and turning up his great sides flashing in the sun. At last he was near the bank. The keeper gave his master the rod, waded back into the river and seized the salmon by the tail. Then the great fish burst away from him, but was seized again immediately, and triumphantly brought to land. When the salmon was held up we could see he was a long heavy fish. The men round us said he was not less than twenty-five pounds. Mr Bulten knocked him on the head with great gusto and then proceeded to weigh him with a pocket steelyard. We were in the very lap of luck to arrive at that moment for Jones had never seen a salmon killed and particularly wished to witness the catching of one. He might not have such a piece of luck again for years. The salmon was splendidly played and landed within ten minutes from the time when he was first hooked. Alluding to Mr Bulten, who was at the moment vigorously knocking the salmon on the head across the river, one of the men said, addressing Pope, 'I don't know whether I ought to speak of it to you, Sir. You'll excuse my mentioning it, but that old gentleman has had five wives'.

THE VERY REV. PATRICK MURRAY SMYTHE: from *The Diary of an All-round Angler: 1872* (edited by Patrick C. Smythe 1956).

11 March [twelve years old] We went a walk to the Pit and Bradney had a bit of stick on a string which he lent me and I took two fishes. In the afternoon Ward and I got leave to get violets in that field so we set two to catch some more and I got fourteen four of which I got by two at a time he caught some others.

Altogether sixteen sticklebacks.

16 June Coming back from Church caught a minnow with my hands. I ate minnow.

13 August Went to fish in the Almond with Frankie, Mr Cowan and Jimmy Scott at a bridge near Lynedoch. Having fished for about an hour without a bite got two which I missed then left my rod for a little while I crossed the bridge to get a worm when I came back I found my rod shaking so lugged it out and found my first eel a very small one on the end in a few minutes I caught MY FIRST TROUT very soon I caught another then I went to a rapid where I caught a small trout and then under a stone a big one of a quarter of a pound or five ounces after which I caught two more and tumbled in to finish my fun.

Altogether six trout, one eel.

FRANK BUCKLAND: from *A Familiar History of British Fishes* (1873).

Tittler Fishing

Most anglers will confess that they were first entered into the sport by fishing for sticklebacks, which abound in all the ponds and ditches in the neighbourhood of London, they are also very common in canals, especially in the Regent's Park Canal. In the summer-time, thousands of little boys go out fishing for 'tittlers', their apparatus consisting of a stick, a piece of thread, and a short piece of worm tied in the middle without any hook; if expert, they sometimes pull out two at a time in this way. The fashion is to take them home in pickle-bottles; and the boys generally sell them, sometimes getting as much as sixpence a bottleful. I always encourage these boys, as the little urchins are thus taken out of the London streets, and have a chance of learning a little natural history. There are seven species of sticklebacks.

Pickled Minnows

The *Minnow*, or Pink (*Cyprinus phoxinus, Leuciscus phoxinus*), is a lovely little fish, especially in spawning time, when the gentlemen wear green and red coats. It is a very gregarious species, and shoals are to be found in almosty every shallow river, especially in clear weather; for they seem to delight in warmth and sunshine. The flesh of the minnow is delicate and of good flavour. When at Winchester, I used to pickle minnows with vinegar and spice, and keep them in pickle bottles. They were capital eating, especially when, as 'a junior', I was not over-fed, and had to look out for what extra 'grub' I could get hold of. Wherever there are plenty of minnows the trout are always good: minnows should be introduced into trout streams.

Another small and familiar species is the *Loach*, or Beardie (*Cobitis barbatula*), always readily distinguished by having six barbules about the mouth. Like other fishes provided with these appendages, it feeds at, or near, the bottom of the river, and, from its habit of lurking beneath stones, it is so often overlooked as to be sometimes considered scarce. It is, however, not uncommon in our rivers and brooks. From its slimy smoothness and activity it is very difficult to catch. The Winchester boys used to spear this fish with an ordinary fork tied on to the end of a stick, and then pickle him with the minnows. It forms an excellent bait for eels, and Mr Thames Trout will sometimes take him, if he is properly and artistically spun.

CHARLES HALLOCK: from *The Fishing Tourist* (1873).

There are some kinds of fish, comely in appearance, bold biters, and rather successful torturers of fine tackle, which are styled *game-fish* and angled for as such, but which by no means deserve the name and reputation. Such customers may possibly 'pass in a crowd', as the shabby genteel frequently do among the masses of human society. But the superior qualities and attributes of the true game-fish are readily detected.

Define me a *gentleman* and I will define you a 'game' fish; which the same is known by the company he keeps, and recognized by his dress and address, features, habits, intelligence, haunts, food, and manner of eating. The true game-fish, of which the trout and salmon are frequently the types, inhabit the fairest regions of nature's beautiful domain. They drink only from the purest fountains, and subsist upon the choicest food their pellucid streams supply. Not to say that all fish that inhabit clear and sparkling waters are game fish: for there are many such, of symmetrical form and delicate flavor, that take neither bait nor fly. But it is self-evident that no fish which inhabit foul or sluggish waters can be 'game-fish'. It is impossible from the very circumstances of their surroundings and associations. They may flash with tinsel and tawdry attire; they may strike with the brute force of a blacksmith, or exhibit the dexterity of a prize-fighter, but their low breeding and vulgar quality cannot be mistaken. Their haunts, their very food and manner of eating, betray their grossness.

GERARD MANLEY HOPKINS: from his Journal (1873).

8 August Wan white sea with a darker edge on the skyline, very calm. At sunset from above it looked milky blue with blue cording of waves. Sunset fine – spokes of dusty gold; long wing of brownish cloud warping in the perspective. I marked well how the sea fell over from the other side of the bay, Fort Hillion and the lighthouse, to the cliff's foot, quite like the rounding of a waterfall.

9 August Mackerel fishing but not much sport. Besides I was in pain and could not look at things much. When the fresh-caught fish flounced in the bottom of the boat they made scapes of motion, quite as  strings do, nodes and all, silver bellies upwards – something thus. Their key markings do not correspond on the two sides of the backbone. They changed colour as they lay. There was sun and wind. I saw the waves to seaward frosted with light silver surf but did not find out much, afterwards from the cliffs I saw the sea paved with wind – clothed and purpled all over with ribbons of wind.

W. C. PRIME: from *I go a-fishing* (1873).

Fishermen never lose their love for the employment. And it is notably true that the men who fish for a living love their work quite as much as those who fish for pleasure love their sport. Find an old fisherman, if you can, in any sea-shore town, who does not enjoy his fishing. There are days, without doubt, when he does not care to go out, when he would rather that need did not drive him to the sea; but keep him at home a few days, or set him at other labour, and you shall see that he longs for the toss of the swell on the reef, and the sudden joy of a strong pull on his line. Drift up alongside of him in your boat when he is quietly at his work, without his knowing that you are near. You can do it easily. He is pondering solemnly a question of deep importance to him, and he has not stirred eye, or hand, or head for ten minutes. But see that start and sharp jerk of his elbow, and now hear him talk, not to you – to the fish. He exults as he brings him in, yet mingles his exultation with something of pity as he baits his hook for another. Could you gather the words that he has in many years flung on the sea-winds, you would have a history of his life and adventures, mingled with very much of his inmost thinking, for he tells much to the sea and the fish that he would never whisper in human ears. Thus the habit of going a-fishing always modifies the character. The angler, I think, dreams of his favourite sport oftener than other men of theirs. There is a peculiar excitement in it, which perhaps arises from somewhat of the same causes which make the interest in searching for ancient treasures, opening Egyptian tombs, and digging into old ruins. One does not know what is under the surface. There may be something or there may be nothing. He tries, and the rush of something startles every nerve. Let no man laugh at a comparison of trout-fishing with antiquarian researches. I know a man who has done a great deal of both, and who scarcely knows which is most absorbing or most remunerating; for each enriches mind and body, each gratifies the most refined tastes, each becomes a passion unless the pursuer guard his enthusiasm and moderate his desires.

It is nothing strange that men who throw their flies for trout should dream of it.

As long ago as when Theocritus wrote his Idyls, men who caught fish dreamed of their sport or work, whichever it was. It can not, indeed, be said that the Greek fisherman dreamed of the mere excitement of fishing, for to him the sea was a place of toil, and his poor hut was but a miserable hovel. He fished for its reward in gold; and he dreamed that he took a fish of gold, whose value would relieve him from the pains and toils of his life, and when he was awake he feared that he had bound himself by an oath in his dream, and his wise companion – philosopher then, as all anglers were, and are, and will be evermore – relieved him by a brief sermon, wherein lies a moral. Look it up, and read it. What angler does not dream of great fish rising with heavy roll and plunge to seize the fly? What dreams those are!

Is there anything strange, then, in the question whether Peter in his slumber never dreamed of the great fish in the Sea of Galilee, or the gentle John, in his old age and weary longing for the end, did not sometimes recall in sleep other and more earthly scenes than the sublime visions of inspiration? Do you doubt – I do not – that his great soul, over which had swept floods of emotion such as few other human souls have ever experienced, was yet so fresh and young, even in the days of rock-bound Patmos, and long after at Ephesus, when he counted a hundred years of life, that in sleep he sometimes sat in his boat, rocked by the waves of the blue Gennesaret, his black locks shaking in the breeze that came down from Hermon, his eyes wandering from Tabor to Gilboa, from Gilboa to Lebanon, from Lebanon to the wild hills of the Gadarenes, while he caught the shy but beautiful fish that were born in the Jordan, and lived in the waters that were by Capernaum and Bethsaida?

To you, my friend, who know nothing of the gentle and purifying associations of the angler's life, these may seem strange notions – to some, indeed, they may even sound profane. But the angler for whom I write, will not so think them, nor may I, who, thinking these same thoughts, have cast my line on the Sea of Galilee, and taken the descendants of old fish in the swift waters of the Jordan.

* * *

In the name of sense, man, if God made fish to be eaten, what difference does it make if I enjoy the killing of them before I eat them? You would have none but a fisherman by trade do it, and then you would have him utter a sigh, a prayer, and a pious ejaculation at each cod or haddock that he killed; and if by chance the old fellow, sitting in the boat at his work, should for a moment think there was, after all, a little fun and a little pleasure in his business, you would have him take a round turn with his line, and drop on his knees to ask forgiveness for the sin of thinking there was sport in fishing.

I can imagine the sad-faced, melancholy-eyed man, who makes it his business to supply game for the market as you would have him, sober as the sexton in Hamlet, and for ever moralizing over the gloomy necessity that has doomed him to a life of murder! Why, sir, he would frighten respectable fish, and the market would soon be destitute.

The keenest day's *sport* in my journal of a great many years of sport was when, in company with some other gentlemen, I took three hundred blue-fish in three hours' fishing off Block Island, and those fish were eaten the same night or the next morning in Stonington, and supplied from fifty to a hundred different tables, as we threw them up on the dock for anyone to help himself. I am unable to perceive that I committed any sin in taking them, or any sin in the excitement and pleasure of taking them.

It is time moralists had done with this mistaken morality. If you eschew animal food entirely, then you may argue against killing animals, and I will not argue with you. But the logic of this business is simply this: the Creator made fish and flesh for the food of man, and as we can't eat them alive, or if we do we can't digest them alive, the result is we must kill them first, and (see the old rule for cooking a dolphin) it is sometimes a further necessity, since they won't come to be killed when we call them, that we must first catch them. Show first, then, that it is a painful necessity – a necessity to be avoided if possible – which a good man must shrink from and abhor, unless starved into it, to take fish or birds, and which he must do when he does it with regret, and with sobriety and seriousness, as he would whip his child, or shave himself when his beard is three days old, and you have your case. But till you show this, I will continue to think it great sport to supply my market with fish.

J. J. MANLEY: from *Notes on Fish and Fishing* (1877).

'De minimis non curat Lex' – 'The Law regards not minims' – is an old adage, but one which I must disregard for the nonce in continuing my notes on 'Small Fry', as I now come to 'Nature's minim', the Minnow, so called because he is a 'minim', the tiniest (Latin, *minimus*) of our fresh-water fish. The word 'Minnow' is seen in the old French *men-uise*, 'small fish', 'fry', – from *menu* 'small'.

An old English name for the minnow was 'pink'. Thus in the *Angler's Ballad*, in Cotton, we read –

> And full well you may think,
> If you troll with a *pink*,
One [ie fishing-rod,] too weak will be apt to miscarry.

This name, it is said, was given to our little fish from the 'pink' or rosy colour of its belly in summer. Or is the word really the old English *pink*, a small eye, an eyelet (*œillet*), eyelet-hole, and given as a title to the minnow on account of his smallness; or again is it the flower 'pink', also *œillet* in French?

The little fish, though a humble member of the family, takes his place among the *Cyprinidæ*, or Carp, which I have had occasion to mention so often as supplying most of our English fresh-water fish; and he is of the subgenus *Leucisci*, or White Fish, to which the roach and dace belong. His ichthyological name is *Leuciscus phoxinus* (Cuvier), or *Phoxinus lævis*; the Greek φοξός (connected with ὀξύς – 'sharp'?) signifying 'pointed'. Thersites, in the *Iliad*, has this term applied to his head, which was of the sugar-loaf type. But why it should be specially applied to the minnow I cannot understand, as he is no more 'pointed', or sugar-loafed, as to either head or tail, than many other fish.

But never mind – what a pretty little fellow he is! Not a prettier fish disports itself in our waters. Lay one, when in full season in the height of summer, on the palm of your hand, and examine and admire him. Mark his shape – a miniature salmon in symmetrical configuration.

Mark his beautiful colouring – every shade of olive, white, pale brown, silver, pink, and rosy, harmoniously blended, and producing that beautifully mottled appearance which reminds one of the mackerel and of the *Salmo fontinalis*, the lovely American brook-trout, which I hope before long will be naturalized in many of our rivers. Izaak Walton describes him in this way: 'The minnow when he is in perfect season hath a kind of dappled or waved colour, like a panther, on his sides, inclining to a greenish or sky colour'. These are evidently meant to be words of enthusiastic admiration, though, with all deference to our old master, somewhat unintelligible. But however we may describe him, no one with an eye to beauty can fail to admire the pretty little minim.

RICHARD JEFFERIES: from *The Gamekeeper at Home* (1878).

Fresh fish – that is, those who are new to that particular part of the brook – are, the poachers say, much more easily captured than those who have made it their home for some time. They are, in fact, more easily discovered; they have not yet found out the nooks and corners, the projecting roots and the hollows under the banks, the dark places where a black shadow falls from overhanging trees and is with difficulty pierced even by a practised eye. They expose themselves in open places, and meet an untimely fate.

Besides pike, tench are occasionally wired, and now and then, even a large roach; the tench, though a bottom fish, in the shallow brooks may be sometimes detected by the eye, and is not a difficult fish to capture. Every one has heard of tickling trout: the tench is almost equally amenable to titillation. Lying at full length on the sward, with his hat off lest it should fall into the water, the poacher peers down into the hole where he has reason to think tench may be found. This fish is so dark in colour when viewed from above that for a minute or two, till the sight adapts itself to the dull light of the water, the poacher cannot distinguish what he is searching for. Presently, having made out the position of the tench, he slips his bared arm in slowly, and without splash, and finds little or no trouble as a rule in getting his hand close to the fish without alarming it: tench, indeed, seem rather sluggish. He then passes his fingers under the belly and gently rubs it. Now it would appear that he has the fish in his power, and has only to grasp it. But grasping is not so easy; or rather it is not so easy to pull a fish up through two feet of superincumbent water which opposes the quick passage of the arm. The gentle rubbing in the first place seems to soothe the fish, so that it becomes perfectly quiescent, except that it slowly rises up in the water, and thus enables the hand to get into proper position for the final seizure. When it has risen up towards the surface sufficiently far – the tench must not be driven too near the surface, for it does not like light and will glide away – the poacher suddenly snaps as it were; his thumb and fingers, if he possibly can manage it, closing on the gills. The body is so slimy and slippery that there alone a firm hold can be got, though the poacher will often flick the fish out of the water in an instant so soon as it is near the surface. Poachers evidently feel as much pleasure in practising these tricks as the most enthusiastic angler using the implements of legitimate sport.

ROBERT LOUIS STEVENSON: from *An Inland Voyage* (1878).

It was a fine, green, fat landscape, or rather a mere green water-lane going on from village to village. Things had a settled look, as in places long lived in. Crop-headed children spat upon us from the bridges as we went below, with a true conservative feeling. But even more conservative were the fishermen, intent upon their floats, who let us go by without one glance. They perched upon sterlings and buttresses and along the slope of the embankment, gently occupied. They were indifferent like pieces of dead nature. They did not move any more than if they had been fishing in an old Dutch print. The leaves fluttered, the water lapped, but they continued in one stay, like so many churches established by law. You might have trepanned every one of their innocent heads and found no more than so much coiled fishing line below their skulls. I do not care for your stalwart fellows in india-rubber stockings breasting up mountain torrents with a salmon rod; but I do dearly love the class of man who plies his unfruitful art forever and a day by still and depopulated waters.

J. A. FROUDE: from *Cheyneys and the House of Russell*. From *Fraser's Magazine* (September 1879).

There was no longer any alarm for the tackle, and it was but to throw the fly upon the river, near or far, for a trout instantly to seize it. There was no shy rising where suspicion balks the appetite. The fish were swallowing with a deliberate seriousness every fly which drifted within their reach, snapping their jaws upon it with a gulp of satisfaction. The only difficulty was in playing them when hooked with a delicate, chalk-stream casting-line. For an hour and a half it lasted, such an hour and a half of trout-fishing as I had never seen and shall never see again. The ease of success at last became wearisome. Two large baskets were filled to the brim. Accident had thrown in my way a singular opportunity which it would have been wrong to abuse, so I decided to stop. We emptied out our spoils upon the grass, and the old keeper said that long as he had known the river he had never but once seen so many fish of so large size, taken in the Ches in a single day by a single rod.

How can a reasonable creature find pleasure in having performed such an exploit? If trout were wanted for human food, a net would have answered the purpose with less trouble to the man and less annoyance to the fish. Throughout creation man is the only animal – man, and dogs and cats which have learnt from him – who kills, for the sake of killing, what he does not want, and calls it sport. All other animals seize their prey only when hungry, and are satisfied when their hunger is appeased.

Such, it can only be answered, is man's disposition. He is a curiously formed creature, and the appetite for sport does not seem to disappear with civilization. The savage in his natural state hunts, as the animals hunt, to support his life; the sense of sport is strongest in the elaborately educated and civilized. It may be that the taste will die out before 'Progress'. Our descendants perhaps, a few generations hence, may look back upon a pheasant battue as we look back on bear-baiting and bull-fighting, and our mild offspring, instructed in the theory of development, may see a proof in their fathers' habits that they come of a race who were once crueller than tigers, and will congratulate themselves on the change. So they will think, if they judge us as we judge our forefathers of the days of the Plantagenets and Tudors, and both we and they may be perhaps mistaken. Half the lives of men in medieval Europe was spent in fighting. Yet from medieval Europe came the knightly graces of courtesy and chivalry. The modern soldier, whose trade is war, yet hates and dreads war more than civilians dread it. The sportsman's knowledge of the habits of animals gives him a kindly feeling towards them notwithstanding, and sporting tends rather to their preservation than their destruction. The human race may become at last vegetarians and water-drinkers. Astræa may come back, and man may cease to take the life of bird, or beast, or fish. But the lion will not lie down with the lamb, for lambs and lions will not be allowed to consume grain which might have served as human food, and will be extinct as the dodo. It may be all right and fit and proper: a world of harmless vegetarians may be the appropriate outcome of the development of humanity. But we who have been born in a ruder age do not aspire to rise beyond the level of our own times. We have toiled, we have suffered, we have enjoyed, as the nature which we have received has prompted us. We blame our fathers' habits; our children may blame ours in turn; yet we may be sitting in judgment, both of us, on matters of which we know nothing.

The storm has passed away, the dripping trees are sparkling in the warm and watery sunset. Back then to our inn, where dinner waits for us, the choicest of our own trout, pink as salmon, with the milky curd in them, and no sauce to spoil the delicacy of their flavour. Then bed, with its lavender-scented sheets and white curtains, and sleep, sound sweet sleep, that loves the country village and comes not near a London bedroom. In the morning, adieu to Cheneys, with its red gable ends and chimneys, its venerable trees, its old-world manners, and the solemn memories of its mausoleum. Adieu, too, to the river, which, 'though men may come and men may go', has flowed and will flow on for ever, winding among its reed beds, murmuring over its gravelly fords, heedless of royal dynasties, uncaring whether Cheney or Russell calls himself lord of its waters, graciously turning the pleasant corn mills in its course, unpolluted by the fetid refuse of manufactures, and travelling on to the ocean bright and pure and uncharged with poison, as in the old times when the priest sung in the church upon the hill and the sweet soft matins bell woke the hamlet to its morning prayers.

WILLIAM HENDERSON: from *My Life as an Angler* (1880).

Few scenes offer so great a variety as a running stream, and still fewer
are so well calculated to fill the heart with gratitude for being brought
into such close communion with the Maker and Preserver of all things.
I have related much of happy days passed with dear friends by Glen
and Coquet, Teviot and Tweed, and the very name of those rivers
recalls many a face fondly cherished by memory, but never more to be
seen in this world. But stepping beyond this inner circle, I have made
many acquaintances by the riverside of whom I still think with
pleasure, and that from every grade of society. Angling is in its way a
leveller, and intimacies often spring up whose basis is simply piscatorial. It were an 'ow'r long tale' to tell how I fraternized with the old
soldier, who having lost his right arm in his country's service used his
left to such good purpose that few could throw so fine a fly; or how day
by day I sought the companionship of the village postman who, driven
by a penurious Government to eke out the scanty pittance he received,
shouldered his creel between his hours of duty, and rarely failed to
bring a welcome addition to the evening meal he had so well earned.
Happily, in many districts, the riverside is still a free territory, where
persons incapable of hard labour may pass their time pleasantly and
earn something towards a living.

On a cold day in the month of April, while fishing for salmon in the
Tweed, I once observed a man trouting in a sharp running stream. He
lingered there so long that my attention was drawn to him, and seeing
that he was without wading boots, I enquired of the boatman how it
was possible for a man to remain so long in cold running water. 'Oh,
that's old Timbertoes,' was the reply. 'No fear of his feeling the cold.
There's nothing like a pair of wooden legs for warmth. But that's not
the best of it; look close, an' ye'll see he has gotten a third leg which he
claps on to his tail and sits down as cozy as if he were in the chimney
neuk.' So the mystery was explained; seated on his wooden tripod, the
old fellow fished at his ease and drew the trout towards him in true
epicurean style.

Let me here mention that I once had an excellent opportunity of
watching the wonderful success of William Ranken, the blind fisherman of St Boswell's. The month was June and the locality a beautiful
stream not far from Mertoun Bridge. The sun had long set, and as the
darkness prevented me from distinguishing my flies any longer I was in
the act of leaving the river when a young man came down from the

village and began to put on his fishing tackle. He did this with as much speed as is usual with anglers, though it soon became evident that he was quite blind. It promised to be too dark for what is ordinarily termed 'night-fishing', but my curiosity was excited, and I determined to wait and see what would come next.

Presently the young man walked to the edge of the stream, and choosing the most suitable place waded as far into the water as could be done with safety. Here casting his flies exactly by the edge of the main current, he began playing them with that peculiar motion which bespoke him at once to be a master of the art. It was not long ere he basketed a goodly trout, and then he pursued his course steadily downwards, taking fish after fish of a size that might excite the envy of an angler accustomed to labour under day's garish eye.

Every now and then the blind man's large water dog circled close round him, and I noticed that on each occasion he paused or took a step backwards. It was evident that the dog watched affectionately over his master's safety, and was accustomed to give timely notice of danger.

A thick fog had now gathered over the bosom of the stream, such as under ordinary circumstances would have driven me homewards, but there was a fascination in the scene which was irresistible to me, and I stood a long time on the river bank, listening to the slight noise the fisherman caused now and then in the water, and to the constant spattering of the trout on its surface as he drew them reluctantly to his feet.

CHARLES DICKENS: from *A Dictionary of the Thames* (1883).

Sturgeon occasionally come up the Thames, but they were never numerous in this river. Provision was made in ancient Acts excepting them from the vulgar fate of other fish, and in the instructions to the City water-bailiffs for the time being, orders were issued that the sturgeon 'was not to be secreted', and that all royal fishes taken within the jurisdiction of the Lord Mayor of London, as namely, whales, sturgeons, porpoises, and such like, should be made known, and the name and names of all such persons as shall take them shall be sent in to the Lord Mayor of London for the time being. The sturgeon therefore is always, when taken, sent direct to grace the table of majesty. The presence of mud (if it is *clean* mud) does not, from their bog-like habit of ploughing up the deposit of the stream, form any obstacle to their progress into fresh water, nor does the latter appear to affect them, even immediately from their presence in the sea. They have never been known to be taken by line and bait, but they often get entangled in the nets of the fishermen, which they greatly mutilate, from their amazing strength, in their efforts to escape.

The flesh of the sturgeon is looked upon with suspicion little short of aversion by some persons, but it, according to the parts submitted to the operations of the cook, may be rendered into the choicest of dishes – one portion simulating the tenderest of veal, another that of the sapid succulence of chicken, and a third establishing its reputation to a claim to most of the gastronomic virtues of the flesh of many acceptable fish in combination. The great *chefs*, Francatelli and Ude, used to aver that there were one hundred different ways of rendering sturgeon fit for an emperor; and Soyer would boast that he had added two more methods of its culinary preparation to these apparently exhaustive receipts.

CHARLES HALLOCK: from *Etchings on a Salmon Stream*. From *Fishing with the Fly* (edited by Orvis and Cheney 1883–6).

I love to see the salmon leap in the sunlight on the first flood of a 'June rise', and I love to hear his splash in the darkness of the still night, when the place where he jumped can be determined only by the sound, unless perchance his break in the water disturbed the reflection of a star. I have stood on heights afar off at the opening of the season, ere my unconsecrated rod had chance to exercise its magic, or my lips and feet to kiss the river, and with the combined exhilaration of impatience, desire, and joy, watched the incessant spurts of silvery spray until my chained and chafed spirit almost broke at the strain; and I have lain on my couch at midnight sleepless and kept awake by the constant splash of the salmon leaps. More interesting, if not so stimulating, is the leap of the salmon at obstructing falls, with the air filled with dozens of darting, tumbling, and falling fish – the foam dashing and sparkling in the sun, the air resonant with roar, and damp with the ever-tossing spray. Nay, more: I have seen a fall whose breast was an unbroken sheet thirty feet perpendicular, inclosed by lateral abutments of shelving crags which had been honey-combed by the churning of the water in time of flood; and over these crags the side-flow of the falls ran in struggling rivulets, filling up the holes and providing little reservoirs of temporary rest and refreshment for the running salmon; and I have actually seen and caught with my hands a twelve-pound salmon which had worked its way nearly to the counterscarp of the topmost ledge in its almost successful effort to surmount a barrier so insuperable! Surely, the example of such consummate pertinacity should teach men to laugh at average obstacles which stand in the pathway of their ambition!

RICHARD JEFFERIES: from *Nature near London* (1883).

It was at the tail of one of the arches of the bridge over the brook that my favourite trout used to lie. Sometimes the shadow of the beech came as far as his haunts, that was early in the morning, and for the rest of the day the bridge itself cast a shadow. The other parapet faces the south, and looking down from it the bottom of the brook is generally visible, because the light is so strong. At the bottom a green plant may be seen waving to and fro in summer as the current sways it. It is not a weed or flag, but a plant with pale green leaves, and looks as if it comes there by some chance; this is the water-parsnip.

By the shore on this, the sunny side of the bridge, a few forget-me-nots grow in their season, water crow's-foot flowers, flags lie along the surface and slowly swing from side to side like a boat at anchor. The breeze brings a ripple, and the sunlight sparkles on it; the light reflected dances up the piers of the bridge. Those that pass along the road are naturally drawn to this bright parapet where the brook winds brimming full through green meadows. You can see right to the bottom; you can see where the rush of the water has scooped out a deeper channel under the arches, but look as long as you like there are no fish.

The trout I watched so long, and with such pleasure, was always on the other side, at the tail of the arch, waiting for whatever might come through to him. There in perpetual shadow he lay in wait, a little at the side of the arch, scarcely ever varying his position except to dart a yard up under the bridge to seize anything he fancied, and drifting out again to bring up at his anchorage. If people looked over the parapet that side they did not see him; they could not see the bottom there for the shadow, or if the summer noonday cast a strong beam even then it seemed to cover the surface of the water with a film of light which could not be seen through. There are some aspects from which even a picture hung on the wall close at hand cannot be seen. So no one saw the trout; if any one more curious leant over the parapet he was gone in a moment under the arch.

Folk fished in the pond about the verge of which the sedge-birds chattered, and but a few yards distant; but they never looked under the arch on the northern and shadowy side, where the water flowed beside the beech. For three seasons this continued. For three summers I had the pleasure to see the trout day after day whenever I walked that way, and all that time, with fishermen close at hand, he escaped notice, though the place was not preserved. It is wonderful to think how difficult it is to see anything under one's very eyes, and thousands of people walked actually and physically right over the fish.

However, one morning in the third summer, I found a fisherman standing in the road and fishing over the parapet in the shadowy water. But he was fishing at the wrong arch, and only with paste for roach. While the man stood there fishing, along came two navvies; naturally enough they went quietly up to see what the fisherman was doing, and one instantly uttered an exclamation. He had seen the trout. The man who was fishing with paste had stood so still and patient that the trout, re-assured, had come out, and the navvy – trust a navvy to see anything of the kind – caught sight of him.

The navvy knew how to see through water. He told the fisherman, and there was a stir of excitement, a changing of hooks and bait. I could not stay to see the result, but went on, fearing the worst. But he did not succeed; next day the wary trout was there still, and the next, and the next. Either this particular fisherman was not able to come again, or was discouraged; at any rate, he did not try again. The fish escaped, doubtless more wary than ever.

In the spring of the next year the trout was still there, and up to the summer I used to go and glance at him. This was the fourth season, and still he was there; I took friends to look at this wonderful fish, which defied all the loafers and poachers, and above all, surrounded himself not only with the shadow of the bridge, but threw a mental shadow over the minds of passers-by, so that they never thought of the possibility of such a thing as trout. But one morning something happened. The brook was dammed up on the sunny side of the bridge, and the water let off by a side-hatch, that some accursed main or pipe or other horror might be laid across the bed of the stream somewhere far down.

Above the bridge there was a brimming broad brook, below it the flags lay on the mud, the weeds drooped, and the channel was dry. It was dry up to the beech tree. There, under the drooping boughs of the beech, was a small pool of muddy water, perhaps two yards long, and very narrow – a stagnant muddy pool, not more than three or four inches deep. In this I saw the trout. In the shallow water, his back came up to the surface (for his fins must have touched the mud sometimes) – once it came above the surface, and his spots showed as plain as if you had held him in your hand. He was swimming round to try and find out the reason of this sudden stinting of room.

Twice he heaved himself somewhat on his side over a dead branch that was at the bottom, and exhibited all his beauty to the air and sunshine. Then he went away into another part of the shallow and was hidden by the muddy water. Now under the arch of the bridge, his favourite arch, close by there was a deep pool, for, as already mentioned, the scour of the current scooped away the sand and made a hole there. When the stream was shut off by the dam above his hole remained partly full. Between this pool and the shallow under the beech there was sufficient connection for the fish to move into it.

My only hope was that he would do so, and as some showers fell, temporarily increasing the depth of the narrow canal between the two pools, there seemed every reason to believe that he had got to that under the arch. If now only that accursed pipe or main, or whatever repair it was, could only be finished quickly, even now the trout might escape! Every day my anxiety increased, for the intelligence would soon get about that the brook was damned up, and any pools left in it would be sure to attract attention.

Sunday came, and directly the bells had done ringing four men attacked the pool under the arch. They took off shoes and stockings and waded in, two at each end of the arch. Stuck in the mud close by was an eel-spear. They churned up the mud, wading in, and thickened and darkened it as they groped under. No one could watch these barbarians longer.

Is it possible that he could have escaped? He was a wonderful fish, wary and quick. Is it just possible that they may not even have known that a trout was there at all; but have merely hoped for perch, or tench, or eels? The pool was deep and the fish quick – they did not bale it, might he have escaped? Might they even, if they did find him, have mercifully taken him and placed him alive in some other water nearer their homes? Is it possible that he may have almost miraculously made his way down the stream into other pools?

There was very heavy rain one night, which might have given him such a chance. These 'mights', and 'ifs', and 'is it possible' even now keep alive some little hope that some day I may yet see him again. But that was in the early summer. It is now winter, and the beech has brown spots. Among the limes the sedges are matted and entangled, the sword-flags rusty; the rooks are at the acorns, and the plough is at work in the stubble. I have never seen him since. I never failed to glance over the parapet into the shadowy water. Somehow it seemed to look colder, darker, less pleasant than it used to do. The spot was empty, and the shrill winds whistled through the poplars.

RICHARD JEFFERIES: from *Mind Under Water* (1883).

Does he hear the stream running past him? Do the particles of water, as they brush his sides and fins, cause a sound, as the wind by us? While he lurks beneath a weed in the still pool, suddenly a shoal of roach rush by with a sound like a flock of birds whose wings beat the air. The smooth surface of the still water appears to cover an utter silence, but probably to the fish there are ceaseless sounds. Water-fowl feeding in the weedy corners, whose legs depend down into the water and disturb it; water-rats diving and running along the bottom; water-beetles moving about; eels in the mud; the lower parts of flags and aquatic grasses swinging as the breeze ruffles their tips; the thud, thud of a horse's hoofs, and now and then the more distant roll of a hay-laden waggon. And thunder – how does thunder sound under the surface? It seems reasonable to suppose that fish possess a wide gamut of hearing since their other senses are necessarily somewhat curtailed, and that they are peculiarly sensitive to vibratory movements is certain from the destruction a charge of dynamite causes if exploded under water. Even in the deep sea the discharge of a torpedo will kill thousands of herrings. They are as it were killed by noise. So that there are grounds for thinking that my quiet jack in the pool, under the bank of the brook, is most keenly alive by his sense of hearing to things that are proceeding both out and in the water. More especially, no doubt, of things in the water itself. With all this specialized power of hearing he is still circumscribed and limited to the groove of the brook. The birds fly from field to field, from valley to mountain, and across the sea. Their experience extends to whole countries, and their opportunities are constant. How much more fortunate in this respect than the jack! A small display of intelligence by the fish is equivalent to a large display by the bird.

When the jack has been much disturbed no one can do more than obtain a view of him, however skilfully he may conceal himself. The least sign of further proceedings will send the jack away; sometimes the mere appearance of the human form is sufficient. If less suspicious, the rod with the wire attached – or if you wish to make experiments, the rod without the wire attached – can be placed in the water, and moved how you choose.

GUY DE MAUPASSANT: *Two Friends* (1883). Translated from the French by Ernest Boyd and others, 1928.

Paris was blockaded, famished, at the last gasp. Sparrows were getting scarce on the roofs, and the sewers were depleted of their rats. People were eating anything.

As he was strolling sadly along the outer boulevard on a fine January morning, with his hand in the pockets of his military trousers, and his stomach empty, Monsieur Morissot, a watchmaker by profession, and a man of his ease when he had the chance, came face to face with a brother in arms whom he recognized as a friend, and stopped. It was Monsieur Sauvage, an acquaintance he had met on the river.

Before the war Morissot had been in the habit of starting out at dawn every Sunday, rod in hand, and a tin box on his back. He would take the train to Argenteuil, get out at Colombes, then go on foot as far as the Island of Marante. The moment he reached this place of his dreams he would begin to fish, and fish until nightfall. Every Sunday he met there a little round jovial man, Monsieur Sauvage, a draper of the rue Notre Dame de Lorette, also an ardent fisherman. They would often pass half the day side by side, rod in hand, feet dangling above the stream, and in this manner had become fast friends. Some days they did not talk, other days they did. But they understood each other admirably without words, for their tastes and feelings were identical.

On spring mornings, about ten o'clock, when the young sun was raising a faint mist above the quiet-flowing river, and blessing the backs of those two passionate fishermen with the pleasant warmth of a new season, Morissot would sometimes say to his neighbour: 'I say, isn't it heavenly?' and Monsieur Sauvage would reply: 'Couldn't be jollier!' which was quite enough to make them understand and like each other.

In autumn, as the day was declining, when the sky, reddened by the glow of the setting sun, reflected the crimson clouds in the water, stained the whole river with colour, the horizon flaming when our two friends looked as red as fire, and the trees, already russet and shivering at the touch of winter, were turned to gold, Monsieur Sauvage would look smilingly at Morissot, and remark: 'What a sight!' and Morissot, not taking his eyes off his float, would reply ecstatically: 'It beats the boulevard, eh?'

As soon as they recognized each other, they shook hands heartily, quite moved at meeting again in such different circumstances.

With a sigh, Monsieur Sauvage murmured: 'Nice state of things!' Morissot, very gloomy, groaned: 'And what weather! Today's the first fine day this year!'

The sky was indeed quite blue and full of light.

They moved on, side by side, ruminative, sad. Morissot pursued his thought: 'And fishing, eh? What jolly times we used to have!'

'When shall we go fishing?' asked Monsieur Sauvage.

They entered a little café, took an absinthe together, and started off once more, strolling along the pavement.

Suddenly Morissot halted: 'Another absinthe?' he said.

'I'm with you!' responded Monsieur Sauvage. And in they went to another wine-shop. They came out rather light-hearted, affected as people are by alcohol on empty stomachs. The day was mild, and a soft breeze caressed their faces.

Monsieur Sauvage, whose light-headedness was completed by the fresh air, stopped short: 'I say – suppose we go!'

'What d'you mean?'

'Fishing!'

'Where?'

'Why, at our island. The French outposts are close to Colombes. I know Colonel Dumoulin; he'll be sure to let us pass.'

Morissot answered, quivering with eagerness: 'All right; I'm on!' And they parted, to get their fishing gear.

An hour later they were marching along the high road. They came presently to the villa occupied by the Colonel, who, much amused by their whim, gave them leave. And furnished with his permit, they set off again.

They soon passed the outposts, and, traversing the abandoned village of Colombes, found themselves at the edge of the little vineyard fields that run down to the Seine. It was about eleven o'clock.

The village of Argenteuil, opposite, seemed quite deserted. The heights of Orgemont and Sannois commanded the whole countryside; the great plain stretching to Nanterre was empty, utterly empty of all but its naked cherry-trees and its grey earth.

Monsieur Sauvage, jerking his thumb towards the heights, muttered: 'The Prussians are up there!' And disquietude stole into the hearts of the two friends, looking at that deserted country. The Prussians! They had never seen any, but they had felt them there for months, all round Paris, bringing ruin to France, bringing famine; pillaging, massacre, invisible, yet invincible. And a sort of superstitious terror was added to their hatred for that unknown and victorious race.

Morissot stammered: 'I say – suppose we were to meet some?'

With that Parisian jocularity which nothing can suppress, Monsieur Sauvage replied: 'We'd give 'em some fried fish.'

None the less, daunted by the silence all round, they hesitated to go farther.

At last Monsieur Sauvage took the plunge. 'Come on! But be careful!'

They got down into a vineyard, where they crept along, all eyes and ears, bent double, taking cover behind every bush.

There was still a strip of open ground to cross before they could get to the riverside; they took it at the double and the moment they reached the bank plumped down amongst some dry rushes.

Morissot glued his ear to the ground for any sound of footsteps. Nothing! They were alone, utterly alone.

They plucked up spirit again, and began to fish.

In front of them the Island of Marante, uninhabited, hid them from the far bank. The little island restaurant was closed, and looked as if it had been abandoned for years.

Monsieur Sauvage caught the first gudgeon, Morissot the second, and every minute they kept pulling in their lines with a little silvery creature wriggling at the end. Truly a miraculous draught of fishes!

They placed their spoil carefully in a very fine-meshed net suspended in the water at their feet, and were filled by the delicious joy that visits those who know once more a pleasure of which they have been deprived too long.

The good sun warmed their shoulders; they heard nothing, though of nothing, were lost to the world. They fished.

But suddenly a dull boom, which seemed to come from underground, made the earth tremble. The bombardment had begun again.

Morissot turned his head. Away above the bank he could see on his left the great silhouette of Mont Valérien, showing a white plume in its cap, a puff of smoke just belched forth. Then a second spurt of smoke shot up from the fort's summit, and some seconds afterwards was heard the roar of the gun.

Then more and more. Every minute the hill breathed out death, sending forth clouds of white smoke, which rose slowly to the calm heaven, and made a crown of cloud.

Monsieur Sauvage shrugged his shoulders. 'At it again!' he said.

Morissot, who was anxiously watching the bobbing of his float, was seized with the sudden fury of a man of peace against these maniacs battering against each other, and he growled out: 'Idiots I call them, killing each other like that!'

'Worse than the beasts!' said Monsieur Sauvage.

And Morissot, busy with a fish, added: 'It'll always be like that, in my opinion, so long as we have governments.'

Monsieur Sauvage cut him short. 'The Republic would never have declared war—'

Morissot broke in: 'Under a monarchy you get war against your neighbours; under a republic – war amongst yourselves.'

And they began tranquilly discussing and unravelling momentous political problems with the sweet reasonableness of peaceable, ignorant men, who agreed at any rate on one point, that Man would never be free.

And Mont Valérien thundered without ceasing, shattering with its shells the homes of France, pounding out life, crushing human beings, putting an end to many a dream, to many an expected joy, to many a hope of happiness; opening everywhere, too, in the hearts of wives, of girls, of mothers, wounds that would never heal.

'Such is life!' declared Monsieur Sauvage.

'You mean "Such is death",' said Morissot, and laughed.

They both gave a sudden start; there was surely someone coming up behind them. Turning their eyes they saw, standing close to their very elbows, four men, four big, bearded men, dressed in a sort of servant's livery, with caps on the heads, pointing rifles at them.

The rods fell from their hands and floated off downstream.

In a few seconds they were seized, bound, thrown into a boat, and taken over to the island.

Behind the house that they had thought deserted they perceived some twenty German soldiers.

A sort of hairy giant, smoking a great porcelain pipe, and sitting astride of a chair, said in excellent French: 'Well, gentlemen, what luck fishing?'

Whereupon a soldier laid at his officer's feet the net full of fish, which he had carefully brought along.

The Prussian smiled. 'I see – not bad. But we've other fish to fry. Now listen to me, and keep cool. I regard you as two spies sent to watch me. I take you, and I shoot you. You were pretending to fish, the better to disguise your plans. You've fallen into my hands, so much the worse for you. That's war. But, seeing that you passed through your outposts, you must assuredly have been given the password to get back again. Give it me, and I'll let you go.'

Livid, side by side, the two friends were silent, but their hands kept jerking with little nervous movements.

The officer continued: 'No one will ever know; it will be all right; you can go home quite easy in your minds. If you refuse, it's death – instant death. Choose.'

They remained motionless, without a word.

The Prussian, calm as ever, stretched out his hands towards the water, and said: 'Think! In five minutes you'll be at the bottom of that river. In five minutes. You've got families, I suppose?'

Mont Valérien went on thundering. The two fishermen stood silent.

The German gave an order in his own language. Then he moved his chair so as not to be too near his prisoners. Twelve men came forward, took their stand twenty paces away, and grounded arms.

The officer said: 'I give you one minute; not a second more.'

And, getting up abruptly, he approached the two Frenchmen, took Morissot by the arm, and, drawing him aside, whispered: 'Quick, that password. Your friend need never know. It will only look as though I'd relented.' Morissot made no answer.

Then the Prussian took Monsieur Sauvage apart, and asked him the same question.

Monsieur Sauvage did not reply.

Once again they were side by side. The officer gave a word of command. The soldiers raised their rifles.

At that moment Morissot's glance alighted on the net full of gud-geons lying on the grass a few paces from him. The sun was shining on that glittering heap of fishes, still full of life. His spirit sank. In spite of all effort his eyes filled with tears.

'Goodbye, Monsieur Sauvage!' he stammered out.

Monsieur Sauvage answered: 'Goodbye, Monsieur Morissot.'

They grasped each other's hands, shaken from head to foot by a trembling they could not control.

'Fire!' cried the officer.

Twelve shots range out as one.

Monsieur Sauvage fell forward like a log. Morissot, the taller, wavered, spun around, and came down across his comrade, his face upturned to the sky; blood spurted from his tunic, torn across the chest.

The German gave another order. His men dispersed. They came back with ropes and stones, which they fastened to the feet of the two dead friends, whom they carried to the river-bank. And Mont Valérien never ceased rumbling, crowned now with piled-up clouds of smoke.

Two of the soldiers took Morissot by the head and heels, two others laid hold of Monsieur Sauvage in the same manner. The bodies, swung violently to and fro, were hurled forward, described a curve, then plunged upright into the river, where the stones dragged them down feet first.

The water splashed up, foamed, and rippled, then fell calm again, and tiny waves rolled out towards the banks.

A few bloodstains floated away.

The officer, calm as ever, said quietly: 'Now it is the fishes' turn!' and went back towards the house.

But suddenly catching sight of the net full of gudgeons on the grass, he took it up, looked it over, smiled, and called out: 'Wilhelm!'

A soldier in a white apron came running up. The Prussian threw him the spoil of the two dead fishermen.

'Get these little things fried at once while they're still alive. They will be delicious.'

And he went back to his pipe.

FRANK S. PINCKNEY: from *Winter Angling*. From *Fishing with the Fly* (edited by Orvis & Cheney 1883–6).

I went over the other day to Bright's Run. I don't know exactly where it is, and I consider it (next to Bright's disease of the kidneys) the very worst thing Bright has developed. It is a stream such as might properly empty into the Dismal Swamp, and find itself quite at home there. It is totally devoid of romantic beauty – and nearly so of trout. I never worked so hard in my life for twenty-two little ones, that put me to the blush as I put them in the basket. I was perpetually in a row with the overhanging thickets and the underlying logs, and my thoughts were a monologue of exclamation points. I would not angle in Bright's turgid waters again for all the trout the most minute analysis might discover in them.

Yesterday I had a much more agreeable day without a seven-mile ride on a pesky buck-board. I went quite alone, up the Buckhill as far as the Fall. This is a pleasant stream full of Nature – and sawdust – with here and there a speckled trout and here and there a black snake. (By special permission of Mr Tennyson.) There really are now and then cool little nooks which make one envy the trout; and an occasional spring dripping with a fresh *rat-tat-tat* over rocks and moss and into one's whiskey in spite of all one can do. This sort of thing is what makes a trout-stream after all. You may catch a whale in a goose-pond but it isn't angling. To me much depends upon surroundings. I like to form a picturesque part of a picturesque whole. Even when there is no audience in the gallery.

Given a dark glen fringed with pines that sigh and pine high up aloft – a pool whose sweep is deep, around which rocks in tiers, mossy as tombstones centuries old, bow their heads in mourning – heads crowned with weeds, and grave-mounds of mother earth, and pallid flowers, pale plants and sapless vines that struggle through shadows of a day in coma, laid in the hearse of night, without a proper permit, and I am happy. I don't know just why, but if I meet an undertaker I mean to ask him. All these deep, dark hiding spots of nature seem but so many foils to the keen sense of life and thrills of vitality that fill me. My nervous system sparkles against such sombre back-grounds.

Then, too, the Fall was lovely. Next to Niagara, the Kauterskill and Adams', this Buckhill Fall is one of the most successful, in a small way, that I know of. It might be bigger and higher and have twenty-five cents worth more water coming over it out of a dam; but for a mere casual Fall gotten up inadvertently by nature, it is very good, in an amateurish sort of way, you know!

There is, I believe (hang it, there *always* is!) a romantic legend connected with – but stay! – you already guess it. Big Buck Indian – years ago – in love with mother-in-law – commits suicide – jumps over the ledge – ever since on moonlight nights, water the colour of blood (probably tannery just above the Fall), Buck Kill, now corrupted into Buckhill. In the march of civilization the last *impedimenta* to be left by the wayside are the beautiful superstitions of ignorance.

I am now quite alone here. A young music composer, hitherto my companion, left yesterday, so I am hand-cuffed to nature in solitary confinement.

By the way, my composer was a voluntary exile from the domestic arena. He had but recently married – to formulate it by proportions – say about a ton of mother-in-law to about an ounce of wife, and when the contest waxed fiercer than became the endurance of a sensitive nature, he packed his bag and came a-fishing. He was a capital angler – a phenomenal musician and had an appetite and digestion like one or more of the valiant trencher men of England's merrie days, so he solaced his grief with Sonatas and buckwheat cakes in the mornings and tears and ginger-bread in the evenings. He was a born genius and as beautiful as a dream, so I advised him to go home, choke his m-in-l, kiss his wife and live happily all the days of his life. I think he has gone to try the plan.

Speaking of buckwheat cakes, you can go out here most any time and catch a nice mess running about a half a pound and *game* all the way through. No! No! I'm thinking of the trout! I mean they are light as a feather, and taste to me just as did those I never had half enough of when I was a lad with my good old Presbyterian grandmother, who would not 'set' the batter on Saturday night lest it should 'work' on the Sabbath.

JOHN BURROUGHS: from *Locusts and Wild Honey* (1884).

Indeed there is no depth of solitude that the mind does not endow with some human interest. As in a dead silence the ear is filled with its own murmur, so amid these aboriginal scenes one's feeling and sympathies become external to him, as it were, and he holds converse with them.

Then a lake is the ear as well as the eye of a forest. It is a place to go and listen and ascertain what sounds are abroad in the air. They all run quickly thither and report. If any creature had called in the forest for miles about I should have heard it. At times I could hear the distant roar of water off beyond the outlet of the lake. The sound of the vagrant winds purring here and there in the tops of the spruces reached my ear. A breeze would come slowly down the mountain, then strike the lake, and I could see its footsteps approaching by the changed appearance of the water. How slowly the winds move at times, sauntering like one on a Sunday walk! A breeze always enlivens the fish; a dead calm and all pennants sink; your activity with your fly is ill-timed, and you soon take the hint and stop. Becalmed upon my raft, I observed, as I have often done before, that the life of nature ebbs and flows, comes and departs, in these wilderness scenes; one moment her stage is thronged and the next quite deserted.

Then there is wonderful unity of movement in the two elements, air and water. When there is much going on in one, there is quite sure to be much more going on in the other. You have been casting, perhaps, for an hour with scarcely a jump or a sign of life anywhere about you, when presently the breeze freshens and the trout begin to respond. And then, of a sudden, all the performers rush in; ducks come sweeping by, loons laugh and wheel overhead, then approach the water on a long, gentle incline, ploughing deeper and deeper into its surface until their momentum is arrested, or converted into foam; the fish hawk screams, the bald eagle goes flapping by, and your eyes and hands are full. Then the tide ebbs, and both fish and fowl are gone.

PIERRE LOTI: from *An Iceland Fisherman* (1886). Translated from the French by Clara Cadiot, 1888.

About a month later, around Iceland, the weather was of that rare kind which the sailors call a dead calm; in other words, in the air nothing moved, as if all the breezes were exhausted and their task done.

The sky was covered with a white veil, which darkened towards its lower border near the horizon, and gradually passed into dull grey leaden tints; over this the still waters threw a pale light, which fatigued the eyes and chilled the gazer through and through. All at once, liquid designs played over the surface, such light evanescent rings as one forms by breathing on a mirror. The sheen of the waters seemed covered with a net of faint patterns, which intermingled and reformed, rapidly disappearing. Everlasting night or everlasting day, one could scarcely say what it was; the sun, which pointed to no special hour of the day, remained fixed, as if presiding over the fading glory of dead things; it appeared but as a mere ring, being almost without substance, and magnified enormously by a shifting halo.

Yann and Sylvestre, leaning against one another, sang 'Jean-François de Nantes', the song without an end, amused by its very monotony, looking at one another from the corner of their eyes as if laughing at the childish fun, with which they recommenced the verses over and over again, trying to put fresh spirit into them each time. Their cheeks glowed ruddily under the sharp freshness of the morning; the pure air they breathed was strengthening, and they inhaled it deep down in their chests, the very fountain of all vigorous existence. And yet, around them, was a semblance of non-existence, of a world either finished or not yet created; the light itself had no warmth; all things seemed without motion, and as if chilled for eternity under the great ghostly eye which represented the sun.

The *Marie* projected over the sea a shadow long and black as night, or rather appearing deep green in the midst of the polished surface, which reflected all the purity of the heavens; in this shadowed part, which had no glitter, could be plainly distinguished through the transparency, myriads upon myriads of fish, all alike, gliding slowly in the same direction, as if bent towards the goal of their perpetual travels. They were cods, performing their evolutions all as parts of a single body, stretched full length in the same direction, exactly parallel, offering the effect of grey streaks, unceasingly agitated by a quick motion which gave a look of fluidity to the mass of dumb lives. Sometimes, with a sudden quick movement of the tail, all turned round at the same time, showing the sheen of their silvered sides; and the same movement was repeated throughout the entire shoal by slow undulations, as if a thousand metal blades had each thrown a tiny flash of lightning from under the surface.

The sun, already very low, lowered further; so night had decidedly come.

As the great ball of flame descended into the leaden-coloured zones which surrounded the sea, it grew yellow, and its outer rim became more clear and solid. Now it could be looked straight at, as if it were but the moon. Yet it still gave out light, and looked quite near in the immensity; it seemed that by going in a ship, only as far as the edge of the horizon, one might collide with the great mournful globe, floating in the air just a few yards above the water.

Fishing was going on well; looking into the calm water, one could see exactly what took place; how the cods came to bite, with a greedy spring, then feeling themselves hooked, wriggled about, as if to hook themselves still firmer. And every moment, with rapid action, the fishermen hauled in their lines, hand-over-hand, throwing the fish to the man who was to clean them and flatten them out.

The Paimpol fleet was scattered over the quiet mirror, animating the desert. Here and there appeared distant sails, unfurled for mere form's sake, considering there was no breeze. They were like clear white outlines upon the greys of the horizon. In this dead calm, fishing off Iceland seemed so easy and tranquil a trade that ladies' yachting was no name for it.

L. M. TURNER: from *The Vákhnya, or Tom-Cod.* From *Contributions to the Natural History of Alaska* (1886).

The Eskimo fisherman, or woman, goes out early in the morning to the hole, which has been made the day before, for while cutting it out the fish are frightened away from it and nothing will be caught at that time. The person takes a grass sack or basket along to carry the fish home in. A piece of old sealskin or grass mat is taken to sit on. On arrival at the place it is carefully cleaned out by means of seine-like scoops with as little disturbance as possible, the line prepared and let down into the water. Ere many seconds one or two fish will be drawn out and slung high in the air; and, as they slap down on the ice they invariably become detached from the hook. The native is now in good humour, as an abundance of fish is indicated by their taking the hook when first put down. He takes off his glove and contentedly reaches behind his right ear for the quid of tobacco, which has lain there for the last twelve hours, covered by his abundant locks of hair; and, thrusting it far back between the teeth and cheek, calmly lets it soak while he pulls out dozens of Vákhni. When he has caught a sufficient number he gives a signal for those on the lookout to come with a dog and sled to carry them home. During favourable times two or three bushels may be caught by a single fisherman. Any that are not wanted for home

consumption are brought to the trading post and sold for so much per
basketful of about 75 to 125 fish, the price being fifteen to twenty cents
in trade, which represents six to nine cents in money. During the
winter fishing a short pole is used, while in summer a long pole is held
over the projecting ledge of rocks. The number of fish of this species
consumed by the inhabitants of Norton Sound is enormous. They are
used as food for man and dog. The natives either cook them by boiling,
or else freeze and eat them raw. I have never eaten a boiled Vákhnya,
neither do I desire to eat it. The flesh is rather firm, but in a very short
time it becomes watery. When they are fried hard and brown they do
well enough as a change but not as a regular diet month after month. I
have eaten them while frozen so hard that the flesh had to be shaved
off with a knife, but there is so little fleshy fibre and so much water in
the meat that it is like eating ice made from the water in which they
were boiled.

ROBERT LOUIS STEVENSON: *To Andrew Lang.* From
Underwoods, Book 1 (1887).

> Dear Andrew, with the brindled hair,
> Who glory to have thrown in air,
> High over arm, the trembling reed,
> By Ale and Kail, by Till and Tweed:
> An equal craft of hand you show
> The pen to guide, the fly to throw:
> I count you happy starred; for God,
> When He with inkpot and with rod
> Endowed you, bade your fortune lead
> Forever by the crooks of Tweed,
> Forever by the woods of song
> And lands that to the muse belong;
> Or if in peopled streets, or in
> The abhorred pedantic sanhedrin,
> It should be yours to wander, still
> Airs of the morn, airs of the hill,
> The plovery Forest and the seas
> That break about the Hebrides,
> Should follow over field and plain

And find you at the window pane;
And you again see hill and peel,
And the bright springs gush at your heel.
So went the fiat forth, and so
Garrulous like a brook you go,
With sound of happy mirth and sheen
Of daylight – whether by the green
You fare that moment, or the gray;
Whether you dwell in March or May;
Or whether treat of reels and rods
Or of the old unhappy gods:
Still like a brook your page has shone,
And your ink sings of Helicon.

ANDREW LANG: *The Last Chance.* From *Grass of Parnassus* (1888).

Within the streams, Pausanias saith,
    That down Cocytus valley flow,
Girdling the gray domain of Death,
    The spectral fishes come and go;
The ghosts of trout flit to and fro,
    Persephone, fulfil my wish,
And grant that in the shades below
    My ghost may land the ghosts of fish.

SIR RANDAL H. ROBERTS: from *The Philosophy of Angling.* From
The Silver Trout and Other Stories (1888).

Are there many of these unsuccessful anglers in Paris? At a rough
guess I should say close upon 1,000. Statistics reveal the presence of
12,000 anglers with the rod in France; but, judging from the aspect of
the river's side for ten months in the year, and that no licence is
required, this must be underrated, and out of the one thousand I
should say at least four hundred have never felt the joy of landing ever
so small a fish upon the bank. 'Never mind the result, the excitement
and emotions of the chase alone suffice,' says my friend. This philoso-

phy must be a true one, or else the angling records of France would not be so crowded with illustrious names.

The Curator of the Bibliothèque Nationale once told me that fifty per cent of his most valuable *personnel* were anglers with the rod. M. Messonier is an enthusiastic votary. M. Ambroise Thomas, the composer of the opera of *Mignon*, is supposed to find his most tuneful airs whilst watching his float. Rossini acknowledged to having found one of his magnificent trios whilst angling on the estate of Mr Aguado. Alphonse Karr, Emile Augier, Jules Sandeau swell the list of French anglers. But the most striking feature of the philosophy of the Parisian angler is the persistency with which he will select a spot and stick to it in spite of failure. Should he by chance vacate it, there are a dozen successors ready to take his place. His inopportune return gives rise to comic scenes; for the inveterate French angler, though peaceful enough whilst plying his craft, is pugnacious.

A few years ago, a friend of mine, an eminent Parisian journalist, had the misfortune to institute a comparison between the fly-fisher and the bottom fisher. He opined that the former was more active, more intelligent, more skilful, and consequently more prone to resent a slight. A gentleman of the latter persuasions felt offended at this insinuation, and challenged him to single combat. They did not fight.

Again, while the Hôtel de la Monnaie was burning during the Commune, several anglers who had helped to set it on fire returned to their peg by the river-side, telling their companions to call them if they were wanted. They expressed no joy at the destruction they had wrought, but they eagerly enquired if anyone had caught a fish during their absence.

As a rule, the French angler, when engaged in his favourite pursuit, is profoundly indifferent to surrounding events. During the first day of the July revolution, Compigny, the well-known friend of Mlle Mars, and the head of a department at the Ministry of Public Education, remained peacefully seated beneath the Bridge of Arts plying his rod, while on both sides of the bridge the terrific struggle was going on, and over his head the artillery was thundering. M. Salvady, Minister of Public Instruction during the reign of Louis Philippe, reinstated a provincial professor whom he had dismissed because the latter had by the merest accident settled himself in his favourite spot under the bridge *de la Concorde*. 'I should have yielded my position in the Ministry to my most persistent political adversary,' he said, 'in order to get rid of him.' What becomes of these ardent votaries during the close time? Some fish, in spite of the law, but they do not use rods. They attach a line to their ankle and dangle it for hours beneath the surface of the stream. Among these is Barre, a *sociétaire* of the Comédie Française, a very eminent actor. Others go to Sceaux, where they fish upon a piece of private water for fifty centimes and a fee for their tackle. The water abounds in carp, but the administration makes the angler pay for every fish he catches. It provides a new emotion. The angler's pride prompts him to wish for good sport. His spirit of economy makes him furious at a bite. The other day I met five French anglers who had not heard of the Expulsion Bill, and when told of it they expressed their sympathy with one member of the Orleans family only, and that was because he was a good fisherman.

ANNIE TRUMBULL SLOSSON: from *Fishing Jimmy* (1888).

'As I was tellin' ye,' he said, 'I allers loved fishin' an' know'd 't was the best thing in the hull airth. I knowed it larnt ye more about creeters an' yarbs an' stuns an' water than books could tell ye. I knowed it made folks patienter an' commonsenser an' weather-wiser an' cuter gen'ally; gin 'em more fac'lty than all the school larnin' in creation. I knowed it was more fillin' than vittles, more rousin' than whisky, more soothin' than lodlum. I knowed it cooled ye off when ye was het, an' het ye when ye was cold. I knowed all that, o' course – any fool knows it. But – will ye b'l'eve it? – I was more'n twenty-one year old, a man growed, 'fore I foun' out why 't was that away. Father an' mother was Christian folks, good out-an'-out Calv'nist Baptists from over East'n way. They fetched me up right, made me go to meetin' an' read a chapter every Sunday, an' say a hymn Sat'day night a'ter washin'; an' I useter say my prayers mos' nights. I wa'n't a bad boy as boys do. But nobody thought o' tellin' me the one thing, jest the one single thing that'd ha' made all the diffunce. I knowed about God, an' how he made me an' made the airth, an' everythin', an' once I got thinkin' about that, an' I asked my father if God made the fishes. He said 'course He did, the sea an' all that in 'em is, but somehow that did n't seem to mean nothin' much to me, an' I lost my int'rist agin. An' I read the Scripter account o' Jonah an' the big fish, an' all that in Job about pullin' out levi'thing with a hook an' stickin' fish spears in his head, an' some parts in them queer books nigh the end o' the ole Test'men about fish-ponds an' fish-gates an' fish-pools, an' how the fishers shall l'ment – everything I could pick out about fishin' an' sech; but it didn't come home to me; 't wa'n't my kind o' fishin' an' I did n't seem ter sense it.

'But one day – it's more'n forty year ago now, but I rec'lect it same's 't was yest'day, an' I shall rec'lect it forty thousand year from now if I'm 'round, an' I guess I shall be – I heerd – suthin' – diffunt. I was down in the village one Sunday; it wa' n't very good fishin' – the streams was too full; an' I thought I'd jest look into the meetin'-house 's I went by. 'T was the ole union meetin' house, ye know, an' they had n't got no reg'lar s'pply, an' ye never knowed what kind ye'd hear, so 't was kind o' excitin'.

''T was late, 'most 'leven o'clock, an' the sarm'n had begun. There was a strange man a-preachin', some one from over to the hotel. I never heerd his name, I never seed him from that day to this; but I knowed his face. Queer enough I'd seed him a-fishin'. I never knowed he was a min'ster; he did n't look like one. He went about like a real fisherman, with old clo'es an' an ole hat with hooks stuck in it, an' big rubber boots, an' he fished, reely fished, I mean – ketched 'em. I guess 't was that made me liss'n a leetle sharper 'n us'al, for I never seed a fishin' min'ster afore. Elder Jacks'n, he said 't was a sinf'l waste o' time, an' old Parson Loomis, he'd an idee it was cruel an' onmarciful; so I thought I'd jest see what this man 'd preach about, an' I settled down to liss'n to the sarm'n.

'But there wa'n't no sarm'n; not what I'd been raised to think was the on'y true kind. There wa'n't no heads, no fustlys nor sec'ndlys, nor fin'ly bruthrins, but the first thing I knowed I was hearin' a story, an' 't was a fishin' story. 'T was about Some One – I had n't the least idee then who 't was, an' how much it all meant – Some One that was dreffle fond o' fishin' an' fishermen, Some One that sot everythin' by the water, and useter go along by the lakes an' ponds, an' sail on 'em, an' talk with the men that was fishin'. An' how the fishermen all liked him, 'nd asked his 'dvice, an' done jest 's he telled 'em about the likeliest places to fish; an' how they allers ketched more for mindin' him; an' how he was a-preachin' he wouldn't go into a big meetin'-house an' talk to rich folks all slicked up, but he'd jest go out in a fishin' boat, an' ask the men to shove out a mite, an' he'd talk to the folks on shore, the fishin' folks an' their wives an' the boys an' gals playin' on the shore. An' then, best o' everythin', he telled how when he was a-choosin' the men to go about with him an' help him an' larn his ways so's to come a'ter him, he fust o' all picked out the men he'd seen every day fishin', an' mebbe fished with hisself; for he knowed 'em an' knowed he could trust 'em.

'An' then he telled us about the day when this preacher come along by the lake – a dreffle sightly place, this min'ster said; he'd seed it hisself when he was trav'lin' in them countries – an' come acrost two men he knowed well; they was brothers, an' they was a-fishin'. An' he jest asked 'em in his pleasant-spoken, frien'ly way – there wa'n't never sech a drawin', takin', lovin' way with any one afore as this man had, the min'ster said – he jest asked 'em to come along with him; an' they lay down their poles an' their lines an' everythin', an' jined him. An' then he come along a spell further, an' he sees two boys out with their ole father, an' they was settin' in a boat an' fixin' up their tackle, an' he asked 'em if they'd jine him, too, an' they jest dropped all their things, an' left the ole man with the boat an' the fish an' the bait an' follered the preacher. I don't tell it very good. I've read it an' read it sence that; but I want to make ye see how it sounded to me, how I took it, as the min'ster telled it that summer day in Francony meetin'. Ye see I'd no idee who the story was about, the man put it so plain, in common kind o' talk, without any come-to-passes an' whuffers an' .thuffers, an' I never conceited 't was a Bible narr'tive.

JEROME K. JEROME: from *Three Men in a Boat* (1889).

I knew a young man once, he was a most conscientious fellow and, when he took to fly-fishing, he determined never to exaggerate his hauls by more than twenty-five per cent.

'When I have caught forty fish,' said he, 'then I will tell people that I have caught fifty, and so on. But I will not lie any more than that, because it is sinful to lie.'

But the twenty-five-per-cent plan did not work well at all. He never was able to use it. The greatest number of fish he ever caught in one day was three, and you can't add twenty-five per cent to three – at least, not in fish.

So he increased his percentage to thirty-three-and-a-third, but that, again, was awkward, when he had only caught one or two; so, to simplify matters, he made up his mind to just double the quantity.

He stuck to this arrangement for a couple of months, and then he grew dissatisfied with it. Nobody believed him when he told them that he only doubled, and he, therefore, gained no credit that way whatever, while his moderation put him at a disadvantage among the other anglers. When he had really caught three small fish, and said he had caught six, it used to make him quite jealous to hear a man, whom he knew for a fact had only caught one, going about telling people he had landed two dozen.

So, eventually he made one final arrangement with himself, which he has religiously held to ever since, and that was to count each fish he caught as ten, and to assume ten to begin with. For example, if he did not catch any fish at all, then he said he had caught ten fish – you could never catch less than ten fish by this system; that was the foundation of it. Then, if by any chance he really did catch one fish, he called it twenty, while two fish would count thirty, three forty, and so on.

It is a simple and easily worked plan, and there has been some talk lately of its being made use of by the angling fraternity in general. Indeed, the committee of the Thames Anglers' Association did recommend its adoption about two years ago, but some of the older members opposed it. They said they would consider the idea if the number were doubled, and each fish counted as twenty.

If ever you have an evening to spare up the river, I should advise you to drop into one of the little village inns, and take a seat in the tap-room. You will be nearly sure to meet one or two old rod-men, sipping their toddy there, and they will tell you enough fishy stories in half an hour to give you indigestion for a month.

George and I – I don't know what had become of Harris; he had gone out and had a shave, early in the afternoon, and had then come back and spent full forty minutes in pipe-claying his shoes, we had not seen him since – George and I, therefore, and the dog, left to ourselves, went for a walk to Wallingford on the second evening, and, coming home, we called in at a little riverside inn, for a rest, and other things.

We went into the parlour and sat down. There was an old fellow there, smoking a long clay pipe, and we naturally began chatting.

He told us that it had been a fine day to-day and we told him that it had been a fine day yesterday, and then we all told each other that we thought it would be a fine day to-morrow; and George said the crops seemed to be coming up nicely.

After that it came out, somehow or other, that we were strangers in the neighbourhood, and that we were going away the next morning.

Then a pause ensued in the conversation, during which our eyes wandered round the room. They finally rested upon a dusty old glass-case, fixed very high up above the chimney-piece, and containing a trout. It rather fascinated me, that trout; it was such a monstrous fish. In fact, at first glance, I thought it was a cod.

'Ah!' said the old gentleman, following the direction of my gaze, 'fine fellow that, ain't he?'

'Quite uncommon,' I murmured; and George asked the old man how much he thought it weighed.

'Eighteen pounds six ounces,' said our friend, rising and taking down his coat. 'Yes,' he continued, 'it wur sixteen year ago, come the third o' next month, that I landed him. I caught him just below the bridge with a minnow. They told me he wur in the river, and I said I'd have him, and so I did. You don't see many fish that size here now, I'm thinking. Good night, gentlemen, good night.'

And out he went, and left us alone.

We could not take our eyes off the fish after that. It really was a remarkably fine fish. We were still looking at it, when the local carrier, who had just stopped at the inn, came to the door of the room with a pot of beer in his hand, and he also looked at the fish.

'Good-sized trout, that,' said George, turning round to him.

'Ah! you may well say that, sir,' replied the man; and then, after a pull at his beer, he added, 'Maybe you wasn't here, sir, when that fish was caught?'

'No,' we told him. We were strangers in the neighbourhood.

'Ah!' said the carrier, 'then, of course, how should you? It was nearly five years ago that I caught that trout.'

'Oh! was it you who caught it, then?' said I.

'Yes, sir,' replied the genial old fellow. 'I caught him just below the lock – least ways, what was the lock then – one Friday afternoon; and the remarkable thing about it is that I caught him with a fly. I'd gone out pike fishing, bless you, never thinking of a trout, and when I saw that whopper on the end of my line, blest if it didn't quite take me aback. Well, you see, he weighed twenty-six pound. Good night, gentlemen, good night.'

Five minutes afterwards a third man came in, and described how *he* had caught it early one morning, with bleak; and then he left, and a stolid, solemn-looking middle-aged individual came in, and sat down over by the window.

None of us spoke for a while; but, at length, George turned to the newcomer, and said:

'I beg your pardon, I hope you will forgive the liberty that we – perfect strangers in the neighbourhood – are taking, but my friend here and myself would be so much obliged if you would tell us how you caught that trout up there.'

'Why, who told you I caught that trout?' was the surprised query.

We said that nobody had told us so, but somehow or other we felt instinctively that it was he who had done it.

'Well, it's a most remarkable thing – most remarkable,' answered the stolid stranger, laughing; 'because, as a matter of fact, you are quite right. I did catch it. But fancy your guessing it like that. Dear me, it's really a most remarkable thing.'

And then he went on, and told us how it had taken him half an hour to land it, and how it had broken his rod. He said he had weighed it carefully when he reached home, and it had turned the scale at thirty-four pounds.

He went in his turn, and when he was gone, the landlord came in to us. We told him the various histories we had heard about his trout, and he was immensely amused, and we all laughed very heartily.

'Fancy Jim Bates and Joe Muggles and Mr Jones and old Billy Maunders all telling you that they had caught it. Ha! ha! ha! Well, that is good,' said the honest old fellow, laughing heartily. 'Yes, they are the sort to give it *me*, to put up in *my* parlour, if *they* had caught it, they are! Ha! ha! ha!'

And then he told us the real history of the fish. It seemed that he had caught it himself, years ago, when he was quite a lad; not by any art or skill, but by that unaccountable luck that appears to always wait upon a boy when he plays the wag from school, and goes out fishing on a sunny afternoon, with a bit of string tied on to the end of a tree.

He said that bringing home that trout had saved him from a whacking, and that even his schoolmaster had said it was worth the rule-of-three and practice put together.

He was called out of the room at this point, and George and I turned our gaze upon the fish.

It was really a most astonishing trout. The more we looked at it, the more we marvelled at it.

It excited George so much that he climbed up on the back of a chair to get a better view of it.

And then the chair slipped, and George clutched wildly at the trout-case to save himself, and down it came with a crash, George and the chair on top of it.

'You haven't injured the fish, have you?' I cried in alarm, rushing up.

'I hope not,' said George, rising cautiously and looking about.

But he had. That trout lay shattered into a thousand fragments – I say a thousand, but they may have only been nine hundred. I did not count them.

We thought it strange and unaccountable that a stuffed trout should break up into little pieces like that.

And so it would have been strange and unaccountable, if it had been a stuffed trout, but it was not.

That trout was plaster of Paris.

WILLIAM McGONAGALL: from *Loch Leven*. From *Poetic Gems* (1890).

Beautiful Loch Leven, near by Kinross,
For a good day's fishing the angler is seldom at a loss,
For the loch it abounds with pike and trout,
Which can be had for the catching without any doubt;
And the scenery around it is most beautiful to be seen,
Especially the Castle, wherein was imprisoned Scotland's ill-starred
    Queen.

Then there's the lofty Lomond Hills on the eastern side,
And the loch is long, very deep, and wide;
Then on the southern side there's Benarty's rugged hills,
And from the tops can be seen the village of Kinross with its spinning
    mills.

ANDREW LANG: from *Angling Sketches* (1891).

These are the waters with which our boyhood was mainly engaged; it is a pleasure to name and number them. Memory, that has lost so much and would gladly lose so much more, brings vividly back the golden summer evenings by Tweedside, when the trout began to plash in the stillness – brings back the long, lounging, solitary days beneath the woods of Ashiesteil – days so lonely that they sometimes, in the end,

begat a superstitious eeriness. One seemed forsaken in an enchanted
world; one might see the two white fairy deer flit by, bringing to us, as
to Thomas Rhymer, the tidings that we must back to Fairyland. Other
waters we knew well, and loved: the little salmon-stream in the west
that doubles through the loch, and runs a mile or twain beneath its
alders, past its old Celtic battlefield, beneath the ruined shell of its
feudal tower, to the sea. Many a happy day we had there, on loch or
stream, with the big sea-trout which have somehow changed their
tastes, and today take quite different flies from the green body and the
red body that led them to the landing-net long ago. Dear are the twin
Alines, but dearer is Tweed, and Ettrick, where our ancestor was
drowned in a flood, and his white horse was found, next day, feeding
near his dead body, on a little grassy island. There is a great pleasure
in trying new methods, in labouring after the delicate art of the dry
fly-fisher in the clear Hampshire streams, where the glassy tide flows
over the waving tresses of crow's-foot below the poplar shade. But
nothing can be so good as what is old, and, as far as angling goes, is
practically ruined, the alternate pool and stream of the Border waters,
where

> The triple pride
> Of Eildon looks over Strathclyde,

and the salmon cast murmurs hard by the Wizard's grave. They are all
gone now, the old allies and tutors in the angler's art – the kind
gardener who baited our hooks; the good Scotch judge who gave us
our first collection of flies; the friend who took us with him on his
salmon-fishing expedition, and made men of us with real rods, and
'pirns' of ancient make. The companions of those times are scattered,
and live under strange stars and in converse seasons, by troutless
waters. It is no longer the height of pleasure to be half-drowned in
Tweed, or lost on the hills with no luncheon in the basket. But, except
for scarcity of fish, the scene is very little altered, and one is a boy
again, in heart, beneath the elms of Yair, or by the Gullets at Ashiestiel. However bad the sport, it keeps you young, or makes you young
again, and you need not follow Ponce de Léon to the western wilderness, when, in any river you knew of yore, you can find the Fountain of
Youth.

WILLIAM R. LE FANU: from *Seventy Years of Irish Life* (1893).

In the year 1826, my father having been appointed Dean of Emly and Rector of Abington, we left Dublin to live at Abington, in the county of Limerick. Here our education, except in French and English, which our father taught us, was entrusted to a private tutor, an elderly clergyman, Stinson by name, who let us learn just as much, or rather as little, as we pleased. For several hours every day this old gentleman sat with us in the schoolroom, when he was supposed to be engaged in teaching us classic lore, and invigorating our young minds by science; but being an enthusiastic disciple of old Isaak, he in reality spent the whole, or nearly the whole, time in tying flies for trout or salmon and in arranging his fishing gear, which he kept in a drawer before him. Soon after he had come to us, he had wisely taken the precaution of making us learn by heart several passages from Greek and Latin authors; and whenever our father's step was heard to approach the schoolroom, the flies were nimbly thrown into the drawer, and the old gentleman in his tremulous and nasal voice, would say, 'Now, Joseph, repeat that ode of Horace', or 'William, go on with that dialogue of Lucian'. These passages we never forgot, and though more than sixty years have passed, I can repeat as glibly as then the dialogue beginning, ῏ω πάτερ οἷα πέπονθα and others. As soon as our father's step was heard to recede, 'That will do,' said our preceptor; the drawer was reopened, and he at once returned, with renewed vigour, to his piscatory preparations, and we to our games. Fortunately my father's library was a large and good one; there my brother spent much of his time in poring over many a quaint and curious volume. As for me, under the guidance and instructions of our worthy tutor, I took too ardently to fishing to care for anything else. I still profit by those early lessons. I can to-day tie a trout or salmon fly as well as most men.

* * *

When fishing in Connemara, in the summer of 1869, I started one morning very early from Glendalough Hotel, our headquarters, for the Snave Beg ('The Little Swim'), so called because it is the narrowest part of Ballinahinch Lake, in fact little more than a strait joining the upper to the lower lake. My wife and two children were, after their breakfast, to meet me there. By half-past nine I had killed two salmon, and in order to cast my fly over a fish that was rising a long way out, I stepped out from stone to stone on some slippery rocks. Just as I reached the point I was making for my feet went from under me, and I fell flat on my back into the lake. All my clothes, I need not say, required drying, so, as the sun was hot, I spread them on the rocks, and ran about across the heather to warm and dry myself. While I was still in this unusual fishing costume I heard the sound of a car rapidly approaching, and saw, to my horror, that not only were my wife and children upon it, but also another lady. Fortunately there was a large rock close by; behind this I carefully concealed myself, and despatched one of my boatmen to stop the car, and to ask them to send me a rug and as many pins as they could muster. The rug was pinned round me, my arms left free, and my legs sufficiently so to allow me to walk, and thus attired I fished for three full hours, until my clothes were dry.

HERBERT SPENCER: from *An Autobiography* (1894).

Shortly before the close of the London season, I wrote to John Mill on some matter which I forget, and, referring to my approaching departure for Scotland, suggested, more in jest than in earnest, that if he would join me, I would initiate him in salmon-fishing. The following passage from his reply refers to this offer.

> My murderous propensities are confined to the vegetable world. I take as great a delight in the pursuit of plants as you do in that of salmon, and find it an excellent incentive to exercise. Indeed I attribute the good health I am fortunate enough to have, very much to my great love of exercise, and for what I think the most healthy form of it, walking.

Having in boyhood had little or no experience of the ordinary boyish sports, Mill had a somewhat erroneous conception of them. Hence the inappropriate use of the word 'murderous'; as though the gratification were exclusively in killing. But I quite agree in the implied objection he makes to pursuits that inflict pain. Though so fond of fishing as a boy, my dislike to witnessing the struggles of dying fish, becoming stronger as I grew older, had the result that between twenty-one and thirty-five I never fished at all. It was only because, on being prompted to try the experiment at the latter age, I found fishing so admirable a sedative, serving so completely to prevent thinking, that I took to it again, and afterwards deliberately pursued it with a view to health. Nothing else served so well to rest my brain and fit it for resumption of work.

J. P. WHEELDON: from *Sporting Facts and Fancies* (1894).

Under the willow was the deepest hole of all, and many a goodly trout therein found comfortable, shady lodgings. There was one fish in particular, which the divine and I had watched upon numerous occasions, when he was feeding upon the countless minnows incessantly wriggling, like a little black and olive-green cloud, close in under the loamy bank. This trout had a white patch or mark upon his side, looking like the trace of a bruise against the sides of a hatch-hole, or mayhap the effects of a blow. He was a three-pounder if he weighed an ounce, and now and again the vicar tried his hand over him. In his youth he had been an admirable fly-fisher, but with the frosts of seventy winters powdering his head, he found, as he said, that the possession of old bones, in the process of plashing along by the side of sedgy water-courses, did not agree. Thus, about all that he did do, in those days which I recollect so well, was to stand on the bridge at the farther side of the stream, on warm summer evenings, and throw a fly with a beautiful underhanded cast, which I tried over and over again in vain to imitate, right under the boughs of the willow, and into the deep swirly hole sheltered by its roots. He was exceedingly fond of fishing with a sunk fly, and when his lure had been swept full in the throat of the eddy he would joggle gently at the point of the rod, so as to produce a counterfeit presentment, nearly as might be, of the struggles of a drowning insect. At the slightest twitch of the line, or jar through the supple rod, the dear old boy was death upon a trout, and, in spite of all the gallant upward leaps, the lithe, bounding body, flashing like a lusty bar of gold, flushed with rose hues in the light of the summer evening, he had him out and tumbling and rolling in mid-stream, from whence he would presently be tumbled into my landing-net.

One night – I recollect it as well as if it were only yesterday – he and I stood upon the little bridge. It was in the thick of the May-fly season, and hundreds of the dainty gauze-winged insects were dancing up and down, up and down, over the tops of the feathery rustling sedges. The sun was just sinking in a blood-red and orange streaked sky, and the boughs and whispering leaves of the willow looked dark overhead against a sea of pale apple-green and faintest azure. The rich lush meadows, where lazy sleepy-eyed cattle stood knee-deep in the fat pastures, yellow with millions of buttercups, and flooded with pale golden glory from the dying sun, lay bathed in a soft, misty, Cuyp-like haze of light. There was no motion anywhere, save for the dancing insects, the quick sweep and dash of a little knot of swifts and swallows, the swoop of a spotted flycatcher from the arm of a tree, and the ever-shifting swirl of the hurrying waters. There was no voice, except the murmurous ripple and plash of the stream; now and again the 'plop' of a rising fish, the plunge of a water-rat, the shrill twitter and scream of the circling birds, and the low mutterings and grumblings of a far-off angry bull.

Every now and again there was a plunge, followed by a rolling eddy of the dark waters in the hole under the tree. I doubt not that many a score of dead and dying drakes were there washing back and forth in the swirling water. At last, after seeing the big trout come up boldly and suck down fly after fly, my good old friend could stand it no longer, and sent me into the house for his rod and fly-book. Then he put up a beautiful cork-bodied fly, and after well soaking his cast, sent it with a gentle flick right on to the overhanging roots of the old tree.

'Ah me, that's very bad!' said he, with a kindly, humorous smile, doubtless thinking that the fly was fast. But raising the point of the rod very gently, it dropped beautifully, and in an instant the big trout had it. He was probably cruising at that very moment under the bank. Anyhow, the steel was in him, and in the very next second's space, with a tremendous dash and upward fling into the sun-lit air, the bright drops falling in a twinkling shower from his bent and bow-like body, he was down again, and pulling like a mad trout twenty yards below us. With never a thought of old bones then, the dear old warrior, with only thin dinner shoes on, plashed through the wet and sedgy ground, forever ejaculating such phrases as 'Holy Father! got him at last! May He forgive me for using His name. Hold up, you great beast! Ah me, he's in the weeds! – Saints above us, he isn't! Prayers and praises! what a ponderous trout! Devil take him for a pigheaded thing!' and so on, until after a glorious fight, the perspiration streaming down the dear old fellow's head the while, he got him to the side, thoroughly done up, and grappled him. Then he actually crouched down, the tails of his old-fashioned coat dabbling in the stream, while water was oozing up from amongst the aquatic weeds all round his thin shoes, so that he might weigh his prize in his withered leaden-veined hands, and say over and over again, the light of victory brightening his dim blue eyes, 'Eh me, what a beauty! What a beauty he is, to be sure! And Lord forgive me for swearing'.

ROBERT LOUIS STEVENSON: from a letter to J. M. Barrie,
Vailima, 13 July 1894.

By the way, I was twice in Kirriemuir, I believe in the year '71, when I
was going on a visit to Glenogil. It was Kirriemuir, was it not? I have a
distinct recollection of an inn at the end – I think the upper end – of an
irregular open place or square, in which I always see your characters
evolve. But, indeed, I did not pay much attention; being all bent upon
my visit to a shooting-box, where I should fish a real trout-stream, and
I believe preserved. I did, too, and it was a charming stream, clear as
crystal, without a trace of peat – a strange thing in Scotland – and alive
with trout; the name of it I cannot remember, it was something like the
Queen's River, and in some hazy way connected with memories of
Mary, Queen of Scots. It formed an epoch in my life, being the end of
all my trout-fishing. I had always been accustomed to pause and very
laboriously to kill every fish as I took it. But in the Queen's River I took
so good a basket that I forgot these niceties; and when I sat down, in a
hard rain shower, under a bank, to take my sandwiches and sherry, lo!
and behold, there was the basketful of trouts still kicking in their
agony.

I had a very unpleasant conversation with my conscience. All that
afternoon I persevered in fishing, brought home my basket in triumph,
and sometime that night, 'in the wee sma' hours ayont the twal', I
finally forswore the gentle craft of fishing. I dare say your local
knowledge may identify this historic river; I wish it could go farther
and identify also that particular Free kirk in which I sat and groaned on
Sunday.

W. ST LEGER: *A Gallop of False Analogies*. Reprinted from *Punch*
(1894).

There is a fine stuffed chavender,
   A chavender or chub,
That decks the rural pavender,
   The pavender or pub,
Wherein I eat my gravender,
   My gravender or grub.

How good the honest gravender!
How snug the rustic pavender!
From sheets as sweet as lavender,
    As lavender or lub,
I jump into my tavender,
    My tavender or tub.

Alas, for town and clavender,
    For business and my club!
They call me from my pavender
To-night – ay, there's the ravender,
    Alas, there comes the rub!

To leave each blooming shravender,
    Each spring-bedizened shrub,
And meet the horsey savender,
    The very forward sub,
At dinner in the clavender,
    At billiards soundly drub
The self-sufficient cavender,
    The not ill-meaning cub,
Who me a bear will davender
    A bear unfairly dub,
Because I sometimes snavender,
    Not too severely snub,
His setting right the clavender,
    His teaching all the club.

Farewell to peaceful pavender,
    My river-dreaming pub,
To bed as sweet as lavender,
To homely, wholesome gravender,
And you, inspiring chavender,
    Stuffed chavender or chub.

R. D. BLACKMORE: from *Crocker's Hole*. From *Slain by the Doones and Other Stories* (1895).

The Culm used to be a good river at Culmstock, tormented already by a factory, but not strangled as yet by a railroad. How it is now, the present writer does not know, and is afraid to ask, having heard of a vile 'Culm Valley Line'. But Culmstock bridge was a very pretty place to stand and contemplate the ways of trout; which is easier work than to catch them. When I was just big enough to peep above the rim, or to lie upon it with one leg inside for fear of tumbling over, what a mighty river it used to seem, for it takes a treat there and spreads itself. Above the bridge the factory stream falls in again, having done its business, and washing its hands in the innocent half that has strayed down the meadows. Then, under the arches, they both rejoice and come to a slide of about two feet, and make a short, wide pool below, and indulge themselves in perhaps two islands, through which a little river always magnifies itself, and maintains a mysterious middle. But after that, all is used to come together, and make off in one body for the meadows, intent upon nurturing trout with rapid stickles, and buttercuppy corners where fat flies may tumble in. And here you may find in the very first meadow, or at any rate you might have found, forty years ago, the celebrated 'Crocker's Hole'.

The story of Crocker is unknown to me, and interesting as it doubtless was, I do not deal with him, but with his Hole. Tradition said that he was a baker's boy who, during his basket-rounds, fell in love with a maiden who received the cottage-loaf, or perhaps good 'Households', for her master's use. No doubt she was charming, as a girl should be, but whether she encouraged the youthful baker and then betrayed him with false *rôle*, or whether she 'consisted' throughout – as our cousins across the water express it – is known to their *manes* only. Enough that she would not have the floury lad; and that he, after giving in his books and money, sought an untimely grave among the trout. And this was the first pool below the bread-walk deep enough to drown a five-foot baker boy. Sad it was; but such things must be, and bread must still be delivered daily.

ANON: *De Clickin' ob de Reel* (19th century).

I's heard de bullfrog bellow,
　De fatty 'possum squeal;
But dat's no music like unto
　De clickin' ob de reel.

I's heard de locus' singin',
　De killdea's noisy peal;
But dat don't wake de heart up
　Like de clickin' ob de reel.

I's heard de farm bell ringin',
　De call fer fiel' han's meal;
But dat don't hab no 'traction
　Like de clickin' ob de reel.

I's heard de foxhoun' barkin',
　He's scent de rabbit's heel;
But dat were mighty dulness
　'Gin de clickin' ob de reel.

Is yer eber bin a-boatin'
　In de ship widout de keel.
En seen de rod a-bendin'
　To de clickin' ob de reel?

De trow dey call de 'castin'',
　En when de 'strike' ye's feel,
De line she go a-sizzin'
　To de clickin' ob de reel.

Yer begin ter wind 'er in den
　Wid all ye's nigga zeal,
Fer ye's like ter cotch'd er bass, sah,
　Wid de clickin' ob de reel.

From ebery nook en connor
　Natur's mel'dies roun' me steal,
But nun ob dem am in it
　Wid de clickin' ob de reel.

G. F. BROWNE, Bishop of Stepney: from *A Night with a Salmon*. From *Off The Mill: Some Occasional Papers* (1895).

It is now half-past three o'clock, and we are rapidly approaching Newburgh. A council of war determines that, at all hazards, we must get to shore; and, as if in furtherance of our determination, the fish makes towards the island. We push on, parallel with him, and regardless of the splice, until the boat actually touches the bottom for a moment, imparting to the third man the most pleasurable sensation he has yet felt. The next moment we are rowing hard out into mid channel, for a sudden rush has run all the line off the reel but ten yards or so. That is our first and last contact with the shore from the beginning to the end. He still makes seawards; but we observe with much satisfaction that the tide shews signs of turning, and we hope soon to find ourselves moving homewards. The change of tide seems to make the fish frantic. We are never still for half a minute, and never cease wondering what his size must be if his strength is so enormous and so untiring. Finally, he decides on going up with the tide, and he goes at so merry a rate that the third man is encouraged to bring out three sandwiches of potted grouse – our whole supply of food – and eats his share. A strong cold wind from the sea, and a heavy fall of rain, soon come to damp his satisfaction, and he is reduced to the verge of despair. Double himself up as he will, his waterproof will not cover the whole of him; and as he must sacrifice either his legs or his head, he elects to save the legs. The waves become embarrassing, and the boat is no longer easy to manage. A new fiend enters the fish, and makes him play the maddest pranks imaginable. We have for some time discussed the probability of his being a strong fish hooked foul, which would account for some part of his power; but just when the waves are at the highest and the boat is blowing up the river close upon the fish, out he springs two feet into the air, a monster as large as a well-grown boy, with the line leading fair up to his snout. 'Never land that fellow with a couple of trout-lines, or any other line,' is the fisherman's verdict; and as if to confirm it a cry comes the next minute, 'The line has parted!' Sure enough one strand has gone, owing to the constant friction of the wet line running through the rings for so many hours, and within twenty yards of the end of the line there is an ugly place two inches long, with only two strands out of three remaining. There is no longer a moment's safety unless that flaw is kept on the reel; and the necessity of pressing close on the fish leads Jimmy such a life as he will probably not forget. We are hungry and cold and somewhat wet; it is growing very dusk, and if we could not land him with 120 yards of line, how can we with twenty? We have caught a Tartar indeed. The non-combatant determines to go overboard and swim to land; but the fish seems inclined to save him the trouble, and once more makes for the favourite north shore. We near the haven, are within fifteen yards of land. Our friend gets on to the seat to jump, but waits for one weak moment to have a shorter swim, when off goes the fish, and off we go, too, into mid-channel. The disappointed man resigns himself, for the Tay, with a strong tide half up, is no pleasant bath in the twilight of a rough October day.

And now night comes on in earnest. It is half-past six, and all but dark, before we reach the pier whence we started seven hours before. Here there are several boats kept, and we shout with the utmost confidence for 'Ro-bairt' to come and take our friend ashore. Alas! all the boats are far up in the reeds, and will not be available for two or three hours yet, so on we go into the deepening darkness. The clock at home strikes seven, and we hear our passenger groaning over the fact that they are just going in to dinner. Lights peep on the hillsides and in the plain, and a gathering cluster of bright points at the water's edge reminds us that we are nearing Inchyra, where we shall certainly get a boat to come out to us. We shout in concert, 'Boat!' – 'Boo-o-at' the hills all round return, with echoes marvellously prolonged; but there is no other reply. The whole village must have heard – probably takes it for a hoax. Again and again we cry, now in harmony, now in discord; and anything more horrible than a loud body of discord borne on repeating echoes it is difficult to conceive. At length a measured sound of oars is heard, and a black pirate-like boat comes down upon us. We state our need. Can he take this gentleman down to the pier, and bring us back some food? 'Na!' And that is all he will vouchsafe to say as he sheers off again. Soon, however, a more Christian boat appears, and with many complicated manoeuvres, to keep the line clear of the boats in the dark, we tranship our friend about eight o'clock, loaded with injunctions to send off food and a light. The light would be of the greatest service, for a frozen finger and thumb are not sufficiently certain indicators of the passage of the frayed portion of the line from the reel; and as the fish has never ceased to rush from one side to the other, frequently passing sheer under the boat, and requiring the utmost care to keep the line clear of the oars, we think almost more of the coming lantern than of the sorely needed food. It is an hour before the boat returns, with an excellent lantern, a candle and a half, a bottle of whisky, and cakes and cheese enough for a week. Before setting to work upon the food we attempt to put in execution a plan we have long thought of and carefully discussed. A spare rod, short and stiff, is laid across the seats of the boat, with the reel all clear, and a good salmon-line on, with five or six yards drawn through the rings. We wait till the fish is quiet for a moment or two under the boat, and, taking gently hold the line he is on, pass a loop of it through the loop at the end of the salmon-line. As if he divined our intention, off he goes at once, running the flaw off the reel, and costing us some effort to catch him up again. This is repeated two or three times. At last we get the loop through, get a good knot tied, snap the old line above the knot, and there is our friend careering away at the end of a hundred yards of strong salmon-line, with some seven or eight yards only of the thinner line. When we examine the now innocuous flaw, we find it is seven inches long, and half of one of the remaining strands is frayed through. The only thing now to be avoided is coming into very close contact with the fish, as the new loop will not run easily through the rings. Unfortunately the light in the boat seems to attract him to us, for he does little else than rush from one side of the boat to the other, and we are obliged to take the oars in and let her drift. For a few moments, we propose to hang the light over the stern, and gaff him when he comes up to it; but that method is at once rejected as unfair to so noble a foe. Jimmy, however, will not abandon it. 'I should be ashamed all my life,' the fisherman declares. 'There's never a body need know,' Jimmy replies. '*I* should know,' was the moral rejoinder. 'Deed I wudna tell.'

Time passes on as we drift slowly up the river towards Elcho. Ten o'clock strikes, and we determine to wait till dawn, and then land and try conclusions with the monster that has had us fast for ten hours. The tide begins to turn, and Jimmy utters gloomy forebodings of our voyage down to the sea in the dark. The fish feels the change of tide, and becomes more demoniacal than ever. For half an hour he is in one incessant flurry, and at last, for the first time, he rises to the surface, and through the dark night we can hear and see the huge splashes he makes as he rolls and beats the water. He must be near done, Jimmy thinks. As he is speaking the line comes slack. He's bolting towards the boat, and we reel up with the utmost rapidity. We reel on; but no sign of resistance. Up comes the minnow, minus the tail hook. Jimmy rows home without a word; and neither he nor the fisherman will ever get over it.

Note – A large fish was taken in the nets at Newburgh the next year, which was popularly recognized as the fish of the above account. It had a mark just where I saw the tail hook of the minnow when the fish shewed itself once in the strong water above Newburgh; and a peculiarity of form of the shoulder, which I then noticed, was seen in the great fish taken in the nets. Correspondence with Mr Frank Buckland, who took a cast of the fish, appeared to establish the identity of the two. It was the largest salmon ever known to be taken, weighing seventy-four pounds as weighed at Newburgh, and seventy pounds in London the next day. Fish are usually found not to decrease, but to increase largely in weight after their capture. My boatman on Loch Frenchie once told me, à propos of a 'four pound trout' caught by a Stirling gentleman in the loch, that the fish must have grown two-and-a-half pounds between that and Stirling.

VISCOUNT GREY OF FALLODON: from *Fly Fishing* (1899).

As a rule, we find our pleasures in our own way for ourselves, and do not take or learn them from others. What we really care for we have at first hand, the beginning of the feeling being within us or not at all, though what we read or hear from others helps and stimulates it. It is indeed almost impossible to justify a particular pursuit to some one else who has not got the sense of it. One man has a hobby and may talk about it to another easily, or even with eloquence and power; but if that other has not shared the hobby, he will not understand the language, and the speaker has no right to expect that he should. On the other hand, to any one who does share it, even a little imperfectly told becomes interesting, and weak words begin to stir kindred memories. When a man has a hobby it is to be hoped that he will learn reticence; that he will never go into the world at large without a resolve not to talk about what he cares for most; that in society and places where they talk, he will carry his delight within him like a well-guarded treasure, not to be unlocked and disclosed in all its fullness on any slight or trivial inquiry. Rather let him not use his own key for himself, being sure that the test of any really kindred spirit will be the possession of a master key which will open this special door of his mind for him. It is seldom enough that this happens. Most of us live wherever circumstances decide that we should, and live the life that our work requires. We think of our pleasures in night watches, in passing from one place to another, upon the pavement, in trains and cabs; but the prospect on any given occasion of meeting such a really kindred spirit seems almost too good to be true. If, then, a book is written about a pursuit like fishing, it should be not to preach, or to convert, or to dogmatize. Books about sport and country life should be written and read, partly perhaps for the sake of hints, information, and instruction, but much more in the hope that the sense of refreshing pleasure, which has been felt by the writer, may slide into a sympathetic mind.

There remains yet another difficulty, that of expressing pleasure at all. It may be that language lends itself more easily to forms of argument and thought than of feeling. An argument is something which can be caught and held down and strapped into sentences, but after reading an account of a day's fishing, it is continually borne in upon one that, when all has been said, the half has not been told; it is not because there is really nothing to tell, as some cynical and unsympathetic mind may suppose; rather, I think it is because of the nature of joy. Feelings of delight come unsought and without effort – when they are present they are everywhere about and in us like an atmosphere; when they are past it is almost as impossible to give an account of them as it is of 'last year's clouds', and the attempt to analyse and reconstruct the sense of joy that has been and may be again, seems to result in rows of dead words.

* * *

Sometimes I think that sea trout fishing is the best of all sport. It combines all the wildness of salmon fishing with the independence of trout fishing, and one may have all the excitement of hooking large fish without using a heavy rod and heavy tackle. There is less rule and less formality about it than there is about salmon fishing, and there seems more scope for the individuality of the angler. Perhaps this is partly because the sea trout season comes so directly after a long period of work in the stale air of cities in summer, and coincides with the first burst into freedom and fresh atmosphere. The difference is so great in August, after a few days of exercise in the air of the North, that there come times when the angler, who wanders alone after sea trout down glens and over moors, has a sense of physical energy and strength beyond all his experience in ordinary life. Often after walking a mile or two on the way to the river, at a brisk pace, there comes upon one a feeling of 'fitness', of being made of nothing but health and strength so perfect, that life need have no other end but to enjoy them. It is as though till that moment one had breathed with only a part of one's lungs, and as though now for the first time the whole lungs were filling with air. The pure act of breathing at such times seems glorious. People talk of being a child of nature, and moments such as these are the times when it is possible to feel so; to know the full joy of animal life – to desire nothing beyond. There are times when I have stood still for joy of it all, on my way through the wild freedom of a Highland moor, and felt the wind, and looked upon the mountains and water and light and sky, till I felt conscious only of the strength of a mighty current of life, which swept away all consciousness of self, and made me a part of all that I beheld.

(*From the 1930 edition*)

The cottage that I put up by the Itchen in 1890 was intended only as a fishing cottage; a place in which to get food, sleep, and shelter when I was not fishing. It became a sanctuary. The peace and beauty of the spot made it a sacred place. The cottage belongs to angling memories, but the fishing became a small part of the happiness that was associated with it. For thirty-three years the chosen spot remained a place of refuge and delight, not in the fishing season only. For the last four years, indeed, I had been unable to fish with a dry fly, and the original purpose for which the cottage had been put there had ceased to be. Great changes, however, had been taking place that were inseparable from a new epoch. For the first fifteen years there was little change and had been little change for many years before this time. I had seen the old mill at the village not far away replaced by a new building, and the dull, monotonous sound of a turbine had replaced the lively splashing of a water-wheel; but otherwise things remained as they were. The cottage was invisible from any road; it was approached by an old lime avenue, long disused, and the track down this was not suited for any wheels but those of a farm cart. There was a little wayside station on a single railway line close by; but the quickest route from London was to go by a fast train to Winchester, and thence to drive a distance between four and five miles to the nearest point to the cottage that was accessible by wheels. This was a drive of at least half an hour in a one-horse fly. Presently taxi-cabs took the place of the horse conveyance and reduced the time of the drive to a quarter of an hour. Was this an advantage? On balance it was not. For escape from London meant that hurry, noise and bustle had been left behind: I had entered into leisure, where saving of time was no object, and often I would walk from Winchester to enjoy the country. There was a footpath way on each side of the river. By one of these one entered the cottage without, except for the momentary crossing of one road and of three secluded lanes, having had touch or sight of a road. There were thirty-three stiles on this path. It happened not infrequently that I could not get to Winchester till the latest train arriving there some time after eleven o'clock. The walk then lasted well into the midnight hour. In the dusk or dark it was easier to walk by the road than by the path. There was much charm in this midnight walk. Traffic had ceased, cottage lights had been put out, the inmates were all at rest or asleep. Now and then one heard in passing the song of a nightingale or a sedge-warbler, but in the main there was silence. It was pleasant after the hardness of London streets and pavements to feel the soft dust about my feet. On a still summer night there were sweet and delicate scents in the air, breathed forth from leaves and herbs and grass, and from the earth itself. It was as if one's own very being was soothed and in some way refined by the stillness, the gentleness and the sweetness of it all.

Then came the age of motors and tarred roads. Few people, I imagine, seek the smell of tar for its own sake. To me there is nothing unclean or nauseous in it, but it is a coarse, rough smell. The sweet and delicate scents of the night were obliterated by it, as if, overpowered and repelled, they had sunk back into the leaves and earth from which they had ventured into air. The strong smell of the tar seemed to disturb even the stillness of the night: the soft dust was no more, and the road was hard as a paved street. Not all, but much of the charm of the night walk was gone. There were other changes too; small houses of the villa type were built along the road that was nearest to the cottage: doubtless there are more of them now, for the cottage was accidentally destroyed by fire in January 1923, and I have not seen the place for some years. The sense of change was in the air. It may be that change is for the good;

> The old order changeth, yielding place to new,
> And God fulfils himself in many ways,
> Lest one good custom should corrupt the world.

It is not for us, who cannot foresee the future, who perhaps cannot rightly understand the present, to chide or to repine too much. Only it is impossible for us, who in our youth gave our affections to things that are passed or passing away, to transfer our affections to new things in which a new generation finds delight.

The beauty, however, of chalk-stream valleys still remains wonderful. The river still waters meadows that are unspoilt and unchanged, and its clear purity is guarded and protected.

> Still glides the stream and shall for ever glide,
> The form remains, the function never dies.

Thus, as the angler looks back he thinks less of individual captures and days than of the scenes in which he fished. The luxuriance of water meadows, animated by insect and bird and trout life, tender with the green and gay with the blossoms of early spring: the nobleness and volumes of great salmon rivers: the exhilaration of looking at any salmon pool, great or small; the rich browness of Highland water: the wild openness of the treeless, trackless spaces which he has traversed in an explorer's spirit of adventure to search likely water for sea trout: now on one, now on another of these scenes an angler's mind will dwell, as he thinks of fishing. Special days and successes he will no doubt recall, but always with the remembrance and the mind's vision of the scenes and the world in which he fished. For, indeed, this does seem a separate world, a world of beauty and enjoyment. The time must come to all of us, who live long, when memory is more than prospect. An angler who has reached this stage and reviews the pleasure of life will be grateful and glad that he has been an angler, for he will look back upon days radiant with happiness, peaks and peaks of enjoyment that are not less bright because they are lit in memory by the light of a setting sun.

W. B. YEATS: *The Song of Wandering Aengus.* From *The Wind Among the Reeds* (1899).

> I went out to the hazel wood,
> Because a fire was in my head,
> And cut and peeled a hazel wand,
> And hooked a berry to a thread;
> And when white moths were on the wing,
> And moth-like stars were flickering out,
> I dropped the berry in a stream
> And caught a little silver trout.
>
> When I had laid it on the floor
> I went to blow the fire aflame,
> But something rustled on the floor,

And some one called me by my name:
It had become a glimmering girl
With apple blossom in her hair
Who called me by my name and ran
And faded through the brightening air.

Though I am old with wandering
Through hollow lands and hilly lands,
I will find out where she has gone,
And kiss her lips and take her hand;
And walk among long dappled grass,
And pluck till time and times are done
The silver apples of the moon,
The golden apples of the sun.

'A cool curving world'
The Early Twentieth Century

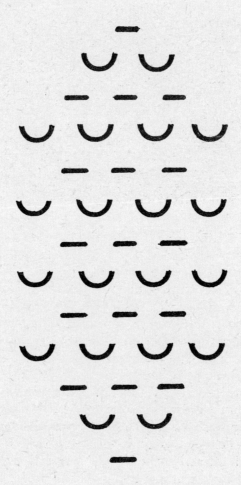

FISCHES NACHTGESANG: (Fish's Nightsong). From *Galgenlieder (Gallows Songs)* by Christian Morgenstern (1905).

CHARLES FREDERICK HOLDER: from *The Big Game Fishes of the United States* (1901).

Around many portions of the Californian coast, especially its islands, there is a submarine forest of great density. The trees are represented by the so-called kelp, the *Macrocystis*, which attains a length of several hundred feet, rising upward in broad deep-green leaves of gigantic size, which swing in the current undulating like living things, forming a maze or forest, which, while easily seen, is a closed region even to the diver owing to the intricate convolutions of the plants. Looking down into this mimic forest when the sun is overhead, the scene, especially when observed through a water-glass, or a glass-bottom boat, is fascinating. Arches, loops, parterres, festoons, colonnades, every possible conception which the imagination might devise, is seen, glorified by the sunlight and bathed in marvellous tints of green, while through every interstice the deep-blue water forms a matchless mosaic. At low tide the long fluted leaves lie like snakes upon the surface, the wind often lifting them, but at the flood they are submerged and swing in the current at an angle of thirty-five or forty degrees; now straightening up or turning, according to the whim or fancy of the mysterious currents which are found about these islands bathed by the Kuroshiwo, the great Black Current of Japan.

This submarine forest is the home of the king of the bass, *Stereolepis gigas* (Ayres), the gigantic black sea-bass, possibly the largest of all the serranoids. In appearance it bears a marked resemblance to the small black bass. Imagine a small-mouth black bass seven feet in length, weighing six or seven hundred pounds, and some idea of this monster, which is a common fish in the region described, may be conceived. It has been my good fortune to see the fish in its native haunts. Lying prone on the deck of a small boat, with my face within a foot of the water, I was watching my bait forty feet down among the stems of the kelp, the water being so clear that every object could be seen. As I looked, into the range of vision, through a curtain of kelp which it seemed to push aside like a portière, came a mighty fish which I recognized as a black sea-bass. It was at least six feet in length, weighing possibly three hundred pounds, and simulated the colour of the weed. At its approach the small fry and numerous sheepshead disappeared before the king. Its movements were slow and dignified, as became its size, and guided either by scent or sight it swam toward my small sardine bait prepared for yellowtail, gazed at it warily and passed on to return and view it from another position. A score of times this gigantic fish, which I had previously imagined a glutton that rushed at food and bolted it, played about the bait with tactful movements, the personification of caution and deliberation; then, as though satisfied, it poised directly over it, depressed its muzzle until it stood upon its head, tail upward, then took the bait and slowly moved off. When it felt the wire leader a whirlwind seemed to have struck the kelp forest, leaves and stems being tossed hither and yon in a vortex as the tail of the mighty bass swept through it beyond my range of vision. I had but two hundred feet of fifteen-thread line on my yellowtail reel, hence the end soon came. The reel uttered a vigorous protest, and the line parted. But I was well paid; I had seen a big sea-bass standing upon its head in the heart of this maze of kelp.

ALFRED RONALD: *Taste and Smell.* From *Flyfisher's Entomology* (1901).

It seemed almost impossible to devise experiments relative to the sense of smell in fishes, which would offer the prospect of satisfactory results, without depriving the animal of sight; the cruelty of which operation deterred me from prosecuting the inquiry.

Observations on the taste of fishes are involved in still greater difficulty. I once threw upon the water, from my hut (by blowing them through a tin tube), successively, ten dead house-flies, towards a Trout known to me by a white mark upon the nose (occasioned by the wound of a hook), all of which he took. Thirty more with *Cayenne pepper and mustard* plastered on the least conspicuous parts of them, were then administered in the same manner. These he also seized, twenty of them at the instant they touched the water, and not allowing time for the dressing to be dispersed; but the other ten remained a second or two upon the surface before he swallowed them, and a small portion of the dressing parted and sank. The next morning several exactly similar doses were taken by the same fish, who probably remembered the previous day's repast, and seemed to enjoy them heartily. From these and similar experiments, such as getting Trout to take flies dipped in honey, oil, vinegar, etc., I concluded that if the animal has taste, his palate is not peculiarly sensitive.

My experience goes to prove, contrary to the opinion of some who say that the Trout will take *every* insect, that he does not feed upon the Honey Bee (*Apis mellifica*), or Wasp (*Vespa vulgaris*), and that he very rarely takes the Bumble Bee (*Bombus*).

FREDERIC M. HALFORD: from *An Angler's Autobiography* (1903).

Looking back, I can see before me plainly the appearance of the Serpentine and Long Water on a fine autumn afternoon and evening. The banks were thickly lined with shabby, quiet-looking old men, patiently sitting on their tackle boxes, each with a long roach pole supported on two wire stands. All eyes were fixed on the points of the slender quill floats just peeping above the surface of the water, and each angler was intently watching to detect the smallest movement, ready to strike, and gently detaching the lower joints of the cumbersome rod, work the big roach or bream, with the three or four upper joints, round to the bank.

I have some recollection of seeing it stated somewhere that the accumulation of mud on the bed of the lake had become so great and so noisome that the authorities, from due regard for the health of the population, were constrained to clean it out. To do this the water was pumped away, the fish removed elsewhere, the depth of the lake largely decreased, and then allowed to fill up again. Why the fish were not returned to the water, or why it was not restocked, is a mystery to most of us. No doubt the present aspect of Hyde Park and Kensington Gardens is far more respectable, and the absence of the great number of ill-clad individuals from the margin of the lake is an advantage in the eyes of the nurses and children who frequent these parts, but to many poor men it suggests a deep injustice.

W. H. HUDSON: from *Hampshire Days* (1903).

Beyond that starved, melancholy wilderness, the sight of which has led me into so long a digression, one comes to a point which overlooks the valley of the Exe; and here one pauses long before going down to the half-hidden village by the river. Especially if it is in May or June, when the oak is in its 'glad light grene', for that is the most vivid and beautiful of all vegetable greens, and the prospect is the greenest and most soul-refreshing to be found in England. The valley is all wooded and the wood is all oak – a continuous oak-wood stretching away on the right, mile on mile, to the sea. The sensation experienced at the sight of this prospect is like that of the traveller in a dry desert when he comes to a clear running stream and drinks his fill of water and is refreshed. The river is tidal, and at the full of the tide in its widest part beside the village its appearance is of a small inland lake, grown round with oaks – old trees that stretch their horizontal branches far out and wet their lower leaves in the salt water. The village itself that has this setting, with its ancient water-mill, its palace of the Montagus, and the Abbey of Beaulieu, a grey ivied ruin, has a distinction above all Hampshire villages, and is unlike all others in its austere beauty and atmosphere of old-world seclusion and quietude. Above all, is that quality which the mind imparts – the expression due to romantic historical associations.

One very still, warm summer afternoon I stood on the margin, looking across the sheet of glassy water at a heron on the farther side, standing knee-deep in the shallow water patiently watching for a fish, his grey figure showing distinctly against a background of bright green sedges. Between me and the heron scores of swallows and martins were hawking for flies, gliding hither and thither a little above the glassy surface, and occasionally dropping down to dip and wet their under plumage in the water. And all at once, fifty yards out from the margin, there was a great splash, as if a big stone had been flung out into the lake; and then two or three moments later out from the falling spray and rocking water rose a swallow, struggling laboriously up, its plumage drenched, and flew slowly away. A big pike had dashed at and tried to seize it at the moment of dipping in the water, and the swallow had escaped as by a miracle. I turned round to see if any person was near, who might by chance have witnessed so strange a thing, in order to speak to him about it. There was no person within sight, but if on turning round, my eyes had encountered the form of a Cistercian monk, returning from his day's labour in the fields, in his dirty black-and-white robe, his implements on his shoulders, his face and hands begrimed with dust and sweat, the apparition on that day, in the mood I was in, would not have greatly surprised me.

The atmosphere, the expression of the past may so attune the mind as almost to produce the illusion that the past is now.

F. G. AFLALO: from *The Salt of My Life* (1905).

One more kind of fishing we tried on the way home to Europe, and, since I have promised not to gloze the failures, it shall here be set forth, though it will be long again before I go to so much trouble with so slight a chance of success.

Long had I treasured the details furnished by a sporting correspondent of the *Field*, a naval officer, of stupendous fishing in the Indian Ocean and Red Sea when under way. Albicore, bonito and other splendid surface-swimming fishes had been taken by this method, and, as we were bound for those hallowed waterways, in a vessel moreover which did nothing to emulate the expedition of a mail-boat, I resolved to try my luck. The *dobash* of the B. I. Company at Batavia procured for me an immense bamboo pole, the which, with the sanction of the skipper and by the help of a well-bribed quarter-master, was rigged up in the correct fashion, so that it projected, seemingly for about a quarter of a mile, from the starboard side, a gigantic fishing-rod indeed. A brand new line, a treble hook dressed with bunting to imitate a flying fish – it might just as well have been a drowned immature hippogriff – and a small bell completed this amazing outfit. The eight knots, which had sufficed our unambitious old tramp *via* the Queensland ports and Barrier Reef, were, on leaving Tanjong Priak increased to nine, probably rather too fast for success; but the skipper,

though not hostile to the idea of fresh fish in the saloon, declined any
further concession. We could fish at nine knots, or 'do the other thing',
whatever that was. The autocrats put in charge of cargo-boats 'fitted to
carry a few passengers' have a charm of manner that distinguishes
them from the other personages of earth. The only construction we
could put upon 'the other thing' was whist all day and pegs all the
evening; and, as these had been tried to exhaustion, we resolved to give
the fishing a turn. Over went the flying-fish on the day that Java faded
from sight, and away it trailed in the direction of that spicy island,
bobbing and dancing in the creamy wake of the pulsing screw, and the
lissom bamboo bent to the pull of it. Then the line and bell were so
connected that as soon as a fish threw additional strain on the former it
set the latter ringing. The first time, the bell remained silent, and after
waiting with waning enthusiasm for three or four hours, six of us,
passengers and crew together, had half-an-hour's back-breaking exercise getting the line in, so appalling was the tension. Next evening,
when some slight finishing touches had been put on the 'fish', till it
now resembled a waterlogged bird, it was once more cast loose to
dance before the eyes of ravening monsters of the deep. It did its work,
but we never saw it again. Just as we were busy at dinner with some
more than usually uninteresting dish, tinkle went the bell, and, without
apology to the Captain, who would not have left his food if the four
beasts of the apocalypse had sat down at the saloon table, we dashed on
deck, just in time to see our precious bamboo bending like a sapling in
a gale. Next minute, we were all hanging on to it, and for a few glorious
moments of suspense, we felt the desperate play of something lively
and ponderous out in the darkening foam, probably one of Lieut.
Howell's dolphin or kingfish. Then the ship's nine knots and the
efforts of the fish combined with a result that sent us tumbling on the
deck, for the line parted, and when we were on our feet again we
hauled in the slack. That was our last attempt. 'Flying-fishes' cost us
half-a-crown apiece, nor, seeing how much they took up of their
maker's time, and what fearful objects of art they were when completed, could they be called dear at that price. The game was, however,
voted not worth the flying-fish, and the ocean-rod joined the list of the
ship's belongings, as I was in no mind to take sixty feet of bamboo on a
cab through the streets of London.

CHARLES MARSON: from *Super Flumina, Angling Observations of a Coarse Fisherman* (1905).

The meditative angler, especially while he is trying some new fetch for the girlish dace, may do well to reflect that the fish reflect not insignificantly the types of his acquaintance. Is not this little dace, like lively young Dashling, who coxed the Queen's eight? I see the very man inpiscate. He ran and boxed too, did Dashling, far beyond his inches, and if I remember rightly, became an explorer in Africa, where he was eaten of lions. This pushing, practical perch in my basket, reminds me of Dollardson, in his rich waistcoats, whom none could ignore or forget. He took a good degree, and became a barrister, renowned for his bullying and sharp cross-examinings. Poor old Dough, now the mild-eyed, perpetual curate of Ramsbotham Minor, who lived in cheap lodgings in Walton Street, and belonged to the unattached, he was a good, but timid roach. He hated extremes did Dough, and had a sad earnestness about him. That wide-eyed fellow, we always thought so lacking in taste – Fallowfield, of Lincoln, I mean – also took Orders and everything else he could get: he was actually made chaplain to Lord Earlscourt, and is now a rotund Canon in the wilds of somewhere. He is the very embodiment of a chub, a two-pound chub. Sallow old Heavyside the solicitor, a quiet family man, with a thick ring and stupid sons, he is a tench. He ought to have been a physician by rights, but he fattens upon his diet of deeds. Call upon him at his office and see him slowly grope in the twilight among his despatch boxes. How he rubs his fat fingers along the red tape! Beckling of the blue blood, the dandy, became a soldier and perished magnificently before his day in some frontier scuffle: he had the dash of a gallant trout about him. The walrus, as we called little Gregson, because of his huge moustache and solemn bearing, ought to have been the gudgeon. He got taken on at Christie's, and dabbles a good deal in Art criticism, taking himself over-seriously. Large Longleat became an Army Contractor and promoted companies. His grin, and those hard eyes, proclaimed him a jack, when he was young. He is now a pike, as his admirers will admit. Cecil Rhodes was much taken with him, and sent a lot of good things his way, which he did not let slip. You, my kind round-eyed Sir, with the cocked hair, made me wonder if you were ever a rock whiting. Painful Higgins, you have assuredly the aspect of a blenny. Forbes, you long-bodied rowing champion, you Ireland scholar and king of good fellows, you are a salmon even to your love of prawns and self-sacrifice. I could easily believe that your flesh would be pink, if some Shylock carved out a pound of it. There is no fish that swims, but has his counterpart in the human brotherhood. Even the ladies have their likenesses in the watery world. Do I not know the pretty dapper pilot fish? The matronly bream?

* * *

Considering how little is really known about the weeds we walk upon, it is not astonishing to find that the weeds we boat upon have attracted such scant study and attention that they are dismissed with short sentences by the botany books. Let us lie upon our stomachs over the bank and peer into the stream. Do you see that dark bank of swelling green? That is Canada's present to us, the beautiful but mischievous water thyme, with its small whorls of translucent leaves tucked into the stem. *Elodea Canadensis* is the creature's name. It came over to Yorkshire in 1847, and is slowly creeping over our quiet rivers. It is too dense for fish, too tart for insects, too bitter for ducks, and too soft and deep for the tools of clearers. Those rich cushions are choking our streams. Why? Have we not undiscovered wealth enough of water weed? Ours, at any rate, are all pock pitted by hungry jaws, but look at this perfect stranger. Nobody bites at him, and he is flourishing when the rest are half rotten.

Those long, waving, leafy things, which sway in the stream, with a sort of dry flake in the axil, are the pond weeds. There are thirty of them, without counting foreigners, and that bit of smooth water, held still by flat lancehead leaves, is the swimming pond weed, and a good friend of the fish. Our perch will often hang their strings of eggs under those leaves, where they are safe always to be in the water, be the river high or low, and, if it were not for the ducks, to be fertilized in peace, through the tiny holes which fit none other sperms than those of perch, and so to hatch out into little inky fry, which themselves begin to breed when they weigh a fifth of a pound. That long, green, hairy tress is the *Conferva* of Pliny. Its name implies that it is good for healing broken bones, (*Confervere*, to knit). We call it flannel wort, and catch roach with it. Those fine, short, fennel leaves belong to the water milfoil, which is of small interest to us, but of enormous joy to the minnows. That bit of bright green wrack is a thing to eye with respect, for it is probably the great grandfather of all the whole vegetable family or most of them. Here is the common ancestor of grass, vines, roses, balm, cabbages, corn and geraniums, and all those modifications of the green leaf, the water leaf.

GROVER CLEVELAND: from *Fishing and Shooting Sketches* (1906).

Daniel Webster, too, was a fisherman – always in good and regular standing. In marshalling the proof which his great life furnishes of the beneficence of the fishing propensity, I approach the task with a feeling of awe quite natural to one who has slept in the room occupied by the great Expounder during his fishing campaigns on Cape Cod and along the shores of Mashpee Pond and its adjacent streams. This distinguished member of our fraternity was an industrious and attentive fisherman. He was, besides, a wonderful orator – and largely so because he was a fisherman. He himself has confessed to the aid he received from a fishing environment in the preparation of his best oratorical efforts; and other irrefutable testimony to the same effect is at hand.

It is not deemed necessary to cite in proof of such aid more than a single incident. Perhaps none of Mr Webster's orations was more notable, or added more to his lasting fame, than that delivered at the laying of the cornerstone of the Bunker Hill Monument. And it will probably be conceded that its most impressive and beautiful passage was addressed to the survivors of the War of Independence then present, beginning with the words, 'Venerable men'! This thrilling oratorical flight was composed and elaborated by Mr Webster while wading waist deep and casting his flies in Mashpee waters. He himself afterwards often referred to this circumstance; and one who was his companion on this particular occasion has recorded the fact that, noticing indications of laxity in fishing action on Mr Webster's part, he approached him, and that, in the exact words of this witness, 'he seemed to be gazing at the overhanging trees, and presently advancing one foot and extending his right hand he commenced to speak, "Venerable Men"!'

Though this should be enough to support conclusively the contention that incidents of Mr Webster's great achievements prove the close relationship between fishing and the loftiest attainments of mankind, this branch of our subject ought not to be dismissed without reference to a conversation I once had with old John Attaquin, then a patriarch among the few survivors of the Mashpee Indians. He had often been Mr Webster's guide and companion on his fishing trips and remembered clearly many of their happenings. It was with a glow of love and admiration amounting almost to worship that he related how this great fisherman, after landing a large trout on the bank of the stream, 'talked mighty strong and fine to that fish and told him what a mistake he had made, and what a fool he was to take that fly, and that he would have been all right if he had let it alone'. Who can doubt that patient search would disclose, somewhere in Mr Webster's speeches and writings, the elaboration, with high intent, of that 'mighty strong and fine' talk addressed to the fish at Mashpee?

ANTWERP E. PRATT: from *Two Years Among New Guinea Cannibals* (1906).

One of the curiosities of Waley, and, indeed, one of the greatest curiosities that I noted during during my stay in New Guinea, was the spiders' web fishing-net.

In the forest at this point huge spiders' webs, six feet in diameter, abounded. These are woven in a large mesh, varying from one inch square at the outside of the web to about one eighth of an inch at the centre. The web was most substantial, and had great resisting power, a fact of which the natives were not slow to avail themselves, for they have pressed into the service of man this spider, which is about the size of a small hazel-nut, with hairy, dark-brown legs, spreading to about two inches. This diligent creature they have beguiled into weaving their fishing-nets. At the place where the webs are thickest they set up long bamboos, bent over into a loop at the end. In a very short time the spider weaves a web on this most convenient frame, and the Papuan has his fishing-net ready to his hand. He goes down to the stream and uses it with great dexterity to catch fish of about one pound weight, neither the water nor the fish sufficing to break the mesh. The usual practice is to stand on a rock in a backwater where there is an eddy. There they watch for a fish, and then dexterously dip it up and throw it on to the bank. Several men would set up bamboos so as to have nets ready all together, and would then arrange little fishing parties. It seemed to me that the substance of the web resisted water as readily as a duck's back.

ERNEST BRIGGS: from *Angling and Art in Scotland* (1908).

Close at hand, on the western shore, stands the keeper's cottage, fringed with straggling spruces. From it comes the reek of peat, whose scent is occasionally wafted to the fisherman as he drifts across the loch. It is interesting, this cottage, for in it lived, for many years, that gem of Scottish gamekeepers, the late Thomas Burnside.

He was a man of a type fast disappearing; one who possessed a certain dry sense of humour, and a picturesque and quaint way of expressing himself, combined with characteristic native caution. His caution, I can recollect, strongly manifested itself on our first visit to the loch, when, after allowing us to take out the boat – a boat so heavy that it was only with difficulty that it could be made to move through the water – he repeatedly warned us, most solemnly, of the danger of running it on the 'stanes', assuring us that it was 'but a wee cawkle-shell of a thing'.

Burnside was an elderly man when I first knew him, fully six feet in height, and of an upright and soldierly carriage. He wore a fringe of iron-grey side-whiskers around his face, which, together with his hands, was tanned, from constant exposure, to a deep brown colour. His eyes were of a yellowish-grey hue, and wore a far-off, somewhat pained expression; and when he was talking to you they never seemed to see any object nearer than the horizon line some three miles distant. Even at the end of the day, when our basket of trout had been displayed for his admiration, and his right hand was mechanically, and apparently unconsciously, thrust slightly forward, palm uppermost, it was difficult to believe that his mind was concentrated on any object within that three-mile radius. He usually spoke through his teeth in a monotonous voice, as though some unseen agency were squeezing the words out under a high pressure, and it gave one the distinct impression that the operation was painful.

Burnside took an enormous pride in Lochinvar: I am sure he believed it to be one of the best lochs in Scotland; consequently, he would never allow that it was a good fishing day, lest you should have bad sport, and so take away the only extenuating excuse which could be offered. When you arrived at the loch-side in the morning, and saw the water dimpled with rising fish, you naturally remarked, 'Good morning, Mr Burnside, this looks a likely morning for the fishing'. 'Na, na!' he would reply; 'thaat's no the right thing at a'; there's a nasty glassy *glare* on the waterr'; or, 'I dinna like thae nasty, white, tourin' paaks (high thunder-clouds); the troot never tak' when they're aboot'. The next day we visit the loch it is possibly brilliantly fine, with no cloud in sight, so we hazard the remark, 'Well, Mr Burnside, there are no white towering packs about this morning'; to be answered with, 'No, but likely they'll get up with the day! I fear there's ower muckle *fire* in the air the day'. Another occasion, I remember – a perfect fishing day with a greyish sky and beautifully steady breeze from the west – on arriving at the loch, I ventured on a word of praise, and was met with several inarticulate murmurs from Burnside – sounds as if he were being wound up somewhere inside. At last these internal noises formed themselves into words, and came out as though under great pressure, with a burst – 'I like not thaat nasty *slated* appearance on the waterr'.

RICHARD JEFFERIES: *The Sun and the Brook.* From *The Hills and the Vale* (1909).

The sun first sees the brook in the meadow where some roach swim under a bulging root of ash. Leaning against the tree, and looking down into the water, there is a picture of the sky. Its brightness hides the sandy floor of the stream as a picture conceals the wall where it hangs, but, as if the water cooled the rays, the eye can bear to gaze on the image of the sun. Over its circle thin threads of summer cloud are drawn; it is only the reflection, yet the sun seems closer seen in the brook, more to do with us, like the grass, and the tree, and the flowing stream. In the sky it is so far, it cannot be approached, nor even gazed at, so that by the very virtue and power of its own brilliance it forces us to ignore, and almost forget it. The summer days go on, and no one notices the sun. The sweet water slipping past the green flags, with every now and then a rushing sound of eager haste, receives the sky, and it becomes a part of the earth and of life. No one can see his own face without a glass; no one can sit down and deliberately think of the soul till it appears a visible thing. It eludes – the mind cannot grasp it. But hold a flower in the hand – a rose, this later honeysuckle, or this the first harebell – and in its beauty you can recognize your own soul reflected as the sun in the brook. For the soul finds itself in beautiful things.

Between the bulging root and the bank there is a tiny oval pool, on the surface of which the light does not fall. There the eye can see deep down into the stream, which scarcely moves in the hollow it has worn for itself as its weight swings into the concave of the bend. The hollow is illuminated by the light which sinks through the stream outside the root; and beneath, in the green depth, five or six roach face the current. Every now and then a tiny curl appears on the surface inside the root, and must rise up to come there. Unwinding as it goes, its raised edge lowers and becomes lost in the level. Dark moss on the base of the ash darkens the water under. The light green leaves overhead yield gently to the passing air; there are but few leaves on the tree, and these scarcely make a shadow on the grass beyond that of the trunk. As the branch swings, the gnats are driven farther away to avoid it. Over the verge of the bank, bending down almost to the root in the water, droop the heavily seeded heads of tall grasses which, growing there, have escaped the scythe.

These are the days of the convolvulus, of ripening berry, and dropping nut. In the gateways, ears of wheat hang from the hawthorn boughs, which seized them from the passing load. The broad after-math is without flowers; the flowers are gone to the uplands and the unstilled wastes. Curving opposite the south, the hollow side of the brook has received the sunlight like a silvered speculum every day that the sun has shone. Since the first violet of the meadow, till now that the berries are ripening, through all the long drama of the summer, the rays have visited the stream. The long, loving touch of the sun has left some of its own mystic attraction in the brook. resting here, and gazing down into it, thoughts and dreams come flowing as the water flows. Thoughts without words, mobile like the stream, nothing compact that can be grasped and stayed: dreams that slip silently as water slips through the fingers. The grass is not grass alone; the leaves of the ash above are not leaves only. From tree, and earth, and soft air moving, there comes an invisible touch which arranges the senses to its waves as the ripples of the lake set the sand in parallel lines. The grass sways and fans the reposing mind; the leaves sway and stroke it, till it can feel beyond itself and with them, using each grass blade, each leaf, to abstract life from earth and ether. These then become new organs, fresh nerves and veins running afar out into the field, along the winding brook, up through the leaves, bringing a larger existence. The arms of the mind open wide to the broad sky.

Some sense of the meaning of the grass, and leaves of the tree, and sweet waters hovers on the confines of thought, and seems ready to be resolved into definite form. There is a meaning in these things, a meaning in all that exists, and it comes near to declare itself. Not yet, not fully, nor in such shape that it may be formulated – if ever it will be – but sufficiently so to leave, as it were, an unwritten impression that will remain when the glamour is gone, and grass is but grass, and a tree a tree.

RUPERT BROOKE: *The Fish* (written 1911).

In a cool curving world he lies
And ripples with dark ecstasies.
The kind luxurious lapse and steal
Shapes all his universe to feel
And know and be; the clinging stream
Closes his memory, glooms his dream,
Who lips the roots o' the shore, and glides
Superb on unreturning tides.
Those silent waters weave for him
A fluctuant mutable world and dim,
Where wave ring masses bulge and gape
Mysterious and shape to shape
Dies momently through whorl and hollow,
And form and line and solid follow
Solid and line and form to dream
Fantastic down the eternal stream;
An obscure world, a shifting world,
Bulbous, or pulled to thin, or curled,
Or serpentine, or driving arrows,
Or serene sliding, or March narrows.
There slipping wave and shore are one,
And weed and mud. No ray of sun,
But glow to glow fades down the deep
(As dream to unknown dream in sleep);
Shaken translucency illumes
The hyaline of drifting glooms;
The strange soft-handed depth subdues
Drowned colour there, but black to hues,
As death to living, decomposes –
Red darkness of the heart of roses,

Blue brilliant from dead starless skies,
And gold that lies behind the eyes,
The unknown unnameable sightless white
That is the essential flame of night,
Lustreless purple, hooded green,
The myriad hues that lie between
Darkness and darkness! . . .

                And all's one,
Gentle, embracing, quiet, dun,
The world he rests in, world he knows,
Perpetual curving. Only – grows
An eddy in that ordered falling,
A knowledge from the gloom, a calling
Weed in the wave, gleam in the mud –
The dark fire leaps along his blood;
Dateless and deathless, blind and still,
The intricate purpose works its will;
His woven world drops back; and he,
Sans providence, sans memory,
Unconscious and directly driven,
Fades to some dank sufficient heaven.

O world of lips, O world of laughter,
Where hope is fleet and thought flies after,
Of lights in the clear night, of cries
That drift along the wave and rise
Thin to the glittering stars above,
You know the hands, the eyes of love!
The strife of limbs, the sightless clinging,
The infinite distance, and the singing,
Blown by the wind, a flame of sound,
The gleam, the flowers, the vast around
The horizon, and the heights above –
You know the sigh, the song of love!

But there the night is close, and there
Darkness is cold and strange and bare;
And the secret deeps are whisperless;
And rhythm is all deliciousness;

And joy is in the throbbing tide,
Whose intricate fingers beat and glide
In felt bewildering harmonies
Of trembling touch; and music is
The exquisite knocking of the blood.
Space is no more, under the mud;
His bliss is older than the sun.
Silent and straight the waters run.
The lights, the cries, the willows dim,
And the dark tide are one with him.

HAROLD RUSSELL: from *Chalkstream and Moorland* (1911).

Yet compared with the serious things of life, fishing is after all a trivial business. The thoughtful angler must frankly confess this. It adds to the difficulty of the problem when he asks himself why the pleasure of catching a few trout is so great and failure so disheartening. The eagerness and excitement with which one sets about fishing water which holds big fish is almost childish. The value of the prize is in no way comparable to the desire it arouses. When the fish are rising and showing themselves, the longing to hook them which one feels is almost insane. And again when we see them feeding regardless of our fly or dashing off terrified at our efforts to delude them, the resentment which the fisherman feels is almost like the anger of a madman. These emotions resemble the longing, the despair, or the indignation of childhood. To tell the truth, fishermen remain always boys so far as their amusement goes. Yet they learn something by experience, and no one will pretend that as we get older the disappointment of losing a big fish, just when it was nearly landed, is quite as bitter as it was when we were younger. With youthful envy we watch experienced fishermen catching fish when we only bungle and fail. Admiration at their skilful powers and humiliation at our own clumsy casting make us ready to give years of our lives to attain the art which they possess. Perhaps in time we reach the same degree of skill and find ourselves able to catch those shy and cautious trout which seemed formerly so impossible to delude. The satisfaction is very great and well worth the labour and time it has cost to attain. But perhaps, like many things in life, when we have got our desired object we take it as our due; and the satisfaction is not as lively as the desire might lead us to expect. So success and failure in fishing show us, as in a mirror, the careers of men in the great world. But it is all in miniature, and the emotions of the actors are those of children. It may be, perhaps, because men become again, as it were, little children that fishing gives those who love it such great pleasure and keeps them young.

H. T. SHERINGHAM: from an article in *The Field* (1 July 1911).

You cannot, of course, fish for big carp in half a day. It takes a month. So subtle are these fishes that you have to proceed with the utmost precautions. In the first week, having made ready your tackle and plumbed the depth, you build yourself a wattled screen, behind which you may take cover. By the second week the fish should have grown accustomed to this, and you begin to throw in ground-bait composed of bread, bran, biscuits, peas, beans, strawberries, rice, pearl barley, aniseed cake, worms, gentles, banana, and potato. This ground-baiting must not be overdone. Half a pint on alternate evenings is as much as can safely be employed in this second week. With the third week less caution is necessary, because by now the carp will be less mindful of the adage concerning those who come bearing gifts. You may bear gifts daily, and the carp will, it is to be hoped, in a manner of speaking, look these gifts in the mouth – as carp should. Now, with the fourth week comes the critical time. All is very soon to be put to the touch.

On Monday you lean your rod (it is ready put up, you remember) on the wattled fence so that its top projects eighteen inches over the water. On Tuesday you creep up and push it gently, so that the eighteen inches are become four feet. The carp, we hope, simply think that it is a piece of the screen growing well, and take no alarm. On Wednesday, Thursday, and Friday you employ the final and great ruse. This is to place your line (the depth has already been plumbed, of course) gently in the water, the bullet just touching the bottom so that the float cocks, and the two feet of gut which lie on the bottom beyond it terminating with a bait in which is no fraudful hook. This so that the carp may imagine that it is just a whim of the lavish person behind the screen (be sure they know you are there all the time) to tie food to some fibrous yet innocuous substance. And at last, on Saturday, the thirty-first of the month, you fall to angling, while the morning mists are still disputing with the shades of night. Now there is a hook within the honey paste, and woe betide any carp which loses its head. But no carp does lose its head until the shades of night are disputing with the mists of evening. Then, from your post of observation (fifty yards behind the screen), you hear a click, click, which tells you that your reel revolves. A carp has made off with the bait, drawn out the five yards of line coiled carefully on the ground, and may now be struck. So you hasten up and strike. There is a monstrous pull at the rod-point, something pursues a headlong course into the unknown depths, and after a few thrilling seconds there is a jar, a slackness of line, and you wind up sorrowfully. You are broken, and so home.

PATRICK CHALMERS: *The First Fisherman*. From *Green Days and Blue Days* (1912).

Beside a vast and primal sea
A solitary savage he,

Who gathered for his tribe's rude need
The daily dole of raw sea-weed.

He watched the great tides rise and fall,
And spoke the truth – or not at all!

Along the awful shore he ran
A simple pre-Pelasgian;

A thing primeval, undefiled,
Straightforward as a little child, –

Until one morn he made a grab
And caught a mesozoic crab!
Then – told the tribe at close of day
A bigger one had got away!

From him have sprung (I own a bias
To ways the cult of rod and fly has)
All fishermen – and Ananias!

H. RIDER HAGGARD: from *The Days of My Life* (1926 – written 1912).

On the whole we enjoyed our fishing very much, and I killed a good number of salmon, though, because of the drought, not nearly so many as I ought to have done. Also there were multitudes of trout. The trout stream ran out of a gloomy lake surrounded by high mountains. The Icelanders vowed that there were no trout in this lake. However we procured an old boat so leaky that we could only row a little way from land and back again before she filled. Ross, who had been an oar at College, rowed, while I managed the two trolling rods. Before we had gone a few yards they were both of them bent almost double. Never before or since did I have such fishing. To what size the trout ran in that lake I had no idea, for the biggest ones invariably tore the hooks off the Phantoms and brass 'devils', or smashed the tackle, but we caught many up to about four pounds in weight. Indeed, the sport was so easy that one grew weary of it. Very charming it was also to stand alone in the blue light at midnight by the banks, or in the water of the wide and brawling salmon river, casting for and sometimes hooking the king of fish. Never shall I forget the impression it produced upon me. The mighty black mountains, the solitude, the song of the river, and the whistling flight of the wild duck – by which the silence alone was broken – and, over all, that low unearthly light just strong enough to show my fly upon the water and the boiling rises of the salmon. It is an experience which I am glad to have known.

GILFRID W. HARTLEY: from *Wild Sport and Some Stories* (1912).

At last, after making both fisherman and boatman very anxious and irritated, he worked his way out by a narrow channel into deep water, and we, rejoicing, followed him. He passed swiftly through 'Bank', through 'Boyces', and at the bottom of this pool we landed, and got on to ideal ground for following a big fish. For hundreds of yards the river ran now, on our side, by a smooth grassy lily-of-the-valley-covered bank, where you could go at any speed, and keep on level and equal terms with your salmon. He passed through the tail of 'Boyces', and into the swiftly running but steady stream of 'Cut bushes'. Two hundred yards or so of this led into a pool called 'Kirkeide', and at the lower end of this latter is a huge backwater, a most desirable and suitable place for landing a tired fish. We had come the best part of a mile: the long continuous strain was telling on him: he still kept well out in the stream, but his strong rushes had ceased, and as we neared a place in the bank where a few days before I had landed a twenty-seven pounder, I thought that we might be able to doubly mark it by also getting ashore this much greater prize. But the salmon was still too strong and too far out in the stream to come in here.

And now surely, never had anglers a better opportunity of gauging, before they handled, their prize. The short sight he gave us of him when he passed under the boat told us little; the glimpse caught of him when sulking, nothing, but that he was big. The weight test on the arms was a very fallible one: a thirty-pounder in a stream feels very heavy. But when he got into the clear smooth water above 'Kirkeide' he showed himself almost as plainly to us as if he had been on the bank. For a hundred yards or more we could see his every movement: follow the line till it went into the water and joined the trace: follow still the trace leading fair up to his mouth, so disproving what at times we had been afraid of – that he was foul-hooked. The great, pale, silvery-green, symmetrical form shone ghostly-like, but with wonderful distinctness, in the dark emerald-green water. We could see his fins working: now and then he pulled impatiently, as it were, at his reins, and sometimes, turning half over, showed the ridge of his back. He might lunge about and give some trouble at the landing, but his real fighting was over: he was becoming tractable, and could be led instead of leading us.

And we began to make almost sure of him. That men who had fished for many years and habitually quoted half a dozen sayings about premature confidence should ever allow themselves to be sure of a salmon before he was on the bank, shows to what a pitch ignorance and presumption can lead mortals. We knew the strength of the tackle. We knew by this time that the fish must be well hooked: we saw ever coming nearer the calm smooth backwater into which he was to be gently and yet firmly towed, and if he should manage to struggle still farther down, we had the boat still with us, dragged behind by a keenly interested farmer, who had left his hay-making to see the sport. With audacity, which no doubt derserved punishment, we even speculated on his weight. 'He is a very big fish,' said Mons. 'I think he is bigger than P.'s,' – a forty-eight pounder which my man had gaffed the year before.

And then – without a struggle or jerk – with no extra strain put on it, the rod-top, which for an hour had formed a fair and beautiful bow flew straight. The fish was free! So done was he that for perhaps eight or ten seconds he stood almost in the same place, giving ample time if he had been nearer the bank for an active man to run down and gaff him even yet. He stood so, almost motionless, and then slowly disappeared into deep water. The splendid trace had parted: either in the hole where he had sulked so long, or, more likely, when he made his first wild rush up-stream in Laxigar, the gut must have got a terrible rub on a rock.

So the long struggle ended. This was the greatest calamity of my fishing life – the greatest blow of the kind I have ever received.

H. T. SHERINGHAM: from *Coarse Fishing* (1912).

Salmon-fishing is good; trout-fishing is good; but to the complete angler neither is intrinsically better than the pursuit of roach, or tench, or perch, or pike. There are moods and seasons, of course. Comes April, and desire is off to the valleys between the mountains, where streams are boisterous and little trout leap in the foam; where the wind comes sparkling off the moors, and a man feels a new life stirring within him. But in July, when the world croons the summer song of heat and light and slumbrous days, it is to the deep, slow river with its cool wealth of shade, and the solemn music of the weir, that we wander for refreshment, there to watch a daintily poised float, or to cozen old loggerhead out of his fastness of lily-pads with an artificial bumblebee.

In truth, the matter needs no longer argument. To the angler the world offers all manner of joys, and it cannot be said that some are better or some worse – rather that they are different. The man richest in them is the man who disdains no kind of fishing, but takes what chances of sport opportunity throws in his way. Some need there is for him to attune his mind to the keynote of the moment, some need to appreciate the niceties by which apparently very small beer can be transformed into sound old October. The artifice of fishing is displayed not only in the delusion of the fish, but to some extent in the delusion of the fisher also. Let him but have the power of persuading himself that the boy in him has never grown up, or, better, let it be so without his knowing it, and the world is his oyster. Childhood says,

'Let's pretend', and forthwith finds itself in a magic land where everything is as it should be, and where the words 'I wish' control the scheme of being. The consciousness of 'pretending' is soon lost in the exhilaration of achievement, and what was unreal at first becomes reality. Perhaps this dream-world *is* real. Who shall say that it is not? If 'beauty is in the eye of the beholder', where is the real to be found?

But I wander too far. I do not propose that the angler should pretend altogether, but rather that he should borrow some of childhood's earnestness, and see things in their right proportions. If he angles in the Puddle where roach are small and catches a pounder, let him not straightway remind himself how, in the Avon last September, he caught one of two pounds two ounces, and then fall to abusing the present hour and place. He must rather forget all about the Avon, concentrate his thoughts on the Puddle, and *realize* how lucky he is to have taken a pounder from its niggardly waters. If he can do this without difficulty, he is capable of extracting from the sport of fishing all the pleasure that it has to offer.

Fifty years ago this long preamble to a book about coarse fishing and the art of catching them would not have been needed. A hundred years ago it would have been an impertinence. But now a good many anglers do seem to need a reminder that trout and salmon are not the only fish worthy of their attention, and that by concentrating their efforts on those twain they wilfully miss a great deal. Trout and salmon are not always or everywhere to be had, and they are expensive luxuries. Hence, you may often hear bitter lamentation from men whose fishing holidays have brought them little but disappointment. Coarse fish, on the other hand, are still reasonably plentiful and accessible, and are more certain to yield some result for the angler's trouble and outlay. A holiday spent in pursuit of them is sure to provide some exciting hours. It is hardly conceivable that a keen fisherman should spend a month on a coarse-fish river without laying some golden memories in store. But the salmon-fisher may well return home after four melancholy weeks in which he has not stirred, and has scarcely seen, a fish. 'Probatum est', as *The Secrets of Angling* says about that obscure unguent, oil of ivy.

* * *

Sport is an intrinsic part of the world-scheme. The spider quite obviously takes an interest in his pursuit of a fly; the dog finds most of his life-pleasure in hunting rabbits; and even the rabbit feels a thrill at sight of a defenceless lettuce.

It is no good telling me that a lettuce does not feel. The principle of life is in a lettuce just as much as in you or me. And your humanitarian will eat lettuces without a pang, also nuts, and apples, and perhaps even eggs. On his own showing he is therefore a brutal fellow, since he is interfering with the principle of life, diverting it from its natural development. Were he to be consistent, he would eat nothing, drink nothing, and cease to breathe, for whatever he does he interferes. So he would die. And even in dying he would be in the wrong of it, since wilfully, of malice prepense, he would have interfered with the development of the life principle within himself. And that is obviously a wrong thing to do.

No; your rabid humanitarian who wants us to give up sport is in a cleft stick. There is no logical way for him to tread. Why, there is brave sport going on within him every day and every hour of the day, even a kind of fishing! In the warm stream of his blood are great battles, leucocytes preying upon bacilli, bacilli marshalling their array against leucocytes. And he is powerless to prevent it. Even if he dies, what happens? His atoms continue the unending conflict, and the very worms that were himself turn one against another. I am profoundly sorry for the man who sees evil, and nothing but evil, in 'Nature red in tooth and claw'. There is nothing before him but the abyss of despair, for how can he endure to go on living in a scheme which makes him an unwilling instrument of red ruin and death, so long as his entities exist, and that is so long as this physical world lasts?

This is no philosophy for us anglers, conscious as we are by frequent intercourse with Nature of a scheme which is intrinsically good and not evil. Look at that wagtail on the end of the beam there. It is a terrible instrument of destruction, that dainty, humorous, happy little thing. The amount of life which that monster destroys every day would make you shudder could you realize it in the true pessimistic spirit. But see if you can detect any signs of remorse in those bright eyes or that perky tail. No, of course you can't because it is *right* that the bird should do these distressing things, just as it is right that you, living in this part of the world, should from time to time eat beef – beef being the result of the regrettable decease of ox. The truth, as I see it, is that the life-principle in all created things is lent, not given, and it must in due course be returned to the hand that lent it. The manner of that return is not for creatures to choose, nor does it matter. We all – men, beasts, birds, fishes, plants – have it in common. How does it concern us in what way it passes from one to another, or which of us for the moment gives it outward form? Thinkers are too much obsessed with the idea of individualism, which is really quite another matter. If by a simple process you become an intrinsic portion of a crocodile, naturally you cease to be the handsome fellow who aforetime sat in this punt and wondered why he did not get any more bites. But you don't stop: you go on.

You think that *I* had better stop? Yes, you are right, and, in fact, I'm getting rather perplexed myself. The problem of the soul wants rather more attention than I have been able to give it so far. A million years hence, if we can then conveniently discuss things . . . But there is one more thing with regard to this humanitarianism. It is evidently meant that we should be responsible for the divergence of the vital principle – that is to say, for death in one form or another. But I grant importance in our mental attitude. There must be no malice. We must not desire to kill simply for the sake of killing, because that reacts on our own natures, besides causing more death than Nature requires. It would be evil to drain a pond dry simply that its inhabitants might gasp away their lives for man's edification, and afterwards lie there to rot. But it is not evil to try and catch them with a hook or (otherwise than in a sporting sense) with a net. Our interest lies not in the killing, but in the contest of wits and skill, in the eating, or perhaps in profit to be made. We are developing natural and healthy faculties, not pandering to a morbid lust of cruelty. It is possible, I maintain, for a sportsman to feel for his quarry both respect and affection, and yet to pursue it none the less. Does this seem a hard saying? Yet you may prove it by the fatherly eye which a fishery owner casts on his fish, and the arrangements he makes for their health and comfort. Nothing is more saddening to an honest angler than the sight of fish dying in polluted water, and that is chiefly because he looks on fish as his familiar friends, and grieves that they should be so sadly used.

W. H. HUDSON: from *Far Away and Long Ago* (1918).

One day I witnessed a very strange thing, the action of a dog by the waterside. It was evening and the beach was forsaken; cartmen, boatmen, fishermen, all gone, and I was the only idler on the rocks; but the tide was coming in, rolling quite big waves on to the rocks, and the novel sight of the waves, the freshness, the joy of it, kept me at that spot, standing on one of the outermost rocks not yet washed over by the water.

By and by a gentleman, followed by a big dog, came down to the beach and stood at a distance of forty or fifty yards from me, while the dog bounded forward over the flat, slippery rocks and through pools of water until he came to my side, and sitting on the edge of the rock began gazing intently down at the water.

He was a big, shaggy, round-headed animal, with a greyish coat with some patches of light reddish colour on it; what his breed was I cannot say, but he looked somewhat like a sheepdog or an otter hound. Suddenly he plunged in, quite vanishing from sight, but quickly reappeared with a big shad of about three and a half to four pounds weight in his jaws.

Climbing on to the rock he dropped the fish, which he had not appeared to have injured much, as it began floundering about in an exceedingly lively manner. I was astonished and looked back at the dog's master, but there he stood in the same place, smoking and paying no attention to what his animal was doing.

Again the dog plunged in and brought out a second fish and dropped it on the flat rock, and again and again he dived, until there were five big shads all floundering about on the wet rock and likely soon to be washed back into the water.

The shad is a common fish in the Plata and the best to eat of all its fishes, resembling the salmon in its rich flavour, and is eagerly watched for when it comes up from the sea by the Buenos Aires fishermen, just as our fishermen watch for mackerel on our coasts. But on this evening the beach was deserted by everyone, watcher included, and the fish came and swarmed along the rocks, and there was no one to catch them – not even some poor hungry idler to pounce and carry off the five fishes the dog had captured. One by one I saw them washed back into the water, and presently the dog, hearing his master whistling him, bounded away.

ROMILLY FEDDEN: from *Golden Days: from the Fishing-log of a Painter in Brittany* (1919).

But the nature of a fisherman's joy is a subtle quality. It cannot be adequately expressed in written characters, nor is it occasioned by the mere catching of fish. Birds come into it, and flowers and the spring sunshine, and there is nature-magic, too, which even winged words would fail to touch. If, therefore, we may share only a little of our joy with brothers of the blood, what fragment of its fringe will others find – our other friends who do not fish? 'But isn't it rather dull?' they ask, remembering Paris, and vaguely a long line of fishers, motionless and vigilant, who guard the river Seine. 'It would require too much patience.' For them it would, and doubtless we are wise to keep a golden silence, thankful for waters yet not over-fished, and friends who still respect a patient, meditative turn of mind, even when they find us odd and very dull. Perhaps, however, that philosophic and contemplative mood which is necessary to perfect contentment in angling only comes with years. Youth is so full of the fever of pursuit, that there is no time to put the rod down even for five minutes while we light a ruminative pipe. Unfortunately, some of us never grow up. We are too keen on excitement. We change our fly often, and rush on from pool to pool, harassed and worried, spoiling what should be the joy of a summer's day. Yet none of us can quite spoil it. Sooner or later we begin to realise a sense of freedom, of mental detachment. We find emotional elbow-room – time to think, to rediscover the things in life which really count. Mother Earth is very near in those hours by the water-side, that are so long and golden.

It was not for nothing that a canon law of the ancient Church prescribed fishing for the clergy as being 'favourable to the health of their body, and specially of their soules'.

Jean Pierre will have it that all good fishermen are good fellows, and that no really bad man ever cares for fishing: *Et vous savez il faut avoir foi dans la pêche, car la foi est un don du bon Dieu.*

W. B. YEATS: *The Fisherman.* From *The Wild Swans at Coole* (1919).

> 'Although I can see him still,
> The freckled man who goes
> To a grey place on a hill
> In grey Connemara clothes
> At dawn to cast his flies,
> It's long since I began
> To call up to the eyes

This wise and simple man.
All day I'd looked in the face
What I had hoped 'twould be
To write for my own race
And the reality;
The living men that I hate,
The dead man that I loved,
The craven man in his seat,
The insolent unreproved,
And no knave brought to book
Who has won a drunken cheer,
The witty man and his joke
Aimed at the commonest ear,
The clever man who cries
The catch-cries of the clown,
The beating down of the wise
And great Art beaten down.

Maybe a twelvemonth since
Suddenly I began,
In scorn of this audience,
Imagining a man,
And his sun-freckled face,
And grey Connemara cloth,
Climbing up to a place
Where stone is dark under froth,
And the down-turn of his wrist
When the flies drop in the stream;
A man who does not exist,
A man who is but a dream;
And cried, 'Before I am old
I shall have written him one
Poem maybe as cold
And passionate as the dawn'.

EDMUND BLUNDEN: *The Pike*. From *The Waggoner and other Poems*
(1920).

From shadows of rich oaks outpeer
The moss-green bastions of the weir,
Where the quick dipper forages
In elver-peopled crevices,
And a small runlet trickling down the sluice
Gossamer music tires not to unloose.

Else round the broad pools hush
        Nothing stirs,
Unless sometime a straggling heifer crush
Through the thronged spinney where the pheasant whirs;
        Or martins in a flash
Come with wild mirth to dip their magical wings,
While in the shallow some doomed bulrush swings
At whose hid root the diver vole's teeth gnash.

And nigh this toppling reed, still as the dead
        The great pike lies, the murderous patriarch
        Watching the waterpit sheer-delving dark,
Where through the plash his lithe bright vassals thread.

The rose-finned roach and bluish bream
And staring ruffe steal up the stream
Hard by their glutted tyrant, now
Still as a sunken bough.

He on the sandbank lies,
        Sunning himself long hours
With stony gorgon eyes:
        Westward the hot sun lowers.

Sudden the grey pike changes, and quivering poises for slaughter;
        Intense terror wakens around him, the shoals scud awry, but
            there chances
        A chub unsuspecting; the prowling fins quicken, in fury he
            lances;
And the miller that opens the hatch stands amazed at the whirl in
            the water.

G. E. M. SKUES: *Hands.* From *The Way of a Trout with a Fly* (1921).

One of the most enviable of the qualities which go to make up the first-rate fly fisherman is that which, in connection with horsemanship, whether in riding or driving, is known as 'hands', the combined certainty and delicacy of correspondence between wrist and eye which mean so much, whether in the despatch of the tiny feathered iron to its coveted quarry, or in the skilful restraint of that quarry when hooked, and its ultimate steering to the net. After all, certainty and delicacy are correlatives – dual manifestations of the same confident power. It is, I believe, the truth that the finest handloom weavers are invariably big, powerful men, with their nerves in fine order, and that for fineness and delicacy their work far excels that of women. Anyone turning over *Who's Who,* and picking out those whose recreation is angling, will probably be surprised to see what a large proportion of these classes comes within the fraternity of fly fishermen – sailors, surgeons, and artists – all of them men of their hands, though those hands may differ in type, and there seems little in common between the long taper fingers of the artist and the skilled mechanic type of hand common among great surgeons and dentists. Probably it would be impossible to classify the hands of the sailor man in this way, but the tendency of quality which drove them seaward made them instinctively handy men. And since the greatest satisfactions of life are to be found in the perfect performance of function, the faculty of handiness, whether in sailor, surgeon, or artist, turns the possessor instinctively to the sport in which the quality finds its finest opportunities of exposition – the sport of fishing with the fly. Watch a company of anglers at the billiard table, and it will be long-odds that those with the most sensitive hands, with that quality of touch which makes for scoring, will also be the best fly fishermen.

It is the quality of hands which enables a man with the shabbiest and most hopeless equipment to make a show of the man whose hopes are built merely on perfection of rods and gear. Wise indeed was George Selwyn Marryat when he said: 'It's not the fly; it's the driver'. It would seem as if there could be no difference between the way a fly presented by *A* and an exact replica presented by *B* floats down dry over a fish when once it has lit upon the water. Yet there is some quality in some men which seems to make the fly at the end of their line exercise a provocative fascination over trout which the average performer fails to achieve. The most conspicuous example of this which I ever came across was a Frenchman, with whom I spent a couple of days on a Norman chalk stream during the May-fly season. There was a very hard-fished hundred yards of right bank in part of the water, with a good trout in every little bay. My French friend courteously gave me the *pas*, and I tried fish after fish, seven or eight in all, I think. I was not conscious of fishing badly, and I put none of these fish down, but I got no rise from any one of them; but no sooner – when I stood aside to let him cast to them – did his fly (the same pattern as mine) drift down over a fish than it rose to it almost as a matter of course. I could see no practical difference in the delivery of our flies; but, like the eliminated fee in the Edinburgh lawyer's corrected bill, it was a case of 'Man, we mayna' see him, but he's there'. Hands!

JOHN BUCHAN: *Fisher Jamie*. From *The Northern Muse* (edited by John Buchan 1924).

Puir Jamie's killed. A better lad
    Ye wadna find to busk a flee
Or burn a pule or wield a gad
    Frae Berwick to the Clints o' Dee.

And noo he's in a happier land –
    It's Gospel truith and Gospel law
That Heaven's yett maun open stand
    To folk that for their country fa'.

But Jamie will be ill to mate;
    He lo'ed nae music, kenned nae tunes
Except the sang o' Tweed in spate,
    Or Talla loupin' ower its linns.

I sair misdoot that Jamie's heid
    A croun o' gowd will never please;
He liked a kep o' dacent tweed
    Whaur he could stick his casts o' flees.

If Heaven is a' that man can dream
  And a' that honest herts can wish,
It maun provide some muirland stream,
  For Jamie dreamed o' nocht but fish.

And weel I wot he'll up and speir
  In his bit blate and canty way,
Wi' kind Apostles standin' near
  Whae in their time were fishers tae.

He'll offer back his gowden croun
  And in its place a rod he'll seek,
And bashfu'-like his herp lay doun
  And speir a leister and a cleek.

For Jims had aye a poachin' whim;
  He'll sune grow tired, wi' lawfu' flee
Made frae the wings o' cherubim
  O' castin' ower the Crystal Sea.

I picter him at gloamin' tide
  Steekin' the backdoor o' his hame
And hastin' to the waterside
  To play again the auld auld game;

And syne wi' saumon on his back
  Catch't clean against the Heavenly law,
And Heavenly byliffs on his track,
  Gaun linkin' doun some Heavenly shaw.

busk, dress   *pule*, pool   *gad*, gaff   *yett*, gate   *speir*, ask
blate and canty, shy and friendly   *leister*, salmon spear   *steekin'*, shutting
linkin', stealing   *shaw*, wood

HARRY PLUNKET GREENE: from *Where the Bright Waters Meet* (1924).

I love Blagdon, not only because it holds great fish, but because I have always been happy there. It would be impossible to find more delightful people than those of the farm who have always taken me in as their guest. I have a vivid recollection, too, of the time, in the middle of the war when we were most severely rationed, when I arrived there starved and tired to death after weeks of work and drill, and sat down to potato-soup, a wild duck, a black-currant pudding, a local 'Wensleydale' cheese and as much cider as I wanted – all farm-grown. But they were (and are) part and parcel of that lovely spot in Somerset typical of southern England at its best.

Blagdon is an artificial reservoir, it is true, but it is only the western end that lets you into that secret. Here is the big embankment of which Sheringham speaks in *Trout-fishing*, where the 'great whales' lie with their noses on the stones. But you can sit on the grass in a dozen places round the shore and swear that you are on the banks of one of the prettiest natural lakes in the kingdom. There is not a lovelier sight (*pace* Ramsbury and Hurstbourne Priors in buttercup-time) in England than Blagdon from the Butcombe end at sundown, with the tiny town straggling up the steep hill-side like a Bavarian village, the red roofs of the houses peeping out of the thick orchards (with never a Methodist Chapel to shock the artist's eye), and the evening sunlight setting the windows of the old church aglow and flushing with purple-pink the glassy surface of the lake. There is a stillness here that belongs to no other valley. You can hear the 'plop' of the big trout far out half a mile away. You can talk to your friend across the water when the sun is down without ever raising your voice, and hear the scream of his reel in the blackness, and Blagdon is about seven miles round, and he may be half the length of the lake from you.

But the dominant impression in my mind is the lovely colour of the evening light upon the valley as you face it looking east. It has a crimson velvet glow which hangs like an aura on the meadows and makes the shores and the scolloped hills burn with fires. It is Devonshire clay here, and the whole landscape warms pink and deepens to purple-black as the sun sinks low.

I know, too, that there was once a witch in the valley and that they drowned her when they let the water in; and one night as I grope my way home in the dark I shall stumble on Hänsel and Gretel asleep on the grass in a mist of white angels, with the myriad million stars of the Milky Way and the golden lights of Blagdon shining on their heads and winking in the watery glass at their feet.

* * *

There never was a river that wanted less looking after than the Bourne before we overstocked it. The fish seemed actually to thrive upon short rations. There were long stretches of bare gravel without a patch of weeds in sight, where wooden artificial 'hides' had actually been put down to give them shelter, and they seemed fatter and healthier and more beautiful there than anywhere. The cattle used to walk into the water and eat the weed, and it made no apparent difference to the food-supply. I have seen two-pounders and three-pounders swimming about the shallows with their back fins out of water and fairly bursting with health and defiance and high spirits. It was a wonder to us all how they managed it, for no one did a thing for them; nature did it all herself.

Exactly – nature did it alone, as she always will if you will not try to go one better. The secret of this river was that its watershed was fed by springs as clear and clean as crystal. In its three miles' run from the source it had no chance to pick up pollution. There were no mills to discharge their waste-products into those pure waters. The spawning-beds were spotless, the weed and the gravel veritable provision-stores, and the only worry in the lives of its inhabitants was the man on the bank. So they were born, and grew up and bred in the open, wild fish every one of them, and models to the Itchen or the Kennet or the Windrush or any other river in the British Isles. It was man that spoiled it all. If the Bourne is to be saved she must be given back to nature.

And so I say goodbye to her. The watercress beds above the viaduct have scarred her face and marred her beauty for ever. The pollard is there still, but the trees with the wild bees are gone. The black death is creeping through the chalk and covering her eyes with a film. Materialism has her in its grasp, and the road-hog must be served.

But somewhere, deep down, I have a dim hope that one night the fairy godmother will walk along the tarry road and stop on the bridge and listen, and send a message to me in the dark; and that when the mists begin to lift and the poplars to shiver and the cock-pheasants crow in the beech-woods, the little Bourne will wake and open her eyes and find in her bosom again the exiles that she had thought were gone for good – the silver trout, and the golden gravel, and the shrimp and the duns – and smell the dust of the road, and see the sun once more, and the red and white cows in the grass, and the yellow buttercups in the meadow and the blue smoke of the cottages against the black elms of the Andover hill – and me, too, perhaps, kneeling beside her as of old and watching the little iron-blue, happy, laughing, come bobbing down to me under the trees below the Beehive bridge on the Whitchurch Road.

J. W. HILLS: from *A Summer on the Test* (1924).

The climax of the year has come, bringing the wild rose, the yellow iris and the mayfly. The iris is another great Hampshire flower, and is everywhere in masses, arranged as though nature had gardened it. And the river now has its summer appearance. Patches of the white cups of the water crowfoot lie on the surface, many a hooked trout takes refuge in one of those thick jungles which fishermen call celery beds, the water grows crystalline, its surface flecked with wind-blown petals and pollen of the grass, trout come suddenly into sight, iron blues sail down in droves, and islands of dead weed form round the piers of bridges. The grass in the hayfields is growing long, large daisies appear in it, moths fly at night, and the hedges are starred with wild roses. The evening rise begins, red sedge flies blunder on to the surface, and you can fish till ten o'clock. Then June passes, birds have hatched their young, and family parties of linnets and goldfinches splash themselves at the shallow edge of the gravelly ford.

As the year runs on, and the hay is cut, the valley loses individuality. It remains beautiful, but less distinctive. There are no flowering trees, and the only bush is the guelder rose, not enough by itself, though graceful. I never see its ivory flowers without thinking of chalk streams. There is a pause in nature, until the late summer flowers come. And they do come, in quantities, and at no time are the banks so gay. Clusters of mimulus with its melted gold, thick spires of purple loosestrife, the homely comfrey, and a few tall columns of mullein make a brilliant garden: ditches are full of meadow-sweet and the air is heavy with its scent: patches of yellow ragwort cover the bottom of the down, and willow herb in the clearing of the wood is so thick that it looks like a pink mist. Some of these flowers last all through the hot days of July and August, until the turn of the year. Then we slip into autumn, catch perhaps a few fish in September, linger as long as we can, and finally say good-bye to the valley until next April.

But, before you go, do not forget to pay a tribute to the loveliest of all Test flowers, the loveliest and the rarest, the balsam. It is unmistakable, with its olive-dark leaves and its red and orange blossoms, looking remote and exotic, more in keeping with an equatorial forest than our keen strenuous air. It is not in full bloom till September. It is a wayward creature, because in some years it disappears entirely and in others it is difficult to find. But when it is plentiful it is one of the great sights afforded by English flowers. There are few places in these islands where it grows at all, and there can be still fewer where it blossoms so luxuriantly as on the Test.

EDMUND BLUNDEN: *Water Moment*. From *English Poems* (1925).

> The silver eel slips through the waving weeds,
> And in the tunnelled shining stone recedes;
> The earnest eye surveys the crystal pond
> And guards the cave: the sweet shoals pass beyond.
> The watery jewels that these have for eyes,
> The tiger streaks of him that hindmost plies,
> The red-gold wings that smooth their daring paces,
> The sunlight dancing about their airs and graces,
> Burn that strange watcher's heart; then the sly brain
> Speaks, all the dumb shoal shrieks, and by the stone
> The silver death writhes with the chosen one.

ERNEST HEMINGWAY: from *Big Two-hearted River*. From *In Our Time* (1925).

He started down to the stream, holding his rod, the bottle of grasshoppers hung from his neck by a thong tied in half hitches around the neck of the bottle. His landing net hung by a hook from his belt. Over his shoulder was a long flour sack tied at each corner into an ear. The cord went over his shoulder. The sack flapped against his legs.

Nick felt awkward and professionally happy with all his equipment hanging from him. The grasshopper bottle swung against his chest. In his shirt the breast pockets bulged against him with the lunch and his fly book.

He stepped into the stream. It was a shock. His trousers clung tight to his legs. His shoes felt the gravel. The water was a rising cold shock.

Rushing, the current sucked against his legs. Where he stepped in, the water was over his knees. He waded with the current. The gravel slid under his shoes. He looked down at the swirl of water below each leg and tipped up the bottle to get a grasshopper.

The first grasshopper gave a jump in the neck of the bottle and went out into the water. He was sucked under in the whirl by Nick's right leg and came to the surface a little way down stream. He floated rapidly, kicking. In a quick circle, breaking the smooth surface of the water, he disappeared. A trout had taken him.

Another hopper poked his face out of the bottle. His antennae wavered. He was getting his front legs out of the bottle to jump. Nick took him by the head and held him while he threaded the slim hook under his chin, down through his thorax and into the last segments of his abdomen. The grasshopper took hold of the hook with his front feet, spitting tobacco juice on it. Nick dropped him into the water.

Holding the rod in his right hand he let out line against the pull of the grasshopper in the current. He stripped off line from the reel with his left hand and let it run free. He could see the hopper in the little waves of the current. It went out of sight.

There was a tug on the line. Nick pulled against the taut line. It was his first strike. Holding the now living rod across the current, he brought in the line with his left hand. The rod bent in jerks, the trout pumping against the current. Nick knew it was a small one. He lifted the rod straight up in the air. It bowed with the pull.

He saw the trout in the water jerking with his head and body against the shifting tangent of the line in the stream.

Nick took the line in his left hand and pulled the trout, thumping tiredly against the current, to the surface. His back was mottled the clear, water-over-gravel colour, his side flashing in the sun. The rod under his right arm, Nick stooped, dipping his right hand into the current. He held the trout, never still, with his moist right hand, while he unhooked the barb from his mounth, then dropped him back into the stream.

He hung unsteadily in the current, then settled to the bottom beside a stone. Nick reached down his hand to touch him, his arm to the elbow under water. The trout was steady in the moving stream, resting on the gravel, beside a stone. As Nick's fingers touched him, touched his smooth, cool, underwater feeling he was gone, gone in a shadow across the bottom of the stream.

He's all right, Nick thought. He was only tired.

He had wet his hand before he touched the trout, so he would not disturb the delicate mucus that covered him. If a trout was touched with a dry hand, a white fungus attacked the unprotected spot. Years before when he had fished crowded streams, with fly fishermen ahead of him and behind him, Nick had again and again come on dead trout, furry with white fungus, drifted against a rock, or floating belly up in some pool. Nick did not like to fish with other men on the river. Unless they were of your party, they spoiled it.

He wallowed down the stream, above his knees in the current, through the fifty yards of shallow water above the pile of logs that crossed the stream. He did not rebait his hook and held it in his hand as he waded. He was certain he could catch small trout in the shallows, but he did not want them. There would be no big trout in the shallows this time of day.

Now the water deepened up his thighs sharply and coldly. Ahead was the smooth dammed-back flood of water above the logs. The water was smooth and dark; on the left, the lower edge of the meadow; on the right the swamp.

Nick leaned back against the current and took a hopper from the bottle. He threaded the hopper on the hook and spat on him for good luck. Then he pulled several yards of line from the reel and tossed the hopper out ahead on to the fast, dark water. It floated down towards the logs, then the weight of the line pulled the bait under the surface. Nick held the rod in his right hand, letting the line run out through his fingers.

There was a long tug. Nick struck and the rod came alive and dangerous, bent double, the line tightening, coming out of water, tightening, all in a heavy, dangerous, steady pull. Nick felt the moment when the leader would break if the strain increased and let the line go.

The reel ratcheted into a mechanical shriek as the line went out in a rush. Too fast. Nick could not check it, the line rushing out, the reel note rising as the line ran out.

With the core of the reel showing, his heart feeling stopped with the excitement, leaning back against the current that mounted icily his thighs, Nick thumbed the reel hard with his left hand. It was awkward getting his thumb inside the fly reel frame.

As he put on pressure the line tightened into sudden hardness and beyond the logs a huge trout went high out of water. As he jumped, Nick lowered the tip of the rod. But he felt, as he dropped the tip to ease the strain, the moment when the strain was too great; the hardness too tight. Of course, the leader had broken. There was no mistaking the feeling when all spring left the line and it became dry and hard. Then it went slack.

His mouth dry, his heart down, Nick reeled in. He had never seen so big a trout. There was a heaviness, a power not to be held, and then the bulk of him, as he jumped. He looked as broad as a salmon.

Nick's hand was shaky. He reeled in slowly. The thrill had been too much, He felt, vaguely, a little sick, as though it would be better to sit down.

The leader had broken where the hook was tied to it. Nick took it in his hand. He thought of the trout somewhere on the bottom, holding himself steady over the gravel, far down below the light, under the logs, with the hook in his jaw. Nick knew the trout's teeth would cut through the snell of the hook. The hook would imbed itself in his jaw. He'd bet the trout was angry. Anything that size would be angry. That was a trout. He had been solidly hooked. Solid as a rock. He felt like a rock, too, before he started off. By God, he was a big one. By God, he was the biggest one I ever heard of.

Nick climbed out on to the meadow and stood, water running down his trousers and out of his shoes, his shoes squelchy. He went over and sat on the logs. He did not want to rush his sensations any.

He wriggled his toes in the water, in his shoes, and got out a cigarette from his breast pocket. He lit it and tossed the match into the fast water below the logs. A tiny trout rose at the match, as it swung around in the fast current. Nick laughed. He would finish the cigarette.

He sat on the logs, smoking, drying in the sun, the sun warm on his back, the river shallow ahead entering the woods, curving into the woods, shallows, light glittering, big water-smooth rocks, cedars along the bank and white birches, the logs warm in the sun, smooth to sit on, without bark, grey to the touch; slowly the feeling of disappointment left him. It went away slowly, the feeling of disappointment that came sharply after the thrill that made his shoulders ache. It was all right now. His rod lying out on the logs, Nick tied a new hook on the leader, pulling the gut tight until it grimped into itself in a hard knot.

He baited up, then picked up the rod and walked to the far end of the logs to get into the water, where it was not too deep. Under and beyond the logs was a deep pool. Nick walked around the shallow shelf near the swamp shore until he came out on the shallow bed of the stream.

On the left, where the meadow ended and the woods began, a great elm tree was uprooted. Gone over in a storm, it lay back into the woods, its roots clotted with dirt, grass growing in them, rising a solid bank beside the stream. The river cut to the edge of the uprooted tree. From where Nick stood he could see deep channels, like ruts, cut in the shallow bed of the stream by the flow of the current. Pebbly where he stood and pebbly and full of boulders beyond; where it curved near the tree roots, the bed of the stream was marly and between the ruts of deep water green weed fronds swung in the current.

Nick swung the rod back over his shoulder and forward, and the line, curving forward, laid the grasshopper down on one of the deep channels in the weeds. A trout struck and Nick hooked him.

Holding the rod far out toward the uprooted tree and sloshing backward in the current, Nick worked the trout, plunging, the rod bending alive, out of the danger of the weeds into the open river. Holding the rod, pumping alive against the current, Nick brought the trout in. He rushed, but always came, the spring of the rod yielding to the rushes, sometimes jerking under water, but always bringing him in. Nick eased downstream with the rushes. The rod above his head he led the trout over the net, then lifted.

The trout hung heavy in the net, mottled trout back and silver sides in the meshes. Nick unhooked him; heavy sides, good to hold, big undershot jaw, and slipped him, heaving and big sliding, into the long sack that hung from his shoulders in the water.

Nick spread the mouth of the sack against the current and it filled, heavy with water. He held it up, the bottom in the stream, and the water poured out through the sides. Inside at the bottom was the big trout, alive in the water.

WILLIAM CAINE: from *Fish, Fishing and Fishermen* (1927).

It is a lie that fishermen lie.

A lie is a statement made with intent to deceive. No fisherman makes such statements. For since every fisherman to whom another fisherman asserts that, on such a day and in such a place, he slew so many trouts or barbels or whitebaits, weighing so much – since every such first fisherman automatically divides number and weight by three, halves that and knocks off ninety per cent from the quotient (or whatever it is), he – I mean the first fisherman – when in his turn he tells a story of the same sort to yet another, a third fisherman, confidently expects that third fisherman to treat his (the first's) in the same fashion. Now such a man may not justly be accused of lying. He does no more than follow a well-recognized and convenient custom.

When I tell you – supposing you to be what some people call A Brother of the Angle – that in one day I killed two hundred trouts weighing exactly two hundred pounds the last time I fished the Barle at Dulverton, you will not for a moment imagine that I am trying to deceive you, but will simply understand that I am speaking of a rather unusually good bit of sport I have once had, and that I did, perhaps, in actual fact, kill sixteen trouts weighing all together fifty ounces.

This instinctive and generous (or is it jealous?) discount which fishermen allow to one another's statements alone perfectly explains why those statements are so generously conceived. It is cruel and wicked and quite unnecessary to assume that they are prompted by any sort of wish to deceive. If I tell another disciple (as they say) of Walton that I have caught – and I speak the very truth – sixteen trouts weighing fifty ounces in the Barle at Dulverton, which mark you, is a very fine performance, he will take me to have meant that I have caught one fish weighing one ounce and risen two others of unknown size. And instead of his admiration, which is my due, I shall earn his contempt, which would be unfair. In order, therefore, to make him understand precisely what happened, I am compelled to speak in hundreds of fishes and in hundreds of pounds. I am not making a statement with intent to deceive – that is to say, lying; I am making a statement with intent to convey an accurate impression – that is to say, I am telling the truth.

Fishermen are simply confirmed and painstaking truthtellers, who all happen to react a little feebly to a certain kind of stimulus. You would not call a paralysed man a liar, would you, because he remains unaffected by an electric battery? Very well, then.

No; if it's liars you're looking for don't search the banks of a stream. Go to the golf-links.

Go, at once, to the golf-links.

* * *

The angler, then, has had his day's fishing. Here, again, is a pleasure peculiar (from another aspect) to the walk home. The day is over. Its miseries are past; its joys remain. He is a fool who dwells upon the fishes he has lost while he carries home a brace of two-pounders, and even if he have nothing to show, there is much of which he may more profitably think than a few trout still swimming in their stream.

The valley – at all times a thing of pure delight – is perhaps at its best in the dusk. Now mystery and suggestiveness take the place of clear colour and bold outline and strong shadow. The river shines pale here and there among the formless meadows. The willows are like grey ghosts trooping down to drink. Above the solemn downs the young stars suddenly make vast the sky, and the dusk is the very hour of the elms. And the angler is observed. From the withy beds naiads, I swear, peep curiously at the odd lumpy figure that plods along so heavily. Soon the valley will be theirs for the night. In half an hour the Green Man will turn out its customers. In an hour at most the last candle will be dowsed in the cottages. But the naiads would be very well assured of the angler's final departure. The indiscreet person has been known to linger by the stream till unconscionable hours. They like to see him well away.

I think that the crunch of brogues sounds oddly pleasant in the dusk; I am sure it is different from the harsh grind they set up under a strong sun. Do they, at memory's moment, soften their voice for memory's sake? Do they hush themselves in sympathy with the soundlessness of the feet which tread the road by the fisherman's side? For each evening as I leave the mill for my walk home through the twilight along this Clere river I am joined always by one silent pair of brogues, and I think I go more slowly than I might (for I have every reason to hurry) because they lag a little, and because I know that I shall never hear them again.

BLISS PERRY: from *Pools and Ripples, Fishing Essays* (1927).

And here comes one of the paradoxes of fishing. By some strange trick of the memory, the fish which you take or lose seem in retrospect only a bit of highlight in the general picture. The exaltation of an instant of perfect skill, the heartbreaking sense of clumsiness or stupidity when you lose a salmon, lessen their poignancy in the presence of the beauty which is always waiting upon the angler. The cardinal flowers blooming twenty years ago on a mossy log upon the shadowed shore of Big Greenough Pond are lovely yet, though not a trout rose that morning from under the log. The big red fox still squats on his haunches upon the far side of Norbert's Pool, wisely criticizing my unsuccessful casting. The ravens bark hoarsely in the black spruces above the Sheerdam. That pair of great horned owls still follow me down the Olmsted brook. The buck that snorted and jumped just behind me as I was making a very careful cast on the Big Magalloway still makes my heart pump – so silent was that lonely afternoon. The moose tracks are still there on the muddy shore of the St Maurice. The cries of strange birds in the twilight haunt the willow copses along the Margaree. The endless hot afternoons on the Miramichi, while we were waiting for falling water, are no longer tedious, for now they are crowded with pictures of friendly purple finches, and mother partridges with their broods, and 'mourning-cloak' butterflies clustering by thousands upon the worn rocks by the river. No, you may forget the fish that you catch or lose, but you can never forget the fishing!

I have no quarrel with the persons who go into the woods to peep and botanize and name all the birds without a gun. There is fun enough in this world, if properly distributed, to give everybody something. But I am stating a truism when I claim that the man with a rod or gun sees more and feels more in the woods than if he were to go empty-handed. In moments of tense excitement in watching for fish or game one's field of vision is wider and sight and hearing are more sensitive than in the moods of mere passive receptivity to 'Nature's teaching'. Never is the dawn more miraculous than when the fog first lifts along the reaches of the river and you tie on a favourite fly with chilled, fumbling fingers, light your first pipe of the day, and wade, shivering, into the chuckling water. Never is the divine and terrifying mystery of the dark so close to you as when you are stumbling campward in the twilight along an unknown trail. The woodsman who cannot understand how a man can be panic-stricken by the dark is no woodsman. He lacks a sense of the situation: of the very narrow line that separates fire, food, and shelter from the desperate horror of 'a man lost'. I helped find one of these men once. He rose up gaunt in the October dusk from a bog back of Spencer Mountain, and waved his arms wildly just as I was holding the rifle on him, taking him for a moose: and I shall never forget how we filled him up with coffee, trout, and venison that night, and put him safely on the 'tote road' in the morning.

And between dawn and dark what infinite variations of air and light and colour and wind play upon the mind of the fisherman as if it were an opal! The wind caresses him one moment, and torments him the next, tossing his fly into treetops or breaking the brittle hook against a rock. But the water is the true opal. In the upper reaches of many of our New England streams the water flowing from a peat bog or cedar swamp has the tone of a very dark sherry; in full sunlight, flecked by shadows, it becomes one of Emerson's leopard-coloured rills; as it pours over granite ledges it changes to something strangely austere and pure. No two successive hours are alike to the angler, for the brook or river is changing its form and hue in every instant, and his mind and mood and artistry are affected by every yard of the gliding, Protean stream. He is watching it, not with the sentimentalist's preoccupation with pure beauty, but rather with the fisherman's trained perception of the effect of wind and light, of deeper or darker-coloured water, of eddy or shallow, upon the next cast of his fly. The paradox is that this very preoccupation with angling seems to make him more sensitive to the enfolding beauty of the landscape.

ARTHUR RANSOME: *Fishermen's Patience.* From *Rod and Line* (1929).

Nothing is more trying to the patience of fishermen than the remark so often made to them by the profane: 'I have not patience enough for fishing'. It is not so much the remark itself (showing a complete and forgivable ignorance of angling as it does) that is annoying as the manner in which it is said, the kindly condescending manner in which Ulysses might tell Penelope that he had not patience for needlework. What are they, these dashing, impatient sparks? Are they d'Artagnans all, rough-riders, playboys of a western world, wild desperate fellows who look for a spice of danger in their pleasure? Not a bit of it. They hit a ball backwards and forwards over a net or submit to the patient trudgery of golf, a laborious form of open-air patience in which you hit a ball, walk earnestly after it and hit it again. These devotees of monotonous artificial pleasures who say that fishing is too slow a game for them seem to imagine that fishing is a sedentary occupation. Let them put on waders and fish up a full river and then walk down it on a hot summer day. Let them combine for an afternoon the arts of the Red Indian and the mountaineer and, in the intervals of crawling through brambles and clambering over boulders, keep cool enough to fill a basket with the up-stream worm. Let them discover that they have to take their coats off when salmon fishing on a day when the line freezes in the rings. Let them spin for pike in February, or trout in August. They will find that they get exercise enough. Some forms of fishing are sedentary, in the purely physical sense, in that after a man has baited a spot for carp or roach, or anchored a boat for perch, he keeps still. But he has not attained a sort of Nirvana, like a crystal gazer, isolating himself from nature by concentration on a miserable ball. His mind is not dulled but lively with expectation and, of all the virtues, patience is the one he least requires. Of all kinds of fishing only one requires patience and that is trailing a bait after a boat when someone else is doing the rowing. Even in those forms of fishing which do not mean moving about, it never occurs to an angler to pride himself on his patience. Self-control, if you like, but not the most leisurely of all the virtues. There would be patience needed to watch a float which (there being no fish in the water) you knew would never budge, but none in watching a float that may at any moment make a demand for instant action.

What other people mistake for patience in anglers is really nothing of the sort but a capacity for prolonged eagerness, an unquenchable gusto in relishing an infinite series of exciting and promising moments, any one of which may yield a sudden crisis with its climax of triumph or disaster. Something rather like patience may be required by the kind of fisherman who casts a fly mechanically and uniformly and is jerked into consciousness only by some extraordinarily altruistic little trout who in a passion of benevolence hangs himself on the end of a undeserving line. But such fishermen seldom persist and, if they do persist, learn to fish in a different manner. Fishing, properly so called, is conducted under continuous tension. The mere putting of fly or bait on or in the water is an action needing skill, an action that can be done well or ill and consequently a source of pleasure. Many an angler returns with an empty basket after a day made delightful by the knowledge that he was putting his float exactly where he wanted it, casting his fly a little better than usual, or dropping his spinner with less splash at greater distances. The mere athletics of casting give the fishermen all the golfer's pleasure in good driving or putting. But, and here is the point, there is no red flag to show the angler in what direction he should aim, to take from him all initiative, to put him, as it were in blinkers. His free will is limited only by his skill in execution. If he is a trout fisher he is watching the river for a rise, for a boil, for the slight swirl in the water that betrays a fish feeding below, for the roll in the surface made by a submerged stone above which may be a motionless pocket, below which may be a minute eddy, either a fit place for a trout to lie in wait for his dinner. Now and again, if the river is new to him, he will find a hole in what he had thought was continuous shallow and will tell himself to remember next time to fish that spot before he comes to it. All the time he is watching for cover and will use the hole that he kicked himself for not seeing before he came to it to keep low and out of sight while he casts to another likely spot above. He marks where the water runs slow under the banks. At the hang of a pool he tries to put his flies at once just where the fish is likeliest to be. He knows that a mistake is all but irrevocable, that a first cast has a better chance than a third. His day is a long series of crises and demands on his presence of mind. Even in float-fishing so much depends on observation, on watercraft, on the reading of barely perceptible signs, that those who imagine that a good fisherman can watch his float and think of something else beside his fishing are very much mistaken. So completely does fishing occupy a man that if a good angler had murdered one of those people who prate about patience and were allowed to spend his last day at the river instead of in the condemned cell, he would forget the rope.

The ultimate test is one of time. Patience is a virtue required when times goes slowly. In fishing time goes too fast. Fishermen's wives are unanimous in deploring the hopeless unpunctuality of their husbands at the fag-end of the day. Fishermen rarely have time to eat all the sandwiches provided for their luncheons. If, on occasion, they do eat in leisure at the waterside it is with the peculiar relish that accompanies stolen fruit. They run a race with the sun, and are always finding that it has beaten them and is casting their shadow on the water long before they had expected to have to cross the river. The only time that seems to the fishermen longer than it is is that in which he is playing a big fish. Then, indeed, his drawn-out anxiety makes him apt to think he spent an hour in landing a salmon which was actually on the bank in fifteen minutes. But no one will suggest that those minutes were so dull that they needed to be patiently borne.

ROBERT BRIDGES: *Summer on Thames.* From *Shorter Poems* (1931).

> A rushy island guards the sacred bower,
> And hides it from the meadow, where in peace
> The lazy cows wrench many a scented flower,
> Robbing the golden market of the bees:
>> And laden barges float
>> By banks of myosote;
> And scented flag and golden flower-de-lys
>> Delay the loitering boat.
>
> Sometimes an angler comes, and drops his hook
> Within its hidden depths, and 'gainst a tree
> Leaning his rod, reads in some pleasant book,
> Forgetting soon his pride of fishery,
>> And dreams, or falls asleep,
>> While curious fishes peep
> About his nibbled bait, and scornfully
>> Dart off and rise and leap.

PATRICK CHALMERS: from *At the Tail of the Weir* (1932).

And the other Thames names – are not they England too, are they not kingcups, rooks in April elms, the white owl sweeping and a nightingale in the dark? Listen to them, Bablock Hythe, Bray, Long Wittenham, Bisham, Hedsor, Iffley, Medmenham – I could fill a page with such music and, reading, you would remember, in the sound of it, the big trout below Marsh that I wanted to tell you of. I tell the tale as it was told to me, I do not vouch for the truth of it, I only say that you will learn, when you fish for a much fished for Thames Trout, that he is an exceptional fellow and, like Habakkuk, *capable*, almost, *de tout*.

The eleven-pounder lived, when first I heard of him, *above* Marsh Lock. He was a glorious fish, short, thick and deep, as I know because once in May he followed my spinning-bait almost into the bank. He meant business; like a bullet he came, full speed and wide open. But he came too late. Perforce the bank stopped my minnow's flight. The trout, undeceived, turned aside from the sham with a flounce and a wallop, that, literally, splashed me with Thames water, and was gone. Later in the summer it was told to me that a young Scotchman, going from Shiplake to Henley, approached the lock in a rowing boat. As he came, he, resting upon his oars, sought in his flannel trousers for the three coppers which his lock ticket must, presently, cost him. He found but two pennies and so he must break into a sixpenny bit. In his hand he held the little coin when, to avoid the wash of the steam-launch *Wargrave*, he picked up his oars all of a sudden. The sixpence fell into the water. The young man, like the Scot in the comic papers, looked outboard as his sixpenny piece spun, silverly dropping in the slow current, down into green deeps. He saw a great fish shoot across the path of his little silver coin and absorb it as though it were a silver dace that wobbled so seductively. That was all.

Next June the Best Thames Angler Ever anchored his fishing punt on the bright shallows below the Lock. The bright shallows where the spawned barbel, rolling like cats roll sidealong in the sun, clean themselves and preen themselves at the tail of the weir. Then, standing up, the angler tossed a spinning-bait hither and yon. Presently, as the blue phantom sped among the piles of the footbridge, a yard-long shadow dashed aslant at it. The little rod bent into a kicking arc, the reel shrieked, and forty yards away – but you've read this sort of thing before, I think?

To make a long tale short then, an hour or so later when the Trout was opened in the kitchen, within him was found, and sent upstairs to his captor upon a salver, three coppers and a lock ticket.

T. H. WHITE: from *England Have My Bones* (first published 1936).

Entry for 23. vii. xxxiv.

The salmon, and the fact that my trouting rod has been stolen, and the frenzy for aeroplanes, have put me off trout fishing for the time being. It is the old story of never having enough time for what one wants to do. Flying over Wiltshire yesterday, we followed the course of a little river. Hanging over Cobbett's favourite country, with the sharp downs to provide a skyline of *useful* beauty, and the fertile valleys full of comfort and richness between them, it was almost an agony of affection to look down into the clean water. You could see the whole geography of the stream, the bright green cresses, almost the shadowy trout with their undershadows.

Nothing will beat the dry-fly. One may have momentary crazes, stunning super-pleasures like the buoying aeroplane and the freezing spring salmon, but ultimately one will come back. For the dry-fly is the highest of the arts. You have got to endure for a salmon, and there is a pleasure in the absolutely straight sizzle of gut culminating in the plop of a lure that will be fishing efficiently through the whole arc, and the ten minutes with the fish on are at the tip of life. But you can't stalk a salmon. You don't caress your cast on to the water with a feathery anxiety.

There is something in our effete old English waters after all. Though they don't go red and quick and talkative, the sun dances on their ripple. The birds sing beside them in the crystal light, the artificial may-fly goes zzt-zzt in the air above them. And in them stands absorbed the ruminant angler, unconscious of time, deft with his fingers, puzzling his beloved fly-box, breathing his pale smoke regularly in the bliss of concentration, pitting his quivering wits and tackle against the rosy-spotted tiger-fighters of the drinkable water, sun-struck into another infinite universe like the heron. I suppose the heron must be the happiest of living creatures.

Entry for 20. ii. xxxv

I get this feeling now at the beginning of seasons, when it is a question of recollection. You have forgotten the stuffy feathery ball of a dead partridge turning over in the air, or the nuisance of keeping Silver into his bridle so that he will not forget. You think about tomorrow, and suddenly it is there before you in the full colours of life, and the pony's reaction happens of its own accord. Something physical runs down your back.

It happens to me most with fishing. I bought a new rod from Hardy's yesterday, and took it down to the lake today, to see if I could remember anything about casts. (I used to fish this lake last year with a trout rod. It is possible to cast a spoon accurately without a spinning reel, by coiling the line in the punt and allowing it to pick itself up. On a trout rod a nine-pound pike – it is *not* particularly difficult to drive the hooks in – is just worth catching. But my trout rod, which had come to no good by this handling, was stolen; and I didn't trouble to buy another. This year I have only fished once, on a borrowed casting rod, and again had a nine-pounder: but it was not worth pulling him out.) Today I took the new rod down, and cast bitterly into a fierce wind. I was enjoying myself, but only normally, when I remembered the cuckoo.

I heard him last year on the 6th of April. It would be nice to give the feeling. The cuckoo is essentially the Coln in Gloucestershire, a thing mixed up with clear water and cresses. Cuckoo, it said, twice: and there on my fingers was the sticky, the grassy, the fishy smell of trout. There were his rosy stipples, his buck in the hand, the olive dun in the tender nook of his lip. The gut gets in the way as you make to disgorge. He was in my nose and ear and spine.

HENRY WILLIAMSON: from *Salar the Salmon* (1935).

Salar slept. The water lightened with sunrise. He lay in shadow. His eyes were fixed, passively susceptible to all movement. The sun rose up. Leaves and stalks of loose weed and water-moss passing were seen but unnoticed by the automatic stimulus of each eye's retina. The eyes worked together with the unconscious brain, while the nerves, centres of direct feeling, rested themselves. One eye noticed a trout hovering in the water above, but Salar did not see it.

The sun rose higher, and shone down on the river, and slowly the shadow of the ledge shrank into its base. Light revealed Salar, a grey-green uncertain dimness behind a small pale spot appearing and disappearing regularly.

Down there Salar's right eye was filled with the sun's blazing fog.

His left eye saw the wall of rock and the water above. The trout right forward of him swam up, inspected that which had attracted it, and swam down again; but Salar's eye perceived no movement. The shadow of the trout in movement did not fall on the salmon's right eye.

A few moments later there was a slight splash left forward of Salar. Something swung over, casting the thinnest shadow; but it was seen by the eye, which awakened the conscious brain. Salar was immediately alert.

The thing vanished. A few moments later, it appeared nearer to him.

With his left eye Salar watched the thing moving overhead. It swam in small jerks, across the current and just under the surface, opening and shutting, gleaming, glinting, something trying to get away. Salar, curious and alert, watched it until it was disappearing and then he swam up and around to take it ahead of its arc of movement. The surface water, however, was flowing faster than the river at mid-stream, and he misjudged the opening of his mouth, and the thing, which recalled sea-feeding, escaped.

On the bank upriver fifteen yards away a fisherman with fourteen-foot split-cane rod said to himself, excitedly, 'Rising short'; and pulling loops of line between reel and lowest ring of rod, he took a small pair of scissors from a pocket and snipped off the thing which had attracted Salar.

No wonder Salar had felt curious about it, for human thought had ranged the entire world to imagine that lure. It was called a fly; but no fly like it ever swam in air or flew through water. Its tag, which had glinted, was of silver from Nevada and silk of a moth from Formosa; its tail, from the feather of an Indian crow; its butt, black herl of African ostrich; its body, yellow floss-silk veiled with orange breast-feathers of the South American toucan, and black Macclesfield silk ribbed with silver tinsel. This fly was given the additional attraction of wings for water-flight, made of strips of feathers from many birds: turkey from Canada, peahen and peacock from Japan, swan from Ireland, bustard from Arabia, golden-pheasant from China, teal and wild duck and mallard from the Hebrides. Its throat was made of the feather of an English speckled hen, its side of Bengal jungle-cock's neck feathers, its cheeks came from a French kingfisher, its horns from the tail of an Amazonian macaw. Wax, varnish, and enamel secured the 'marriage' of the feathers. It was one of hundreds of charms, or materialized river-side incantations, made by men to persuade sleepy or depressed salmon to rise and take. Invented after a bout of seasickness by a Celt as he sailed the German Ocean between England and Norway, for nearly 100 years this fly had borne his name, Jock Scott.

While the fisherman was tying a smaller pattern of the same fly to the end of the gut cast, dark stained by nitrate of silver against under-water glint, Salar rose to mid-water and hovered there. Behind him lay the trout, which, scared by the sudden flash of the big fish turning, had dropped back a yard. So Salar had hovered three years before in his native river, when, as parr spotted like a trout, and later as a silvery smolt descending to the sea, he had fed eagerly on nymphs of the olive dun and other ephemeridae coming down with the current.

He opened his mouth and sucked in a nymph as it was swimming to the surface. The fisherman saw a swirl on the water, and threw his fly, with swish of double-handed rod, above and to the right of the swirl. Then, lowering the rod point until it was almost parallel to the water, he let the current take the fly slowly across the stream, lifting the rod tip and lowering it slightly and regularly to make it appear to be swimmng.

Salar saw the fly and slowly swam up to look at it.

JOHN TAINTER FOOTE: from *Broadway Angler* (1937).

We got out of town and Bruce began to tell me what great stuff this trout fishing was. He called it an art. He began to hand me a line that went over my head like a proscenium arch. He talked about a guy named Isaac something-or-other that I had never heard of, and I know a lot of Jewish boys. Then he went Chinese on me. He talked about Fan Wing. He said Yellow May was a warm number this time of year. Pretty soon he forgot his chinks and began to babble about Ginger Quill. I said the only Ginger I knew was Ginger Rogers, but he gave me one of those looks, so I just sat back and let him rave.

All this time we'd been trying to pass trucks, with the sun beating down. My feet got so hot they began to swell, and I thought my new riding boots were going to cripple me for life. I tried to think of something else. I tried to think about the new routine the dance director had promised me for our September opening. I tried to think about how cool the starlight roof of the Waldorf would be with Wayne King's orchestra playing. I tried to think of a way to stop the stage manager's babe from hogging the mirror and chiselling in on my cold cream. I even tried to listen to Bruce. He was talking about another of the Quill girls by the name of Olive.

All of a sudden he slammed on the brakes and stopped right in the middle of a bridge. He had a wild look in his eye that made me think of George White at rehearsal when a number won't click.

I said, 'Now what? Out of gas?' Bruce said, 'The Willowemoc! It joins the Beaver Kill at Roscoe'.

Believe it or not, he sat there in the sun for ten minutes watching the water that ran under the bridge. He said he was looking for rises. I said he wasn't looking in the right place. I told him there was blisters rising on me, from the neck down, on account of that leather seat . . . How about a cigarette? . . . Thanks!

We got to the Bancrofts' fishing lodge not long after that. It turned out to be a flop – just a joint made of logs like some of those Stop and Eats you see along the road. There was a few chairs and benches that needed painting on a porch made of tree branches with the bark on.

Something came out on the porch and yoohooed, and that was the tip-off it was human. I said, 'Hold everything! Do you see what I see?' Bruce yoohooed back. He said, 'It's Lucille. She's still in her waders'. I forgot my feet, looking this one over while she came down the path to the car. Picture a dame in a pair of rubber pants made for Man Mountain Dean, with shoes to match, and you'll get it. Above the pants was an old tan flannel shirt and – I wouldn't try to kid you – suspenders. Men's suspenders, I mean. Now I ask you! But wait a minute. I keep forgetting you're a trout fisher yourself. Maybe you think that's a hot costume. Maybe a babe in outsize rubber pants just knocks you dead. I dunno. Me, I've been raised different. I don't see what chasing fish gets you, and anyone letting herself look like that just seems screwy to me.

When she got to the car, I saw she could of been a pretty fair looker, but she didn't have a scrap of make-up on – not even lipstick – and her face was shiny and red, and her nose was peeling. She said, 'So this is Violet!' She gave me the up and down. Then she said, 'Now that I see her, Bruce, I'm beginning to understand'.

PATRICK CHALMERS: from *The Angler's England* (1938).

No longer is sea angling as I first remember it. I can recall a pier that bestrid the blue Southampton Water. I can recall how a small boy in a sailor suit, myself, unwound a line, that would have carried a week's washing comfortably, from off a frame – a hollow square of wood. At the line's end was a lump of lead about as big as a duck's egg. Below the lead there fell a foot or so of wire with a two-foot cross-piece, likewise of wire, depending therefrom. Upon the extremities of the cross-piece there hung, still on wire, two large hooks. From a red tin bucket the angler produced a dead clam, two dead clams. He baited his hooks. He swung the lead with a circular movement and let go suddenly. Then, if he were lucky, lead, line and appanage, describing an entrancing parabola in blue air, fell, forty yards from the pier-end, splash, into blue water. If he were unlucky, the lead and line released, wound itself about the pier railing or made a Laocoon of a spectator. Once indeed it was the attendant nursemaid's chignon (the lead struck it fairly and squarely) that saved her head. Fortunately her woven plaits were those of a Rapunzel and small harm was done. But, all being well and the baits duly upon the ocean bed, the frame, to which the line was attached, was hitched about the railing and the outfit was left to fish itself. But every ten minutes the hooks would be hauled in for examination, when occasionally it would be found, to acclamation, that a codling had occurred or a crab.

I can remember, at the same time of life, how we put out in a brown sailing boat from a little northern harbour, loud with gulls and strong with the intoxicating smell of tar and sunshine and low tide. Other boats lay along the sea-weedy wall of the little pier. We hauled past them and out into the bay. We anchored. We dropped the hand lines as before and as fast as (another small boy and myself) could pull them up again and rebait them, we caught whiting-pout and flounders. Occasionally our host, a young cavalry officer, glanced carelessly at a small military formation a mile away, upon the cliff-top above the harbour. The members of the company seemed vaguely interested in ourselves since the sun now and again, had one time to look, caused the lens of an official field-glass, turned towards us, to coruscate. Then, some hundreds of yards from our bows, a furious fountain of white water shot into the air, and another and another as the duck-and-drake ricochet fled on, hop, skip and jump. Boom – the report rolled sullenly over the water. It was Mr Leech to the life. 'Oh, Mr

Boatman, what's that?' 'That, Mum? Nothin', Mum, honly the har-tillerie a-practisin', Mum', etc., etc.

It was then that I heard expressed (and I have always recollected it) the splendid contempt of a regular officer, and a cavalryman at that, for a volunteer. 'I wouldn't budge', our host muttered, not to us but to his moustache, 'if they were shooting at me, but –' He hauled up the mud-hook and we changed ground.

EDWARD THOMAS: from *The Childhood of Edward Thomas, a Fragment of Autobiography* (1938).

I fished for sticklebacks and gudgeon in the long pond* on the far side of the railway, which owed its name of 'Backaruffs' or 'Pack of Roughs', so I always thought, to the poor ill-dressed boys who used to swarm to it from Battersea on Saturdays and bank holidays. I fished with a worm either tied on the cotton line or impaled on a bent pin, and put my stickleback or my rare lovely spotted gudgeon in a glass jam-jar. Once at least I did as I had seen others do, hauling a heavy fruit basket out into the pond and dragging it in full of weed and mud and the little 'blood worms' that breed in mud, and sticklebacks, even a red-throated one, but never a gudgeon. The gudgeon was so attractive, partly for its looks, perhaps chiefly for its comparative size, that many times I willingly paid a halfpenny for one and let it be believed that I had caught it. Even when dead it was hard to part with, so smooth and pure was it. I liked even its smell, yet never dreamed of catching it. There were carp, too, in this pond and in the roundish Box Pond that lay half-way between the top of our street and the railway. By the longer pond I once saw a carp many times as big as a gudgeon in the possession of a rough: he had torn its head off to make it fit his jar. Much larger ones were talked about, caught in the Box Pond by the elder brothers of one boy. I saw them fishing there once or twice without a motion of the float in the motionless water. Once I tried there myself all alone. My expectations were huge: that I failed com-pletely only increased my respect for the sacred pond. Bigger boys used to fish in the Penn Ponds at Richmond Park and allowed me to buy from them a perch of four or five inches long, which looked magnificent with its dark bars, standing almost on its head in my little

*On Wandsworth Common.

round bowl. There in spite of worms and breadcrumbs it shortly afterwards died. I was pained at coming down in the morning and finding such a magnificent, uncommon and costly creature dead. Nor did I ever like the perch's stiff prickly corpse, faded in death, and looking much smaller out of the bowl than inside.

GEORGE ORWELL: from *Coming Up For Air* (1939).

I was rather an ugly little boy, with butter-coloured hair which was always cropped short except for a quiff in front. I don't idealize my childhood, and unlike many people I've no wish to be young again. Most of the things I used to care for would leave me something more than cold. I don't care if I never see a cricket ball again, and I wouldn't give you threepence for a hundredweight of sweets. But I've still got, I've always had, that peculiar feeling for fishing. You'll think it damned silly, no doubt, but I've actually half a wish to go fishing even now, when I'm fat and forty-five and got two kids and a house in the suburbs. Why? Because in a manner of speaking I *am* sentimental about my childhood – not my own particular childhood, but the civilization which I grew up in and which is now, I suppose, just about at its last kick. And fishing is somehow typical of that civilization. As soon as you think of fishing you think of things that don't belong to the modern world. The very idea of sitting all day under a willow tree beside a quiet pool – and being able to find a quiet pool to sit beside – belongs to the time before the war, before the radio, before aeroplanes, before Hitler. There's a kind of peacefulness even in the names of English coarse fish. Roach, rudd, dace, bleak, barbel, bream, gudgeon, pike, chub, carp, tench. They're solid kind of names. The people who made them up hadn't heard of machine-guns, they didn't live in terror of the sack or spend their time eating aspirins, going to the pictures, and wondering how to keep out of the concentration camp.

Does anyone go fishing nowadays, I wonder? Anywhere within a hundred miles of London there are no fish left to catch. A few dismal fishing-clubs plant themselves in rows along the banks of canals, and millionaires go trout-fishing in private waters round Scotch hotels, a sort of snobbish game of catching hand-reared fish with artificial flies. But who fishes in mill-streams or moats or cow-ponds any longer? Where are the English coarse fish now? When I was a kid every pond and stream had fish in it. Now all the ponds are drained and when the streams aren't poisoned with chemicals from factories they're full of rusty tins and motor-bike tyres.

My best fishing-memory is about some fish that I never caught. That's usual enough, I suppose.

When I was about fourteen Father did a good turn of some kind of old Hodges, the caretaker at Binfield House. I forget what it was – gave him some medicine that cured his fowls of the worms, or something. Hodges was a crabby old devil, but he didn't forget a good turn. One day a little while afterwards when he'd been down to the shop to buy chicken-corn he met me outside the door and stopped me in his surly way. He had a face like something carved out of a bit of root, and only two teeth, which were dark brown and very long.

'Hey, young 'un! Fisherman, ain't you?'

'Yes.'

'Thought you was. You listen, then. If so be you wanted to, you could bring your line and have a try in that they pool up ahind the Hall. There's plenty bream and jack in there. But don't you tell no one as I told you. And don't you go for to bring any of them other young whelps, or I'll beat the skin off their backs.'

Having said this he hobbled off with his sack of corn over his shoulder, as though feeling that he'd said too much already. The next Saturday afternoon I biked up to Binfield House with my pockets full of worms and gentles, and looked for old Hodges at the lodge. At that time Binfield House had already been empty for ten or twenty years. Mr Farrel, the owner, couldn't afford to live in it and either couldn't or wouldn't let it. He lived in London on the rent of his farms and let the house and grounds go to the devil. All the fences were green and rotting, the park was a mass of nettles, the plantations were like a jungle, and even the gardens had gone back to meadow, with only a few old gnarled rose-bushes to show you where the beds had been. But it was a very beautiful house, expecially from a distance. It was a great white place with colonnades and long-shaped windows, which had been built, I suppose, about Queen Anne's time by someone who'd travelled in Italy. If I went there now I'd probably get a certain kick out of wandering round the general desolation and thinking about the life that used to go on there, and the people who built such places because they imagined that the good days would last for ever. As a boy I didn't give either the house or the grounds a second look. I dug out old Hodges, who'd just finished his dinner and was a bit surly, and got him to show me the way down to the pool. It was several hundred yards behind the house and completely hidden in the beech woods, but it was a good-sized pool, almost a lake, about a hundred and fifty yards across. It was astonishing, and even at that age it astonished me, that there, a dozen miles from Reading and not fifty from London, you could have such solitude. You felt as much alone as if you'd been on the banks of the Amazon. The pool was ringed completely round by the enormous beech trees, which in one place came down to the edge and were reflected in the water. On the other side there was a patch of grass where there was a hollow with beds of wild peppermint, and up at one end of the pool an old wooden boathouse was rotting among the bulrushes.

The pool was swarming with bream, small ones, about four to six inches long. Every now and again you'd see one of them turn half over and gleam reddy-brown under the water. There were pike there too, and they must have been big ones. You never saw them, but sometimes one that was basking among the weeds would turn over and plunge with a splash that was like a brick being bunged into the water. It was no use trying to catch them, though of course I always tried every time I went there. I tried them with dace and minnows I'd caught in the Thames and kept alive in a jam-jar, and even with a spinner made out of a bit of tin. But they were gorged with fish and wouldn't bite, and in any case they'd have broken any tackle I possessed. I never came back from the pool without at least a dozen small bream. Sometimes in the summer holidays I went there for a whole day, with my fishing-rod and a copy of *Chums* or the *Union Jack* or something, and a hunk of bread and cheese which Mother had wrapped up for me. And I've fished for hours and then lain in the grass hollow and read the *Union Jack,* and then the smell of my bread paste and the plop of a fish jumping somewhere would send me wild again, and I'd go back to the water and have another go, and so on all through a summer's day. And the best of all was to be alone, utterly alone, though the road wasn't a quarter of a mile away. I was just old enough to know that it's good to be alone occasionally. With the trees all round you it was as though the pool belonged to you, and nothing ever stirred except the fish ringing the water and the pigeons passing overhead. And yet, in the two years or so that I went fishing there, how many times did I really go, I wonder? Not more than a dozen. It was a three-mile bike ride from home and took up a whole afternoon at least. And sometimes other things turned up, and sometimes when I'd meant to go it rained. You know the way things happen.

One afternoon the fish weren't biting and I began to explore at the

end of the pool farthest from Binfield House. There was a bit of an
overflow of water and the ground was boggy, and you had to fight your
way through a sort of jungle of blackberry bushes and rotten boughs
that had fallen off the trees. I struggled through it for about fifty yards,
and then suddenly there was a clearing and I came to another pool
which I had never known existed. It was a small pool not more than
twenty yards wide, and rather dark because of the boughs that overhung it. But it was very clear water and immensely deep. I could see
ten or fifteen feet down into it. I hung about for a bit, enjoying the
dampness and the rotten boggy smell, the way a boy does. And then I
saw something that almost made me jump out of my skin.

It was an enormous fish. I don't exaggerate when I say it was
enormous. It was almost the length of my arm. It glided across the
pool, deep under water, and then became a shadow and disappeared
into the darker water on the other side. I felt as if a sword had gone
through me. It was far the biggest fish I'd ever seen, dead or alive. I
stood there without breathing, and in a moment another huge thick
shape glided through the water, and then another and then two more
close together. The pool was full of them. They were carp, I suppose.
Just possibly they were bream or tench, but more probably carp. Bream
or tench wouldn't grow so huge. I knew what had happened. At some
time this pool had been connected with the other, and then the stream
had dried up and the woods had closed round the small pool and it had
just been forgotten. It's a thing that happens occasionally. A pool gets
forgotten somehow, nobody fishes in it for years and decades and the
fish grow to monstrous sizes. The brutes that I was watching might be
a hundred years old. And not a soul in the world knew about them
except me. Very likely it was twenty years since anyone had so much as
looked at the pool, and probably even old Hodges and Mr Farrel's
bailiff had forgotten its existence.

Well, you can imagine what I felt. After a bit I couldn't even bear the
tantalization of watching. I hurried back to the other pool and got my
fishing things together. It was no use trying for those colossal brutes
with the tackle I had. They'd snap it as if it had been a hair. And I
couldn't go on fishing any longer for the tiny bream. The sight of the
big carp had given me a feeling in my stomach almost as if I was going
to be sick. I got on to my bike and whizzed down the hill and home. It
was a wonderful secret for a boy to have. There was the dark pool
hidden away in the woods and the monstrous fish sailing round it – fish
that had never been fished for and would grab the first bait you offered

them. It was only a question of getting hold of a line strong enough to hold them. Already I'd made all the arrangements. I'd buy the tackle that would hold them if I had to steal the money out of the till. Somehow, God knew how, I'd get hold of half a crown and buy a length of silk salmon line and some thick gut or gimp and Number 5 hooks, and come back with cheese and gentles and paste and meal-worms and brandlings and grasshoppers and every mortal bait a carp might look at. The very next Saturday afternoon I'd come back and try for them.

But as it happened I never went back. One never does go back. I never stole the money out of the till or bought the bit of salmon line or had a try for those carp. Almost immediately afterwards something turned up to prevent me, but if it hadn't been that it would have been something else. It's the way things happen.

I know, of course, that you think I'm exaggerating about the size of those fish. You think, probably, that they were just medium-sized fish (a foot long, say) and that they've swollen gradually in my memory. But it isn't so. People tell lies about the fish they've caught and still more about the fish that are hooked and get away, but I never caught any of these or even tried to catch them, and I've no motive for lying. I tell you they were enormous.

'The orders of bliss'
The Later Twentieth Century

THREE WORLDS by M. C. Escher (1955).

NEGLEY FARSON: from *Going Fishing* (1942).

A true surf-caster is a man who loves the sea. Far beyond the prize of any great fish he might land, is the exhilaration of the waves. In the summer along the New Jersey coast they came in in sets of three, in great, racing combers. You could hear their dull booms far inland. Then there was the smell of the salt marsh. When the wind was off-shore these arching sea-horses raced in with long white manes streaming from their tips. From the marsh at sunset you heard the cry of shore-fowl. The haunting, space-hinting cry of the curlew; is there a more moving call by any sea? There were days of dull mist which blurred the headlands. Then a white fog, with the hot sun behind it, when the hissing surf shone like burnished silver. And then the long hot afternoons when the mirage came and the liners far off the yellow coast came past in streamers, or sailed upside down.

These are the things which fill the eye, and heart, and mind of the veteran surfcaster. These are often all that he brings home after a hard day's work, with the sandpipers dancing along the shore. Surf-casting is not a duffer's sport. And you are sure to catch many more fish from a boat.

For some reason, perhaps experience, we held the belief that the striped channel bass always struck best by night. There was a rod-maker along that coast who gave as a prize each year 'a handsome snakewood rod', with German silver mounting, and agate guides, to the person who caught the biggest channel bass. One year the man who lived next door to me won it with a forty-two pounder. He was very professional, having taken a house where he could command the sea, and having a glass case in that house full of greenheart, snakewood, and split-cane rods. Below the case was a chest of drawers containing Vom Hofe reels, Pfluegers, with ratchet and drag, and cast-off so that the spool could run free without turning the handle. Being an intensely religious man he never fished on Sundays; but that had nothing to do with 'practising'. So, when other people were at church, he and some of his old cronies would totter stiffly down to the beach and practise casting with just the sinker. For some reason – because of the ecstasy of it, I suppose – he seemed to get his strength back the minute he took his stance to make a cast.

It was a delight to watch the even parabola of his sinker, sailing surely to precisely where he had intended it. A back-lash, from him, would have been sacrilege. But there were other casters, among the summer lot, who were not so skilful. One summer day a novice, making the sweeping sidewise cast among a lot of enthusiasts at the end of our local wooden pier, rotated with all his might to shoot his sinker out to sea, but, unfortunately, caught a Japanese in the ear.

The hook was driven with such force that it pulled the ear forward and entered the Jap's skull. The lead sinker then swiftly spun around his head, and, *clunk!* hit him on the forehead and almost brained him.

But we, we locals, detested pier fishing. It meant a crowd; and that meant you lost the chief thing in surf-casting – the luxury of your own solitude. That, and trying to solve the sea – guessing whether this or that sand-bar had shifted – these things are the very essence of surf fishing. Then, to haul two-or three-pound fish up like a bucket is an entirely different thing from beaching a fighting twenty-five pounder through heavy waves. There, every bit of your skill and intelligence is called upon. And quickly. In these conditions, with a heavy undertow and the last receding wave adding pounds to your line-pull, you can make a mistake only once.

Not able to play Sancho Panza to my revered neighbour, and feeling (quite correctly) that I had little chance of ever winning that fine prize rod myself, I attached myself to the next-best fisherman I knew along that stretch of coast. He was an old ex-German. I did not know what his profession was, or his politics; nor did I care. All I knew was that if I did want to be in at the killing of one of these monster fish, he was the man for me. He felt likewise.

You cannot buy enthusiasm. Nor a small boy who will run a mile to fetch your bait. Or someone who will sit silent, for hours, while you ruminate. Someone who will eagerly hold your rod while you take a snooze. Or, even more wondrous companion, a boy who will collect driftwood for a fire on cold nights, when the driftwood burns green from the copper in it; and you two sit, avidly eating the bait – the fat clams you have roasted in the embers. Clams scorned by the channel bass.

But one moonlit night they did not scorn them. The German had waded far out and made his cast. Now he was drying himself by our fire. He had taken up all slack. With the click on, his rod was leaning over a 'Y' that he always brought along to rest it on – for these surf rods are not light things; if you can afford it, you use a heavy belt with a leather cup to hold the butt of your rod against you while you are fighting a fish. *And the reel screamed!*

I did not know a word of German then. But I heard a sputter of them. He was into a big fish. There was no doubt about that, the way the German's rod was bending – *and jerking.* Joe's bark showed that even he had realized this moment's significance. For the German nearly went crazy. What had happened was that he had jammed his reel. If my wealthy neighbour had reels with gadgets that made me envious, this German had tackle which made my heart ache. His reel not only had a drag, but super-super-drags. And one of them had 'frozen'. The spool was locked solid. The only thing to do now was run back and forth to the surf, or up and down the coast, *as the fish played him!*

In this unforseen tug-of-war the fat German showed almost an indecent agility. One minute he would be shouting commands to me from atop the sand dunes (though what I could do about it, I could not see!); the next he would be racing past me towards the surf. The bass had made a run out for deep water. The fish had the upper hand for some time. 'Big von! Big von!' the German kept shouting at me. But the bend of his rod had already told me that. Finally loud Teuton yelps from the sand dunes announced that the German was beaching him.

And very skilfully he did it! Watching for an incoming wave, he went backwards with it. The fish was tired. The German got him just ahead of the wave and raced shorewards with it, keeping a taut line, bringing the fish with it as the wave surged far up the sands. Then he held it. The wave retreated. And there in the moonlight flapped a huge striped channel bass.

Then I broke the line.

I had tried to pull the fish farther upwards with it. Fatal ignorance! His dead weight snapped the Cuttyhunk forthwith. But I landed it. I ran down and fell upon it, thrusting my hand and arm well up through its gills. A scratchy gesture. But when the next wave came we were holding the prize up in the moonlight – just to look at it.

KEITH DOUGLAS: *Behaviour of Fish in an Egyptian Tea Garden*
(written 1943).

> As a white stone draws down the fish
> she on the seafloor of the afternoon
> draws down men's glances and their cruel wish
> for love. Her red lip on the spoon
>
> slips-in a morsel of ice-cream. Her hands
> white as a shell, are submarine
> fronds, sink with spread fingers, lean
> along the table, carmined at the ends.
>
> A cotton magnate, an important fish
> with great eyepouches and a golden mouth
> through the frail reefs of furniture swims out
> and idling, suspended, stays to watch.
>
> A crustacean old man clamped to his chair
> sits near her and might coldly see
> her charms through fissures where the eyes should be;
> or else his teeth are parted in a stare.
>
> Captain on leave, a lean dark mackerel,
> lies in the offing, turns himself and looks
> through currents of sound. The flat-eyed flatfish sucks
> on a straw, staring from its repose, laxly.
>
> And gallants in shoals swim up and lag,
> circling and passing near the white attraction –
> sometimes pausing, opening a conversation –
> fish pause so to nibble or tug.

But now the ice-cream is finished, is
paid for. The fish swim off on business
and she sits alone at the table, a white stone
useless except to a collector, a rich man.

ED ZERN: *The Truth About Izaak Walton.* From *To Hell with Fishing*
(1945).

If you think *this* book is dull, go curl up with *The Compleat Angler, or
The Contemplative Man's Recreation.* Then try to uncurl.

Of course, Izaak Walton wrote *The Compleat Angler* a long time ago.
Even nonfishermen could not spell very good in those days.

The Compleat Angler is all about a character named Piscator. Later, in
disgust, he became a stage director.

Izaak Walton pretended to be an expert on fishing. In his introduction, he refers to 'the honest Angler'. That's how much *he* knew.

The Compleat Angler is chock-full of useful information for fishermen. For example, in Part 1, Chapter IV, it says: 'And next you are to
notice, that the Trout is not like the Crocodile'. Walton was observant.

In Chapter VIII, he tells of a man who caught a pike by using a mule
as bait. Fortunately for Ike, it was several hundred years before anybody read beyond Chapter 1.

In the same chapter, he also tells of a pike that bit a Polish girl's foot.
Personally, I would prefer this type of bait over mules.

I once knew a Polish girl in Hamtramck, Mich., who . . .

Skip it.

VIRGINIA WOOLF: *Fishing* (a review of the angling writer
J. W. Hills). From *The Moment and Other Essays* (edited by Leonard
Woolf 1947).

While there is a Chinese proverb which says that the fisherman is pure
at heart 'as a white sea-shell', there is a Japanese poem, four lines long,
which says something so true but at the same time so crude about the
hearts of politicians that it had better be left in its original obscurity. It
may be this contradiction – Major Hills, says his publisher, 'has been a

member of the House of Commons for thirty years . . . Throughout his
long parliamentary life he has remained faithful to his favourite sport' –
which has produced a collision in his book; a confusion in the mind of
the reader between fish and men.

All books are made of words, but mostly of words that flutter and
agitate thought. This book on the contrary, though made of words, has
a strange effect on the body. It lifts it out of the chair, stands it on the
banks of a river, and strikes it dumb. The river rushes by; a voice
commands: 'Stand absolutely motionless . . . Cast up and slightly
across . . . Shoot the line out . . . Let the flies come well round . . . On
no account pull . . . Do not be in a hurry to lift . . .' But the strain is too
great, the excitement too intense. We have pulled – we have lifted. The
fish is off. 'Wait longer next time,' the voice commands, 'wait longer
and longer.'

Now, if the art of writing consists in laying an egg in the reader's
mind from which springs the thing itself – whether man or fish – and if
this art requires such ardour in its practitioners that they will readily,
like Flaubert, give up all their bright spring mornings to its pursuit,
how does it come about that Major Hills, who has spent thirty years in
the House of Commons, can do the trick? Sometimes at four in the
morning, in the early spring dawn, he has roused himself, not to
dandle words, but to rush down to the river – 'the exquisite river, with
its vivid green wooded banks, its dark rose-coloured sandstone rocks,
its rushing crystaline water', and there he has stood with his rod.
There we stand too.

Look at the rod. It was bought of Strong of Carlisle and cost one
pound. 'It consisted of a piece of whole bamboo with a lancewood top
spliced on . . . Never have I had a rod sweeter to cast with and
throwing a longer line.' It is not a rod; it is a tool, more beautiful than a
Persian pot, more desirable than a lover. '. . . A friend broke it . . . and
I could never get another like it . . . and I grieved sorely, for bamboo
cannot be mended.' What death or disaster could be more pungent?
But this is no time for sentiment. There deep under the bank lies the
old male salmon. What fly will he take? The grey turkey, with a body of
violet silk, the archdeacon in fact, number one? The line is cast; out it
floats; down it settles. And then? '. . . The fish went perfectly mad,
overran my reel . . . jammed it, and broke my twisted gut trace. It all
happened in a few seconds . . .' But they were seconds of extraordinary
intensity, seconds lived alone 'in a world of strong emotion, cut off
from all else'. When we look up, Corby's walks have changed. 'The
trees had their young light leaves, some of them golden, the wild

cherry was covered with drifts of snow and the ground was covered with dog mercury, looking as though it had been newly varnished . . . I felt receptive to every sight, every colour and every sound, as though I walked through a world from which a veil had been withdrawn.'

Is it possible that to remove veils from trees it is necessary to fish? – our conscious mind must be all body, and then the unconscious mind leaps to the top and strips off veils? Is it possible that, if to bare reality is to be a poet, we have, as Mr Yeats said the other day, no great poet because since the war farmers preserve or net their waters, and vermin get up? Has the deplorable habit of clubs to fetter anglers with ridiculous restrictions, to pamper them with insidious luxuries, somehow cramped our poets' style? And the novelists – if we have no novelist in England today whose stature is higher than the third button on Sir Walter's waistcoat, or reaches to the watchchain of Charles Dickens, or the ring on the little finger of George Eliot, is it not that the Cumberland poachers are dying out? 'They were an amusing race, full of rare humour, delightful to talk to . . . We often had chats on the banks and they would tell me quite openly of their success.' But now 'the old wild days are over'; the poachers are gone. They catch trout, commercially, innumerably, for hotels. Banish from fiction all poachers' talk, the dialect, the dialogue of Scott, the publicans, the farmers of Dickens and George Eliot, and what remains? Mouldy velvet; moth-eaten ermine; mahogany tables; and a few stuffed fowls. No wonder, since the poachers are gone, that fiction is failing . . . 'But this is not catching trout,' the voice commands. 'Do not dawdle . . . Start fishing again without delay.'

It is a bad day; the sun is up; the trout are not feeding. We fail again and again. But fishing teaches a stern morality; inculcates a remorseless honesty. The fault may be with ourselves. 'Why do I go on missing at the strike? . . . If I had more delicacy in casting, more accuracy, if I had fished finer, should I not have done better? And the answer is – Yes! . . . I lost him through sinning against the light . . . I failed through obstinate stupidity.' We are sunk deep in the world of meditation and remorse. 'Contradiction lies at the root of all powerful emotions. We are not ruled by reason. We follow a different law, and recognize its sanctions . . .' Sounds from the outer world come through the roar of the river. Barbarians have invaded the upper waters of the Eden and Driffield Beck. But happily the barbarians are grayling; and the profound difference that divides the human race is a question of bait – whether to fish with worms or not; some will: to others the thought is unutterably repulsive.

But the summer's day is fading. Night is coming on – the Northern night, which is not dark, for the light is there, but veiled. 'A Cumberland night is something to remember,' and trout – for trout are 'curious pieces of work' – will feed in Cumberland at midnight. Let us go down to the bank again. The river sounds louder than by day. 'As I walked down I heard its varied cadence, obscured during sunlight, at one moment deep, then clamorous, then where thick beech trees hid the river subdued to a murmur . . . The flowering trees had long since lost their blossoms, but on coming to a syringa bush I walked suddenly into its scent, and was drenched as in a bath. I sat on the path. I stretched my legs. I lay down, finding a tuft of grass for pillow, and the yielding sand for mattress. I fell asleep.'

And while the fisherman sleeps, we who are presumbly reading – but what kind of reading is this when we see through the words Corby's trees and trout at the bottom of the page? – wonder, what does the fisherman dream? Of all the rivers rushing past – the Eden, the Test, and the Kennet, each river different from the other, each full of shadowy fish, and each fish different from the other; the trout subtle, the salmon ingenious; each with its nerves, with its brain, its mentality that we can dimly penetrate, movements we can mystically anticipate, for just as, suddenly, Greek and Latin sort themselves in a flash, so we understand the minds of fish? Or does he dream of the wild Scottish hill in the blizzard; and the patch of windless weather behind the rock, when the pale grasses no longer bent but stood upright; or of the vision on top – twenty Whooper swans floating on the loch fearlessly, 'for they had come from some land where they had never seen a man'? Or does he dream of poachers with their whisky-stained weather-beaten faces; or of Andrew Lang, drinking, and discussing the first book of Genesis; or of F. S. Oliver, whose buttons after a meal 'kept popping off like broom pods in autumn'; or of Sparrow, the hunter, 'a more generous animal never was seen'; or of the great Arthur Wood and all his bees? Or does he dream of places that his ghost will revisit if it ever comes to earth again – of Ramsbury, Highhead, and the Isle of Jura?

For dream he does. 'I always, even now, dream that I shall astonish the world. An outstanding success . . .' The Premiership is it? No, this triumph, this outstanding success is not with men; it is with fish; it is with the floating line. 'I believe it will come . . .' But here he wakes 'with that sense of well-being which sleep in the open air always engenders. It was midnight, moonless and clear. I walked to the edge of the flat rock . . .' The trout were feeding.

RODERICK HAIG-BROWN: from *A River Never Sleeps* (1948).

A river is water in its loveliest form; rivers have life and sound and movement and infinity of variation, rivers are veins of the earth through which the life blood returns to the heart. Rivers can attain overwhelming grandeur, as the Columbia does in the reaches all the way from Paco to the sea; they may slide softly through flat meadows or batter their way down mountain slopes and through narrow canyons; they may be heavy, almost dark, with history, as the Thames is from its mouth at least up to Richmond; or they may be sparkling fresh on mountain slopes through virgin forest and alpine meadows.

Lakes and the sea have great secret depths quite hidden from man and often almost barren of life. A river too may have its deep and secret places, may be so large that one can never know it properly; but most rivers that give sport to fly fishermen are comparatively small, and one feels that it is within the range of the mind to know them intimately – intimately as to their changes through the seasons, as to the shifts and quirks of current, the sharp runs, the slow glides, the eddies and bars and crossing places, the very rocks of the bottom. And in knowing a river intimately is a very large part of the joy of fly fishing.

One may love a river as soon as one sets eyes upon it; it may have certain features that fit instantly with one's conception of beauty, or it may recall the qualities of some other river, well known and deeply loved. One may feel in the same way an instant affinity for a man or a woman and know that here is pleasure and warmth and the foundation of deep friendship. In either case the full riches of the discovery are not immediately released – they cannot be; only knowledge and close experience can release them. Rivers, I suppose, are not at all like human beings, but it is still possible to make apt comparisons; and this is one: understanding, whether instinctive and immediate or developing naturally through time or grown by conscious effort, is a necessary preliminary of love. Understanding of another human being can never be complete, but as it grows towards completeness, it becomes love almost inevitably. One cannot know intimately all the ways and movements of a river without growing into love of it. And there is no exhaustion to the growth of love through knowledge, whether the love be for a person or a river, because the knowledge can never become complete. One can come to feel in time that the whole is within one's compass, not yet wholly and intimately known, but there for the knowing, within the last little move of reaching; but there will always be something ahead, something more to know.

I have known very few rivers thoroughly and intimately. There is not time to know many, and one can know only certain chosen lengths of the few. I know some miles of the Dorsetshire Frome and of the little river Wrackle that cuts away from the Frome by Stratton Mill and rejoins it farther down, because I grew up with them and had all the quick instinctive learning power of the very young when I fished there. It was a happy and proud thing to know those streams, and the knowing paid great dividends in fish; it paid even greater dividends in something that I can still recapture – sheer happiness in remembering a bend or a run or the spread below a bridge as I saw them best, perhaps open in sunlight with the green weeds trailing and a good fish rising steadily, or perhaps pitted by rain under a grey sky, or white and black and golden, opaque in the long slant of the twilight. I knew those streams through fishing them, through cutting the weeds in them, through shooting ducks and snipe all along them, through setting nightlines in them, through exploring them when the hatches were down and the water was very low. I carry them with me wherever I go and can fish them almost as well sitting here as I could were I walking the meadow grass along their banks six thousand miles from here.

I learned other waters almost as easily, though more superficially, when I was very young. The lower reaches of the Frome, between Wool and Wareham, where we used to fish for salmon, were harder to know than the best of the trout water because the river was deeper and darker and slower down there, more secret within itself. But I fished with a man who knew all the secrets and we used the prawn a lot, fishing it deep down and slow, close to bottom and close under the banks. Fish lay where he said they should lie and took hold as he said they would take, and one remembered and fished it that way for oneself until the knowledge was properly one's own. I think I could still start at Bindon Mill and work on all the way down to Salmon Water without missing so very many of the good places. And then, perhaps, I could walk back along the railroad track towards evening with a decent weight of salmon on my back.

'B. B.': from *Confessions of a Carp-fisher* (1950).

As I have mentioned, your true habitual carp fisher is almost unique in that he pursues his craft – or suffers most acutely from his afflictions, whichever way you will have it – during the heat of summer. His memories (with those of the entomologist), therefore, are mostly pleasant sunny ones; few places are more tranquil than a wood embowered pool on a summer's evening. Also he is early astir and more than any other angler senses the beauty and unimpaired freshness of the summer dawn. He has no recollection of the wintry leaden waves chasing before a keen nor'easter such as the pike fisher remembers, when it is so cold you must stamp your feet as if in a wine press and swing your arms like a demented bear. No – there is the memory of the unbelievable scents which come to the watcher in that late hour when the sun has gone, when the heated air rises up from the fields and woods, lanes and hedgerows, when the moths click among the glimmering wild rose bushes, and the little people of the night stir secretly among the reeds. To him, when he hears the heavy splash of some big questing carp, there comes a delicious shiver to visit his spine, running up and down it like the flicker of a serpent's tongue. And how many are the noises one hears beside the water at fall of night! Some can be guessed at and mental pictures formed of what manner of creatures they are – others leave one mystified. Nor is the water really still when the sun has gone. Ever and again a ripple passes through the reeds, something patters and squeaks, lily pads stir and shudder, hidden gleams come and go. It is an hour bewitched.

J. W. DUNNE: from *Caveat Juvenis*. From *Sunshine and the Dry Fly* (second edition 1950).

A sport is not, and should never, I think, be regarded as, a game. The difference between the two forms of amusement is fundamental. A game is essentially a constructed thing: its rules and regulations are the bones and body of its being. Deprived of these, it would have nothing left to offer that could appeal to a grown man. But hunting and fishing are amusements rich in exactly that quality which is lacking in a game – a basic charm and fascination existing quite apart from any embroidery of rules. Stalking deer and catching fish are things immensely exciting in themselves; indeed, it was just the discovery of this which led to their preservation as pastimes. The origin of that excitement may possibly be traced to the days when success or failure in these pursuits meant, to primitive man, all the stark difference between satiety and starvation. But that is a side issue. The point to be observed is that this queer, fundamental charm is the thing which gives form and meaning to the whole modern edifice; and those who lose sight of this fact in a passion for redundant ornamentation have little right to feel surprised when they find, as they usually do, that the structure has somehow ceased to please.

Nor is this all. In a game, your opponent is merely another rule-bound man. But in a sport your opponent is no less a personage than *Nature herself*, – Nature, wild and free and entirely lawless, – Nature, wayward, cheating, laughing, alluring, infinitely diversified, entrancingly mutable. And to come to such a playfellow equipped with a book of set rules is more than an absurdity – it is to miss the whole spirit of the meeting.

ZANE GREY: from *South to Virgin Seas*. From *Zane Grey's Adventures in Fishing* (edited by Ed Zern 1952).

We came at length to a place that, the moment my eyes fell upon it, struck me with the singular thrilling appreciation and realization that it must be recorded in my memory book for rare fishing spots. And the charm of living over my experience of them never dies.

The outermost island of this group was a long, low, black ledge absolutely covered with pelicans. Perhaps this rock island was half an acre in extent and rose twenty feet or so above the sea. It marked the end of the reef, and around it the current heaved with swelling power and resonant music. There was a tide-rip that set in from the open sea, and which met the offshore current just around the corner of this island. I could see amber and yellow rock running out some rods, under the green water. Over this submerged ledge the left-hand current poured to meet presently the incoming tide-rip. The result was a foaming maelstrom, and in the boiling water below shone a great crimson patch a hundred feet long and half as wide. Fish! Red snapper! There were thousands of them. And when we ran into that current the crimson patch disintegrated and appeared to string out after our boats.

The redsnapper followed us. Each angler was playing a fish at the same time, and that, while hundreds of great red-golden fish, hungry ad fierce, almost charged the boats. They ran in weight from ten to forty, perhaps fifty pounds. They were gamy, hard-fighting fish, and when first out of the water seemed the most gorgeously flaming creatures I had ever seen come from the sea. While the boys were having such splendid sport I happily remembered that we could use some fresh food fish, and that the natives would also welcome some.

When the swell rolled in, slow and grand, and heaved up on the island to the very feet of the comical pelicans, it made a roar that shook my heart and made me turn fearfully. But it had only expended its force on the rock barrier and had foamed back to slide down that long golden ledge, like a millrace, and mingle with the white foam and green current so beautifully spotted with flashing red fish.

I saw one great amberjack, between seventy-five and a hundred pounds, strike at Romer's spoon and miss it. I saw a huge silver shield-shaped fish that must go nameless. There are myriads of small green-coloured yellow-barred fish, very shy and swift. I caught a gleam of a golden dolphin.

Over our heads, while the anglers trolled and struck and pulled, and the boatmen handled wheels and levers, the screaming wild fowl sailed around and to and fro. The deep, low, melodious roar of the surge was never still. What fascinated me most, as I stood high on the bow, was the millrace current pouring over the amber ledge to meet that incoming tide-rip. The two formed a corner apart from the tranquil sea beyond, a foaming, eddying, dimpling, rippling triangular pool full of red flashing shadows of fish.

It was a wonderful place and I had to force myself to leave it, though I had not laid my hand on a rod. Some privileges should be respected. And as we ran away from that white-wreathed and bird-haunted rock I knew another marvelous fishing place had been added to my gallery of pictures. Such possessions as that are infinitely precious. In the years to come, when perhaps I cannot fish any more – though imagination halts here – I shall have that gray pelican-dotted rock to recall, and the swell and thundering surge, and golden ledge and swarm of red fish. The places that we cannot return to, if they are enchanting, may not be best beloved, but they are most regretted.

ERNEST HEMINGWAY: from *The Old Man and the Sea* (1952).

The line rose slowly and steadily and then the surface of the ocean
bulged ahead of the boat and the fish came out. He came out
unendingly and water poured from his sides. He was bright in the sun
and his head and back were purple and in the sun the stripes on his
sides showed wide and a light lavender. His sword was as long as a
baseball bat and tapered like a rapier and he rose his full length from
the water and then re-entered it, smoothly, like a diver and the old man
saw the great scythe-blade of his tail go under and the line commenced
to race out.

'He is two feet longer than the skiff,' the old man said. The line was
going out fast but steadily and the fish was not panicked. The old man
was trying with both hands to keep the line just inside of breaking
strength. He knew that if he could not slow the fish with a steady
pressure the fish could take out all the line and break it.

He is a great fish and I must convince him, he thought. I must never
let him learn his strength nor what he could do if he made his run. If I
were him I would put in everything now and go until something broke.
But, thank God, they are not as intelligent as we who kill them;
although they are more noble and more able.

The old man had seen many great fish. He had seen many that
weighed more than a thousand pounds and he had caught two of that
size in his life, but never alone. Now alone, and out of sight of land, he
was fast to the biggest fish that he had ever seen and bigger than he
had ever heard of, and his left hand was still as tight as the gripped
claws of an eagle.

It will uncramp though, he thought. Surely it will uncramp to help
my right hand. There are three things that are brothers: the fish and
my two hands. It must uncramp. It is unworthy of it to be cramped.
The fish had slowed again and was going at his usual pace.

I wonder why he jumped, the old man thought. He jumped almost
as though to show me how big he was. I know now, anyway, he
thought. I wish I could show him what sort of man I am. But then he
would see the cramped hand. Let him think I am more man than I am
and I will be so. I wish I was the fish, he thought, with everything he
has against only my will and my intelligence.

He settled comfortably against the wood and took his suffering as it
came and the fish swam steadily and the boat moved slowly through
the dark water. There was a small sea rising with the wind coming up

from the east and at noon the old man's left hand was uncramped.

'Bad news for you, fish,' he said and shifted the line over the sacks that covered his shoulders.

He was comfortable but suffering, although he did not admit the suffering at all.

'I am not religious,' he said. 'But I will say ten Our Fathers and ten Hail Marys that I should catch this fish, and I promise to make a pilgrimage to the Virgen de Cobre if I catch him. That is a promise.'

ELIZABETH BISHOP: *The Fish.* From *Poems* (1956).

> I caught a tremendous fish
> and held him beside the boat
> half out of water, with my hook
> fast in the corner of his mouth.
> He didn't fight.
> He hadn't fought at all.
> He hung a grunting weight,
> battered and venerable
> and homely. Here and there
> his brown skin hung in strips
> like ancient wallpaper,
> and its pattern of darker brown
> was like wallpaper:
> shapes like full-blown roses
> stained and lost through age.
> He was speckled with barnacles,
> fine rosettes of lime,
> and infested
> with tiny white sea-lice,
> and underneath two or three
> rags of green weed hung down.
> While his gills were breathing in
> the terrible oxygen
> – the frightening gills
> fresh and crisp with blood,
> that can cut so badly –
> I thought of the coarse white flesh

packed in like feathers,
the big bones and the little bones,
the dramatic reds and blacks
of his shiny entrails,
and the pink swim-bladder
like a big peony.
I looked into his eyes
which were far larger than mine
but shallower, and yellowed,
the irises backed and packed
with tarnished tinfoil
seen through the lenses
of old scratched isinglass.
They shifted a little, but not
to return my stare.
– It was more like the tipping
of an object toward the light.
I admired his sullen face,
the mechanism of his jaw,
and then I saw
that from his lower lip
– if you could call it a lip –
grim, wet and weapon-like,
hung five old pieces of fish-line,
or four and a wire leader
with the swivel still attached,
with all their five big hooks
grown firmly in his mouth.
A green line, frayed at the end
where he broke it, two heavier lines,
and a fine black thread
still crimped from the strain and snap
when it broke and he got away.
Like medals with their ribbons
frayed and wavering
a five-haired beard of wisdom
trailing from his aching jaw.
I stared and stared
and victory filled up
the little rented boat,

from the pool of bilge
where oil had spread a rainbow
around the rested engine,
to the bailer rusted orange,
the sun-cracked thwarts,
the oarlocks on their strings,
the gunnels – until everything
was rainbow, rainbow, rainbow!
And I let the fish go.

H. E. BATES: *The Little Fishes.* From *Sugar for the Horse* (1957).

My Uncle Silas was very fond of fishing. It was an occupation that helped to keep him from thinking too much about work and also about how terribly hard it was.

If you went through the bottom of my Uncle Silas's garden, past the gooseberry bushes, the rhubarb and the pigsties, you came to a path that went alongside a wood where primroses grew so richly in spring that they blotted out the floor of oak and hazel leaves. In summer wild strawberries followed the primroses and by July the meadows beyond the wood were frothy with meadow-sweet, red clover and the seed of tall soft grasses.

At the end of the second meadow a little river, narrow in parts and bellying out into black deep pools in others, ran along between willows and alders, occasional clumps of dark high reeds and a few wild crab trees. Some of the pools, in July, would be white with water lillies, and snakes would swim across the light flat leaves in the sun. Moorhens talked to each other behind the reeds and water rats would plop suddenly out of sight under clumps of yellow monkey flower.

Here in this little river, my Uncle Silas used to tell me when I was a boy, 'the damn pike used to be as big as hippopotomassiz'.

'Course they ain't so big now,' he would say. 'Nor yit the tench. Nor yit the perch. Nor yit the—'

'Why aren't they so big?'

'Well, I'm a-talkin' about fifty years agoo. Sixty year agoo. Very near seventy years agoo.'

'If they were so big then,' I said, 'all that time ago, they ought to be even bigger now.'

'Not the ones we catched,' he said. 'They ain't there.'

You couldn't, as you see from this, fox my Uncle Silas very easily, but I was at all times a very inquisitive, persistent little boy.

'How big were the tench?' I said.

'Well, I shall allus recollect one as me and Sammy Twizzle caught,' he said. 'Had to lay it in a pig trough to carry it home.'

'And how big were the perch?'

'Well,' he said, rolling his eye in recollection, in that way he had of bringing the wrinkled lid slowly down over it, very like a fish ancient in craftiness himself, 'I don' know as I can jistly recollect the size o' that one me and Arth Sugars nipped out of a September morning one time. But I do know as I cleaned up the back fin and used it for a horse comb for about twenty year.'

'Oh Uncle Silas,' I would say, 'let's go fishing! Let's go and see if they're still as big as hippopotomassiz!'

But it was not always easy, once my Uncle Silas had settled under the trees at the end of the garden on a hot July afternoon, to persuade him that it was worth walking across two meadows just to see if the fish were as big as they used to be. Nevertheless I was, as I say, a very inquisitive, persistent little boy and finally my Uncle Silas would roll over, take the red handkerchief off his face and grunt:

'If you ain't the biggest whittle-breeches I ever knowed I'll goo t'Hanover. Goo an' git the rod and bring a bit o' dough. They'll be no peace until you do, will they?'

'Shall I bring the rod for you too?'

'*Rod?*' he said. 'For *me. Rod?*' He let fall over his eye a tremulous bleary fish-like lid of scorn. 'When me and Sammy Twizzle went a-fishin', all we had to catch 'em with wur we bare hands and a drop o' neck-oil.'

'What's neck-oil?'

'Never you mind,' he said. 'You git the rod and I'll git the neck-oil.'

And presently we would be walking out of the garden, past the wood and across the meadows; I carrying the rod, the dough and perhaps a piece of carraway cake in a paper bag, my Uncle Silas waddling along in his stony-coloured corduroy trousers, carrying the neck-oil.

Sometimes I would be very inquisitive about the neck-oil, which was often pale greenish-yellow, rather the colour of cowslip, or perhaps of parsnips, and sometimes purplish-red, rather the colour of elder-berries, or perhaps of blackberries or plums.

On one occasion I noticed that the neck-oil was very light in colour, almost white, or perhaps more accurately like straw-coloured water.

'Is it a new sort of neck-oil you've got?' I said.

'New flavour.'

'What is it made of?'

'Taters.'

'And you've got two bottles today,' I said.

'Must try to git used to the new flavour.'

'And do you think,' I said, 'we shall catch a bigger fish now that you've got a new kind of neck-oil?'

'Shouldn't be a bit surprised, boy,' he said, 'if we don't git one as big as a donkey.'

That afternoon it was very hot and still as we sat under the shade of a big willow, by the side of a pool that seemed to have across it an oiled black skin broken only by minutest winks of sunlight when the leaves of the willow parted softly in gentle turns of air.

'This is the place where me and Sammy tickled that big 'un out,' my Uncle Silas said.

'The one you carried home in a pig trough?'

'That's the one.'

I said how much I too should like to catch one I could take home in a pig trough and my Uncle Silas said:

'Well, you never will if you keep whittlin' and talkin' and ompolodgin' about.' My Uncle Silas was the only man in the world who ever used the word ompolodgin'. It was a very expressive word and when my Uncle Silas accused you of ompolodgin' it was a very serious matter. It meant that you had buttons on your bottom and if you didn't drop it he would damn well ding your ear.

'You gotta sit still and wait and not keep fidgetin' and very like in another half-hour you'll see a big 'un layin' aside o' that log. But not if you keep ompolodgin'! See?'

'Yes, Uncle.'

'That's why I bring the neck-oil,' he said. 'It quiets you down so's you ain't a-whittlin' and a-ompolodgin' all the time.'

'Can I have a drop of neck-oil?'

'When you git thirsty,' my Uncle Silas said, 'there's that there spring in the next medder.'

After this my Uncle Silas took a good steady drink of neck-oil and settled down with his back against the tree. I put a big lump of paste on my hook and dropped it into the pool. The only fish I could see in the pond were shoals of little silver tiddlers that flickered about a huge fallen willow log a yard or two upstream or came to play inquisitively about my little white and scarlet float, making it quiver up and down like the trembling scraps of sunlight across the water.

Sometimes the bread paste got too wet and slipped from the hook and I quietly lifted the rod from the water and put another lump on the hook. I tried almost not to breathe as I did all this and every time I took the rod out of the water I glanced furtively at my Uncle Silas to see if he thought I was ompolodgin'.

Every time I looked at him I could see that he evidently didn't think so. He was always far too busy with the neck-oil.

I suppose we must have sat there for nearly two hours on that hot windless afternoon of July, I not speaking a word and trying not to breathe as I threw my little float across the water, my Uncle Silas never uttering a sound either except for a drowsy grunt or two as he uncork-ed one bottle of neck-oil or felt to see if the other was safe in his jacket pocket.

All that time there was no sign of a fish as big as a hippopotamus or even of one you could take home in a pig trough and all the time my Uncle Silas kept tasting the flavour of the neck-oil, until at last his head began to fall forward on his chest. Soon all my bread paste was gone and I got so afraid of disturbing my Uncle Silas that I scotched my rod to the fallen log and walked into the next meadow to get myself a drink of water from the spring.

The water was icy cold from the spring and very sweet and good and I wished I had brought myself a bottle too, so that I could fill it and sit back against a tree, as my Uncle Silas did, and pretend that it was neck-oil.

Ten minutes later, when I got back to the pond, my Uncle Silas was fast asleep by the tree trunk, one bottle empty by his side and the other still in his jacket pocket. There was, I thought, a remarkable expression on his face, a wonderful rosy fogginess about his mouth and nose and eyes.

But what I saw in the pool, as I went to pick my rod from the water, was a still more wonderful thing.

During the afternoon the sun had moved some way round and under the branches of the willow, so that now, at the first touch of evening, there were clear bands of pure yellow light across the pool.

In one of these bands of light, by the fallen log, lay a long lean fish, motionless as a bar of steel, just under the water, basking in the evening sun.

When I woke my Uncle Silas he came to himself with a fumbling start, red eyes only half open, and I thought for a moment that perhaps he would ding my ear for ompolodgin'.

'But it's as big as a hippopotamus,' I said. 'It's as big as the one in the pig trough.'

'Wheer, boy? Wheer?'

When I pointed out the fish, my Uncle Silas could not, at first, see it lying there by the log. But after another nip of neck-oil he started to focus it correctly.

'By Jingo, that's a big 'un,' he said. 'By Jingo, that's a walloper.'

'What sort is it?'

'Pike,' he said. 'Git me a big lump o' paste and I'll dangle it a-top of his nose.'

'The paste has all gone.'

'Then give us a bit o' carraway and we'll tiddle him up wi' that.'

'I've eaten all the carraway,' I said. 'Besides you said you and Sammy Twizzle used to catch them with your hands. You said you used to tickle their bellies—'

'Well, that wur—'

'Get him! Get him! Get him!' I said. 'He's as big as a donkey!'

Slowly, and with what I thought was some reluctance, my Uncle Silas heaved himself to his feet. He lifted the bottle from his pocket and took a sip of neck-oil. Then he slapped the cork back with the palm of his hand, wiped his lips with the back of his hand and put the bottle back in his pocket.

'Now you stan' back,' he said, 'and dammit, don't git ompolodgin'!'

I stood back. My Uncle Silas started to creep along the fallen willow-log on his hands and knees. Below him, in the band of sunlight, I could see the long dark lean pike, basking.

For nearly two minutes my Uncle Silas hovered on the end of the log. Then slowly he balanced himself on one hand and dipped his other into the water. Over the pool it was marvellously, breathlessly still and I knew suddenly that this was how it had been in the good great old days, when my Uncle Silas and Sammy Twizzle had caught the mythical mammoth ones, fifty years before.

'God A'mighty!' my Uncle Silas suddenly yelled. 'I'm a-gooin' over!'

My Uncle Silas was indeed gooin' over. Slowly, like a turning spit, the log started heeling, leaving my Uncle Silas half-slipping, half-dancing at its edge, like a man on a greasy pole.

In terror I shut my eyes. When I opened them and looked again my Uncle Silas was just coming up for air, yelling 'God A'mighty, boy, I believe you ompolodged!'

I thought for a moment he was going to be very angry with me. Instead he started to cackle with crafty, devilish, stentorian laughter, his wet lips dribbling, his eyes more fiery than ever under the dripping water, his right hand triumphant as he snatched it up from the stream.

'Jist managed to catch it, boy,' he yelled and in triumph he held up the bottle of neck-oil.

And somewhere downstream, startled by his shout, a whole host of little tiddlers jumped from the water, dancing in the evening sun.

ALAN SILLITOE: from *Saturday Night and Sunday Morning* (1958).

He sat by the canal fishing on a Sunday morning in spring, at an elbow where alders dipped over the water like old men on their last legs, pushed by young sturdy oaks from behind. He straightened his back, his fingers freeing nylon line from a speedily revolving reel. Around him lay knapsack and jacket, an empty catch-net, his bicycle, and two tins of worms dug from the plot of garden at home before setting out. Sun was breaking through clouds, releasing a smell of earth to heaven. Birds sang. A soundless and miniscular explosion of water caught his eye. He moved nearer the edge, stood up, and with a vigorous sweep of his arm, cast out the line.

Another solitary man was fishing further along the canal, but Arthur knew that they would leave each other in peace, would not even call out greetings. No one bothered you: you were a hunter, a dreamer, your own boss, away from it all for a few hours on any day that the weather did not throw down its rain. Like the corporal in the army who said it was marvellous the things you thought about as you sat on the lavatory. Even better than that, it was marvellous the things that came to you in the tranquillity of fishing.

He drank tea from the flask and ate a cheese sandwich, then sat back to watch the red and white float – up to its waist in water under the alder trees – and keep an eye always close to it for the sudden indication of a fortunate catch. For himself, his own catch had been made, and he would have to wrestle with it for the rest of his life. Whenever you caught a fish, the fish caught you, in a way of speaking, and it was the same with anything else you caught, like the measles or a woman. Everyone in the world was caught, somehow, one way or another, and those that weren't were always on the way to it. As soon as you were born you were captured by fresh air that you screamed against the minute you came out. Then you were roped in by a factory, had a machine slung around your neck, and then you were hooked up by the arse with a wife. Mostly you were like a fish: you swam about with freedom, thinking how good it was to be left alone, doing anything you wanted to do and caring about no one, when suddenly: SPLUTCH! – the big hook clapped itself into your mouth and you were caught. Without knowing what you were doing you had chewed off more than you could bite and had to stick with the same piece of bait for the rest of your life. It meant death for a fish, but for a man it might not be so bad. Maybe it was only the beginning of something better in life, better than you could ever have thought possible before clamping your avid jaws down over the vital bait. Arthur knew he had not yet bitten, that he had really only licked the bait and found it tasty, that he could still disengage his mouth from the nibbled morsel. But he did not want to do so. If you went through life refusing all the bait dangled before you, that would be no life at all. No changes would be made and you would have nothing to fight against. Life would be as dull as ditchwater. You could kill yourself by too much cunning. Even though bait meant trouble, you could not ignore if for ever. He laughed to think that he was full of bait already, half-digested slop that had certainly given him a share of trouble, one way or another.

Watching the float so intently made him sleepy: he had been with Doreen until two the night before. They spoke of getting married in three months, by which time, Arthur said, they would have collected a good amount of money, nearly a hundred and fifty pounds, not counting income-tax rebate, which will probably bump it up to a couple of hundred. So they would be sitting pretty, Doreen replied, because Mrs Greatton had already offered to let them stay with her for as long as they liked, paying half the rent. For she would be lonely when Chumley left. Arthur said he would be able to get on with Mrs Greatton, because living there he would be the man of the house. And if there was any argument, they could get rooms somewhere. So it looked as though they'd be all right together, he thought, as long as a war didn't start, or trade slump and bring back the dole. As long as there wasn't a famine, a plague to sweep over England, an earthquake to crack it in two and collapse the city around them, or a bomb to drop and end the world with a big bang. But you couldn't concern yourself too much with these things if you had plans and wanted to get something out of life that you have never had before. And that was a fact, he thought, chewing a piece of grass.

He fixed the rod firmly against the bank and stood to stretch himself. He yawned widely, felt his legs weaken, then strengthen, then relax, his tall figure marked against a background of curving canal and hedges and trees bordering it. He rubbed his hand over the rough features of his face, upwards over thick lips, grey eyes, low forehead, short hair, then looked up at the mixture of grey cloud and blue patches of sky overhead. For some reason he smiled at what he saw, and turned to walk some yards along the towpath. Forgetting the stilled float in the water he stopped to urinate against the bushes. While fastening his trousers, he saw the float in violent agitation, as if it were suddenly alive and wanted to leap out of the water.

He ran back to the rod and began winding in the reel with steady movements. His hands worked smoothly and the line came in so quickly that it did not seem to be moving except on the reel itself where the nylon thread grew in thickness and breadth, where he evened it out with his thumb so that it would not clog at a vital moment. The fish came out of the water, flashing and struggling on the end of the line, and he grasped it firmly in his hand to take the hook from its mouth. He looked into its glass-grey eye, at the brown pupil whose fear expressed all the life that it had yet lived, and all its fear of the death that now threatened it. In its eye he saw the green gloom of willow-sleeved canals in cool decay, an eye filled with panic and concern for the remaining veins of life that circled like a silent whirlpool around it. Where do fishes go when they die? he wondered. The glow of long-remembered lives was mirrored in its eyes, and the memory of cunning curves executed in the moving shadows from reed to reed as it scattered the smaller fry and was itself chased by bigger fish was also pictured there. Arthur felt mobile waves of hope running the length of its squamous body from head to tail. He removed the hook, and threw it back into the water. He watched it flash away and disappear.

One more chance, he said to himself, but if you or any of your pals come back to the bait, it's curtains for 'em. With float bobbing before him once more he sat down to wait. This time it was war, and he wanted fish to take home, either to cook in the pan or feed to the cat. It's trouble for you and trouble for me, and all over a piece of bait.

The fattest worm of the lot is fastened to the hook, so don't grumble when you feel that point sticking to your chops.

And trouble for me it'll be, fighting every day until I die. Why do they make soldiers out of us when we're fighting up to the hilt as it is? Fighting with mothers and wives, landlords and gaffers, coppers, army, government. If it's not one thing it's another, apart from the work we have to do and the way we spend our wages. There's bound to be trouble in store for me every day of my life, because trouble it's always been and always will be. Born drunk and married blind, misbegotten into a strange and crazy world, dragged-up through the dole and into the war with a gas-mask on your clock, and the sirens rattling into you every night while you rot with scabies in an air-raid shelter. Slung into khaki at eighteen, and when they let you out, you sweat again in a factory, grabbing for an extra pint, doing women at the weekend and getting to know whose husbands are on the night-shift, working with rotten guts and an aching spine, and nothing for it but money to drag you back there every Monday morning.

Well, it's a good life and a good world, all said and done, if you don't weaken, and if you know that the big wide world hasn't heard from you yet, no, not by a long way, though it won't be long now.

The float bobbed more violently than before and, with a grin on his face, he began to wind in the reel.

HENRY WILLIAMSON: from *A Clear-water Stream* (1958).

Just as a huntsman knows every hound in his pack, by both tongue and look, as a shepherd knows his ewes, so I came to know every fish in the clear water above the bridge. Most conspicuous was an old brownie, which when first I had seen him, during the previous year had been big-headed, dark and thin. I guessed his weight to be a pound, his age to be nine or ten years. A trout is in its prime between three and a half and four years. This old creature, being slow, could not compete for flies and nymphs with the younger, more lively fish. He was probably an occasional cannibal, past spawning. Nor was he in the least sociable – at first. When the new fish had jumped about for food, he had waggled his tail and moved into the obscurity of mud under the floating alder roots by the bank.

He was there after the winter, occasionally visible during the spring showers of food, but remaining aloof; but not so sullenly as before. Sometimes he would cruise among the lively shoal, swish his tail as though excited by his daring, and then drift back to his hide again. Perhaps he had been hooked a year or two before, and had not forgotten it. I hoped he would take the food, and change his sombre coat into one of greenish-blue, like the native fish that were taking the food.

I bought an eel-trap, from an advertisement in *The Fishing Gazette*. Having been baited with head, feet and entrails of a hen, it was dropped on a rope by some alder roots in the bank above the bridge. The next day the dour old fish was missing, and I imagined he had been taken by an otter which had travelled up the river the night before. The water-beast's claw-marks were to be seen, where it had climbed out below the first waterfall, by the tall beech trees. Thence it had run some way along a path in the meadow parallel to the bank. This was a well-worn otter path. It ended by an ant-hill, the grass of which had been killed during the previous summer by otters' urine. During the winter, when the otters kept to the lower reaches of the river, perhaps hunting salmon in the big pools, the anthill never showed the marks of spraints; and by March it was the greenest thing in the deer park, the numerous eel-bones upon and around it hidden in rank grass. And the day the old trout was missed, fresh, dark-green spraints lay on the anthill, where an otter had touched the night before.

But when I hauled in my eel-trap, a cylinder of galvanized wire netting, and lifted it out, dripping with weed, I saw a dark-brown fish flapping within. It was the old brownie. Five smaller trout were with him. The bait was uneaten.

The head of the trap, which had lain upstream, was clogged with weed. I wondered if the trout had swum up the narrow one-way funnel at the rear of the trap, not for food, but for shelter.

Lugging the trap well back from the bank, I opened the door in the top, and tipped the cylinder for the fish to slither out. The small trout jumped about, but the old fellow, whose head and jaws suggested a crocodile, began to writhe through the grasses to the river. As he seemed to need no help, I let him continue until his nose stuck in some soft mud made by the feet of cattle. Then, having wetted my hand, I eased him into the water. He swam forward, his snout tipped with mud. Having put back the other fish, I ran up to the parapet of the bridge, to watch what the big fish would do. He was lying on the gravel.

A spoonful of food, and at once the water was rocking; jaws snapping, tails swishing through the broken surface. To my surprise the old trout, hitherto so sluggish and suspicious, was quicker than the others. He raised a wave as he came downstream, he made a slashing rise as he leapt to take a piece of floating food before the opening mouth of a Loch Leven. I threw in more food. He cut and swirled after it. The mud was still on his snout. He behaved as a dog behaves when released from its mournful wait at the end of a chain; or an innocent man reprieved from death, when the shock is passing away.

Whether or not the fish was a mindless creature of 'automatic reflex actions', I saw a fish behaving as I would have behaved had I been that fish. And from that moment he ceased to be shy of human presence on the bridge. He came down with the others when he saw my figure, to await food. He had no feeling for me, as a person (I think); and I wondered if what he saw of me on land was different from his underwater vision of the figure on the bridge. Would he not be short-sighted on land, with the lens of each eye adjusted to sub-aqueous vision?

I re-baited the trap with rabbits' pots; and when I hauled it out the next day from the pool below the bridge, the old trout was again inside. I tipped him once more upon the grass, in the same place, and helped him to wriggle back into the water above the bridge. Back in the water, he behaved like a clown, skittering about among the fish waiting for the food showers.

As summer advanced more fish joined that little watery Band of Hope, including salmon parr and one or two small peal (sea-trout) which, escaping the thirty-six nets working in the estuary from two hours before to two hours after every low tide, ran up from the sea in the silver sea-dresses which covered the spots of their river-coats.

How well-behaved they were! Each fish knew its place, maintaining order of precedence, the bold reformed Clown at their head, where he could get (theoretically) the pick of each cast. Sometimes I threw short, and he came down speedily to claim his rights. He had by now lost his dark colour; his flanks were pale gold, the dull maroon pennant, or adipose fin, bore a bright vermilion spot. His blue-black head had changed to brown, and no longer looked too big. He lay beside fingerling trout, rejuvenated and benevolent.

* * *

Returning to the bridge just before dusk, I saw mist drifting down the valley. Windless air flows as water, and since sunset the colder air of the high moor had been moving down into the coombes and valleys. When it touched the bridge, its chill was upon me. The late egg-laying flies seemed to have lost heart, or life, for no more rises showed on the surface. The innumerable tongues of the water, upon stone and rock and root, were muted.

The mist spread out upon, or arose from, the meadows. Star-points, which before had been wavering in the gentle ripples of spreading trout-rings, were dimmed. How quickly the benison of the day had gone, the feelings of eternity, which is sunshine, with it. The spirit, like that of the ephemeral flies, sank down. What was a man's life, his hopes, set against the rocks, themselves but whirling atoms sprung from outer space? How did it differ, essentially, from that of fish or winged insect, except that for a brief while man's eyes beheld the stones and trees and ferns and intervolving streams, the birds of water – ousel, sandpiper, heron, kingfisher, grey wagtail, each one a morsel of happiness twisted with anxiety, each one owning or claiming for its span a vision of this pleasaunce, this valley of almost complete seclusion, which for week upon week had seemed to be my very own, wherein the spirit of wonder could spread to all life about it, until the illusion arose that such things were eternal; but when I was gone, what would remain of the self which found such wonder there?

V. M. COPPLESON: from *Shark Attack* (1959).

It is always an interesting experience to open up a large shark. Inside its stomach there is likely to be anything from a lady's fur coat or a bottle opener to a brick or a pedigreed pup. Bottles, tins and sundry junk are often found. One shark caught in Sydney Harbour had in its stomach half a ham, several legs of mutton, the hind quarter of a pig, the head and forelegs of a bulldog with a rope tied round its neck, a quantity of horseflesh, a piece of sacking and a ship's scraper. Inside another shark, caught at Bondi, was a full-grown spaniel complete with collar, several sea birds, a mass of fish, a porpoise's skull and the spines of a porcupine. A shark caught in the Adriatic produced three over-coats, a nylon raincoat and a motor car licence.

A. A. LUCE: from *Fishing and Thinking* (1959).

Now comes the hardest part of my task. I have to state a case for a psychological factor, or something like it, in the conditions of the take. It is not a mystical factor; the case is based on angling experience. It is not a religious factor necessarily, though it disposes of the case for irreligion and materialism. But it is a factor that transcends our workaday categories of mechanical explanation. Every angler of experience meets strange happenings, such as the rise and take, described in the previous chapter. Such happenings are of a piece with happenings in a much wider sphere; and they remain unexplained and inexplicable unless we assume that there are more things in heaven and earth than materialism can explain or even recognize. The psychological factor requires the thoughtful angler to assume a spiritual basis for life and existence. If trout and other living things are regarded as machines that react mechanically to external stimuli, their behaviour in general, and in particular their exceptional mass movements and impulses, are inexplicable.

In calling this factor 'psychological' we do not credit fish with possessing a 'psyche' or mind, like the human mind. Trout do not look before and after; they do not expect and remember, as we do; they have little or no centre of individuality; they have no responsibility. Still they are not machines; they feel pain and pleasure; they partake in the world soul or life, and that was the original meaning of the Greek word *psyche;* hence this aspect of their behaviour may be called, and is, psychological. *Sociological* would be a better term in some respects; for fish live largely in their *societas* or species or community; but 'sociology' has become identified in the public mind with the study of human society; and therefore the broader term 'psychological factor', in its original Greek sense, is to be preferred.

The ancient Greeks were firmly convinced that there was a bond of sympathy between all living things. Some of their philosophers maintained that the world itself was alive. 'All things share the breath of life', said one of them. Without some such principle which we may call *the principle of psychological sympathy* it is impossible to give a rational account of the mass movements of fish and other living things. Two anglers are comparing notes on a day's fishing; one has fished the north end of the lake, the other the south end, and twenty miles of water lay between them. 'What time did the trout come on, Tom?' 'There was a short rise at eleven, and a longer rise at five-thirty,

William.' 'That is curious, Tom; it was exactly the same with us.' Curious or not curious, that experience is a commonplace with anglers; and we are inclined to pass it over lightly with the observation, 'Oh, yes; the same causes produce the same effect.' But we are not doing full justice to the facts, unless we include 'psychological sympathy' among the 'same causes'. The individualism that dominates our workaday thinking about ourselves and our environment breaks down in all such cases. Individualism is not the whole truth, or the sole truth about the individual; nor is socialism the whole truth, or the sole truth, about society. Man is a social individual; and there is a bond of sympathy between socialized or socializing individuals, that extends beyond the species *man*, and to a degree is found universally.

Michael has watched the ways of trout at close quarters for over half a century. He is a shrewd observer, and he says that a yawning angler rarely gets a trout; he means that if the angler is sleepy, probably the fish are sleepy, too. Conditions, within limits, that get us down, put them down. Conditions that cheer us, cheer them. If the angler feels 'nesh', as folk in Gloucestershire say, the fish feel 'nesh', too; if the angler is 'sprack', the fish will be 'sprack', too. All things 'conspire'; they share the breath of life.

When the cattle are lying down at the water's edge, or standing in the shallows with drooped heads, flicking the flies away with lazy tail, as if no blade of grass was left, when the raucous seagulls are silent and still, or preening their feathers on rock and stone, when there is not a swallow to be seen, and the air is thick and humid, and Mount Nephin is wrapped in cloud, and there is a halo round the milky sun, and white wisps of fog rise from the water-meadows, accept the verdict, tireless angler. Give it up for the time being; acquiesce in the general feeling; put down the rod; go ashore, and have a cup of tea; for under those conditions not even the apostle's 'south wind blowing softly' could give you a trout.

But see, a change is coming. Michael is staring at the mountain; yes, the cloud is lifting; a shift of wind has scattered the mist, and cleared the air, and whipped up the dancing waves, and melted their leaden hue. The cattle have left the shore, and are munching in the pastures; the swallows are chivying the flies, and the gulls and shapely terns are scouting far and wide. Into your boat, angler; out on the drift, and do not strike too hard!

The fellow-feeling in nature, the natural sympathy between kind and kind, is raised to a higher power and reaches its climax in the mass movements of individuals within the kind of species. The flighting of duck at dusk and dawn, the wheeling squadrons of golden plover in a high wind, the evening exercises of rooks and starlings, the mad, purposeful dance of the myriad spinners on a summer's evening, the buzzing beehive and teeming anthill – these familiar wonders show that individual living organisms are not imitative machines, but are instinct with some family life and family feeling of a semi-spiritual character that must at times be taken into account; and if we call it the 'psychological factor', we shall not be far wrong; for it is a phase of the Life Force, the *élan vital*, or World Soul, and ultimately, for Christians and other theists, it is the gift of the Universal Spirit in whom we live and move, have our being and do our thinking.

TED HUGHES: *Pike.* From *Lupercal* (1960).

Pike, three inches long, perfect
Pike in all parts, green tigering the gold.
Killers from the egg: the malevolent aged grin.
They dance on the surface among the flies.

Or move, stunned by their own grandeur,
Over a bed of emerald, silhouette
Of submarine delicacy and horror.
A hundred feet long in their world.

In ponds, under the heat-struck lily pads –
Gloom of their stillness:
Logged on last year's black leaves, watching upwards.
Or hung in an amber cavern of weeds.

The jaws' hooked clamp and fangs
Not to be changed at this date;
A life subdued to its instrument;
The gills kneading quietly, and the pectorals.

Three we kept behind glass,
Jungled in weed: three inches, four,
And four and a half: fed fry to them –
Suddenly there were two. Finally one

With a sag belly and the grin it was born with.
And indeed they spare nobody.
Two, six pounds each, over two feet long,
High and dry and dead in the willow-herb –

One jammed past its gills down the other's gullet:
The outside eye stared: as a vice locks –
The same iron in this eye
Though its film shrank in death.

A pond I fished, fifty yards across,
Whose lilies and muscular tench
Had outlasted every visible stone
Of the monastery that planted them –

Stilled legendary depth:
It was as deep as England. It held
Pike too immense to stir, so immense and old
That past nightfall I dared not cast

But silently cast and fished
With the hair frozen on my head
For what might move, for what eye might move.
The still splashes on the dark pond,

Owls hushing the floating woods
Frail on my ear against the dream
Darkness beneath night's darkness had freed,
That rose slowly towards me, watching.

SVEN BERLIN: from *Jonah's Dream, A Meditation on Fishing* (1964).

Jonah is my name. I am a solitary person not given to seeking much human company in this life. If anyone appears by the lake or on the bank of a river wherein I may be fishing, like the heron I am in retreat. There are a few friends with whom I would angle – not chosen because I am considered rare company, but chosen because they too seem to understand that fishing is a kind of meditation. Only those who pretend but fail to understand this; those who have shown a perversity of nature or distention of themselves, like the model aircraft that fly incessantly round their owners' heads for their own amusement and satisfaction, but not understanding the stillness of the mind and the quest of fish, have I carefully eliminated as unsuitable; for like any adventure on the brink of the unknown wherein a dream may be caught, the true fisherman is on a search for wisdom – and of that nothing can be spoken. What he does not catch – therein hides the meaning of his long vigil and the purpose of his understanding.

Often when I am by the water – by a river or in a ship or on the edges of an inland sea, a great lake – I dream I am inside a fish and the whole world is the cathedral of his great rib-case and spine, the sunset colours his slippery spongy inside, the salt sting of his strong enzymes bleach me white down one side, as they must have bleached my namesake after seventy-two hours in the belly of a whale. The low murmur of the turbines that power his heart and fins, the elaborate system that picks up vibration and sound in changing patterns, like a radar set, and translates them into images in his prehistoric brain and finally to his eye, are immeasurably marvellous to my inner mind. For just as this image he is hunting goes full circuit and is finally devoured into the body of the fish, so it seems that the memories of my most early experience, even before man was created, of the sea and the great rivers that run to the sea are returning by the miracle of consciousness and render me a more complete person when I have absorbed them. If, as it seems in my dream, I am inside a fish, how much more truly then is the fish inside me when I awake? Surely such things as this help to cease the raging of the mind and make the troubled seas to calm!

Chuang-Tzŭ dreamed he was a butterfly; when he awoke he did not then know if he was a man dreaming he was a butterfly or a butterfly dreaming he was a man. I sometimes find it enchantingly difficult to tell whether I am a man fishing for a pike or the pike for whom a man is fishing; or indeed, the ledge under which the pike lies, as in the rock-drawing at Perche Merle, fused into one by the magic of imagination.

A good fisherman has just that amount of natural contact with the other world to be able to enter it without reason; for reason in fishing belongs only to those other men whose fishing is to compete with one another to catch so many fish that their egos, like their slime-destroying keep-nets, are bulging with their pathetic achievement. Whereas the just man has exactly that amount of cruelty and truth which sharpen the edge of the ecstatic moment when the float runs, and a being from another world withholds its own life and the fight begins; the hunter and hunted, both using all the cunning and the skill that nature has evolved to preserve and destroy life.

But not with the more brutal cruelty of the fisherman who will slit the envelope-mouth of a live flounder with a blunt knife to retrieve his hook, disembowel a roach, maim a weaver because its self-protection is to sting, gouge out the eyes of a pike with the fingers and return him blind to the waters, never to hunt again; dismember a crab and lift its shell because its defence of life is to pinch; but worst of all, to stamp one of these beautifully constructed creatures to death for the only reason that that man hates his own heritage. They are the unrecorded crimes of the river bank, pierhead and shore.

A fully evolved fisherman is interested in everything but the fish's death, and this is because in the heart of that ruthlessness which makes the true hunter there is love, a deep love for the quarry, therefore an understanding of the tragedy of its death and of the miracle of its life, shown so profoundly in the Salmon Shelter carving at Val d'Enfer in the Dordogne, done twenty thousand years ago. The heart of man and the heart of fish beat little differently then as now.

A young fisherman has the making of a man of vision who might learn to tie his own fly, fight his fish and then release it into the great stream of life for another migration. Until the time comes when the catching of fish is not the purpose of fishing. When asked why he used no bait the Chinese sage said: 'The idea is *not* to catch fish!' He became so in harmony with natural laws that he could hold the greatest fish on the slenderest silken thread. So also will the hunter put away his gun and the soldier his flame-thrower, for in the end the spectacle of life is more beautiful and more deeply rewarding to the spirit of man than the carnival of death.

Those who fish are for ever on the shores of the Great Lake into which all rivers must run and there are no longer any frontiers. For them the seasons change, the coot claps his cymbal, the bittern booms on his invisible euphonium, the kingfisher crackles on his electric journey across the lake and the salmon goes on his fanatical migration to the clean gravel of the mountain streams and falls back after his mighty orgasm, a sick creature seeking the comfort of the sea. Pike wait in ambush for the crucified dace. The mayfly, like a queen, beguiles a trout with her magnetic dress which contains an hook. A nymph splits open on a burning reed and becomes an aeroplane. And he knows again the dark horrors of the waters where the dytiscus meet the huge idiot eels from the Sargasso Sea, moving like submarines through the mud with minute pitiless brains. He knows the lady of the evening and her lovely gown.

Often when I have been alone with some sudden fright, the scales down my back have been torn by teeth; and a great fear comes upon me when the evening is pike-skin green, locking in my loneliness on a winter bank.

Fishing therefore is not only a matter of meditation, of peaceful moments in which the reflected images are as real as those above the water, through which fish move and thought is seen upon the fin, turning, nuzzling the mud, searching with its golden eye for a pearl. It is also a dream of prehistory. We touch fintips with the coelacanth, who may well have emerged from the sea to negotiate with the problems on land. It is to the great ocean behind life from which all things emerge and to which all must return, to the Spirit that moves upon the face of the waters and to my brother, that I present my tale.

HUGH FALKUS: from *The Stolen Years* (1965).

We stayed in a hillside cottage overlooking the sea. And there Father and I fished for eels in long, straight, flashing fleets which stretched like knives across the marsh between banks of yellowing reeds.

We fished with great fervour. Day after day, with thermos flask and sandwiches and tin of worms; sitting side by side on little stools, watching our floats. Gentle days of sun and summer rain, with only the sound of wind and the plovers' and curlews' crying, and the wash of the sea on distant shingle.

Sometimes we threw out lines from the beach for plaice and codling, stalked rabbits among the sand dunes, or waited at dusk for duck which flighted from the sea to marshland pools. But mostly we fished for eels.

You may think it strange that anyone should want to fish for eels. One usually catches and curses them when fishing for something else. But eels are fascinating creatures, just as mysterious in their habits as those other migratory fish: salmon and sea-trout. Besides, whether fried or smoked, they are delicious to eat.

We caught a great many. And large eels, as eels go. The biggest weighed nearly three pounds, which is a big eel – although not big enough to satisfy Father who had set his heart on hooking a monster. As the holiday drew all too rapidly to an end, such a capture seemed unlikely.

Then, on our penultimate day I left Father in the garden struggling with a home-made smoking chamber – with characteristic confidence he had promised gifts of smoked eel to all his friends – and wandered off to fish on my own.

Far out across the marshes in the middle of a large reed bed I discovered to my joy a wide dark pool. It had a very eely look. If ever there were a piece of water likely to harbour a whopper this, I felt certain, was it. Little imagination was needed to picture something vast lurking beneath that weedy surface.

The pool was formed by the junction of several of the big fleets which ribboned the marsh, and could be fished very conveniently at one point from an overhanging grassy bank. I sat down on this bank and cast in my bait: boiled shrimp, a food which eels very much enjoy.

How I loved to sit and watch a float. And still do. Ledgering may be a more efficient method of catching fish, but there is nothing, *nothing* quite so fascinating as a float.

I sat there for a long time in the drowsy summer stillness, and nothing happened. My float remained unmoving on the placid surface, the shrimp untouched, and after a while I began to wonder whether this reed-girt pool of sinister enchantment did in fact hold any eels. My attention wandered. Lying flat on the sheep-nibbled turf I listened to the skylarks, and watched the black-headed gulls twisting lazily high overhead in a blue sky.

Suddenly, although there was no sound or movement, nor even a twitch at the line, something caused me to sit upright, instantly alert. In a moment of breathless anticipation I saw that my float had disappeared.

I lifted the rod and tightened. The line stretched taut into the depths, but there was no movement of any sort. No exciting wriggle. Nothing. It felt disappointingly solid. My heart, which at the disappearance of the float had started to thump, returned to normal.

With a sense of anti-climax I pulled some slack from the reel, walked a few yards along the bank and tugged again from a different angle. No good. The hook remained immovable. Clearly, it was snagged in something on the bottom. I began to shorten line preparatory to breaking the cast when without warning, as though attracted by some strange and invisible force, my rod tip was dragged down into the water. Then the reel handle was snatched from my fingers and the line went whizzing out. As I clung to the rod hardly realizing what had happened, there was a bubbling swirl in the centre of the pool .. and a huge eel broke surface.

Nothing I had ever seen in fresh water could be compared to the creature that writhed out there in front of me.

I had seen river eels of up to five pounds in weight; and they were pygmies by comparison. We had caught congers often enough when fishing off-shore, so that I knew something of the comparative weight and size of eels. And I suppose it is not impossible that the leviathan coiling slowly out there on the surface was in fact a conger which had found its way in from the sea through one of the sea-wall sluices. It had, I remember, a curious light-grey back, not unlike that of some conger I have seen.

But at the time I was not concerned with problems of identification. Whatever its species, this eel was far beyond the breaking strain of my tackle. Realizing the danger of letting it get its tail among the reed stems, I tried desperately to coax it in towards the bank. Not liking this treatment, the eel plunged. It was an irresistible rush. Over-run line jammed tight on the reel and bit down into the loose coils beneath. The stiff bamboo rod bent and bent. There was the short, sickening moment of truth familiar to all fishermen when a large fish demands line they are unable to give. Then the humming line went limp. The rod straightened. And that was that.

Sadly, I pulled in the broken cast and sat dry-mouthed as ripples spread across the pool and lapped the bank at my feet. My biggest eel ever, and I had lost it. Worse – it had broken me! To be broken is a fisherman's ultimate disgrace.

I had no heart for further fishing. Back across the marshes I went in search of Father.

He was still at it. On hands and knees amid a litter of spent matches, a bucket of charred eels nearby, puffing away with blackened face at a pile of smouldering chips. Evidently his smoking chamber was not being the success envisaged. Something was not quite right somewhere, and with customary single-mindedness he was concentrating on getting the thing to burn properly; fishing for the time being, forgotten.

It was difficult to engage his attention at such moments. And not until later that evening – after the injudicious use of extra fuel had sent his smokery, like some condemned privy, up in flames – could I get him to listen to my story of the huge eel.

'Hugh! Why didn't you tell me of this before?'

'Well,' I said. 'I tried, but . . .'

'*How* big did you say it was?'

I repeated the story in detail, omitting nothing. Father listened eagerly. This was the eel of his dreams, and he immediately set about preparing for its capture. But it was soon evident that he regarded my estimation of the eel's size as childish exaggeration, for to my dismay he rigged up some fancy tackle on a cut-down greenheart trout rod of great age. Ever experimenting, he pursued everything to extremes and his tackle at times inclined to the bizarre. In no way could I make him appreciate the magnitude of the task in hand.

The return match took place the following afternoon. It was a Saturday, the last day of our stay in Norfolk, and we spent the morning packing. At long last we escaped, and breathless with excitement I hurried Father across the marshes to my dark, mysterious pool.

He glanced appreciatively at the water, baited his hook with care and cast out. We sat waiting in silence, side by side on the soft springy turf.

It was a windless sultry afternoon, and the pool's unrippled surface mirrored the tall reeds which almost completely encircled us. An oppressive stillness enveloped the marshes. A great anvil of cumulus cloud was building far out over the sea, and every now and again from the distance came an ominous rumble. Undeterred by threat of thunder and a sizeable storm, Father puffed patiently at his pipe his eyes never moving from the red-tipped float which lay motionless on the polished black water.

Looking back, I find it interesting to reflect on the certainty with which we anticipated the hooking of that eel. The inestimable fishing gift of absolute confidence. If we waited long enough we should get a bite. Thunder was bad for fishing? Very well, we might have longer to wait. But if still at home our eel would have a go sooner or later. It was simply a question of time.

We sat there sweltering, and gradually the purple storm clouds loomed larger and larger. A gust of wind swept the marsh, rustling the reeds, tipping Father's float and swinging it round towards the bank. Then the first big drops of rain began to splash as lightning flashed over the sea and thunder rumbled all around us.

In the eerie half-light, Father's float suddenly vanished.

The events of the next few seconds are fixed in my memory with great clarity. As though it were happening at this instant I can hear the rush of wind and rain, and see the dark swaying reeds, with Father outlined against that lurid sky. He stood heaving at the line, his rod bent double, the hook seemingly fast in something on the bottom. Then, as though giving a repeat performance, the eel surfaced and began to lash about.

'By damn!' said Father, staggered. His pipe fell from his mouth and bounced into the pool. It went unnoticed. The eel had set off like a torpedo and his reel was screaming.

'Look out!' I shouted. 'It's in the reeds!'

There was a flash of lightning. For a few seconds the monster thrashed among the reeds in a cloud of spray. Then, with a crack and a splintering, father's rod flew into pieces. He gave a howl of anguish, slipped on the wet bank, and fell over backwards. He lay there, speechless, clutching his broken tackle, the rain gleaming on his weatherbeaten face. His line hung from the bank trailing loosely on the surface, and even as I sprang forward to assist I knew we had seen the last of that astonishing eel.

And so it was. For long afterwards we talked hopefully of going back one day to fish again in that magic Norfolk pool among the reeds. But we never did.

SEAMUS HEANEY: *Trout.* From *Death of a Naturalist* (1966).

Hangs, a fat gun-barrel,
deep under arched bridges
or slips like butter down
the throat of the river.

From depths smooth-skinned as plums
his muzzle gets bull's eye;
picks off grass-seed and moths
that vanish, torpedoed.

Where water unravels
over gravel-beds he
is fired from the shallows
white belly reporting

flat; darts like a tracer-
bullet back between stones
and is never burnt out.
A volley of cold blood

ramrodding the current.

RICHARD BRAUTIGAN: *The Hunchback Trout.* From *Trout Fishing in America* (1967).

The creek was made narrow by little green trees that grew too close together. The creek was like 12,845 telephone booths in a row with high Victorian ceilings and all the doors taken off and all the backs of the booths knocked out.

Sometimes when I went fishing in there, I felt just like a telephone repairman, even though I did not look like one. I was only a kid covered with fishing tackle, but in some strange way by going in there and catching a few trout, I kept the telephones in service. I was an asset to society.

It was pleasant work, but at times it made me uneasy. It could grow dark in there instantly when there were some clouds in the sky and they worked their way on to the sun. Then you almost needed candles to fish by, and foxfire in your reflexes.

Once I was in there when it started raining. It was dark and hot and steamy. I was of course on overtime. I had that going in my favour. I caught seven trout in fifteen minutes.

The trout in those telephone booths were good fellows. There were a lot of young cut-throat trout six to nine inches long, perfect pan size for local calls. Sometimes there were a few fellows, eleven inches or so – for the long distance calls.

I've always liked cut-throat trout. They put up a good fight, running against the bottom and then broad jumping. Under their throats they fly the orange banner of Jack the Ripper.

Also in the creek were a few stubborn rainbow trout, seldom heard from, but there all the same, like certified public accountants. I'd catch one every once in a while. They were fat and chunky, almost as wide as they were long. I've heard those trout called 'squire' trout.

It used to take me about an hour to hitchhike to that creek. There was a river nearby. The river wasn't much. The creek was where I punched in. Leaving my card above the clock, I'd punch out again when it was time to go home.

I remember the afternoon I caught the hunchback trout.

A farmer gave me a ride in a truck. He picked me up at a traffic signal beside a bean field and he never said a word to me.

His stopping and picking me up and driving me down the road was as automatic a thing to him as closing the barn door, nothing need be said about it, but still I was in motion travelling thirty-five miles an hour down the road, watching houses and groves of trees go by, watching chickens and mailboxes enter and pass through my vision.

Then I did not see any houses for a while. 'This is where I get out,' I said.

The farmer nodded his head. The truck stopped.

'Thanks a lot,' I said.

The farmer did not ruin his audition for the Metropolitan Opera by making a sound. He just nodded his head again. The truck started up. He was the original silent old farmer.

A little while later I was punching in at the creek. I put my card above the clock and went into that long tunnel of telephone booths.

I waded about seventy-three telephone booths in. I caught two trout in a little hole that was like a wagon wheel. It was one of my favourite holes, and always good for a trout or two.

I always like to think of that hole as a kind of pencil sharpener. I put my reflexes in and they came back out with a good point on them. Over a period of a couple of years, I must have caught fifty trout in that hole, though it was only as big as a wagon wheel.

I was fishing with salmon eggs and using a size fourteen single egg hook on a pound and a quarter test tippet. The two trout lay in my creel covered entirely by green ferns, ferns made gentle and fragile by the damp walls of telephone booths.

The next good place was forty-five telephone booths in. The place was at the end of a run of gravel, brown and slippery with algae. The run of gravel dropped off and disappeared at a little shelf where there were some white rocks.

One of the rocks was kind of strange. It was a flat white rock. Off by itself from the other rocks, it reminded me of a white cat I had seen in my chidhood.

The cat had fallen or been thrown off a high wooden sidewalk that went along the side of a hill in Tacoma, Washington. The cat was lying in a parking lot below.

The fall had not appreciably helped the thickness of the cat, and then a few people had parked their cars on the cat. Of course, that was a long time ago and the cars looked different from the way they look now.

You hardly see those cars any more. They are the old cars. They have to get off the highway because they can't keep up.

That flat white rock off by itself from the other rocks reminded me of that dead cat come to lie there in the creek, among 12,845 telephone booths.

I threw out a salmon egg and let it drift down over that rock and WHAM! a good hit! and I had the fish on and it ran hard downstream, cutting at an angle and staying deep and really coming on hard, solid and uncompromising, and then the fish jumped and for a second I thought it was a frog. I'd never seen a fish like that before.

God-damn! What the hell!

The fish ran deep again and I could feel its life energy screaming back up the line to my hand. The line felt like sound. It was like an ambulance siren coming straight at me, red light flashing, and then going away again and then taking to the air and becoming an air-raid siren.

The fish jumped a few more times and it still looked like a frog, but it didn't have any legs. Then the fish grew tired and sloppy, and I swung and splashed it up the surface of the creek and into my net.

The fish was a twelve-inch rainbow trout with a huge hump on its back. A hunchback trout. The first I'd ever seen. The hump was probably due to an injury that occurred when the trout was young. Maybe a horse stepped on it or a tree fell over in a storm or its mother spawned where they were building a bridge.

There was a fine thing about that trout. I only wish I could have made a death mask of him. Not of his body though, but of his energy. I don't know if anyone would have understood his body. I put it in my creel.

Later in the afternoon when the telephone booths began to grow dark at the edges, I punched out of the creek and went home. I had that hunchback trout for dinner. Wrapped in cornmeal and fried in butter, its hump tasted sweet as the kisses of Esmeralda.

TED HUGHES: from *Poetry in the Making* (1967).

Now where did the poet learn to settle his mind like that on to one thing? It is a valuable thing to be able to do – but something you are never taught at school, and not many people do it naturally. I am not very good at it, but I did acquire some skill in it. Not in school, but while I was fishing. I fished in still water, with a float. As you know, all a fisherman does is stare at his float for hours on end. I have spent hundreds and hundreds of hours staring at a float – a dot of red or yellow the size of a lentil, ten yards away. Those of you who have never done it, might think it is a very drowsy pastime. It is anything but that.

All the little nagging impulses, that are normally distracting your mind, dissolve. They have to dissolve if you are to go on fishing. If they do not, then you cannot settle down: you get bored and pack up in a bad temper. But once they have dissolved, you enter one of the orders of bliss.

Your whole being rests lightly on your float, but not drowsily: very alert, so that the least twitch of the float arrives like an electric shock. And you are not only watching the float. You are aware, in a horizonless and slightly mesmerized way, like listening to the double bass in orchestral music, of the fish below there in the dark. At every moment your imagination is alarming itself with the size of the thing slowly leaving the weeds and approaching your bait. Or with the world of beauties down there, suspended in total ignorance of you. And the whole purpose of this concentrated excitement, in this arena of apprehension and unforeseeable events, is to bring up some lovely solid thing like living metal from a world where nothing exists but those inevitable facts which raise life out of nothing and return it to nothing.

So you see, fishing with a float is a sort of mental exercise in concentration on a small point, while at the same time letting your imagination work freely to collect everything that might concern that still point: in this case the still point is the float and the things that concern the float are all the fish you are busy imagining.

HOWARD MARSHALL: from *Reflections in a River* (1967).

I think I particularly realized a sense of the eternal in angling one hot September day in France, on the River Charente near Angoulême. I was staying at a riverside inn, and the landlord's brother, an angler of note locally, offered to take me out for a day after the tench. The Charente, he told me, was famous for its tench, and undoubtedly we should fill a large sack with our catch. He took me to a wood through which the river ran, and where we found that a clearing had been made in order that anglers might come close to the water. The river flowed steadily and slowly, so slowly that it was difficult to detect any movement. It was deep, at least fifteen feet right in at the water's edge. It was clear and green, and down below us we would see, patrolling in an endless series of circles, the dark shadows which were clearly tench, and large tench at that. Undoubtedly, I thought, my friend was right. We shall catch many tench, and big ones.

We baited with brandlings, threw out our lines, and waited while our quill floats gently settled till only the red tips were showing. We, in turn, settled back in our folding chairs and watched our floats with keen concentration. We watched with optimism also, for we knew the fish were there, and that brandlings were their favourite food on this stretch of the Charente. Nothing stirred except that occasionally there was a tiny tap on the floats as if a cruising tench had touched the line with his tail. As time went by without success, I asked my companion whether we should change our tactics or our bait.

'Monsieur,' he replied, 'one cannot interfere with destiny. If we are to catch these tench, we shall catch them, never fear. To change is to waste time. It is also to show ourselves as unbelievers.' He then returned to his contemplation, and we were enfolded in an absolute silence.

Hour after hour went by and, except for an interlude for a bottle of wine, we watched our motionless floats. At last, as the shadows grew longer and the sun began to sink towards the horizon, my friend stood up and shook himself. 'I am sorry, monsieur,' he said, 'that my tench have treated us with such disdain, but that is fishing, is it not? If the fish neglect us, that is the way things are planned. We may not have caught tench, but if fishing were not so unpredictable, it would not be worthwhile. As it is, we have stolen a day of quietude in a noisy world, and all through these peaceful hours we have been plugged into eternity.' He pointed to our floats and lines. 'These,' he said, 'are our connections with the unseen forces of nature. Even if we do not catch fish, they link us to a larger life.' This charming French philosopher was a happy man. He was not a Richard Walker or he would have caught more tench. Even so, even if he had sometimes to plunge into the workaday world, always he had his re-entry through his rod and line in that jade-green water.

Not long afterwards I met a different kind of angler on the River Loire. I was fishing unsuccessfully for roach from a moored punt when I heard a shout from an angler similarly moored some fifty yards down-stream. 'Come here!' he shouted. 'Untie your boat and drift down to me.' This I did, and when, after some manoeuvring, I came alongside, the fisherman made my boat fast to his and helped me to manage the perilous journey from one to the other. He was a robust, elderly man and introduced himself to me as a retired police inspector of the Sûreté in Paris, a sort of Maigret of the Loire, who told me that he recognized me as a foreigner from my fishing tackle and was anxious to prove that his river could really produce fish. He had, moreover, a large keg of cider with him.

For a time I was content to watch him fishing, using a long, bamboo rod rather like a roach pole, with the line attached to its top ring by a piece of elastic. The river there was deep and slow-moving, and from time to time the inspector threw in handfuls of cloud ground bait. He was using a single maggot for hook bait, and every slow swim down his float would flicker or turn sideways and he would catch a small roach or dace. He fished with great concentration, and his striking was extremely fast, and all went well until suddenly his float disappeared in a flash and he was into something much larger than he had touched before. He gave a shout of triumph and said, 'This is the one – the big chevenne. I shall make him into quennelles.' But at that moment he held too hard and his nylon line broke above the float.

We could see the float bobbing away downstream, and for a moment or two he considered whether we should up-anchor and pursue it. He watched it dejectedly for a while, and then, 'Ah well,' he said, 'it's like crime. The little criminals are easy to catch but the big ones break away. It is strange, is it not, but even I from the Sûreté could not arrest that one!' This was philosophy of a different kind, and I am glad that my friend, by the end of the day, had enough small fish for a fritture. I helped him to eat it at the local inn that evening, and quite excellent it was.

DYLAN THOMAS: from *Ballad of the Long-legged Bait.* From *Collected Poems* (1967).

> The bows glided down, and the coast
> Blackened with birds took a last look
> At his thrashing hair and whale-blue eye;
> The trodden town rang its cobbles for luck.
>
> Then good-bye to the fishermanned
> Boat with its anchor free and fast
> As a bird hooking over the sea,
> High and dry by the top of the mast,
>
> Whispered the affectionate sand
> And the bulwarks of the dazzled quay.
> For my sake sail, and never look back,
> Said the looking land.
>
> Sails drank the wind, and white as milk
> He sped into the drinking dark;
> The sun shipwrecked west on a pearl
> And the moon swam out of its hulk.

Funnels and masts went by in a whirl.
Good-bye to the man on the sea-legged deck
To the gold gut that sings on his reel
To the bait that stalked out of the sack,

For we saw him throw to the swift flood
A girl alive with his hooks through her lips;
All the fishes were rayed in blood,
Said the dwindling ships.

Whales in the wake like capes and Alps
Quaked the sick sea and snouted deep,
Deep the great bushed bait with raining lips
Slipped the fins of those humpbacked tons

And fled their love in a weaving dip.
Oh, Jericho was falling in their lungs!
She nipped and dived in the nick of love,
Spun on a spout like a long-legged ball

Till every beast blared down in a swerve
Till every turtle crushed from his shell
Till every bone in the rushing grave
Rose and crowed and fell!

Good luck to the hand on the rod,
There is thunder under its thumbs;
Gold gut is a lightning thread,
His fiery reel sings off its flames,

The whirled boat in the burn of his blood
Is crying from nets to knives,
Oh the shearwater birds and their boatsized brood
Oh the bulls of Biscay and their calves

Are making under the green, laid veil
The long-legged beautiful bait their wives.
Break the black news and paint on a sail
Huge weddings in the waves,

Good-bye to chimneys and funnels,
Old wives that spin in the smoke,
He was blind to the eyes of candles
In the praying windows of waves

But heard his bait buck in the wake
And tussle in a shoal of loves.
Now cast down your rod, for the whole
Of the sea is hilly with whales,

She longs among horses and angels,
The rainbow-fish bend in her joys,
Floated the lost cathedral
Chimes of the rocked buoys.

Where the anchor rode like a gull
Miles over the moonstruck boat
A squall of birds bellowed and fell,
A cloud blew the rain from its throat;

He saw the storm smoke out to kill
With fuming bows and ram of ice,
Fire on starlight, rake Jesu's stream;
And nothing shone on the water's face

But the oil and bubble of the moon
Plunging and piercing in his course
The lured fish under the foam
Witnessed with a kiss.

SEAMUS HEANEY: *Bait.* From *A Lough Neagh Sequence.* From *Door Into The Dark* (1969).

Lamps dawdle in the field at midnight.
Three men follow their nose in the grass
The lamps' beam their prow and compass.

The bucket's handle better not clatter now:
Silence and curious light gather bait.
Nab him, but wait.

For the first shrinking, tacky on the thumb.
Let him re-settle backwards in his tunnel.
Then draw steady and he'll come.

Among the millions whorling their mud coronas
Under dewlapped leaf and bowed blades
A few are bound to be rustled in these night raids,

Innocent ventilators of the ground
Making the globe a perfect fit,
A few are bound to be cheated of it

When lamps dawdle in the field at midnight,
When fishers need a garland for the bay
And have him, where he needs to come, out of the clay.

CHARLES RITZ: *Oola on the Alta.* From *A Flyfisher's Life* (revised edition 1972).

I had taken bigger fish on the Alta, while fishing as Tony Pulitzer's guest on the Jöraholmen farm, but never under circumstances as bizarre as the day I found myself being ghillied by a girl.

This came about by chance, as it was my day to fish a very fine salmon pool, adjoining a great rocky point, which is ordinarily fished by boat. But I had offered my boat to a friend who was leaving for home that evening. His fishing had been unlucky and we all wanted to give him a last chance. My host concurred, and suggested that I try fishing the pool from the rocky promontory, as long as I would have no boat at my disposal until after 2 p.m. when the other guest would have to leave.

This was challenging, as if I did succeed in hooking a fish, casting from the rocks, the only possible gaffing place would be on the lower part of the rocky point, where the footing for gaffing is on a narrow ledge, about three feet wide and twelve feet long and some three feet above the water level.

I pondered the problem through a late breakfast and at 11 a.m. decided to go look at this difficult landing spot, to see if I could figure out a way to cope with a fish there with nobody around to gaff it for me.

The cook was busy in the kitchen, the Jöraholmen family was out on the farm, the chauffeur had left with Tony Pulitzer, and I was about to give up the idea when suddenly I remembered that in passing the house I had seen somebody hanging up the laundry out in back. That would be Oola, I realized, the young Lapp girl who had only a few days before begun working as kitchen helper and laundress.

Nobody knew much about Oola, who was short and stocky and very round, except that young as she was she already had several children, back in the village of Kaiteno, from lumberjacks, village boys and slate quarry workers. She had explained, in applying for the job, that she needed money to send back to the Lapp woman who was taking care of her kids, the result of her too great kindness to mankind. Oola was high in the front and low in the rear, with a very round face, dark but extremely smooth skin and Asiatic eyes. She was a very sweet girl, with a most comprehensive viewpoint, always looking at us men hungrily, I thought, and we all felt sorry for the poor creature.

'Hello Oola, how would you like to go fishing with me for an hour?'

She jumped up in the air saying, 'Yes, yes.'

I picked up my rod and the gaff and we started for the trail, of about half a mile, that led to the pool, Oola following along behind me until we reached the first barbed wire fence.

I snaked under it, as it was too high to climb over, and when I reached the other side Oola passed me the rod and the gaff and started to imitate me. She stopped with a yell, as the barbed wire caught in her skirt. I managed to get her loose and urged her on and just as she started to crawl again there was another, louder yell, reflecting a more serious problem. This time the wire was taut and stretching almost to the limit across that area of Oola which resembled two honeydew melons. After several failures I finally succeeded a second time in giving her full freedom of movement and Ooola was at last able to pass and join me.

This she did, however, in such a confused and excited state that she threw her arms around me and I had to explain with many gestures that this was not part of salmon fishing and I almost told her I did not want to increase her little tribe. So off we went again towards the pool through the mossy grass and the birch trees.

When we reached the top of the rock, I decided to show Oola what I expected her to do and exactly how to use the gaff. She became more and more excited and I stepped away from her so as to keep clear of her weapon which she was waving frantically. We went to the rocky point and I started casting. 'Oola: all you have to do is to hold the gaff and keep away from my line while I am casting and always stay a reasonable distance behind me until I have the salmon at the foot of the rock, ready for gaffing.' She was holding the gaff and started to dance around me, again waving her weapon dangerously. I somehow managed to calm her and get her back to normal. After a few minutes I located two salmon just where the slack and fast waters met. This was a very good sign. I decided to use a medium size Arctic wolf hair tubefly and started casting.

All of a sudden I thought my fly had caught in a tree and when I turned I noticed the leader wrapped around the gaff and Oola standing close behind me. I stared at her and said: 'Now Oola, come and sit on the rock and leave the gaff on the ground and if you don't obey, you will have to go back to your chores.'

On the third cast, I was into a good fish. He immediately jumped twice and made for deep water and then up again for another jump as he tried to reach the current and swim downstream. He succeeded in doing this and took out a lot of line. I had to follow him trying to prevent the line from breaking on the jagged edges of the rock. I finally managed to stop the fish, then heard some wild yells, just as I had a slack line and the fish turned upstream. Suddenly I saw Oola, gaff in hand, doing some kind of a wild Lapp dance. By that time, my nervous system had almost reached its peak and I had the hardest time to control myself, the fish and Oola. At the end, in despair, I threatened to throw Oola in the pool. She began to cry and, gaff still in hand, started to return to the camp.

'Oola, come back at once, otherwise I will have to send you home to Kaiteno.'

She stopped, came back and sat down on a big stone. I was then able to concentrate on the salmon. Three more runs then he started to show signs of fatigue and I began to think that my usual luck was back. The fish tried twice to swim downstream and reach the current, but without success. He was finally almost still. I could start to bring him close enough for the gaffing. Then the great tragedy of my fisherman's life happened. I had decided I could not trust Oola with the gaff and the only solution was to hand her the rod realizing that any additional delay would increase the chances of the fly tearing loose. I could see it on the edge of the mouth. Now I explained to Oola how to handle the rod.

'Oola, here is the rod, hold it high with both hands, one on the reel and don't move. Remain as still as a statue!'

I took the gaff and immediately had it fast into the fish and lifted him out of the water, on to the rocky ledge. But the salmon was still lively and got off the gaff while I was trying to grab him with my hands. Oola then pulled on the rod with all her strength and broke the leader which had already been frayed on the rocks.

As I was scared of losing him, I did the only logical thing that came to my mind. I flopped down on the salmon. All of a sudden, I felt a tremendous weight on me. Oola was so excited and wanted to be so helpful that she lay on top of me. When the fish had quietened down and I managed to get Oola off me, I looked around for a stone to kill the poor salmon but not seeing one, I sent Oola to find a suitable stone. She soon returned with a rock of about twenty pounds which she wanted to drop on the salmon and probably on me also. I ordered her to lay it down and succeeded in making her understand the need to find a small stone. Soon she returned with a smaller stone, but still too heavy. On the third trip she brought the right sized stone. I killed the poor salmon and finally he was ours! We were shaking and then looked at each other and I felt like giving her a brotherly kiss, but at the last moment I changed my mind because she was looking at me with such spawning eyes.

The salmon tipped the scales at twenty-nine pounds. From that day on every time I saw Oola she gave me such a hungry look that I always had to tell her to stick to her laundry and that I had a French Oola waiting for me in Paris.

Upon my return to Paris, Ludwig Bemelmens was staying with us at the Ritz and when I told him Oola's story, he said: 'Charles, if you write about it, I will gladly make a sketch for you,' which he very kindly did.

But all my friends could say was: 'Oola indeed. Ooh-la-la, you wicked old Frenchman!'

And what kind of remark is that to make to a Swiss?

HUNTER S. THOMPSON: from *The Great Shark Hunt* (1974).

It was late Saturday night, as I recall, when we learned that Frank Oliver had officially won the tournament – by one fish, ahead of the balls-out poor-boy crew on *Lucky Striker*. I wrote this down in my notebook as we roamed round the deck where the boats were tied up. Nobody urged us to come aboard for 'a friendly drink' – as I heard some of the anglers put it to others on the deck – and, in fact, there were only a few people who spoke to us at all. Frank and his friends were sipping beers at the open-air bar nearby, but his kind of hospitality was not in tune with this scene. Jack Daniel's and heavy petting on the foredeck is about as heavy as the Striker crowd gets … and after a week of mounting isolation from this scene I was supposed to be 'covering', I was hung on the dark and ugly truth that 'my story' was fucked. Not only did the boat people view me with gross disapproval but most of them no longer even believed I was working for *Playboy*. All they knew, for sure, was that there was something very strange and off-centre, to say the least, about me and all my 'assistants'.

Which was true, in a sense, and this feeling of alienation on both sides was compounded, on ours, by a galloping drug-induced paranoia that honed each small incident, with every passing day, to a grim and fearful edge. The paranoid sense of isolation was bad enough – along with trying to live in two entirely different worlds at the same time – but the worst problem of all was the fact that I'd spent a week on this goddamn wretched story and I still didn't have the flimsiest notion of what deep-sea fishing *felt like*. I had no idea what it was like to actually catch a big fish. All I'd seen was a gang of frantic redneck businessmen occasionally hauling dark shadows up to the side of various boats, just close enough to where some dollar-an-hour mate could cut the leader and score a point for 'the angler'. During the whole week, I'd never seen a fish out of the water – except on the rare occasions when a hooked sail-fish had jumped for an instant, 100 or so yards from the boat, before going under again for the long reeling-in trip that usually took ten or fifteen minutes of silent struggle and always ended with the fish either slipping the hook or being dragged close enough to the boat to be 'tagged' and then cut loose.

The anglers assured me it was all a great thrill, but on the evidence, I couldn't believe it. The whole idea of fishing, it seemed to me, was to hook a thrashing sea monster of some kind and actually *boat* the bastard. And then eat it.

All the rest seemed like dilettante bullshit – like hunting wild boar with a can of spray paint, from the safety of a pickup truck .. and it was this half-crazed sense of frustration that led me finally to start wandering around the docks and trying to hire somebody to take me and Bloor out at night to fish for man-eating sharks. It seemed like the only way to get a real feel for this sport – to fish (or hunt) for something genuinely dangerous, a beast that would tear your leg off in an instant if you made the slightest mistake.

This concept was not widely understood on the dock in Cozumel. The businessmen-anglers saw no point in getting the cockpits of their expensive tubs messed up with real blood, and especially not theirs . . . but I finally found two takers: Jerry Haugen on *Lucky Striker* and a local Mayan captain who worked for Fernando Murphy.

Both of these efforts ended in disaster – for entirely different reasons and also at different times: but for the record, I feel a powerful obligation to record at least a brief observation about our shark-hunting expeditions off the coast of Cozumel. The first is that I saw more sharks by accident while scuba-diving during the daylight hours than I did during either of our elaborate, big-money night-time 'hunts' off the fishing boats: and the second is that anybody who buys anything more complex or expensive than a bottle of beer on the waterfront of Cozumel is opting for serious trouble.

Cerveza Superior, at seventy-five cents a bottle on the porch of the Bal-Hai, is a genuine bargain – if only because you know what you're getting – compared with the insanely and even fatally inept 'deep-sea fishing and scuba-diving tours' offered at dockside shacks like El Timon or Fernando Murphy's. These people rent boats to dumb gringos for $140 a day (or night) and then take you out to sea and dump you over the side with faulty diving gear in shark-filled waters during the day, or run you around in circles during the night – a Fernando Murphy speciality – while allegedly trolling for sharks about 500 yards offshore. There are plenty of bologna sandwiches while you wait for a strike, unable to communicate verbally with the guilt-stricken Mayan mate or the Mayan captain up top, who both understand what kind of a shuck they are running but who are only following Fernando Murphy's orders. Meanwhile Murphy is back in town playing *maître de* at his Tijuana-style night club, La Piñata.

We found Murphy at his nightclub after spending six useless hours 'at sea' on one of his boats, and came close to getting beaten and jailed when we noisily ruined the atmosphere of the place by accusing him of 'outright thievery' on the grounds of what his hired fisherman had already admitted he'd done to us – and the only thing that kept us from getting stomped by Murphy's heavies was the timely popping-off of flash-bulbs by an American photographer. There is nothing quite like the sudden white flash of a professional gringo camera to paralyse the brain of a Mexican punk long enough for the potential victims to make a quick, nonviolent exit.

We were counting on this, and it worked; a sorry end to the only attempt we ever made to hire *local* fishermen for a shark hunt. Murphy had his $140 cash in advance, we had our harsh object lesson in commercial dealings on the Cozumel dock – and with the photos in the can, we understood the wisdom of leaving the island at once.

Our other night-time shark hunt – with Jerry Haugen on *Lucky Striker* – was a totally different kind of experience. It was at least an honest value. Haugen and his two-man crew were the 'hippies' of the *Striker* fleet, and they took me and Bloor out one night for a *serious* shark hunt – a strange adventure that nearly sunk their boat when they hooked a reef in pitch-darkness about a mile out at sea and which ended with all of us on the bridge while a four-foot nurse shark flopped crazily around in the cockpit, even after Haugen had shot it four times in the head with a .45 automatic.

Looking back on all that, my only feeling for deep-sea fishing is one of absolute and visceral aversion. Hemingway had the right idea when he decided that a .45-calibre submachine gun was the proper tool for shark fishing, but he was wrong about the targets. Why shoot innocent fish, when the guilty walk free along the docks, renting boats for $140 a day to drunken dupes who call themselves 'sport fishermen?'

FRANK TUOHY: from *Live Bait*. From *Live Bait, and Other Stories*
(1978).

On the last evening of the holidays, he was back at the lake with his fishing-tackle. As he had expected, the boathouse was securely locked again: he followed the path round until he reached the jetty. Now, in September, the shadows were already long, and some of the trees had golden reflections in the still water.

He took a long time assembling his rods, paying elaborate attention to each knot, in order to avoid tomorrow in his thoughts. His mother had told him that Godfrey Weare had very kindly offered to take him back to Chalgrove Park in the Sunbeam. It would mean leaving him at school a good deal earlier than usual, because Godfrey Weare and his mother would be driving on to Brighton, to dine together and do a show. She couldn't realize the sharp twinges she caused by announcing jolly plans for the time when he would be out of the way.

In some ways he was surprised to find himself here this evening, nearly a month after his last visit. In the village street he had run into Jeremy, returned from Ireland: with a single instinct they had cut each other dead. Then this morning he had discovered three frogs in some long grass at the end of the garden. He had read Isaac Walton's *Compleat Angler* and he remembered the instruction for using them as live bait: 'Use him as though you love him, that he may live the longer'. A frog would not only live longer but swim out into the clear water. Suddenly his passion was aroused all over again. Nevertheless, he was almost sure that this was the last time he would come here. The future was getting fuller and fuller of other things: part of his childhood was being crowded out, not because he wanted to let it go, but because there was nobody to share it with.

In spite of Isaac Walton, he had found the business of hooking on the frog rather appalling: you needed somebody else at hand to encourage you to do such things. He hoped to catch a small fish for live bait on the lighter of the two rods. By the time everything was ready, moths were starting to flutter clumsily and rooks were going home across the pale sky. His two floats lay far out on the pale water, the smaller one motionless, the larger one trembling, agitated by the desperately swimming frog.

Later, he heard footsteps approaching. He thought it better to disappear, in case it was Major Peverill. He climbed to the top of the rocks nearby and, hidden by a holly tree, looked down. It was the girl.

This time she was wearing a flowered dress, a shapeless effort with smocking and puffed sleeves. It was accompanied by the same crinkled stockings and sturdy shoes. The great difference was the hair, no longer in plaits but flowing loose on to her shoulders. It still framed her face but in a way that made it less round and doll-like. He scrambled down the slope towards her.

'I thought these must be your things. What's been happening to you?'

'Oh, I've been very busy,' he said.

She laughed, as though he was too young to be eligible for this word. 'When Uncle Maurice said he had found you down here, I came back several times.'

'I'm sorry.'

'In the end, I guessed that he had probably frightened you and you wouldn't come back. "The poor boy's frightened," I thought.'

He blushed so hard his face was ready to explode. She was teasing him but, now that the pigtails had gone, you couldn't really tell what she mightn't know.

Now she went to the end of the jetty, pushing her hair back behind her ears and posing in profile against the water.

'It's nice that you've come back,' she said.

'This is the last time.'

'Why's that?'

'Because I've got to go back to school tomorrow.'

'Have you caught the big fish yet?'

'Not yet.' He felt embarrassed by something which two months ago had been the most important thing in the world.

'Not yet!'

She laughed. All at once, she pulled her long hair in a curtain over her eyes and, staring through it with a funny spooky face, she turned on him, waving her arms with the hands ready for clutching. He nearly fell off the jetty.

'Nervous, aren't you?'

To get a bit of his own back, he asked: 'Where's that Australian person?'

Rowena stroked her hair into place behind her ears, and looked remote. 'Oh, she left. Ages ago, actually. I'm going to school in Switzerland after Christmas.'

While they were talking he had forgotten to keep watch on his two floats. The smaller one was still there, but the other had vanished. He picked up the sea rod and pulled hard. The float jerked from where the waterlilies had hidden it. He reeled the line in, and prepared to cast again.

'You've caught a little frog. Look, it's wriggling.'

He tried not to let this display of female ignorance put him off his stroke. He cast out smoothly towards the middle of the lake.

'Didn't you see it?' she asked him in wonder.

'That was the bait.When you're fishing for pike, live frogs are good bait.'

She stared as though she could not believe him. 'But that's horrible. It must hurt it dreadfully. Do you know what you are? You're a sadist.'

'What's that mean?'

'If you don't know, I'm certainly not going to tell you. Poor, poor little thing.'

'They don't feel like we do.'

'You little beast. You mean *you* don't feel.'

He laughed. 'No, they don't, really.'

He watched her doubtfully. No boy would ever make a fuss like this: at Chalgrove Park you could easily collect a crowd by burning a worm or an insect with a magnifying glass. He was quite shocked to see that she was crying in earnest.

'They all said you were horrible. They were quite right.'

'Who said?'

Rowena did not answer, but turned round and fled, large and splay-footed, into the darkening woods.

'Who said? Tell me,' he called after her.

He followed her to a point where the path forked, and the rhododendrons were too tall to allow him to see which way she had taken. Her tears had scattered his wits completely. Returning, still thinking about her last statement and not looking where he went, he tripped headlong over an elbow of tree-root sticking out of the path.

With the skin grazed off both his knees, he limped back to the jetty. There, a curious noise hung in the air. He could not identify it until he noticed that the big rod had fallen over and the noise came from the ratchet of the reel as the line was being dragged off it.

He grabbed the rod and held on. Whatever had seized the bait was now out in the middle of the lake, fighting deep down. Though he was still snivelling with pain, the usual mixture of rage and glee took hold of him. Each time he started regaining some line, the fish headed off again, and he knew it must be deeply hooked because its strength was fighting directly against his own. This made him sure that it was the same pike he had hooked on the day Jeremy had gone home early.

After about ten minutes his arms began to ache. Hot water ran down his leg, though he hadn't felt himself peeing, and made the scraped knee sting. His eyes stung too, and he wiped the back of his hand against them. He couldn't see any better because it was getting dark, although a piece of the setting sun was still visible through the trees on the opposite shore.

By now he knew the battle was going his way: the fish had tired itself fighting out there in the open, and each failing effort gave him a little more slack line, so that he could steer it nearer the waterlilies round the jetty. Suddenly he saw the rounded back fin, the one near the tail, break the surface: it was like a dark sail against the luminous water.

All his dreams came to a quiet conclusion as the pike slid gently towards him. To keep it from tangling among the lilies, he held the rod as high as he could. This brought the great head out of the water, the body looped and thrashed widely, but the hook held. Gradually he eased the pike alongside the jetty, like a liner coming into dock, and into the shallow water. He dropped the rod and plunged in on top of the fish and manhandled it on to the bank. In the wild stink of mud and marsh-gas it lay there, huge and terrible to him. While he watched it, a mounting sense of triumph began to break through all the webs of disbelief.

To stop the line tangling, he cut the knot above the wire trace. The pike gave a number of violent heaves, and its scales became covered with dry leaves and earth. The two eyes that glared from the corners of the head belonged now to a monster of the woods more than the water. In the twilight, Andrew lay on the ground and worshipped it.

For a time, the only noise seemed to be of the blood pounding in his ears. This turned into the murmur of voices, not far off. He had just time to heave the big pike down the bank. By the faint shine that still came from the lake, he could see it indignantly right itself and then the furious swirl with which it regained the deep water.

When he had clambered once more on to the top of his rock, he was aware of several people approaching down the path between the rhododendrons. They carried electric torches, and soon you could see the long cylinders of light shifting to and fro, stopped by tree trunks and then reaching out again among the shadows.

He heard Major Peverill's voice, high-pitched like a well-bred sneeze. 'The poor girl got back to the house in a terrible state.'

Other voices answered, in the lower tones of country people accustomed to agreement.

'He should not have been allowed to come here in the first place.' By now Major Peverill was standing about directly below. 'It was a misunderstanding, which must be put right without more ado.'

There was complete darkness under the holly tree on the rock. Andrew kept his head down, in case a beam of torch-light should sweep across to show his face as a pale patch among the bristling leaves. If you hated people enough, he thought, you could hold out as long as they could. In a short while they would find his gear lying where he had left it by the lake. It would hardly make much difference: they knew he was still here, but it was improbable that they would ever find him.

Soon after this, though, he saw other, different torches flash out on the far side of the lake. He heard his mother calling, and he knew he would have to surrender.

ROGER McGOUGH: *The Birderman.* From *Waving at Trains* (1982).

> Most weekends, starting in the spring
> Until late summer, I spend angling.
> Not for fish. I find that far too tame
> But for birds, a much more interesting game.
>
> A juicy worm I use as bait
> Cast a line into the tree and wait.
> Seldom for long (that's half the fun)
> A commotion in the leaves, the job's half done.

Pull hard, jerk home the hook
Then reel him in. Let's have a look . . .
A tiny thing, a fledgling, young enough to spare.
I show mercy. Unhook, and toss it to the air.

It flies nestwards and disappears among the leaves
(What man roasts and braises, he too reprieves).
What next? A magpie. Note the splendid tail.
I wring its neck. Though stringy, it'll pass for quail.

Unlike water, the depths of trees are high
So, standing back, I cast into the sky.
And ledger there beyond the topmost bough,
Until threshing down, like a black cape, screams a crow!

Evil creature! A witch in feathered form.
I try to net the dark, encircling storm.
It caws for help. Its cronies gather round
They curse and swoop. I hold my ground.

An infernal mass, a black, horrific army
I'll not succumb to Satan's origami.
I reach into my coat, I've come prepared,
Bring out my pocket scarecrow – Watch out bird!

It's cross-shaped, the sign the godless fear
In a thunderflap of wings they disappear.
Except of course, that one, ungainly kite
Broken now, and quickly losing height.

I haul it in, and with a single blow
Dispatch it to that Aviary below.
The ebb and flow: magpie, thrush,
    nightingale and crow.
The wood darkens. Time to go.

I pack away the food I've caught
And thankful for a good day's sport
Amble home. The forest fisherman.
And I'll return as soon as I can

To bird. For I'm a birderer. The birderman.

MICHAEL BALDWIN: *The Fish are Retrograde.*
From *King Horn* (1983).

The fish grumble close under weed
And breathe out pop pop:
Do they yearn for the Eighteenth Century Tradition?

A greater backwash of calm
From the pendant weir?

Rousseau could not fish.
Voltaire did not fish,
Having lost his twine in intelligent women.

I sit here through two quarts of wine.
The fish are not reading their Rousseau,
Do not mention Voltaire.

DAVID JAMES DUNCAN: from *The River Why, Chapter 3a:*
Concerning Statistics (1983).

Like gamblers, baseball fans and television networks, fishermen are enamored of statistics. The adoration of statistics is a trait so deeply embedded in their nature that even those rarefied anglers the disciples of Jesus couldn't resist backing their yarns with arithmetic: when the resurrected Christ appears on the morning shore of the Sea of Galilee and directs his forlorn and skunked disciples to the famous catch of *John 21*, we learn that the net contained not 'a boatload' of fish, nor 'about a hundred and a half', nor 'over a gross', but precisely 'an hundred and fifty and three'. This is, it seems to me, one of the most remarkable statistics ever computed. Consider the circumstances: this is *after* the Crucifixion and the Resurrection; Jesus is standing on the beach newly risen from the dead, and it is only the third time the disciples have seen him since the nightmare of Calvary. And yet we learn that in the net there were 'great fishes' numbering precisely 'an hundred and fifty and three'. How was this digit discovered? Mustn't it have happened thus: upon hauling the net to shore, the disciples squatted down by that immense, writhing fish pile and started tossing them into a second pile, painstakingly counting 'one, two, three, four, five, six, seven . . .' all the way up to an hundred and fifty and three, while the newly risen Lord of Creation, the Sustainer of their beings, He who died for them and for Whom they would gladly die, stood waiting, ignored, till the heap of fish was quantified. Such is the fisherman's compulsion toward rudimentary mathematics.

Statistics are a tool upon which anglers rely so heavily that a fish story lacking numbers is just that: a Fish Story. A fish without an exact weight and length is a nonentity, whereas the sixteen-incher or the twelve-pounder leaps out of the imagination, splashing the brain with cold spray. The strange implication is that numbers are more tangible than flesh; fish without vital statistics are fish without being. And this digital fisherman-consciousness has seeped into most facets of life. One of the most telling examples is this: a human child at birth undergoes a ritual almost identical to that inflicted upon trophy trout at death, to wit *1*) the fish is whacked on the head, thus putting it out of its misery; the infant is whacked on the behind, thus initiating it *into* its misery, *2*) the fish is placed on a scale, weighed to the quarter ounce and measured to the quarter inch: the infant endures identical treatment. *3*) the fish is stripped of the coating of slime that protected it in the water; the infant is purposelessly relieved of its equivalent coating. *4*) the fish is placed in a cold rectangular receptacle to await the taxidermist who will stuff it, creating an illusion of healthy flesh on its lifeless body; the infant is placed in a *warm* rectangular receptacle to await the parents who will stuff it, hopefully creating genuine healthy flesh upon its living body.

Further examples of fishlike human predicaments are too numerous to explore at length, but the disquieting analogies between students in public schools and smolts in rearing ponds, dancers in nightclubs and salmon on their spawning beds, suburbanites in housing tracts and hatchery trout in reservoirs, and industrialists who pollute and trash fish who like pollution, should be obvious to any angler.

I was afflicted with as pernicious a case of the numerical lease on life as any I've encountered, but I had the good fortune to discover that the essential pleasures of fishing are as independent of statistics as are the joys of childbirth independent of little Bosco's length in quarter inches. Most of us appear to be plagued by the notion that digits describe a thing (for instance an infant) more accurately than do the qualities the thing possesses (for instance the infant's drooling smiles, watery eyes, redundant dimples, pathetic coiffure, tired chins and helpless unignorable outcries). Accuracy is a useful thing, certainly. A skyscraper designed by an architect with a head for nothing but drooly smiles and tiered chins is likely never to scrape the sky. But there are times and places to employ statistics and times and places not to – and the times-and-places-not-to comprised one of many lessons I was doomed to learn 'the hard way'.

Concerning those disciples huddled over the pile of fish, another possibility occurs to me: perhaps they paid the fish no heed. Perhaps they stood in a circle adoring their Lord while He, the All-Curious Son of His All-Knowing Dad, counted them all Himself!

Index

Index